THROUGH HEAVEN'S VISION

An imaginary journey
of Heaven's perspective,
guided by Scripture

NOLAN J HARKNESS

Trilogy Christian Publishers

A Wholly Owned Subsidiary of Trinity Broadcasting Network

2442 Michelle Drive

Tustin, CA 92780

For information, address Trilogy Christian Publishing

Rights Department, 2442 Michelle Drive, Tustin, Ca 92780.

Trilogy Christian Publishing/ TBN and colophon are trademarks of Trinity Broadcasting Network.

For information about special discounts for bulk purchases, please contact Trilogy Christian Publishing.

Trilogy Disclaimer: The views and content expressed in this book are those of the author and may not necessarily reflect the views and doctrine of Trilogy Christian Publishing or the Trinity Broadcasting Network.

10 9 8 7 6 5 4 3 2 1

Library of Congress Cataloging-in-Publication Data is available.

ISBN 979-8-89333-299-5

ISBN 979-8-89333-300-8 (ebook)

TABLE OF CONTENTS

INTRODUCTION

For many years now God has used me as a prayer intercessor, and evangelist/revivalist. I have spent a large part of those years in youth ministry having been a youth leader or pastor in five different churches building three of them up from scratch. All that I am certain of is that God saved this backslidden country boy first at 9 years old then later as a young man in Jacksonville Florida in 1979. I so love the Lord and endeavor with His help and grace to serve Him with all of my heart.

I felt called to write *Through Heaven's Vision* about three years ago. I specifically felt Him call me to write a fiction piece so that I could paint foggy pictures of many of the stories that I have lived and not offend anyone or organization. I most certainly hold so tight to the Word of God that I do not want anyone to think that I believe anything about Heaven that is in this book that is not specifically in the Bible actually happened. I merely hoped to fill in some back stories with what may have happened or could have happened because God can to anything that is in accordance with His Will.

I hope some of the myths can be dispelled that Heaven will be a boring place or a place like I heard someone confess recently on national television because they weren't sure that they wanted to go when they died. There is so much that the Bible does not choose to tell us about Heaven. I pray that *Through Heaven's Vision* will create an eternal excitement about going there and hope that the thousands of hours that I have spent in prayer in His presence in the last many years pulled a little bit of the glory of Heaven's truth down with it. Please take the time to write me if it blesses you or possibly someone terminal that you know find Christ so that they can spend millions and millions and millions of years in this wonderful golden city where there will be no more sickness or sorrow or tears. Only eternal love, joy, and peace. It will make the many battles and hours of sacrifice in writing it even more of a blessing to my life and my family.

In His Eternal Love...

Nolan

nolanharkness@gmail.com

CHAPTER 1

THE PULLS BETWEEN HEAVEN AND EARTH

In the beginning God created the heaven and the earth. And the earth was without form, and void; and darkness was upon the face of the deep. And the Spirit of God moved upon the face of the waters... And God said, Let the waters under the heaven be gathered together unto one place, and let the dry land appear: and it was so.

GENESIS 1:1-2, 9 (KJV)

As the earth spun upon its axis in joyful obedience to God's enthralling design, the majestic picture of creation began to unfold. First, the unfathomable power of the Holy Spirit was unleashed upon the water-covered planet. The ten fingers of the Holy Spirit plunged into the depth of the great sphere-shaped body of then colorless and lifeless fluid and rammed into the bedrock of the seven continents, simultaneously lifting them off of the ocean floor.

There as yet were no fish, no coral, no whales, or other ocean mammals. Nothing was known of mountain peaks or plunging valleys, as the earth was without form and void. The incomprehensible power of God's Holy Spirit's part in creation was to be God the Father's instrument of glorious artistic expression, as the Great I Am desired to show forth His greatness through the splendor of His creative artistry.

By hands too enormous to measure their size and through power too great to comprehend, all seven continents began to be lifted simultaneously above the existing water levels as great tidal waves raced across the planet's surface, only calming after colliding with each other, catapulting great waterspouts thousands of feet into the air, collapsing back onto each of the continents' solid rock surfaces, baptizing each landmass in fresh saltwater. What was left was the galactically centered canvas, fit for the Master Artist of all time to produce His most beautiful designs, leaving for all to see that which was so spectacular that upon its observance, the viewers of the future would praise Him for the indescribable splendor of His handiwork! No creature that would ever exist, no man-made device of anyone's design, nor could anything ever be imagined that would come close to comparing to His beauty. Everything that He was about to do from that day forward would point to the fact that He was the One and only True God, the Master Designer and Creator of both the natural world and the spiritual world, a world without end forever more, amen! As a pan out on what was just seen began to develop, the focus now began to be shifted from what was taking place to the spectacular view from the upper kingdom of heaven. The other two of the three-member design team knew it was time to listen to the Heavenly Father speak as key components of His plan for eternity moving forward began to unfold.

The Three all-seeing, all-knowing, ever-present members of the Trinitotalum Godhead began discussing the days that would follow and the creation of mankind. The Heavenly Father begins to explain part of His secret plan: "This is what we must do because without it, the wicked one will, through his craftiness, continually subvert the *will*, thus preventing *the kingdom* from being able to establish the strong foundations for which the future church will need to survive. Although we have preexisted throughout all time, far too few people will understand the pinpoint of purpose for every creature that I will have then created." God the Father goes on to say as He points to the enormous banner that hung across from His throne.

Riveting spiral beams of light radiated from the emblazoned brilliance of the *upper kingdom of heaven*, declaring:

Our Father which art in heaven,
hallowed be Your name,
Your kingdom come,
Your will be done on earth,
as it is in heaven.

Give us this day our daily bread
and forgive our debts,
as we forgive our debtors,
and do not lead us into temptation
but deliver us from the evil one.

For Yours is the kingdom and power and
the glory forever. Amen.

The words "Your will be done on earth as it is in heaven" were expressly illuminated with a diffused pulsating golden glory light, reminding the angels before they entered the natural realm of earth's domain of the primary focus of every duty or military assignment.

As the Trinitotalum continued to meet, they discussed the necessity of fulfilling all righteousness as it related to the warfare for the souls of mankind that they would embark on. When the Father speaks, sharing from His heart things that only He has foreknowledge of, all of the heavenly host of angels bow in holy reverence. "Lucifer's evil pride has caused his foolishness and fall, and although he is evil, we must still abide by righteous standards. The day will come when Lucifer will feel that he has dealt a crippling blow to My Kingdom; however, I have a plan using the ultimate gift of My love to save my creation from eternal destruction. Just as Lucifer will be able to operate at levels of his own deceptive power, affecting the will of mankind, so we will be able to operate at the levels of our own power to counter his deceptions with truth. He will be able to operate with unfair deceptions of the heart, yet we must be righteous in all of the counter strategies we will use to pull mankind back to the truths of My work...

"Windrose," the Father goes on to ask, "do you have everyone chosen for the next six millennia assembled in the arena?"

"Yes, I do, sir, and their emotilliance is preprogrammed into their restricted recall mode so that they will have no memory of these next weeks of classes until just the right point in history for which we are preparing them. The enemy of all souls and his many schemes will be less effective against those who have sought with all of their hearts for Your power and have diligently filled their hearts with the everlasting truth of Your Word."

Faceless souls filled the arena. Having a mind and a thinking capability, they would be able to respond to what they were about to learn and ask questions for the clarity of their understanding. They were yet to be implanted into human beings. The Father, in His omniscient ability, knows which of these souls will be dispersed at key times at different points in history. Their ability to discern darkness from light and good from evil during these time-targeted pivot points would have a critical effect on the future of mankind. They would be "seeds" that would grow at just the right time!

Windrose calls the meeting to order and says, "Ladies and gentlemen, we are going to begin today to look at things that are yet to happen in the future. They will all one day be written down for all the world to see and for all of those who will one day delight in knowing the truth. The Father, in His creation plan, will start by creating the first two humans, called Adam and Eve. Due to their wrong choices, a sinful nature will begin to grow in all mankind, in everyone who will be born from that day forth. Adam and Eve will have two sons called Cain and Abel. Watch now as we are going to project their story up on the omniciscreen, showing how it will happen in the not-too-distant future."

As the giant screen begins to illuminate, two boys are shown playing together in a field. "Go and get this, Abel," Cain shouts to his little brother as he throws Abel's favorite wooden horse that his father had carved for him out of gopher wood down into the small ravine, landing in a muddy puddle right next to the creek.

"Cain, no!" Abel shouts as he makes his way over jagged rocks down to where it lays.

"Ha-ha, I hope it floats away before you get there," Cain responds.

"I'm telling Mom! Where is your cow that Dad carved for you, Cain?"

"Oh, I don't know what happened to that stupid cow. I hate that thing; the next thing we know, we are going to have to be helping Mom milk and do chores on top of all the other things we have to do!"

The giant screen fades for a minute to all white as Windrose continues: "As boys growing up, there was constant tension between them. Cain, being the older of the boys, was always bullying Abel and looking for the upper hand, taking advantage of every opportunity. Adam and Eve tried their best to be fair with them in everything they did and made sure that they learned how to pray and find the fellowship with God the Father, which they had lost in person but now could still enjoy through prayer. It was through pride and rebellion that first Eve, then Adam, fell into the serpent's deception in the garden. The Father then did not give up on humanity but clothed them with lamb skin to cover their nakedness and provided something that was the opposite of pride and rebellion, namely, humility and submission in prayer. Adam would often take the boys for a walk in the big forest to a special place that he had designed among the floral trees to talk with the Father in prayer. Abel always seemed to take delight in the experience; however, Cain seemed to be easily distracted by the animals scurrying about there."

A question arose from Jackson-6: "Windrose, wouldn't that be a normal reaction from a young boy to want to play with the animals rather than pray?"

"Yes, Jackson," Windrose responded. "However, Adam and Eve both knew that it was important to teach them to honor their Heavenly Father by focusing on Him only during prayer time, so Cain often had to be corrected and told to keep his eyes closed during prayer time and to keep his thoughts on the Creator."

Windrose then raised his hand, and the omniciscreen began to show another scene from a different time in Cain and Abel's life. Cain and Abel come riding across a rolling mountaintop on black and white horses. Cain's black horse takes a quick left as Cain pulls hard on its reins, then gallops up towards a steep mountain trail. "Cain, where are you going?" Abel yells.

"There are some huge fig trees up here," Cain responds.

"Yes, but it's a dangerous trail, and your horse could sprain its leg!"

"Yeah, yeah, whatever; Dad has so many horses I will just get another one!"

"Yes, but these were given to us on the same day that they celebrate redemption by sacrificing a goat for our sins!"

"Okay, I know, I know; I will be careful," Cain yells as he rides off into the woods.

Suddenly, Able hears a *whoo-hoo*, and a few minutes later, Cain comes riding recklessly back down the trail with a couple of large fig tree branches loaded with figs draped over his horse's back, chewing one as fig juice flows down both sides of his face. "Here, have some," he says as he throws a small branch at Able, startling Abel's horse.

"Cain!" Able yells as Cain, laughing insanely, rides off. Succeeding in calming his horse, Able follows Cain at a distance to their parents' cabin by Emerald Lake. Once again, the screen fades out to white, and the souls can be heard talking among themselves.

Windrose asks, "Does anyone have any questions?"

Juan-14 says, "Yes, I have no way of knowing what I seem to know already, but why are we watching two young men engaging in a field in what seems to be a normal exchange of teenage activity?"

Windrose responds, "In a later session, we are going to witness something with those two boys that will be a critical indicator of what is really inside their hearts. It will help you understand something that will hinder the Heavenly Father's will from being done on the earth throughout time. For now, we are going to catapult thousands of years further into the future, and your cerebrums that have such large capacities that they will never be fully utilized all the days of your life will now have the R-11 factors of your emotilliance activated so that you can understand the future culture that you are about to visit. To help you to comprehend, in this scene, God the Father has just poured out His Holy Spirit in a school that is educating teenagers for the professional world that they are about to enter once they complete their studies. A few young people had stumbled across the thought, *What would happen if we prayed longer than usual, or what would happen if we sang songs and worshiped God longer than just for twenty minutes? Also, what would happen if we just focused wholeheartedly on praying, "Thy will be done on earth as it is in heaven?"* When they did, they turned the golden key of heaven and loosed the great blessing of God's Holy Spirit! What you are about to witness, however, is their reaction as they realize that their school is going to discontinue the extra worship services they have been holding for weeks!"

At that, groans are heard from all the thousands of souls throughout the whole arena. Windrose responds, "Let's watch their reaction together now!"

"I can't believe it! I just can't believe it," Hakeem keeps shouting, repeatedly pounding his fists on the desk while looking up towards heaven.

"Believe what?" Sonya responded.

Hakeem is so angry that his eyes are bugging out of his head! He answers, "It's been what, eighty years since there was any record of God showing up on this campus in this powerful of a way and what? They are just going to shut it down. Send everyone home? Just so everyone can write about it in their journals or write a paper for a grade? Do they realize what just happened in our gray, dusty, old little chapel? Eric Reichmann just received Christ as his Savior, and not only Savior but his Messiah! Not to mention at least thirty other students, including the fullback from the lacrosse team! So what if it interrupted classes? So what if people started driving here from all over the country? So what if classes had to shut down? Do they realize this is God who is doing this? God, you know, God the Creator of the universe? Do they not think that He cares?"

"I know He cares," Sonya responds. "And I know the Bible says that there will one day be no more tears in heaven, but right now, I think that this is all breaking God's heart!" Just at that moment, Justin walked through the door.

"What's up?"

"What's up, Justin?" Hakeem replied. "I will tell you what's up! This school is telling God to go home after He has visited us in a huge way, changing many lives in the last few weeks!"

Justin responds, "Yes, Hakeem, but you must understand this is a school of higher learning, and classes do have to go on. People have to earn their degrees, and graduation is only a few months away! Besides, it's religion, and that's cool for Sundays and stuff, but people must work and eat, you know? Remember that this went all the way to the trustee board, and they brought it to a vote. Those folks are all very educated people whose job is to keep this school open. Doesn't it say somewhere in the Bible that God works through people of authority?"

Hakeem cups his head in his hands and says, "All I know is that I have found Jesus as my Lord and Savior, and His Holy Spirit has filled me with His beautiful presence, which to me is worth everything! I have given Him my whole life, and all that I want to do is accomplish all of His will for me in my lifetime and see His kingdom advance on the earth through thousands of people finding out about Him!"

"Yes, amen!" Sonya shouts.

Justin just starts grumbling, "You guys have turned into a bunch of fanatics," and walks out the door.

As the screen fades out to white, Windrose again stands up while the arena is filled with murmurs of the souls once again talking with each other. Judy-35 speaks up, asking, "Windrose, is what we just witnessed actually going to happen sometime in the future? It is so hard for us to imagine how anyone could ever do this."

"For some of you, yes, Judy, and that is why the Father has you in these classes: so that your cerebrum can retain certain bits of truth that will help you to later recognize and sort out this type of misconception. These 'seeds of thought' will grow up within you someday so that the enemy's schemes can be thwarted. Unless...."

"Unless what?" a large group of souls seem to all ask simultaneously.

"Unless the evil one gets a stronghold in your lives, and you die before your appointed time!"

Brenda-21 speaks up and asks, "Is that possible?"

"Sadly, yes," Windrose responds. "Far too many allow, as you will one day learn more in-depth, the deceitfulness of riches and the cares of this life to choke out God's truth from their lives, causing them to become spiritually unfruitful and, in some cases, make foolish choices that can lead to an untimely death." At that point, Windrose's head drops in his hand, and tears drop down as he once again directs all the souls to look to the big white screen.

"Ladies and gentlemen, now we are going back to the story of Cain and Abel, but at this point, they are young men. You will see that Cain is a tiller of the ground, and Abel is a shepherd. They have both continued to learn about the Heavenly Father through their father, Adam, and in the process of time, you will see that each of them will bring God a sacrifice. This is where we are going to begin."

"Abel, where are you going?" Cain shouts.

"I'm going to prepare my sacrifice for the Lord; when are you going to get yours ready?"

"Ha-ha," Cain responds, "I have it right over there in a pile. Remember that beautiful black horse Dad gave me? Well, you were right about being careful with him. He broke his ankle stepping on a rock yesterday—stupid horse. That's okay. I don't care; he will be good dog food for our hounds. I have gotten another horse from Dad's farm, but now I must break him in! So, I'm just grabbing a bunch of my best wheat and barley and carrying it to our special worship place among the floral trees."

"Really?" Abel responded. "That's it? That's all you are going to give to the Lord for your offering?"

"Yeah," Cain says, giving a big yawn, "I did pray and told Him what I was going to do, and He didn't question me about it, so He knows, right?"

Abel responds, "I built Him an altar just beyond the floral trees where the sun shines through when it rises in the morning, and I am giving Him the firstborn lamb of my flock this year as a sacrifice there at sunrise!"

"Good for you, Abel!" Cain comments sarcastically.

The next day, when both brothers offer their sacrifices, the Lord is pleased with Abel's sacrifice and blesses it. However, He is not pleased with Cain's sacrifice and does not bless it. This angers Cain. Abel, not realizing how angry Cain is, suggests that they go for a ride together with his new horse, but unfortunately, the invitation only angers Cain further.

"I have work to do, young brother; I will see you later!" Ominously, as Cain walks away, more and more anger rises in his heart against his brother. Thoughts of evil begin to fill his mind. "That goodie-goodie Abel is always outdoing me in everything." An inner rage, which had actually been building for years, comes to a climax and poisons his thinking. As Cain looks down, his eyes light on a round fist-sized rock. Seizing it, he waits for Abel to ride by on his horse. Cain then throws the rock, striking his brother in the back of his head. Abel falls to the ground, breaks his neck and dies. *There*, Cain thinks as he quickly scurries down another trail into the woods, *he won't be outdoing me anymore!*

As he hurries away, the Lord speaks to him, saying, "Cain, where is your brother, Abel?"

Cain replies, "I do not know. Am I my brother's keeper?"

Then the Lord responds, saying, "What have you done? The voice of your brother's blood cries out to me from the ground, and now you will be cursed all the days of your life on the earth!" After God finishes explaining the specifics of His curse on Cain, Cain flees to a land called Nod, and the screen goes to white again.

"What do you see," Windrose asks the souls, "concerning any parallels between these two stories, which are several thousand years apart?" Several souls began to try to answer at once, talking over top of each other. Windrose restores order by saying, "Hold on, hold on, one at a time, please!"

Jane-3 speaks up and answers, "Some people seem to have hearts that are less dedicated to the Heavenly Father than others!"

"That's correct, Jane!" Windrose then goes on to ask, "How many people can this type of relationship affect spiritually?" Some souls say two, thinking of Cain and Abel; some say three, thinking of Hakeem, Sonia, and Justin.

With a very sad countenance, Windrose raises his voice to a level that he had not used until that day. "Before these classes are through, ladies and gentlemen, you will see how just one person who is halfhearted regarding the things of our Heavenly Father and the Kingdom of God can impact thousands and even millions...." A deep groan echoes across the arena as tears can once again be seen rolling down Windrose's face...

CHAPTER 2

GOOD GIFTS, BAD GIFTS, AND THE GIFT

There was a lot of mumbling and discussion between the souls about the thought of something actually being able to affect millions of lives for all of eternity, but everyone quieted as Windrose began to point to the omniciscreen again. "Okay, soldiers," Windrose said, which created a new level of discussion between the souls. Everyone looked puzzled by the statement, so Windrose spoke up and explained this new title. "Yes, you are a type of soldier in God's spiritual army, and when your time comes, you will each have an assignment that will require a soldier's commitment and a soldier's discipline. Some of you will be used as mere children to say or do just the right thing at precisely the right time. The evil one's plan will have been implemented through an unlikely person to try to block God's specific will from being done, and your action or reaction will stop Satan's plan in its tracks. All that I can tell you is that as a result of this training, you will subconsciously know what it is like when the time comes. Others will be used while you are teens, young adults, or in your senior years on the planet. In each case, someone who is being led by their own will or flesh to try to deter or stop God's perfect will from being accomplished will be intercepted by what you do because, at that time, you will automatically be able to recognize it!

Therefore, from now on, to remind you of your future roles, I will call you soldiers from time to time! However, sadly, in other cases, because to fulfill the requirements of righteousness, God the Father must yield to man's will,

His will on earth will not be able to be done in that instance. Let us now view part of Noah's life story, who will be one of the greatest men of God who ever lived! Although he will accomplish the awesome task of building a huge wooden ship called 'the ark,' thus fulfilling the Father's will, one of his children will greatly offend Noah at the end of his life. We will see how the enemy of all souls will try to use one of Noah's sons to discredit him and his example of godliness throughout history."

At that time, the omniciscreen projector's capabilities changed, and a cylndricron projected a life-size three-dimensional image of a wooden ship onto the arena's main floor. Animals of every member of God's design, in groups of two by two, can be seen entering as pairs into the large ship. Because the large door in the side of the Ark is wide open, the assembled souls can also see the thousands of animals already inside. The souls begin to cheer and applaud at this new way of seeing into the future, so Windrose begins moving both of his hands up and down to calm their enthusiasm in order that the story can continue. "Ladies and gentlemen, let's take a look at a day in the life of this special man of God."

As the scene opens, the souls can see Noah and his sons brushing some of the last board seams of the ark with pine tar. They also noticed Noah's wife coming down the path, bringing the men lunch and fresh flasks of wine.

While still a ways off, she says, "Noah, have the boys be sure to take the trail past the waterfall and get cleaned up before dinner. It has been a very hot day, and I have spent most of the morning cleaning our curahutt because we are celebrating Shem's birthday tonight with a special meal. It was so nice of you, Noah, to go out early this morning, harvest a turkey, and cut fresh white lilies. Everything at home smells and looks beautiful, and I would like to keep it that way!" Noah just smiles, but all three boys laugh when Ham makes a sour face after smelling his armpit!

"Yes, I think she is right," Ham says.

"Okay, let's stop for lunch and then get right back to work," Noah interjects.

As the image of the ark fades on the arena floor, the white screen begins to look once again farther into the future.

Windrose starts to speak again, reminding the souls of their God-given abilities.

"Ladies and gentlemen, your abilities to look far into the future and see things and understand them within that time and place in history is part of your sovereign enablement, given to you by your Heavenly Father. From time to time, we are going to start giving you a '*will lesson*,' which will further your understanding of the fact that the enemy of all souls will try to confuse or negate the importance of the will in the hearts and minds of God's creation. The *will lesson* for today is to understand that when it comes to an understanding of '*Thy will be done on earth as it is in heaven*,' there are two structural categories. First, there is the Father's sovereign will, which, within the limits of perfect righteousness, permits Him to supersede all human will, of both good and evil, and alter the course of all mankind by a sovereign act or series of actions. These deeds are righteous because He is steering world events to accomplish a holy mission. Secondly, there are the things that are within the limits of righteousness in the battle between good and evil, which He can only accomplish through the actions of the free will of man. One day, the most important person that God the Father will ever send to earth will teach His followers to pray a certain way. In that prayer outline, that person will make it clear to always include this desire in their prayers. 'Your will be done on earth even as it is in heaven.'

"Souls, this will be the major thrust of all your training! Here is where your will as God's created human vessels will be able to recognize and act, bringing the heart of the Father into play and allowing His will to be done on earth, just as it is continually done in heaven! This will be the avenue through which the people living on the earth can see the goodness of God in the land of the living. In just this same way, when the perfect time comes, the Father will eventually accomplish the unimaginable through one soul that is very special to Him."

All of a sudden, an emotion arises among the thousands of souls that had yet to have been expressed. First, it starts with a few souls clapping their hands together almost spontaneously and saying, "So may it ever be." Then others join in, saying, "May Your will be done."

In response, Windrose shouts out, "Here is the word you are looking for: 'amen,'" which leads to spontaneous shouts of praise to God with the accompaniment of the roar of clapping hands and everyone shouting, "Amen, amen, amen!" to the Father's will being done on the earth just as it is in heaven!

To this, Windrose responds, "Perfect righteousness, perfect love, perfect kindness, perfect peace towards one another for years without end forever and ever! Amen, amen, amen!"

Windrose laughs out loud and smiles, seemingly stretching from one ear to the other, and tears of joy run down both cheeks. Then he looks upward, and he laughs, which makes everyone laugh with him. "Thank You, Father," he says. "This is joy unspeakable and full of glory!" As he turns back to the omniciscreen, he adds, "What you are going to look at now will take place in 1996 by the calendar they will use during that time. Look with me as we join this family on its way to the church, which is what they will call their place of worship then."

As the car goes into a pothole in the road, Shelley yells out, "My lands, George, can't you try to miss those? I just spilled my coffee on my phone. Karen, hand Mommy up that box of tissues beside the car seat."

"Dad, why do we have to go to church so much?" Kevin blurts out. "None of my friends go every service, I mean, Sunday morning, Sunday night, and even on Wednesdays. Doesn't God understand that we have a life?"

"Kevin, that's enough. You know that we have talked about this before. We believe that God has called us as parents to 'train up a child in the way that he should go.'"

"I know, I know, Dad; I have heard it a hundred times; maybe next year, when I get my license, I will at least be able to drive myself!"

"Kevin, do not be disrespectful to your father," Shelley warned sternly. "Honor your mother and father that your days be long upon the earth!"

"Well, all I know is that when I raise my family...." Kevin grumbles.

George responds laughingly, "Oh, yes, I cannot wait to watch that one!"

As the white screen fades off again to blank... Windrose seems to be motionless for a minute and then begins to address the souls once again: "Soldiers, as you will learn throughout these sessions, the human will is very fragile. As I activate the learning capability in your emotilliance, I want you to imagine the operating functions of a mechanical compass. Visualize how the tiny compass needle seems to float on the head of a pin. The slightest turn of the user changes the position of the needle. That is how easily the human's will can shift away from what God is calling them to do. Sometimes, it takes just a nudge to steer them back on track, but other times, it takes bolts of lightning to get their attention! God will have to send bolts of lightning in the fifteenth century to get the attention of a very important priest named Martin Luther. However, we will not be viewing that today on the omniciscreen."

Moans of disappointment could be heard going across the souls seated in the arena.

"What is so important, ladies and gentlemen," Windrose continues, "is that you will be able to sense that you must respond in a way that will seem at the time to be just a simple reaction to what you are witnessing. However, your simple word of encouragement, your simple question about the decision that you see someone making, or even your simple prayer at just the right time will have the power to release God's intervention into certain peoples' lives in a way that may also affect countless other lives. Let us now take a trip back into Noah's life. In this scene, soldiers of the Most High God, you will be viewing a time period after the great flood when life has returned to normal on the earth. Noah had returned to the trade he knew before he was called to build the ark, the trade of a husbandman; he was a planter of vineyards. As the scene opens, we find Noah is sleeping in his tent."

This time, the omniciscreen is sufficient to display this part of Noah's life, and as the white screen lights up, we see Noah's son Ham reorganizing a few of the flasks of wine in the sun after the recent harvest. "What are you doing, Ham?" Shem asks.

"Oh, nothing, just keeping things in good order like you know Father wants us to," Ham replies.

"What were you laughing about? I heard you laughing when I came up the trail," Shem asks.

"No worries," chuckles Ham. "You know how when something just hits you, and I am just so relieved that all of those years of hard work are finally over, and now we can finally return to a more normal life."

"Well, normal or not, there is still lots of work to do, Ham. Did you dig those potatoes for Mother and put those fish that Japheth and I netted this morning on the smoke pit so that they do not spoil?"

"Yes, I did, and where is Japheth anyway?" Ham spouted.

"Oh, Father asked him to see if he could go and take a wild deer as he was hungry for some fresh venison. Japeth took that ashwood bow that Father had made him for his birthday and went hunting. He should be back soon. Oh, here he comes now!"

"Hey, guys, look at this young buck I got," Japheth shouted. Its meat should be nice and tender. Come and help me skin and prepare it for tonight's dinner."

"Well, there is something that you guys should know," Ham grumbles. "Father got a little too happy celebrating and drinking last month's wine, and he is lying in the tent totally naked!"

"And you did nothing to cover him?" Shem shouts angrily.

"What could I do?" Ham retorted.

"Come on, let's pray about it, and God will show us what to do. After all, Father taught us to pray when we face circumstances that seem to have no answer."

Ham seems to agree half-heartedly as the three sons pray together for God to give them an idea.

Shem shouts out, "I got it! Come on, Japheth, grab that robe hanging over there and do exactly what I tell you."

The two brothers can be seen hanging the large robe over their shoulders and walking backward towards where their father lay in his tent. They covered him very carefully without looking at him, as their tender hearts towards God knew that they should not look upon another person's nakedness. Shem looks up at Ham and says, "Now, was that so difficult, Ham?"

"How could I do that by myself?" Ham responds sarcastically.

Japheth scolds, "Well, you could have come right away and gotten one of us. How did he happen to get a flask of the old wine anyway? You know, once it ferments, we pour it out, as we have an abundance of new wine!"

"I do not know anything about that," Ham replies angrily.

"Yeah, right, uh-huh," both brothers say, both replying at the same time.

Noah wakes up from the wine and knows what his younger son has done to him. He becomes very angry and says, "'Cursed be Canaan; a servant of servants He shall be to his brethren.' And he said: 'Blessed be the LORD, the God of Shem, and may Canaan be his servant. May God enlarge Japheth, and may he dwell in the tents of Shem; and may Canaan be his servant.[1]'"

As the omniciscreen fades to white, Windrose begins to ask the souls questions once again. "Who can tell me why Noah was so angry at Ham and why he pronounced a prophetic curse against Ham's son and not against Ham himself?" There is a low rumble as the souls, obviously perplexed, begin discussing the question quietly among themselves.

Finally, Brian-37 queries: "Windrose, how did Noah know upon waking up about something that had happened while he was asleep?"

"Brian, I sense that almost everyone is asking this same question. You see, when the Spirit of God is on a man who has been gifted to be a leader for the Heavenly Father's special purposes, that man can supernaturally know things without actually having seen them happen. Noah knew not only what Ham had done, but he also had the ability to see the attitude of Ham's heart and to know why Ham had done what he did. Also, Noah understood the importance of not only parental but also godly discipline when it was needed. Ham had spent 120 years helping his father build the ark. Noah was aware that Ham knew better than to disrespect his father as he did. That is why Noah gave Ham the worst punishment that he could think of. Punishing Ham by making Ham's son suffer for the rest of his life would hurt worse than anything Noah could do to Ham directly."

The souls notice that, once again, Windrose seems to be crying. With a gentle voice that seems to be breaking up, he says, "Someday, another son will have to suffer for other people's sins. As unfair as this seems, Noah understood that it would be a punishment that would send a message to everyone to never dishonor their mother or father throughout all time or there will be severe consequences." Windrose then raises his voice in a more authoritative tone. "Ladies and gentlemen, it is time for another *will lesson*. In this view into Noah's life, can you see any factors that might have influenced anyone's will in any way to make right or wrong choices?"

Suzette-4 speaks up and says, "Yes, Windrose, I can see the tension between the two older brothers and Ham, and it appears that Ham's choice not to cover his father's nakedness may have something to do with his tension towards his brothers. I believe the *will lesson* here is that our choices can be the direct result of our feelings towards others or even our resentment towards our parents, when actually our choices should be based on what we are taught is right or wrong."

"Well said, Suzette." Windrose replies, "What you have said is so important for created beings to understand. God's people must learn to trust that He knows what is best! Is there anyone else who got something different from this *will lesson*?' Please understand, however, like the needle on a compass, a person's will can so easily change with just the slightest turn of events."

Christine-2 speaks up, declaring, "I see what you are saying, Windrose!"

Speaking to the multitude of souls present in the arena, Windrose states, "Yes, everyone is doing really well. With so many souls present in the arena, however, I must remind everyone to make sure we are maintaining order by everyone being careful to not talk over the top of someone else! Thank you, Christine, that is so true, and remember again, it is why it will be taught in the disciple's prayer to pray to the Father: 'Thy will be done on earth as it is in heaven.' God's angels have open access to the throne of God as He wills it and immediate awareness of His select plans and what His will is in every situation. Even in the environment of heaven itself, where God's will is always being accomplished every minute of every day, God's will must be the continual focus of every angel. This will prevent them from ending up like the great fallen one who committed the ultimate sin after pride rose up in his heart. The former archangel foolishly thought that he could overthrow God and become greater than God the Father Himself. Lucifer will pay for such a foolish sin for all of eternity.

"Now, soldiers, let's turn once again via the omniciscreen way into the future to the year 2023. The children that you viewed before are now much older and have families of their own. As the omniciscreen comes on, we see the father, George, having coffee with his wife, Rhoda, while they are away for a week's vacation at a cottage rental at Rose Diamond Lake."

"I sure miss having the kids with us on vacation, George," Rhoda quietly comments as she looks out across the dock at the beautiful Canadian sunset.

"I know, me too," George replies. "I'm kind of glad that last year we did not realize that we were actually on the last of a long string of vacations together, going clear back to when they were little."

Rhoda's eyes fill with tears as she struggles to say all that was on her heart. "Oh, and the grandkids, I just can't think about them not being here chasing each other around. I even miss Darren's huge dog!"

"Don't cry, honey; we need to thank God every day for them and hope that somehow we can all be back here next year! Besides, with nobody else here, miles from town, and the only other cabin being vacant for renovation, we don't have to worry about the kids and can go skinny-dipping!"

"George!" Rhoda exclaims and starts giggling. "I swear, as you get older, are you still never gonna slow down a little?"

"Why slow down, honey?" George replies. "God made us to enjoy each other, and now that we are empty nesters, I mean, you know, making love is still my favorite contact sport, sweetie!"

George and Rhoda enjoy a moment of romantic laughter and affectionate hugging. "I know what," George says. "Let's take lots of pictures of our fun while we are here, make a digital scrapbook when we get home using one of those online services, and send one to each of our kids. Who knows? Maybe it will help them start planning for next year so that they can be on vacation with us once again?"

Rhoda sort of perks up and laughingly says, "As long as there are no photos while skinny-dipping, right?"

"Heads only out of the water, and nobody will know but us," George responds, laughing hilariously.

Although the album idea lightens her mood, Rhoda still expresses her doubt, saying, "I don't know if that will work, George. You know Darren is an engineer on that big solar farm in Nevada, and Tonya is only in her third year of teaching at Seattle University. It would be a lot for them to both fly here with the kids, and I don't think the airline has a dog crate big enough for him. What breed of dog is that again, I forgot?"

"It's an English mastiff, Rhoda, but you know where their family goes, he goes; he's a big baby!" George responds.

"So true," Rhoda replies. "Did you get that fire going in the fire ring? I'm hungry for a hot dog cooked over the fire!"

"Yes, I got it ready earlier. It was one match only, Eagle Scout, remember?"

Rhoda laughs. "How can I forget? You say that every year. Come on, after those delicious hot dogs cooked over the fire, let's go snuggle in the glider before that brilliant orange sky goes dark. Maybe we will see the northern lights or some shooting stars? Let me grab the hot dogs and fixings."

As they sit in front of the crackling fire, the orange blazes begin to reflect on their eyeglass lenses as they reminisce together about some of the same things, especially how much they miss their kids and grandkids.

Rhoda suddenly breaks the silence, blurting out, "George, have you talked to Darren yet about his walk with the Lord? Do you know if he and Ginger are even going anywhere to church right now?"

"Not yet, Rhoda. You do realize it is sort of a touchy subject, right? He is making tons of money working for that government subcontractor and must be available on Sundays for any power hookups or shutdowns. This is what he went to college for. You know that he has been interested in green energy since he was a teenager, and his high school biology teacher pushed global warming theory on him. Remember how we prayed and prayed, Rhoda? We felt that Darren had a calling to the ministry on his life, but from that point on, it was hard to keep his attention on the things of God."

"Yes, honey," Rhoda replied, "and sadly, though slightly different, Tonya had her own hurts that I believe we must help pray her through. It was so sad that weekend that she came home her freshman year crying because the sociology professor told the class that 'when it comes to your Christianity and working in the real world, you have to be able to put your Christianity in a bottle!'"

Sadly, George responds, "If that was all that she had to endure, I feel as though her faith would have been strong enough. She also had to live through our youth pastor being fired for inappropriate advances to one of the older girls, and then, just as she was getting her teaching degree, she got an 'F' on the paper she wrote in defense of corporal punishment with children in a loving balance practiced by most Bible-believing Christians."

"I remember, George. You sent that paper to a professor you knew from Liberty University, and he sent her back a wonderful letter saying that if she were his student, he would have given her an 'A+'! You did what you could, George, but both of our kids have had to go through a lot spiritually. Thankfully, our marriage has remained strong as we both believe in praying together often so that God's love will stay strong between us."

"Tell you what," George says, stirring the remaining coals a little as they gradually burn out for the night. "When we get home, let's pray over our calendar for the next year and plan separate trips to see Darron and Ginger and Tonya and Wallace and the grandkids. It will just be short stays, but it will be good for all of us. Maybe we could sow some seeds spiritually while we are there?"

"Oh, thank you, honey, that's a great idea," Rhoda says with a little giggle in her voice. "I'll start looking online for some good travel deals!"

"Don't you think we should figure out some dates for travel first?" George replies.

"Details, George. You always are bringing up the details." She laughs, grabbing and folding up the lawn chairs as they head in for bed.

As the omniciscreen fades back to white, there is a lot of interaction between the souls. Some are laughing over the romantic interaction that they just witnessed between a godly couple who are still very much in love. Others are more somber, obviously affected by the more serious side of the future event that they just witnessed.

The first thing that Windrose asks is, "What is the *will lesson* we can learn from what we just witnessed?"

Jessica-12 speaks up immediately, "I can see how what people believe concerning their faith in God can change over time simply by what they are taught is and isn't true. Why would God the Father allow people to continue living who He knows are going to negatively impact others with their lies?"

Many of the souls seem to be speaking out and agreeing with Jessica as an "amen" sort of ripples through the arena.

Then Glen-47 interjects, "Yes, and especially at a school of higher learning where so many young lives are being impacted by those in the position of being instructors on the truths of life and death!"

Windrose waits for a minute to see if the mumbling and inner discussion calms down and then explains: "The Heavenly Father understands the most basic concepts of love. Those are number one; in order to design humans in His image and likeness, He had to create everyone with a free will. Does everyone understand that it would not be love if every one of His creation was forced to do what He told them to? If He made everyone like machines, without the ability to make choices, and they had to obey some preprogrammed responses to life's situations, then their actions as they related to one another would not be generated by love, would they? You see, in the battle between good and evil, everything hinges on the human will! Love is lived out and tested by the choices humans make every day. That is why it is time to start a new class now that explains '*the gift*' more fully!"

Once again, quite a loud rumbling could be heard as the souls began chatting back and forth between each other, wondering what Windrose meant by "*the gift*."

"The gift of salvation is something that, at a key point in history, God the Father is going to offer from that day forward to every living person on the planet. Starting on the day that this gift is offered, every living, breathing human being will be given the option to leave their sinful, self-centered lives behind them and to begin to be what will then be called '*saved*'! Those people who are truly saved through embracing God's gift will be able to spend eternity in heaven with all those who have been saved and have come up here before them."

A roar of applause, shouts of joy, and loud "amens" erupt following that announcement, and they continue for a very long time.

"*However, however, everyone, there is quite a period of time before that gift of the Father's grace is poured out, so let's not get too excited yet!* Visibly traveling through time will enable us to watch it unfold. There is one key piece of information that the Father wants me to tell you before we move ahead any further, so everyone, please relax a minute and listen very closely. Souls, you do remember the purpose of you being here, correct? The whole process of you being nameless and faceless and in the predevelopment phases of your created form is so that when the time comes, you can, in a true, righteous, and loving way, effect change throughout history. Remember how you have been taught that some of you will be used while you are children, some when teens or young adults, and others will be used in your senior years to be the gentle nudge of someone's will in the correct direction so that God the Father's will can be done on earth as it is every day in heaven! The exciting news that He wants you to all know today is that some of the famous characters that you have witnessed or heard about in the stories up until now were actually some of you who are sitting here now!"

"Wow," first one soul shouts out!

Then, another someone says, "Really?"

Still, another comments, "I was wondering about that." While almost everyone discusses this amazing news among themselves, saying things like, "My goodness, of course, why didn't we recognize that all along?"

Windrose concludes that session by chuckling a little bit and adding, "I think it will inspire everyone to pay a little closer attention," and he laughs even more as the omniciscreen fades back to white...

CHAPTER 3

GOD'S CREATION LEARNING HIS WAYS OF COMMUNICATION

Windrose begins to address the souls who were already eager to hear him explain what he meant by *"the gift."* "Soldiers in God's spiritual army, please understand that the receiving of the gift is like the center pin of the compass of the human will, which all of humanity will swing on. It is, therefore, the most integral component of all decision-making. As I have said before, the slightest turn one way or the other will radically move the needle of a compass. Similarly, the slightest turn in a person's life through a decision he or she makes will affect all the other decisions he or she makes. To help us understand this better, let's turn our attention once again to the omniciscreen, where we are going to go ahead in time a very short distance to look into the Garden of Eden and the story of God's first humans, Adam and Eve."

As the omniciscreen begins to light up, we see Adam and Eve talking in the garden. Eve is pondering everything God has told them concerning their responsibilities there. She begins by asking Adam if he understands completely why God has told them there were certain things they could do and certain things they could not do. She then goes on to say, "Adam, you certainly do have a very big task naming all of the animals that God has made. Tell me, my man, how do you do it?"

Adam replies, "Well, God, our Heavenly Father, has given me, through the power of the Holy Spirit, some unique gifts that enable me to do a supernatural amount of work in a short time. I know that God has given me this task. He has also given me the gift of thinking creatively to help me figure out what to call each one. I cannot explain how it works, but it's also wonderful that even though the animals do not speak, as I spend time with them, I somehow sense some of the things that they are thinking, and I am somehow also able to communicate back to them simply by looking into their eyes."

Eve begins to sing a song as it is born in her heart:

"Oh, God, Your creation is so beautiful, so beautiful, so beautiful to me.
Oh, God, You are so wonderful, so wonderful, so wonderful to me.
Oh, God, all the fruits are delicious; oh, God, so beautiful to view.
Oh, God, if You did more than this, I don't know what, I don't know what I
  would do!"

The souls readily perceive that Adam has already been struck with Eve's beauty, but they now see that even though he has become speechless at the beauty of her singing voice, he is enamored and chuckling happily. He says, "That is so beautiful, my dove. I'm sure the Father is so touched by your song to Him. I think He will want you to sing it to Him again tonight when we walk with Him in the cool of the evening. I will see you later because now I have to go over to the flowering tree grove and work with the group of the animals that live there. I will be back later today."

Windrose reaches up as if to wave some sort of adjustment to the omniciscreen, and the background color goes dark. It begins allowing the souls to begin to look into the murky regions of demonic activity. They hear a very dry, scratchy voice begin to speak braggingly to an assembly of other fallen angels. The souls let out a corporate gasp as this is the first time they have been exposed to the sinister darkness that surrounds the one-third of the fallen angels who were cast out of heaven with Lucifer.

"Well, we see God's first created humans having a wonderful life in the garden He created for them. Let's see how they do when I work some of my form of 'truth' into their lives," Lucifer snarls. Growling, gurgling, and evil laughter can be heard as the other demons delight in their master's evil scheme. "I have just the thing that will make this man Adam cave and reject what God has taught him and submit to his *beauuuuuitul* wifey! Ha-ha-ha-ha-ha; oh, ha-ha-ha-ha-ha."

"What are you going to do, Skenector?" one of his chief demons asks.

"Oh, I'm going to take one of the beautiful things God created in the garden, the forbidden fruit, which He already told them they could not have, and make them want it more than anything else in the whole garden!"

"Ah," Skenector replies, "sweets for the sweet," and starts laughing so hard that he begins choking on his own saliva. This seems to incite the other demons to celebrate evilly, extending their slimy dark arms downward in an expression of debauched praise, signifying the dark force's ultimate goal, namely, to bring God's creation down!

The backdrop of the omniciscreen starts to brighten again so that the souls can see back into the garden. Eve is walking among the fruit trees, still singing praises to God for all of His beautiful creation. She delightfully gathers several pieces of fruit for the dinner that she and Adam will have later. Feeling a little bit hungry, she picks some extra for herself. Biting into one from the Ongor tree, she smiles as its sweet juices run down both sides of her face. "That's *soooo* good," she says, saying the same thing again when she goes on to bite into a piece of fruit from the Tydrum tree and then another from the Grimple tree. "Oh, these are all so good," she sighs. Suddenly, she hears a noise behind her and, turning, spies a tall, man-like creature standing behind her, who has obviously been watching all she is doing. *Oh*, she thinks in her mind, *this must be the serpent that my husband told me about*, as she remembers what Adam had shared with her about how he, by a special gift, was able to look into animals' eyes and be able to tell what they were feeling. While the tall creature's reptile-like skin seems a bit scary to her, she finds his form to be very appealing. When she then decides to move a little closer, something very unusual happens. The serpent speaks to her in a soft, gentle voice.

"Hello," he says.

This causes her to respond in kind, saying, "Hello! How is it that you can speak, not being a human, as Adam and I are?"

The serpent responds, "I can speak this way because I am a very special type of God's creation, which I am sure you have not learned about yet. I also have very special knowledge about the garden and these delicious fruit trees! You can literally ask me any question about any of these trees, and I will be able to answer it for you! Think of me as sort of a keeper of the garden with a vast knowledge of all of it."

"Oh, wow," Eve responds. "I was just picking some fruit for my husband and me for our dinner tonight; then I will gather some vegetables to go with the fish Adam is going to bring back after his work naming more animals."

"Have you considered the fruit from that beautiful tree in the center of the garden? The fruit from it is more delicious than all the other fruit of any of the trees anywhere."

Eve then says to the serpent, "We may eat fruit from the trees of the garden, but God did say, 'You must not eat fruit from the tree that is in the middle of the garden, and you must not touch it, or you will die.'"

Then the serpent scoffs, "You will not certainly die, for God knows that when you eat from it, your eyes will be opened, and you will be like God, knowing good and evil." When Eve listened to the serpent and saw that the fruit of the tree was good for food, pleasing to the eye, and desirable for gaining wisdom, she took some and ate it."

Just then, Adam came walking up behind her, but as she turned to introduce him to the serpent, the serpent, being crafty, quietly slipped away into the other trees because he had already sensed that Adam was returning.

"Adam, you have to try this fruit. It is *soooo* delicious!"

"Oh, no!" Adam responds at first. "Don't you remember? That is the tree of the knowledge of good and evil, which God told us not to eat or even touch!"

"It's okay, my man man. I met the serpent. Why didn't you tell me about the creature that can talk? He was so kind to clear up my misunderstanding about why God did not want us to eat from that tree! Here, take a bite, really. I did, and I did not die; I am fine. Maybe somehow, we misunderstood. What harm is one little bite going to do? I have tasted all the fruit from all these other trees, and none of them even come close to tasting as good as this fruit! Why would God want to withhold from us such great-tasting fruit when He has freely given us access to all of the other trees?"

Adam thinks about her question for a minute. He says to himself, "Maybe we should just wait until tomorrow to ask God that question since we walk with Him every morning?" However, Adam feels this unexplainable urge coming up from inside his body that he simply cannot resist. As he turns back and looks at Eve with her beautiful smile, his urge seems totally harmless to him.

She reaches out with that piece of that forbidden fruit, which already had the bite that she had taken out of it, making one more attempt, saying, "Come on, son of God, surely God will understand that we mean no harm!"

At that point, Adam slowly says, "All right," and accepts the piece of fruit. When he takes a little bite, he immediately says, "Wow, this is good!" Then he takes another and another while Eve watches, giggling triumphantly.

"It's good, isn't it, Adam?"

"Yes, but...." Adam replies.

"But what?" Eve asks.

"Something is different! I feel different inside," Adam responds.

"Well, we didn't die like God said we would," Eve replies.

"Yes, but something is different inside of me. Something has changed; something is missing. I do not feel God's presence like I did before. His peace is gone! You know, how each morning, just before He comes to walk with us, we can always sense that He is close? Then, during the day, we continue to feel His love, even though He was not right here. Eve, all of a sudden, I don't feel that anymore. Do you?"

"No, Adam, now that you mention it, I don't," Eve replies. "And we are naked! What can we find to cover ourselves up with?"

"What have we done, Eve?" Adam responds. "Quick! Grab some of these large fig leaves so we can sew them together to cover ourselves." As they reach for the fig leaves, an evil-sounding raspy laughter is heard just beyond the fruit tree grove, slowly fading away in the distance."

The next morning, Adam and Eve find themselves huddling in a dark and secluded gully a small distance from where they normally meet with God. Somehow, they just don't feel right about what they have done. Adam says to Eve, "I feel terrible about this. I wish so much now that we had listened to what God had told us and didn't eat of that forbidden fruit."

"I know, me too, Adam," Eve agrees.

About that time, a voice rings out in the garden. "Adam, where are you?"

"I heard you call as you were coming, and I hid in the gully because I was naked, so I hid," Adam answers.

God then asks Adam, "Who told you that you were naked, Adam? Have you eaten from the tree that I commanded you not to eat from?"

The man says, "The woman you put here with me—she gave me some fruit from the tree, and I ate it."

God's reply to Adam is, "Because you listened to your wife and ate fruit from the tree about which I commanded you, you must not eat from it. Cursed is the ground because of you; through painful toil, you will eat food from it all the days of your life. It will produce thorns and thistles for you, and you will eat the plants of the field. By the sweat of your brow, you will eat your food until you return to the ground since from it you were taken; for dust you are, and to dust you will return."

Then the Lord says to the woman, "What is this you have done?"

The woman replies, "The serpent deceived me, and I ate."

Then the Lord says to the serpent, "Because you have done this, cursed are you above all livestock and above all animals! You will crawl on your belly, and you will eat dust all the days of your life. And I will put enmity between you and the woman and between your offspring and hers; he will crush your head, and you will strike his heal." To the woman, He says, "I will make your pains in childbearing very severe; with painful labor, you will give birth to children. Your desire will be for your husband, but he will rule over you."

However, because of His unchanging love for His children, God then sacrifices a lamb, taking its skin, whose hide He tans instantaneously through a miraculous process, making clothing for Adam and Eve to use to cover themselves. "I have not given up on you, Adam and Eve," God says, "but I have made a way for your sin to be forgiven. I will also give you the strength that you need to live under the judgments that have been placed not just on you but all who will be born after you. The Garden of Eden will now be forever closed to you. Angels with flaming swords will guard the entrance from anyone who would attempt to trespass here! Because the spiritual realm will be shut off to you, we will no longer be able to walk together, conversing face-to-face, as we did before. Go now and produce offspring who will eventually populate the whole earth through the generations that will follow them! From now on, mankind will be continually tested throughout all history to determine the genuineness of their love for Me. I have a plan that will provide a path for all who choose to follow Me with their whole hearts, a plan that will last until the end of time!"

And the Lord God then said, "'The man has now become like one of us, knowing good and evil. He must not be allowed to reach out his hand and also take from the tree of life and eat and live forever.[2]'" Therefore, the Lord banished Adam from the Garden of Eden, condemning him to work the ground from which he had been taken.

Following their expulsion from the garden, Adam and Eve, as they grew in their relationship, made love and produced one son named Cain and then another named Abel. They were the first family to ever live on earth. They began to grow and work and build their homes and multiply, and for a season, they all sought God in prayer and obeyed Him in whatever they did.

The omniciscreen once again fades to black, and Windrose begins to speak.

"Souls, what *will lesson* can we learn from this peek into Adam and Eve's lives?"

Nelson-23 speaks up: "God the Father gave them specific instructions concerning what they could and could not do in the garden, and they chose as an act of their own will to directly disobey God's instruction."

"That's exactly right, Nelson, and because of that choice, sin entered into the whole world from that day forward, affecting all of mankind!" Windrose responds and goes on to ask, "How were their wills affected by the influence of others? Speaking metaphorically, what made that needle of the compass of their will change direction so easily?"

Jackson-12 replies, "Eve was deceived by the serpent when she allowed him to twist what God said to sound like He said something totally different."

"Very good, Jackson," Windrose states. "What you have just identified will be not only the number one deception that people will fall into throughout time, but in addition, the choices that they make in prayerless states of mind when they are making decisions will do the Kingdom of God more damage than any of the other failures of mankind throughout history! Unless God's children learn how to seek Him in prayer and discern His 'still, small voice' while praying, they will be spiritually clueless. They will not have any idea regarding what it is specifically that He needs them to do in each unique situation. Remember, one-on-one fellowship was lost in the garden, separating the spirit world from the natural world. The kingdom of heaven, where we are now, is a parallel universe that is an exact visual duplicate of the natural world but totally separate from it. Prayer is the pathway that God has designed to allow communication between the two worlds.

"Within every human creation is a tendency towards rebellion. From the time they are little babies, they each want their own way, and they want it now. Submitting to the Heavenly Father's will and time schedule requires humans to surrender *their will* and submit to *the Heavenly Father's will*. In the case of the first sinners, Eve and Adam, they each rebelled against what they knew was God's instruction. Sadly, every man, woman, and child from that day forward has been born into the same sinful nature!"

Whoaaaaaah can be heard, as well as many other mixed-in comments of grief, sadness, and sorrow being uttered by the thousands of souls as they grasp, to the best of their ability, the enormity of this first sin.

At this point, Windrose goes on to strongly exhort the souls. "Everyone, I need to admonish you. Pay close attention to what I am about to tell you. It is so vitally important that your memory has the potential to be reconnected to the instruction of this day throughout your lives on earth. Once again, I cannot emphasize enough how important it is that you realize the fact that, like Adam and Eve, every decision that you make has the potential to affect everyone in your family and everyone within the future circle of influence that God will sovereignly give you. Your decisions will affect not only your children but also your children's children from then on down throughout your entire generational lineage."

It is obvious that souls are once again strongly affected! Pauline-14 declares, "May God burn this truth deeply in our hearts so that we consider it a very high priority to seek His will diligently in everything that we do, so as to never hinder God's work from being done on the earth and thus limit the amount of people who will one day be able to spend eternity with Him in heaven."

"Even the purest of hearts can be distracted or deceived from the gentle leadings of the all-powerful Holy Spirit. You will learn more about this as we go in on other *will lessons*, Pauline," Windrose responds. "For now, I would like to ask all of you if you can tell from our look into the Garden of Eden what God's most important gift was to Adam and Eve and why it was the most important."

Some mumbling and internal discussion is heard among the souls after one shouts out, "Adam was given Eve!"

Another says, "It had to be the garden itself with all of its beauty!"

Still, another says, "It was the gift of having authority over all of creation, and also it was the fact that Adam was given the honor and spiritual gift of being able to name each one of them!"

"You all have good answers," Windrose responds. "Yet the greatest gift of all was when God the Father took the life of an innocent lamb and made clothing to cover their nakedness. This was a very powerful symbol of something that will come in the future of all mankind, namely, '*the gift of salvation*'! You see, God had every right to destroy both Adam and Eve and start the whole process over again, but because "God is love" and because the basis of all that He is and everything that He does is love, He demonstrated that love by forgiving Adam and Eve. As a wise Heavenly Father, He instead instituted a plan of discipline to help them learn a lesson from their rebellion and subsequent sin. At the same time, He also put in place a pathway to enable them to continue to communicate with Him through prayer. Even though the two realms, the natural and the spiritual, have been separated until the end of time, prayer reinstates the communication with God, which was lost when Adam and Eve sinned. Remember, sin entered through pride and rebellion. However, prayer is the opposite of pride and rebellion. As an act of humility and submission, even though the two worlds are separated, through prayer, mankind can once again communicate with God. That is why, throughout time, you will see people praying in humble positions, kneeling or laying prostrate before God. By far, the greatest gift God gave mankind at this point was offering them forgiveness for what they had done, a forgiveness which foreshadowed the future gift of salvation, a forgiveness obtainable through prayer! This gift of salvation, however, should never be taken for granted because even though it was freely given through God's love and grace, we must remember that Adam and Eve were expected to have learned from their mistakes and to live righteously through the strength that He gives through prayer!"

Windrose then goes on to say, "Let's now take a look into the future, to a time period known as CE, when a very important man walked on the earth. Jesus Christ was the very Son of God sent to save mankind from their sins. As the scene opens, we discover that He has agreed to meet at night with Nicodemus, a very influential member of the Jewish ruling body called the Sanhedrin. Nicodemus pre-arranged this meeting at night so that no one would see him talking to Jesus, who was hated by the rest of the Sanhedrin."

As the omniciscreen lights up again, the two men can be seen sitting next to each other on a large stone-carved bench, talking earnestly.

Nicodemus starts out by saying, "Rabbi, we know that you are a teacher who has come from God. For no one could perform the signs you are doing if God were not with him."

Jesus replies, "Very truly, I tell you, no one can see the kingdom of God unless they are born again!"

"How can someone be born when they are old?" Nicodemus asks confusedly. "Surely they cannot enter a second time into their mother's womb to be born!"

Jesus answers, "Very truly I tell you, no one can enter the kingdom of God unless they are born of water and the Spirit. Flesh gives birth to flesh, but the Spirit gives birth to spirit. You should not be surprised at my saying, 'You must be born again.' The wind blows wherever it pleases. You hear its sound, but you cannot tell where it comes from or where it is going. So it is with everyone born of the Spirit."

"How can this be?" Nicodemus replies incredulously.

"You are one of Israel's teachers," questioned Jesus, "and do you not understand these things? Very truly I tell you, we speak of what we know, and we testify to what we have seen, but still you people do not accept our testimony. I have spoken to you of earthly things, and you do not believe; how then will you believe if I speak of heavenly things? No one has ever gone into heaven except the one who came from heaven—the Son of Man. Just as Moses lifted up the snake in the wilderness, so the Son of Man must be lifted up, that everyone who believes may have eternal life in him.

"For God so loved the world that he gave his one and only Son, that whoever believes in him shall not perish but have eternal life. For God did not send his Son into the world to condemn the world, but to save the world through him. Whoever believes in him is not condemned, but whoever does not believe stands condemned already because they have not believed in the name of God's one and only Son. This is the verdict: Light has come into the world, but people loved darkness instead of light because their deeds were evil. Everyone who does evil hates the light and will not come into the light for fear that their deeds will be exposed. But whoever lives by the truth comes into the light, so that it may be seen plainly that what they have done has been done in the sight of God.[3]"

As the omnicisreen fades back to black, the souls once again begin talking among themselves about the things that they have just seen and heard. "What does this mean, Windrose?" Christine-12 asks. His question produces many more from the other souls.

"This, my dear souls, is Jesus the Messiah, the only-begotten Son of God who will come to take away the sins of the world through His death on the cross and His resurrection from the dead, which will happen a short time after the conversation that we see here. Do you remember that when Adam and Eve disobeyed God in the Garden of Eden and fell into sin, God did not give up on them but instead sacrificed the life of a lamb? Do you remember that He then took its skin and supernaturally tanned it and made them a covering for their nakedness? Well, one day, everyone in the world will have access to a book called the '*Word of God*'! It will be a book of sixty-six chapters written by forty different Holy Spirit-inspired authors covering a time period of 4,000 years. Every life situation we have seen on the omnicisreen right up until what is known as CE or the common era of when Jesus Christ walked on the earth will be in that book!"

At this point, all of the souls start cheering, applauding, and shouting, "Amen!" Then, there is so much talking and interaction between them that Windrose has to ask them to quiet themselves.

"Quiet, please! Everyone, quiet, please. I know that this is exciting news, but we must continue our *life lessons*, as there is so much more to cover. Let me remind you once again that you are soldiers of God's spiritual army, and because of that, one day, you will have opportunities to help influence thousands in key positions for God's Kingdom's sake!

"To continue, let me tell you that in that book, life stories will begin with Adam and Eve in the Garden of Eden. Page after page, the history of God's children will be written down, covering the first 4,000 years, right up to the time and place we are going to talk about today! It will be recorded that when

Jesus was getting ready to start His earthly ministry at thirty years old, the Father led Him to the river Jordon to be baptized in water by another special person, the first cousin of Jesus called John the Baptist! The Bible, which is another name for the *Word of God*, will record in the Gospel of John: 'Behold! The Lamb of God who takes away the sin of the world!'[4] Please recognize, souls, that John the Baptist called Jesus the 'Lamb of God'! Who can be the first one to tell me how that is significant to the story in the Garden of Eden with Adam and Eve's sin forgiveness?" Windrose asks.

Zachary-7 immediately shouts out, "Because it was a lamb's skin that God used to make clothing to cover their sin."

"That is exactly right, Zachary. The Father understood that the people had never fully submitted to the practice of offering sacrifice in a correct way. Their hearts were not truly broken over their sins. All too soon, they began to subtly just go through the motions of the sacrifice. In doing so, they converted the act of sacrifice into just another meaningless religious ritual. Sadly, the ritual did not change their hearts at all, so they continued on in their sin. The Bible will one day tell us: 'This is the way of an adulterous woman: She eats and wipes her mouth, and says, "I have done no wickedness."'[5] Even though they sacrificed thousands of burnt offerings throughout history, the offerings did not produce any change in the hearts of the Jewish people. Now, let's journey to another place in history to help us understand this better."

Windrose once again directs everyone to look towards the omniciscreen, saying, "Now we are taking a journey to the year 1984." The scene opens on a small farm where a father and daughter are in the middle of a conversation.

"Dad, look out the window! I can't believe how much it has snowed already! It's so pretty hanging on the trees!"

"Yes, Julie. Hey, I have a great idea. Let's take a trip to the mall. They are open until nine, right?"

"Oh, no, Ryan, you are not going out in this weather!" Sarah says.

"Oh, come on, mother, you know that with my 4WD truck and those big digger tires, that six inches of snow will not be any challenge! Besides, I always like going to the mall during a storm. The place will be like a ghost town, easy in, easy out, with no lines at the registers!"

"Yes, Dad, and remember you promised to take me to get that new jogging suit for gym class that I have been saving up for by helping Mr. Mitchell with his chores after he had knee surgery!"

"Yes, Julie, and remember, Sarah, you wanted Julie and I to have more father-daughter time. It will be fun and plenty safe. Okay?"

"Okay, Ryan, but no donuts spinning that truck in circles in the parking lot, right?"

"Okay, dear!"

As Julie and her dad grab their coats and head out the door, Sarah yells, "Drive safe, dear, and bring me back a salted pretzel!"

"You got it, Sarah!" Ryan replies.

The omniciscreen then fast-forwards to when they were just pulling into the mall parking lot.

"Wow, Dad, you weren't kidding; there are hardly any cars here at all!" Julie comments.

"Yes, and it will be a nice night for a little stroll around the mall to stretch our legs. Lead me to the store that has your jogging suit."

"Okay, Dad, I will. It's right down here."

After Julie buys her jogging suit, Ryan says, "Come on, I would like to head down to the pet store to see if they happen to have any German shepherd puppies. I have been wanting to get another one ever since we had to put Tory down."

"Okay, great, Dad! Even if they don't have any German shepherds, I still love to look at all the other animals."

As Julie and her dad round the corner, she says, "Wow, Dad, it looks like all the people at the mall are at the pet store tonight! Look, there have to be at least twenty people in there!"

As they walk in the store, they see different families, couples, and a few people who seem to be by themselves, laughing and looking around, with some being allowed to hold the puppies and kittens.

"People do love animals so much," her dad replies.

"I know, right, Dad? Just like we love the animals on our farm. It was like we lost a member of our family when Tory died! It's hard when we raise calves for the sale or pigs for organic pork. As hard as we try not to, we do get attached to them, even though we know they are being raised for meat."

Her father reminds her, "Unfortunately, although it is sad, it is part of the cycle of life, and just as God gave mankind teeth for chewing meat, He wants us to understand that He put many of the animals here on the earth for both consumption by humans and also other animals."

"Yes, I know, Dad," Julie responds sadly.

Windrose pauses the omniciscreen. It fades to black and then starts to come back on as He says to the souls, "I only want to pause for a minute to reset the scene as we prepare to go to another very important Bible scene; a story will one day be found written in the Gospel of Matthew. Jesus is preparing for what will later be known as 'His triumphal entry into Jerusalem.' As the scene opens, you will see Jesus riding into Jerusalem on a donkey, thus fulfilling an Old Testament prophecy."

The disciples bring the donkey and its colt to Jesus, first placing their cloaks on its back for Jesus to sit on. As Jesus begins to ride, the souls watch as a very large crowd begins spreading their cloaks on the road while others cut branches from the trees and also spread them on the road.

The crowds that go ahead of him and those that follow shout, "Hosanna to the Son of David! Blessed is he who comes in the name of the Lord! Hosanna in the highest heaven!"

As Jesus enters Jerusalem, the whole city is stirred and asks, "Who is this?"

The crowd answers, "This is Jesus, the prophet from Nazareth in Galilee."

Jesus then enters the temple courts and electrifies the crowd by driving out all who were buying and selling animals for the daily sacrifices. He overturns the tables of the money changers and the benches of those selling doves. "It is written," he said to them, 'My house will be called a house of prayer, but you are making it 'a den of robbers.'"

The blind and the lame then come to him at the temple, and he heals them. But when the chief priests and the teachers of the law see the wonderful things he did and hear the children shouting in the temple courts, "Hosanna to the Son of David," they were indignant.

"Do you hear what these children are saying?" they asked him.

"Yes," replies Jesus, and goes on to ask them, "have you never read, 'From the lips of children and infants you, Lord, have called forth your praise'?"[6] He then leaves them and goes out of the city to Bethany, where he spends the night.

Windrose is then, by a process the souls had not yet seen, able to go back to the spot on the omnicscreen where Jesus was angrily overturning the tables of the money changers in the temple. He pauses the image, freezing it in time. "Souls, I want you to look at this still image for a minute and ask yourselves if you have even the slightest idea, with the light and the knowledge that you have so far, as to why Jesus overturned all of these tables so dramatically and drove all of the buyers and sellers out of the temple? Any thoughts about why He was so angry?"

"Perhaps the money changers were cheating the people by not giving them the correct amount of money in exchange for their currency?" Ahsan-8 speculates.

"Well, actually, Ahsan," Windrose replies, "that ends up being what most people have believed for many hundreds of years since that day. Others thought that it was because they were charging too much for the sacrificial animals that they were selling. However, the heart of Jesus was not made known to the writers inspired by the Father to write the New Testament scrolls. God exposes the real problem going on at the temple that day to those who carefully examine what the scriptures teach about the sacrifices in other places in the Bible. Actually, the problem was something that had been going on for decades!

"In the Bible, it will be written, in the New Testament book of James, 'My brethren, take the prophets, who spoke in the name of the Lord, as an example of suffering and of patience.'[7] James will one day write to instruct us that this lesson regarding the sacrifices can be found in several places in the writings of the Old Testament prophets. People who truly sought God with all of their hearts and who had studied God's displeasure with the way that many were making the Old Testament sacrifice had known this all along. Jesus chose to deal with the problem that day in such a dramatic way that His actions would never be forgotten.

"You see, the most important message that you can ever learn from these trips through time visiting different people is that God knew that people loved animals. He knew that from the beginning of time, people would have to farm to survive. Every family would have animals to serve their basic needs. Even the poorest families would have at least a few doves or a few chickens and most needed goats, lambs, and cows for their milk and wool needs. Although they are practical people, farmers still love their animals. The entire purpose of the sacrifice for sin was so that when a person had to witness a blameless animal that they loved die and have its blood shed for the forgiveness of their sins, their hearts would be broken. In the process of their hearts being broken over an innocent animal having to give its life for their sin, they would cease sinning! We see now what God's plan was from the beginning of time. That's why the lamb died in the garden. It died so that its skin could be tanned to make clothing to cover Adam and Eve's bodies after they sinned!

"Therefore, over time, man, being inherently wicked, developed a subtle plan that ensured that they didn't have to watch their own beloved animals die for their owner's sins." As Windrose continues to explain, his voice begins to crack with emotion, and tears begin to run down his face. "They would go down to the temple and buy an animal that they had no feelings for and quickly, with no true repentance, give it to the priest so it would die for their sins!

"That's why, at times, Isaiah the prophet and other prophets throughout history referred to the animal sacrifices offered by the Hebrew people as an abomination, declaring that the smoke coming up from those sacrifices was a stink in God's nostrils! Allow me to quote to you from what will one day be the book of Isaiah, which would be called the Bible. Listen now closely as I quote it to you:

'To what purpose is the multitude of your sacrifices to Me?'
Says the LORD.
'I have had enough of burnt offerings of rams
And the fat of fed cattle.
I do not delight in the blood of bulls,
Or of lambs or goats.

'When you come to appear before Me,
Who has required this from your hand,
To trample My courts?
Bring no more futile sacrifices;
Incense is an abomination to Me.
The New Moons, the Sabbaths, and the calling of assemblies—
I cannot endure iniquity and the sacred meeting.
Your New Moons and your appointed feasts
My soul hates;
They are a trouble to Me,
I am weary of bearing them.
When you spread out your hands,
I will hide My eyes from you;
Even though you make many prayers,
I will not hear.
Your hands are full of blood.

'Wash yourselves, make yourselves clean;
Put away the evil of your doings from before My eyes.
Cease to do evil,
Learn to do good;
Seek justice,
Rebuke the oppressor;
Defend the fatherless,
Plead for the widow.'"[8]

CHAPTER 4

KEEP THE LIGHT SHINING IN DARK PLACES

As the omniciscreen grows dark again, Windrose notes the solemn and quiet attitude of the souls. "I know that the attitude of God's people being so wrong concerning the sacrifice was a sad state of things, but God has always had a small group of people who would serve Him with all of their hearts. He calls them His remnant. Even though His heart is continually being broken over the stubbornness of the masses, He is still forever trying to reach them with His eternal truths. A very famous king named David, a man whom God will describe as 'a man after His own heart,' will one day write about this devastating spiritual problem. Allow me to quote a passage from Psalms, which will one day be another from the book I told you about, called the Bible. You have to realize that I know the Word, just like someday, you can and will know things when you are placed inside the human children of God who you will become. Listen closely now as I quote it to you:

> 'O Lord, open my lips,
> And my mouth shall show forth Your praise.
> For You do not desire sacrifice, or else I would give it;
> You do not delight in burnt offering.
> The sacrifices of God are a broken spirit,
>
> A broken and a contrite heart—
> These, O God, You will not despise.
> Do good in Your good pleasure to Zion;
> Build the walls of Jerusalem.

Then You shall be pleased with the sacrifices of righteousness,
With burnt offering and whole burnt offering;
Then they shall offer bulls on Your altar.'"⁹

Once again, the souls in the arena sound out with thunderous applause and shouts of praises to God, intermixed with hearty "amens!"

"Ladies and gentlemen, the very future soldiers of God on the earth, we have only begun to prepare you for your many missions on the earth. Our next sessions will detail the exciting other *gifts* that God has for all mankind throughout all of history. Hold on to your seats! It's going to be a wild ride!"

As Windrose begins to address the souls for yet another topic that will explain the gifts that God has for His children on the earth, enabling His Kingdom to come so that His will can be done, he points back to the omniciscreen. "Now, we are going to discuss a troubling occurrence that will happen in many ways multiple times throughout the world's history, stretching until the end of time. However, in order to help you process this very sad illumination, you are also going to actually witness as we view into the future one of you here today being used as a result of this training to steer a church leader and his will back to the right direction.

"The sad truth is that even though Jesus, the only-begotten Son of God, left the beauty of heaven to come down to earth, He also accepted the mission of being born into the form of a man and accepted the call to thirty-three and a half years of suffering in many ways. Not only the suffering surrounding the cross but a lifetime of denying Himself the pleasures of this life so He could become the spotless Lamb of God. In so doing, He was the perfect sacrifice for the sins of the whole world! After He completed this act of love that beggars all description, people began to come up with false teachings, false religions, and all types of deception created by Satan himself to try to hinder the good news of the message of the Gospel of Jesus Christ from reaching people!"

At this point, you could hear the souls begin to groan and make statements such as, "Oh, no! How terrible. That is awful. Oh, I can't stand to think about it." As a matter of fact, the groans and the sighs became so loud and seemed to last for such a long time that Windrose had to ask them to quiet themselves.

"Quiet, everyone! Please calm yourselves. Yes, I know, I know, and as a matter of fact, in the Father's eyes, there is nothing more evil that a person can do in his or her time on earth than to mislead people into a false religion! Intrinsically, one of the many things that the Father has put into place is this training session of you, souls, and you are going to have the delight to see one of you in action over the omniciscreen as God the Holy Spirit brings to your remembrance one of these things that we have taught you!"

"Oh, wow! That will be great! Yes, thank You, Father, for allowing us this privilege of seeing that!" Many words of appreciation were said with exuberance, and so many were commenting that it was almost louder than the groans from the last thing that Windrose had told them!

"I wonder who it will be!" one of them shouted out.

Windrose, laughing, says, "Oh, somebody is about to find out that they were the one chosen for that time period in history to do an important task for the Father. He wants to bless all of you with the experience of seeing one example of how this is going to play out."

The arena began to burst out into a spontaneous expression of praise to the Father, to the Son, and to the Holy Ghost, singing songs of heaven that had never been written but were instantly inspired by God. Windrose then directed the souls to look once again at the omniciscreen as he began to tell them about their next journey.

Windrose then says, "Ladies and gentlemen, we are now visibly traveling to a time period in AD 63 when the Apostle Peter penned his second letter to the church. I am going to read out loud to you what he is writing while the omniciscreen lets us view him writing it. The only sound that you will hear while we are watching the Apostle Peter write will be the sound of my voice."

As the omniciscreen lights up, we see Peter sitting in a dimly lit room with oil lamps on either side of him. As he writes, the souls observe him pausing from time to time to bow his head to pray, and then he continues writing. Then Windrose begins to narrate what Peter is writing.

Windrose starts by saying, "It's important to realize, souls, and we will learn more about this as other time travels take place, but we should understand for a minute that God has different gifts that He gives different people to further the teachings of His Kingdom on the earth. One of those gifts that we see used and explained in the Bible in both the Old and the New Testaments is the gift of the prophet. These individuals, a man or a woman, are those whom God chooses to be His spokespeople on the earth. In this case, the Apostle Peter is being used in the ministry of a prophet speaking forth a revelation of a future event that he knows will one day happen on the earth. God, our Heavenly Father, is omnipresent, meaning that He can be anywhere and everywhere He chooses all of the time. He is also omnipotent, meaning He is all-powerful and has unlimited power, and He is omniscient, meaning that He knows everything all the time in the past, the present, and even in the future. It's where we get the word 'omniciscreen,' from which He lets us, by His all-knowing power, view the future as He wills it!"

At this point, all of the souls in the arena expressed their impressiveness with various groans of amazement and words of thanksgiving and praise.

Windrose goes on to explain, "Peter, one of God's true New Testament prophets, writes a stinging rebuke in his second letter to the church in Asia Minor.[10] He realizes that heresy is a wicked sin that must be strongly dealt with, and he uses very strong words to describe what he sees coming in the future. So here is some of what Peter is writing as we see him now. But there were also false prophets among the people, even as there will be false teachers among you, who will secretly bring in destructive heresies, even denying the Lord who bought them and bring on themselves swift destruction. Many will follow their destructive ways, and because of this, the way of truth will be blasphemed. By covetousness, they will exploit you with deceptive words; for a long time, their judgment has not been idle, and their destruction does not slumber."

At this point, again, the arena is filled with expressions of sadness and sorrow. Aabid-27 speaks out and says, "I understand that even when God grants forgiveness and a way to deal with Adam and Eve's sin, evil will still exist in the world, as we saw in the trip to the story of Cain and Abel. However, when the very Son of God comes to the world and makes such a great sacrifice, His sacrifices will be not only surrounding His death and suffering on the cross but the entirety of His life. He will choose to live in self-denial of what other men enjoy, albeit sinful or not, just so that He will represent perfect holiness. It seems so hard to understand how any human being of God's creation could ever try to create a false version of such a great gift!"

"That is an excellent question, Aabid," Windrose responds. "Keep in mind that you as souls have not been born yet into your physical, sinful natures, so it cannot possibly make sense to any of you how that people can make such evil choices! Let me read to you one of Jesus's quotes from the Gospel of John: 'For God did not send His Son into the world to condemn the world, but that the world through Him might be saved. He who believes in Him is not condemned; but he who does not believe is condemned already, because he has not believed in the name of the only begotten Son of God.'[11] You see, Aabid, all of the unbelievers who will one day live on the earth, who, as we have said, have been born into a sinful nature, do not have access to righteous thinking. Subsequently, not only are they capable of very wicked sin, but they, by that nature, follow Satan's inspiration, and his number one desire is to attack God's creation. As a matter of fact, what God loves the most, Satan hates the most as he is still vindictive towards God's judgment of him."

As Windrose continues, he says, "Let's now look at another passage of scripture that Peter will one day write, which also addresses this issue of false teaching. Once again, let's look into the future and watch Peter as he writes in his second letter to the churches of Asia Minor, as I narrate it:

> *'Beloved, I now write to you this second epistle (in both of which I stir up your pure minds by way of reminder), that you may be mindful of the words which were spoken before by the holy prophets, and of the commandment of us, the apostles of the Lord and Savior, knowing this first: that scoffers will come in the last days, walking according to their own lusts, and saying, "Where is the promise of His coming?*

For since the fathers fell asleep, all things continue as they were from the beginning of creation." For this, they willfully forget: that by the Word of God, the heavens were of old, and the earth standing out of water and in the water, by which the world that then existed perished, being flooded with water. But the heavens and the earth which are now preserved by the same word, are reserved for fire until the day of judgment and perdition of ungodly men.

But, beloved, do not forget this one thing, that with the Lord one day is as a thousand years, and a thousand years as one day. The Lord is not slack concerning His promise, as some count slackness, but is longsuffering toward us, not willing that any should perish but that all should come to repentance.'"[12]

The souls continue to respond in expressions of disdain for what they had just heard that Peter wrote.

Emma-14 speaks out loudly, saying, "Windrose, isn't it great that people can be saved from their sins and become born again and know what it is to become a new person in Christ? That is such a thrilling thing to realize and to celebrate in the goodness of God."

"Oh, Emma, Emma, how wonderful it is of you to bring that up!" Windrose says while laughing and smiling. "If there could be a main purpose for all that we are doing here and all that God the Father will ever do, that would be it! Thank you for sharing that thought with us! Now, everyone, let's look to the omniciscreen again as we visibly travel to our next destination.

"Souls, we are traveling to a Christian summer family camp in Northern Maine, where a group of ministers are about to gather for a Bible study. It is the year 2018. The camp represents several churches of the same denomination in the region, and they are shaking hands as they all enter the large room surrounded by chairs. Hanging on the wall are pictures from the many-year history of this well-known campground called Preston Homestead. As each pastor stops for a minute to grab bottled water or a cup of coffee, a general conversation takes place."

"Hey, Pastor Antwon! How are you doing?"

"Good, Bob, good; how's things? Have you settled into the north country after God called you to leave Florida and move all the way up here?"

"It's all right."

Antwon responds, "However, the winter months have not set in yet, but the presbyter has been great and especially encouraging to my wife, who was reluctant at first to come up here, but God confirmed to her heart that He had a plan and she is perfectly at peace about it now!"

"Great, Antwon, great! Yes, we all have been praying for you here. The people of Maine are great overall, by the way. Don't get burned out on the Bigfoot jokes and the mountain men stories, as they are everywhere, but the people truly will give you the shirt off of their backs here! By the way, you thought the seafood was good in Florida; Maine lobster is worth moving here for all by itself!"

"Looking forward to that, Bob!"

At that point, the evening speaker for the nightly revival meetings comes in with the sectional Presbyter Rev. Ron Steinhour.

"I would like everyone to meet Joe Kensington. He comes to us from the Pennsylvania District, and you will be blessed by his ministry. His heart is to see the church come into revival and to see many people get saved, and he is here to tell us how, in tonight's meetings, he will be sitting in with us during our morning study time this week."

"Hi, Joe," several of the pastors reiterated.

"Welcome to the land of the 'frozen chosen,'" one pastor stated, chuckling; several "amens" from the others in the room were heard.

Sister Sue Jenkins then came in the room, who is home on furlough as a missionary from Uganda.

"Welcome, Sister Jenkins, to our morning study time this week," Brother Steinhour says, chuckling in his jolly senior saint way. "I'm so glad that you could come and join us at camp this week. I want you to take fifteen minutes on one of the nights of your choosing to share a bit about your ministry too.

Perhaps some of the churches here will invite you to come and raise support?"

At that point, Pastor Slydol comes in, bringing his son, a visiting pastor, with him.

"Hello, everyone! I would like you to meet my son, Jim, who pastors in Niagara Falls, New York. He and his family are with us this week, and he and his wife, Emily, will soon be joining me on staff in Baileyville. Some of you pastors may want to get to know him this week as he feels that God has called him to a unique ministry involving specialized counseling."

"Hello, Brother Jim," one of the ministers says, with others nodding their heads and greeting him verbally as well.

"Let's all be seated so that we can have a brief word of prayer and then can get right started with our discussion topic this week for minister's fellowship hour. Our presbytery decided this week's topic to be called 'Modern trends in contemporary ministry.'"

"Oh, praise God!" Jim Slydol exclaims. "That's right up my alley!"

Just then, Brother Kindrick and Brother Richards come through the door.

"Sorry, we are late; we had to drive in from the city this morning, and traffic was horrendous!"

"That's okay, brothers," Rev. Steinhour assured. "We were just about to get started on this week's theme, 'Modern trends in contemporary ministry'! Brother Kindrick, will you lead us in a word of prayer over today's fellowship and discussion time?"

"Sure, Brother Steinhour."

"Father God, may You guide us in all truth today as we discuss some possibly controversial topics. May You fill us with love in our hearts and give us the wisdom to discern between good and evil. May we be polite to others who may hold different viewpoints on varying topics. In Jesus's name, we pray. Amen!"

All of the ministers in the room agreed with a hearty "amen."

Brother Steinhour, being the elder in the room, starts the discussion.

"As an opening scripture for today's discussion, let's look at Jeremiah 33:3

(NKJV): 'Call to Me, and I will answer you, and show you great and mighty things, which you do not know.' I have found in over fifty years of ministry that there are times when you will hear a teaching and something just not set well in your heart about it. In those times, this is one of those scriptures that I have leaned on over and over again. Do you know that God has never disappointed me? He always guides me either through some scripture or by His still, small voice. Truth be told, sometimes we just need to really pray before we accept some new doctrine coming down the pike!"

Pastor Jan Slydol speaks up, "Yes, to be honest, when my son started texting me excited about some of the new truths that he had discovered, I had my doubts. It certainly was different than anything that I had ever heard before! At first, it deeply troubled me when he stated, 'Dad, you have to learn a lot about the occult to be able to understand that there is a lot of spiritual power on both sides of darkness and light!'

"You would have thought I had just heard him say he was addicted to drugs or something, and honestly, that's how upset I was!"

"Dad," Jim said, "you had better back up and explain a few things, or these ministers in the room are going to cock their 'rebukers' to get ready to fire! What I was really trying to explain to my father is that times are different now, and I believe that God understands that fact. If we are going to be effective in reaching this generation, we have to have some flexibility in what we believe."

About that time, Joe Kensington began tapping his toe a little and began changing the position that he was sitting several times, obviously showing signs that he was very uncomfortable with the topic at hand.

Pastor Antwon spoke up and said, "Yes, some of these kinds of things are being talked a lot about in the state of Florida. I have heard of whole churches deciding that they felt being 'born again' was just a religious term and really did not have relevance in today's culture!"

This started a lot of inter-discussion between the ministers in the room, and it was not hard to see that several people were uncomfortable discussing this kind of thing.

Brother Richards clears his throat a minute and then says, "I can remember when I was visiting a major denominational church in Atlanta, my newly acquired in-laws attended. It was a huge church, and I could not help but notice that the parking lot was packed with cars. I thought, *Wow, I'm not sure what this church is doing right*, but I surely wished that our parking lot was that full on Sunday mornings!"

Almost everyone in the room chuckled; that is, everyone but Joe. If you looked closely, you could see a tear in his eye, and he was quietly mumbling a prayer.

Then Brother Richards continued, "Yes, that was until the four of us walked down a long hallway. My father-in-law said, 'That room right there is reserved for special classes only. Former President Jimmy Carter teaches a Sunday school class there from time to time. People have to sign up to have one turn in his class. We have sat in before, and he is such an interesting Bible teacher.' Again, another thought crossed my mind: *Well, I guess if a former president goes here, it must be a pretty good church!* Until we rounded the corner, and there it was: an eight-foot by eight-foot multicolored poster promoting their Sunday school that said, '*All the world is born again!*' Then my heart sank! I thought, *Wait a minute, all the world is not automatically born again! There are steps to take, clearly spelled out in scripture, to receive and believe in the Lord Jesus Christ to be born again.*"

Almost everyone in the room agreed with Brother Richards' statement and experiences; this time, everyone except Jim Slydol! Now it was Brother Slydol who was being ancy in his seat and nibbling a bit on his fingernails. It was at this point that Jim spoke up and spouted words that stirred a strong reaction in the room.

"Listen, brethren and our dear sister present today: I know some take these things too far, and the consequences are less than desirable. However, aren't we supposed to win the masses? Isn't the mission that Jesus set down a mission of love? Why should we argue over terms like 'born again'? You see, I have learned that if we would just all set our doctrine aside for a minute—"

That was about all that he got out of his mouth, and Evangelist Joe Kensington came flying out of his chair across the room with his finger pointed in Jim Slydol's face and shouted, "You listen here! I'm not going to set my doctrine aside for my own grandmother or anyone else ever. Do you understand me?"

"Yes, sir," Jim said, slumping down in his chair a little as Joe continued in his rebuke mode!

"Doctrine is the foundational truth of the Bible, and men and women for generations have laid down their lives for this Bible and its doctrinal truths, and there is no equality in power between the Creator of the universe and a fallen angel! You tell the devil the next time you see him that I refuse to take any counsel from anyone who was foolish enough to believe that he thought that he could overthrow God!"

With that, Evangelist Joe Kensington stormed out of the room, leaving several nodding heads saying, "Amen, amen, yes, amen!"

At that point, Windrose says, "We are now going to fast-forward the omniciscreen a little bit to the evening service where Evangelist Joe Kensington is about to speak."

"Good evening, brothers and sisters! Welcome to Family Camp this year, and it is a real privilege to be invited in from Pennsylvania to be your guest speaker. My wife and kids send their greetings from home, and as I have been in prayer over the past few weeks, God has burdened my heart with several messages this week that nightly will challenge and inspire you to live an abundant life in Christ by seeking Him with all of your hearts in a new way! Not that many years ago, having an evangelist or a revivalist come to your church and hold nightly meetings was a common thing, you know. Now, because of various reasons, which could be a sermon in itself, churches no longer do that. In those meetings, night after night, you got a little more from the Lord, and by the end of the week, God's people would get another jump start for the next months of their lives. Personally, I think we need to go back to that, and whoever attends, so be it, but pastors that are present or within the sound of the recording of this service, please prayerfully consider having regular 'revival' meetings again and trust God to use them! So, in a moment, I will have you turn in your Bibles to tonight's scripture.

"First, however, I would like to take a moment to explain myself and my expressions of a strong conviction in this morning's minister's fellowship meeting. I want to say that I apologize for getting so angry with what I said. You see, the topic being discussed in that moment I know is a flagrant heresy against the cross of Christ, and I let my emotions get the best of me! However, I do not apologize for my position against such thinking, and while some foolishly make fun of biblical doctrine, it is the foundation of everything that we believe! So, please accept my apology for striking the rock instead of speaking to it. Can I hear 'amens' to all those who forgive me so that we can move on with the messages that God has put on my heart for this week of meetings?"

Windrose then steps up to the base of the omniciscreen and turns to begin his discussion, revealing which one of the souls God used in this scenario.

"I know, soldiers, that I promised you that I would reveal to you which soul God used in this last travel through time. I don't suppose that anyone would care to guess which soul was used by God during their travel to the summer camp in Maine in 2018. Just a couple of hints: remember, it will be someone who had been supernaturally trained through these exercises yet had no conscious memory of them in their future state as a human child of God. It will also be somebody who can say just the right thing at just the right time to implement a righteous thought into a particular situation to steer a person or a group of people in a godly direction. Is there anyone bold enough to take a guess? It is okay to confer with those sitting next to you on this one. Just try to keep your discussions in a quiet tone. I will give you a few minutes, and this exercise is just for fun until the soul that was used is acknowledged."

You could hear the souls quietly discussing their thinking with one another, creating a low roar of noise across the arena.

Windrose raises his voice and says, "I can hear a lot of names going around out there! Somebody, shout out a name!"

One soul shouted out, "Was it Reverend Steinhour? He interjected an excellent thought and a Bible reference to help all those who were present that day."

Windrose responded, "No, it was not Reverend Steinhour."

Another soul said, "Was it Jim Slydol, as he was trying to introduce some new thought into the discussion group?"

At that statement, you could hear hundreds of souls groan out a "*noooooooooo!*"

With that, Windrose responded, "Oh, you are so right to recognize that, souls. That actually was the statement that needed the help from the soul in that room that day!"

With that, Gregory-19 spoke up and said, "It had to be Joe Kensington, then!"

"Yes, that's it, and would Joseph-33 please stand in the arena and be acknowledged?"

At that point, applause was heard across the arena from all of the souls, along with shouts of congratulations and many saying, "Good job, Joseph! Well done," and such things as that.

"Joseph, you will not have any memory of this day when that day arrives, but the truths that you learned watching Peter pen that warning today caused something powerful to rise up within you! You were then able to be used in a powerful, exhortative way to stand against the false doctrine that was being introduced by Jim Slydol." The will of many people will turn on that day, and the needle of the Father's compass will be moved in the right direction.

Windrose further explains, "I feel I need to remind everyone of the importance of your mission. At the same time, it may seem like a small thing that Joe Kensington will do that day, but the influence of just one wrong thought can carry rapidly, especially as time passes in history and knowledge increases. Devices similar to the omniciscreen that you see here will one day be in almost every household in the world. Even though it will not have access to God's omniscient knowledge, there will be ways that even false doctrine can be transmitted and affect millions of people in a short time.

"In this last time travel, you have received a basic introduction to the Holy Spirit's special gifts. You will also be special gifts to the world when you are born into God's children on earth. However, there are so many more gifts to talk about and so much more to learn as we go. Stay focused as each session gets more interesting, and each thing that you learn will have the potential of greater influence!"

CHAPTER 5

WHEN THE SOULS SEE WHAT IS ALL WORTH GOING TO PRISON FOR

The souls notice Windrose beginning to walk away from the omnicisreen, gently poking his large staff on the gopher wood plank stairs, his long white robe trailing behind him. As he walks along, they see that his head seems to be slightly bowed, and his lips seem to be moving as if perhaps he is praying. Having descended the long flight of stairs from the arena's projection platform, he steps onto the main floor area, where he is surrounded by all the souls who look at him expectantly from the many rows that fill the arena. He slowly rotates in order to be able to make eye contact with everyone. When he begins to speak, even though his voice is calm and only slightly above a whisper, each one of the souls throughout the arena can hear what he says due to the way the Father designed the space.

"Souls, today we embark on a journey designed to help you gain more understanding of the gifts that the Father will bestow upon the church for the work of the ministry. We will discuss not only what some of them are and how they are used but also what will seem to be a hard-to-understand reality. That reality is that not everyone in God's church will accept God's gifts wholeheartedly!"

With that statement, you can hear gentle groans echoing throughout the arena, coming from the many thousands of souls who have been listening intently. In addition, some are heard saying, "*Nooooooo*," while others say things like, "What?" "Why?" or "How could that possibly be?"

Windrose responds to them by saying, "One day, there will be several situations that will be recorded in the Bible, God's Word to the world, which will not make any sense to you. Please keep in mind that because Lucifer, in his bitter fallen state, hates what God loves the most, he infiltrates the church wherever he can to cause strife, division, confusion, and every evil work in order to slow and, where possible, hinder the Father's work. Jesus will one day be quoted by the Apostle John in the Bible's book of Revelation: 'Now to you I say, and to the rest in Thyatira, as many as do not have this doctrine, who have not known *the depths of Satan*, as they say, I will put on you no other burden.' [13]I know, souls, it is hard to believe, but the evil one will use whoever he can to attack those who are working for God's Kingdom.

"However, the very next gift that we are going to discuss helps to shine a light on and thereby expose some of those diabolical schemes. This gift from the Father will beat Satan at his own game and will turn around for good every success Satan will gloatingly think he has accomplished. As I have previously taught you all, in this ongoing battle of darkness against light, the enemy will incorporate evil schemes into his strategies. However, on the other hand, everything we will do must be on the up and up because it must line up with the just and righteous nature of Almighty God! Because of these up-and-coming hidden tricks of Satan, God understands His children will need special equipment with a supernatural power; a power that you need to know is called 'the anointing of the Holy Spirit.' The power of the Holy Spirit will be the energizing force behind every miracle that will ever take place."

The gathered souls then watch in awe as they peer back in history to the very beginning of time and observe the Father's mighty hands display His great unlimited power as He separates the water from the dry land, simultaneously lifting all seven continents from the bedrock of the ocean floor!

"Souls, you have just observed the powerful ability of the Great Equalizer, who will also become the Great Enabler of God's servants on the earth in their many battles against the forces of evil."

At this point, the souls begin to shout great cries of "amens," cheering with such loudness that a vibration is felt in the platform beneath the feet of everyone in the arena and in the seats in which the souls are sitting.

Windrose can tell that the underlying burden and pangs of sadness that the souls had felt up until this time are being counterpunched with a great hope. Their great sadness, which has been caused by their realization that the fallen angel Lucifer would one day cause such evil, has now been upended by their realization that God has a plan to equip His creation with the power of the Holy Spirit. As he observes the change in the souls' demeanor, Windrose's smile stretches from one side of his face to the other, knowing that the best news is yet to come! Then His smile softens momentarily as he reflects on the great price that Jesus Christ, the only-begotten Son of God, will have to pay so that mankind might receive this gift. However, while the cheering continues on and on, the thought of Jesus's future return to earth for His bride immediately causes Windrose's smile to brighten again. At this point, Windrose himself joins in with the cheers that are celebrating the news of the future gift of the Holy Spirit.

After a few more minutes of joyful celebration, Windrose raises his hand for silence and once again begins to speak as he walks back up the stairs to the omniciscreen. "Souls, sadly, a large part of your mission will be to try to reach people within various church movements with the truths involving the many gifts that God will design for His church. In a previous travel through time, you have already witnessed the opposition that Jesus faced while He was on earth. As you will see, opposition to His message will continue throughout the many millenniums, which will pass when He returns to heaven to prepare many mansions for the coming of His bride. One day, the Apostle Paul, knowing why the Son has gone back to heaven, will write in one of his letters to the people of the church of Corinthians, 'Eye has not seen, nor ear heard, nor have entered into the heart of man the things which God has prepared for those who love Him.'[14] Sadly, however, there will be many groups and individuals throughout time who will not accept the wonderful things that the Son is preparing for them.

"In fact, there will be those who will so desire the acceptance of other people that they will come into the churches pretending to be believers, yet in their hearts, they will have never yet fully accepted the gift of salvation through what Jesus will have done for them on the cross. These people will be known as 'religious' people, but in their hearts, they will still be dead in their sins."

Windrose suddenly interrupts himself to say, "Souls, the Father has just sent me a wonderful word that thrills my heart. He just informed me of the following: 'It is time!' I knew this was coming, but I did not know exactly when. Paul's words, which we just foresaw, lead up beautifully to what the Father is about to show us. He is going to let us see firsthand what heaven looks like!"

Once again, the arena is filled with comments of praise and thanksgiving. The animated crosstalk between the souls is exuberant and loud.

Windrose, while chuckling with delight, raises his hands up to calm the souls in their exuberant expressions of excitement. He tells them, "I know you all might think that this could be a journey into heaven as it exists now, as God has always existed and heaven has always existed; however, the place where mankind will live with Him forever has not been in existence eternally. Jesus will one day say to His followers, as will be recorded in John's Gospel,

> *'Let not your heart be troubled; you believe in God, believe also in Me. In My Father's house are many mansions; if it were not so, I would have told you. I go to prepare a place for you. And if I go and prepare a place for you, I will come again and receive you to Myself; that where I am, there you may be also.'"* [15]

As the three-dimensional projection system lights up, the souls see a small opening off in the distance in a large wall surrounded by nothing but space. Through this opening, however, they see an amazingly bright golden light that is casting beams in all directions.

"This golden light," Windrose explains, "will be unlike any light that was, or ever will be, on the earth. The *glory of God* will be both literal and figurative. The holiness of God is so great that its' brightness shines with more brilliance and more beauty than any light form that will ever exist throughout all time. It will not be like sunlight or moonlight. Even if you were able to visibly travel far into the twenty-third century, where the technology of that day will be such that it produces lighting of all various forms of brightness, nothing will rival the heavenly light you are seeing today. It is true that there will one day be incandescent, fluorescent, mercury-vapor, high-pressure sodium, metal halide, quartz, and light-emitting diode or LED lighting. Man's accomplishments through the years in developing and producing various forms of artificial light will be constantly evolving and improving, yet nothing that man ever produces will come close to the beauty, brightness, and splendor of the heavenly light of God. The Apostle John will one day pen these words in the book of Revelation: 'And the city has no need of sun or moon to shine on it, for the glory of God gives it light, and its lamp is the Lamb.'"[16]

Like the splash of a large hailstone falling from a cloud and landing in a puddle, the souls' joint expressions of joy spread out in every direction at the sight of this amazing light! One of the souls shouts out, "Can we see inside the wall? Can we see inside?" And shortly after, others join in with similarly eager expressions. No sooner are the pleas uttered when suddenly the cylndricron expands and reveals a huge three-dimensional image of such overwhelming beauty that, for the first time ever, the souls are speechless in silent awe!

They gaze open-mouthed at large golden cobblestone streets, streets that seem to go on forever, wrapping endlessly around equally spectacular buildings. Hamilton-61 says, "Wow, we saw that Jesus will predict that He will go to prepare a place for us, and just like Paul will one day write, there are no words that could do justice in describing the beauty of heaven!" The souls then notice in amazement that the big golden cobblestones interlock together in such a way that although they are individually unique, together, they form a beautiful pattern stretching out in every direction.

The golden light of God's glory sparkles, resembling tiny golden flakes that seem to be suspended in the air. "Look! In spite of the brilliance of the light, it is not blinding but is instead captivating! It accentuates the magnificent splendor of everything that we see in front of us!" Hamilton-61 cries out in amazement to a group of souls standing near him.

Everyone nods their heads in agreement, and Susan-65 adds, "Just look at the golden cobblestone walls that line the streets! They are capped with wide, flat gold stones that have rounded edges! And look at all the beautiful flowers growing everywhere all around us!"

Windrose then comments, "Everyone, please keep in mind that this beautiful city is the place where God's children will live forever and ever in time without end! Just think: if God the Father will make the earth and all of creation with all of its beauty, how much more beautiful will the place called heaven be, which His Son will create for His Father to live with His children forever!"

At that moment, the souls see people walking down the streets and notice that they all have similar expressions on their faces. They all have smiles so wide that the souls can only refer to them as "absolutely unhindered childlike smiles." In addition, they also notice that the people are giggling frequently as they talk with each other! Then they hear one of the citizens of heaven say, "Well, I have to go now and meet my great-great-grandfather for lunch." Next, they see him make a tiny dip at his knees and immediately shoot up in the air, flying away right in front of everyone's eyes! "What was that?" one of the souls shouts out. Then another responds, "In heaven, we can fly!" Then, in only a matter of moments, all of the souls join in expressing delighted anticipation of being free from gravity in heaven!

Then, Heather-37 comments, "Well, I guess when Paul will one day say, 'Neither has entered the heart of man the things that God has in store for them that love Him,' he will be thinking of surprises like God's creation being one day able to fly like a bird, just like the angels!"

"Yes, Heather, yes," Windrose laughingly replies. "And Paul will have in mind many more gifts that Jesus will make to equip His church for building the Kingdom of God on the earth. Notice how the buildings are all made of solid gold! Jesus, as you have been told, will one day predict that He will be the one who will design mansions, or dwelling places, for us in heaven. See how beautiful these buildings are! It is no coincidence that Jesus will be raised on the earth by a stepfather named Joseph, whose trade will be that of a carpenter. Even though Jesus was, is, and always will be the Son of God, imagine for a minute that while He works with His earthly stepfather building buildings, all of that time, He will comfort Himself, thinking of the days to come when He will return to heaven. He will be planning ahead, thinking about how He will utilize the help of all of heaven's angels. Together, they will spend the next several thousand years in heaven, building eternal dwelling places for all of God's children.

"Souls, do you notice anything unique about these buildings other than the fact they are made of pure, solid, shining gold? In this case, you may be able to pick up on it through the special enhanced learning capability in your emotilliance, which allows you to perceive the cultural norms of the future."

Mateo-11 shouts out, "Oh, oh, I see that none of the building entrances or windows, although they are all exquisitely designed and artistically arched at the top, have any doors, glass, or shutters in the openings to be able to close them up at night!"

"Well, Mateo," Windrose replies, "do you care to guess why that might be? Once again, you will need to utilize your enhanced emotilliance to figure out the two main reasons for this fact!"

Alexi-7 raises her voice and shouts out, "It's because, in heaven, there is no crime, no dangerous animals, no biting insects, and therefore, no need for anyone to worry about someone breaking into their home or harming them in any way! Windows and doorways can be kept wide open, right, Windrose?"

"Yes, yes, Alexi. That is very true. Is it starting to add up in everyone's mind just how valuable heaven will be and how precious it is to think about living forever and forever, time without end, in such a place where there will be no evil of any kind ever again? There is also another reason why the windows and doors do not have to be closed at night. Can anyone tell me what that is?" Windrose then adds a hint: "This reason might be so common most will overlook it!"

Calandra-3 shrieks out with an exuberant squeal, "It's because there is no nighttime in heaven, right, Windrose?"

"That's exactly right, Calandra," Windrose says with a bright-eyed smile. "Now we are going to look back at the omniciscreen to learn a few more things about heaven. What you learn will infuse you with an eternal passion. It will make you be willing to position yourself in your lives so that you will be able to influence the most people in your lifetime. Can you imagine the enormity of the value of the task of laying down your life for the gospel's sake in order to help people from all over the world to be able to spend all of eternity in heaven? Your influence will help others receive not only the gift of eternal life paid for by Jesus's own blood but so many other spiritual gifts too!"

The cylndricron now opens up a three-dimensional image for the souls, which no one had been expecting. The souls see in front of them the time travel projection system, which they have not seen since the day they learned about Noah and his ark.

Windrose, with a happy grin, says, "Welcome, souls, to the area of heaven known as paradise!"

Off in the distance, the souls see snowcapped endless mountains, which serve as an awe-inspiring background to what seems like hundreds of fields filled with beautiful flowers spread out in front of them. They see animals of various kinds running through the fields, but what puzzles the souls the most, even with their enhanced emotilliance, is the fact that lions are running along playfully among herds of deer and antelope. Grizzly bears are lying down lazily next to sheep and baby goats. Birds of spectacular colors fly about, dipping and diving in brilliant displays of splendor, and little children laugh as they chase exotic butterflies and play with cougars and baby zebras!

Windrose, next unexpectedly, through supernatural power of the Holy Spirit, walks down to the cylndricron and, with one step, is transported directly into the scene. The souls see what they think must be a much younger version of Windrose. As he does that, what seems like hundreds of children come running up to him. Some pull on his robe. Some hug his legs. A few others tug on his arms. He then begins to sing a new song to them:

"Come, little children, come; come to the Father's love.

Although earth could not hold you, heaven was made for you.

Come, little children, come. Come, little children, come; come, little children, come.

Though earth could not hold you, heaven was made for you. Come, little children, come."

The souls, hearing this new song, express a new emotion. In absolute awe, they are completely silent. Gentle smiles appear on their faces, accompanied by tears of joy. With that, the young Windrose bids the children goodbye for now and just walks back towards the omniciscreen and right back into the arena with the souls.

"One day," Windrose adds, "the earth will be filled with all of the wonderful animals God will create. In the limitless days of pre-eternity, before the worlds are formed, the Father will delight in watching His Son create all the animals, fish, and birds, and they will use those eons of time to design every living thing one by one. Each bird, each fish, each land animal, and especially each person, even down to each hair follicle, will be predesigned by God's Son. One day, the Apostle Paul will write, under the inspiration of God's Holy Spirit, in the letter to the Colossian church:

> *'For this reason we also, since the day we heard it, do not cease to pray for you, and to ask that you may be filled with the knowledge of His will in all wisdom and spiritual understanding; that you may walk worthy of the Lord, fully pleasing Him, being fruitful in every good work and increasing in the knowledge of God; strengthened with all might, according to His glorious power, for all patience and longsuffering with joy; giving thanks to the Father who has qualified us to be partakers of the inheritance of the saints in the light. He has delivered us from the power of darkness and conveyed us into the kingdom of the Son of His love, in whom we have redemption through His blood, the forgiveness of sins.*

He is the image of the invisible God, the firstborn over all creation. For by Him all things were created that are in heaven and that are on earth, visible and invisible, whether thrones or dominions or principalities or powers. All things were created through Him and for Him. And He is before all things, and in Him all things consist. And He is the head of the body, the church, who is the beginning, the firstborn from the dead, that in all things He may have the preeminence.'"[17]

Once again, the souls break out in exuberant praise and worship! The roar of praise is so loud that they are not able to talk to each other. Someone shouts out as loud as he can, "When do we get to meet Him? When do we get to meet Jesus? Surely, we can visibly travel through time to a place where He will be. When?" At that, others join in, shouting, "When? When?"

Having to compose himself due to his laughter and joy, Windrose raises his hands up and down again to calm the volume of the souls praising enough so that he can speak. "Soon, everyone, soon... When the Father says that it is time, you will all get to meet Him. I'm sure you will all agree when it does happen, the timing will be right. I know it will be worth the wait."

"Wow!" one soul shouts out. "He is before all things, and in Him, all things consist. Praise Jesus for His awesome power and greatness!"

"He is worthy! He is worthy! He is worthy!" the souls begin, magnifying His wonderful greatness.

"Now," Windrose says, "we are going to go back to the omniciscreen and visibly travel in time to a place of desolation. You will be surprised to find that in spite of the desolation and suffering, it will be a place of victory."

As the cylndricron darkens, the omniciscreen begins to light up again. The souls observe hundreds of men in very scraggly clothing moving about on what appears to be an island because they can see water on the other side of the barren stone-strewn landscape. They see that the ragged men are being supervised by other men in soldier-like attire, with long swords sheathed to their sides, who are also carrying whips or clubs.

Windrose speaks once again, addressing the souls concerning what they were seeing. "The day will come when one of the twelve disciples, the youngest, named John, will, in his more senior years, be arrested by the Roman leadership for his preaching regarding the Bible and the many amazing things that he personally witnessed Jesus do and teach! After they arrest him, the Romans will put him in one of their unique island prisons, the island of Patmos, with hundreds of other hardened criminals, who you see here on the omniciscreen. John will be sent there with one of his young disciples, named Prochorus. This island will be a very barren, hot, and dry place, a multiday journey by ship from the mainland, thus destroying any hope of escape. However, during John's very difficult years of suffering, it will be there that God the Holy Spirit will choose to inspire him to write one of the most powerful books of the Bible. This book, which will be called 'Revelation,' will contain many profound prophecies and will also include seven unique letters to the churches in Asia, located in a country that will one day be known as Turkey."

The souls once again begin to vocalize their reactions to this new information, but this time with mixed emotions. Some are blessed by the thought that God will choose what seems like such a forsaken location to inspire such a powerful book. Others feel grieved in their spirits that this disciple, who will be so very close to Jesus, will experience such prolonged suffering and deprivation in such a barren place. A quiet discussion commences among them. Windrose decides that it is best just to let them talk it out because both perspectives are very important.

After a good amount of time, Windrose begins to once again draw their attention to the omniciscreen. "Souls, at this point in history, because of John's good behavior and out of respect for his advanced age, the guards will have allowed him to spend several recent weeks in prayer in a small, secluded cave. You are now about to see two Roman guards approach John with some parchment, a reed pen, and some ink. We will then be able to witness him begin to write as the Holy Spirit dictates the book of Revelation once again to him.

"As you see, there are no trees on Patmos, but very rustic-looking canopies built by the prisoner's labor hang over some scattered rock outcroppings. At this point in time, John, having emerged from his small cave, will be taking refuge from the intense rays of the noonday sun in one of these places of shade. His skin will have been tanned so dark during his many years of back-breaking work on this seemingly forsaken island that some guards will have asked him what the country of his birth was.

"As the scene opens, we will see him with his head cupped in his hands, which part his long white hair. We will overhear him quietly praying to his Heavenly Father for some form of relief from the brutal island climate. We will notice that although his skin shows the wrinkles of his ninety-year age, his muscular frame seems intact, and he shows no apparent signs of weakness. As he shifts his weight, we will see a Roman guard approach him..."

The souls hear the soldier ask, "Are you John, the one they call the apostle?"

"Yes, sir," John answers.

"Here are more of the writing things that you have requested. Please do not take this lightly. Only limited supplies arrive on this island. Be aware that these items will be removed instantly if you share them with any other prisoners. There is a reason that you have been allowed to have these items. You may not know that a written report was submitted to our superiors when you saved another prisoner from drowning during the ship ride here. We have taken notice of the fact that you have been faithful to work very hard in the stone quarry. In addition, you have never shown any disrespect to any of the guards. When you read what you have written so far at night to the prisoners, we notice that they ask many questions and seem to work more peacefully the next day. You also lead some of the other men each night in singing songs. Nobody else has ever done anything like that, and it has been proven to be good for the morale. Our superiors have been reading our reports carefully and feel that you set a good example for the other prisoners. In addition to the parchment, pens, and ink you requested, you will also be allowed to work at a small wooden table, which we will place in your cave. We will also agree to your request that we make sure that your writings will be preserved from being destroyed by either other inmates or any guards."

"Thank you, sir. I will do all that has been asked of me," John responds with great joy. "Now I can continue with my work, writing some more of the things down that God has shown me will be coming in the future."

Windrose once again is able to adjust the omniciscreen to allow the souls to observe John sitting at his rough table after sunset a few hours later. A single flickering candle, pinched in a crack of a projecting stone in the cave wall, shines some light around his prisoner-hewn stone room. The souls see that John is indeed carefully recording what God, by His Holy Spirit, is inspiring him to write.

As John takes the reed pen and continues to write further revelation on the parchment, the souls are allowed to see what he is writing through a special magnification feature of the omniciscreen. In his book Revelation, John writes,

> *Now I saw a new heaven and a new earth, for the first heaven and the first earth had passed away. Also there was no more sea. Then I, John, saw the holy city, New Jerusalem, coming down out of heaven from God, prepared as a bride adorned for her husband. And I heard a loud voice from heaven saying, "Behold, the tabernacle of God is with men, and He will dwell with them, and they shall be His people. God Himself will be with them and be their God. And God will wipe away every tear from their eyes; there shall be no more death, nor sorrow, nor crying. There shall be no more pain, for the former things have passed away."*
>
> *Then He who sat on the throne said, "Behold, I make all things new." And He said to me, "Write, for these words are true and faithful."[18]*

At this point, something out of the ordinary happens. The omniciscreen suddenly lights up, showcasing with a bright golden light the very words that continually hang across from the throne of God, serving to remind the angels of the number one purpose of their mission:

> *Our Father in heaven,*
> *Hallowed be Your name.*
> *Your kingdom come.*

Your will be done.
On earth as it is in heaven.
Give us this day our daily bread.
And forgive us our debts,
As we forgive our debtors.
And do not lead us into temptation,
But deliver us from the evil one.
For Yours is the kingdom and the power and the glory forever. Amen.[19]

John the Apostle then goes on to write out the part of Revelation, which talks about the glory and the splendor of heaven. At that, the souls begin to cheer and shout "amen" with such volume that all Windrose can do is just smile and laugh and join them in their praises of heaven. Sometime later, after everyone begins to calm down, Windrose observes that the souls are now in a quiet attitude of gratitude. Windrose then concludes the session with these eternal thoughts:

"Souls, what you just witnessed is truly what it is *all* about. In the future, all Christ's followers will live with Him in heaven throughout all of eternity, for millions and millions and millions and millions and millions and millions and millions of years without end. Heaven will be a place where the Father will dwell with you, and you shall be His people. God Himself will be with you and be your God. And God will wipe away every tear from your eyes; there shall be no more death, nor sorrow, nor crying. As you just witnessed John writing in the book of Revelation, there shall be no more pain, for the former things will have passed away. There is nothing better that anyone can ever invest their time in than winning lost souls, knowing that they will spend eternity in heaven. Paul will one day write in his letter to the Roman church, telling them that there will be no suffering on earth that will ever compare to the glorious life in heaven. Souls, allow me to share his words, which the Father enables me to know by heart with you:

> *'For I consider that the sufferings of this present time are not worthy to be compared with the glory which shall be revealed in*

us. For the earnest expectation of the creation eagerly waits for the revealing of the sons of God. For the creation was subjected to futility, not willingly, but because of Him who subjected it in hope, because the creation itself also will be delivered from the bondage of corruption into the glorious liberty of the children of God. For we know that the whole creation groans and labors with birth pangs together until now. Not only that, but we also who have the first fruits of the Spirit, even we ourselves groan within ourselves, eagerly waiting for the adoption, the redemption of our body.'[20]

"That, dear future soldiers of God, is why we will do what we do. No greater battle will ever exist in the entire universe than the battle between good and evil over the eternal souls of men. I have been making you wait a long time to learn about the next awesome gift, but it will be worth the wait! In our next journey, you will learn about a gift that is so powerful that Lucifer himself will wage every battle he can muster to try to stop the church from receiving it. When he fails, he will have to try to smother the next gift with more lies than even the gift of salvation itself. When that still does not stop God's power from being poured out, Satan will begin to use one of his most effective age-old tricks. He will try to infiltrate the church with religious lies about control of this gift. So, soldiers, learn that although God always wins in the end, because of this war of wills, Jesus will one day warn His soldiers, that is, His followers, in the book of Matthew: 'Enter by the narrow gate; for wide is the gate and broad is the way that leads to destruction, and there are many who go in by it. Because narrow is the gate and difficult is the way which leads to life, and there are few who find it.'[21] Soldiers, prepare for war!"

CHAPTER 6

THE WAR WHAT FOR AND THE 500 CLUB

"Souls, the reason that I say 'prepare for war' is because Lucifer, the fallen archangel, hates this next wonderful gift of God almost more than salvation itself. The type of war, however, I am talking about is, shockingly, a spiritual war of opposition from religious people who are not truly born again. From the very day that this gift was poured out from heaven onto God's people on Earth, Satan started opposing it with determined vigor. He feared the impact it would have if every single child of God were to receive the power, a power like that poured out on chosen individuals in Old Testament days. The evil one knew that it would enable ordinary individuals to make huge progress in teaching all people groups. They would be empowered to teach them how real God was and how to be righteous and holy, enabling them to live in a way that would unleash the Father's blessings on them. Satan realized he could lose the grip he had on God's creation, a grip that he had seductively stolen in the garden. Throughout history, whenever God has done something unique with His Holy Spirit, many people end up giving their lives to Christ. Satan then immediately steps in to work through vessels that are submissive to his every whim to try to slow down or stop this process. We saw an example of this in one of your very first lessons!

"Right now, however, souls, we are going to use the omniciscreen again to visibly travel ahead in time to a day exactly fifty days after Jesus rose from the dead. What is truly amazing is that this special day on the Hebrew calendar is known as the day of Pentecost. Although few people will ever know about the conversation you are about to observe, we are now going to travel to a place in the future. When we arrive there, we will discover that the Apostle Luke and the Apostle Paul are sitting down and having a discussion. As the scene opens, we will see that they are sitting in the shade of an olive tree in a Corinthian garden. Both will be enjoying a glass of newly pressed grapes. Luke will be discussing with Paul a letter that he has written to his good friend, Theophilus. It will be obvious that their hearts are thrilled concerning all the wonderful things that God has been doing since Jesus was resurrected from the dead. Souls, pay close attention! You are about to hear about a powerful event that will one day change the world!"

As the souls begin to have a lot of discussion between themselves, Windrose has to once again raise his hands up and down to signal them to quiet down and keep their voices low so that everyone can hear what Paul and Luke are discussing.

"Paul, Paul," Luke says, "it is so wonderful to see you again!"

"As it is you, Paul. You must tell me everything you can about so many people who have been accepting Christ as their Savior during your journeys as you have traveled everywhere, planting of new churches!"

"Luke, yes, it's true! There will be lots of time to do that today, but first, I understand that you just finished a letter to Theophilus telling him many things. I know you tell in the letter about Jesus's ascension into heaven and also about my conversion, which I have told you about in great detail many times."

"Yes, Paul, God put it on my heart to write down what happened, by His design, in that upper room on the Pentecost feast day. He also wanted me to tell your story because I believe He wants all the world to know about your sudden and total about-face. I believe yours is the greatest conversion to Christianity that the world has ever known."

"I guess that is why you asked me to bring the scrolls with me, eh, Paul? Ha-ha-ha!" Luke laughs as he pats Paul on the shoulder.

"Yes, true, true, Luke; I am anxious to hear some of it. Would you mind reading it to me? I always enjoy hearing your voice when you read."

"Of course, of course," Luke says as he begins to unroll the first scroll, which he has marked by tying it up with a red ribbon.

"Slowly, Dr. Luke, slowly, I don't want to miss anything!" Paul emphasizes.

"Okay, Paul. I chose to start out like this:

> *The former account I made, O Theophilus, of all that Jesus began both to do and teach, until the day in which He was taken up, after He through the Holy Spirit had given commandments to the apostles whom He had chosen, to whom He also presented Himself alive after His suffering by many infallible proofs, being seen by them during forty days and speaking of the things pertaining to the kingdom of God. And being assembled together with them, He commanded them not to depart from Jerusalem, but to wait for the Promise of the Father, "which," He said, "you have heard from Me; for John truly baptized with water, but you shall be baptized with the Holy Spirit not many days from now." Therefore, when they had come together, they asked Him, saying, "Lord, will You at this time restore the kingdom to Israel?" And He said to them, "It is not for you to know times or seasons which the Father has put in His own authority. But you shall receive power when the Holy Spirit has come upon you, and you shall be witnesses to Me in Jerusalem, and in all Judea and Samaria, and to the end of the earth." Now when He had spoken these things, while they watched, He was taken up, and a cloud received Him out of their sight. And while they looked steadfastly toward heaven as He went up, behold, two men stood by them in white apparel, who also said, "Men of Galilee, why do you stand gazing up into heaven? This same Jesus, who was taken up from you into heaven, will so come in like manner as you saw Him go into heaven."[22]*

Paul interrupts Luke, "Luke! Oh dear God, how I wish I could have been there to watch Jesus ascend into the clouds…"

"Yes, Paul, I agree. Me too. I made sure to spend enough time with the disciples to be able to take detailed notes about every important detail that took place that day. The fact that you wrote to the Corinthian church, informing them that during Jesus's forty days here on earth, he was seen by over 500 people is certainly an 'infallible proof'!"

As the screen fades to black for a minute, Windrose once again steps forward and begins to address the souls.

"Dear spiritual soldiers of God, I am about to share something with you all that will seem shocking and, yes, even unbelievable!" You see, Satan does not use vividly explosive strategies to try to hide the truths of God's kingdom. He always uses subtle plans, which resemble a slowly approaching cloud. Before you know it, the cloud gradually grows denser and denser until it is so thick that it becomes hard for people to perceive what is right in front of them. Sometimes, it is something dramatic and quick, but other times, it involves cover-ups that will take months or even years to complete. The evil one understands the effectiveness of covert operations. For that reason, future souls of planet Earth, out of millions, you have each been chosen for tasks that you will only recognize in the moment that they happen. As a reminder, in the future, you will have no memory of these classes, classes that were set up before Earth's time began to undermine the devil's schemes. As an act of your own free will, you will be able to say or do something to help circumvent the evil one's destructive plans, which he will engage in constantly until the end of time."

With that, the souls once again began to discuss among themselves the enormity of the responsibility that they would have. They are in awe of the fact that they will be able to contend for the faith, defending the truths surrounding the Father's plan of salvation. Like the gentle sound of distant rumbling thunder, the arena revealed once again the spark of life that exists, multiplied by the thousands of concerned souls. As the souls sit there gazing around at other souls, it is easy to see they are each wondering what their future tasks will be.

As Windrose once again makes his familiar motion up and down with his hands, he smiles and, with a gentle heavenly anointing, says, "Quiet, please, dear souls. Let us take another informative journey into the year 2001. I want you to know that something very horrible is about to happen on the earth shortly after what you will witness tonight, which will change the spiritual landscape of the world forever. The teenagers that we will be seeing will have no way of knowing that some of them will soon be going into the military and that they will be involved in a war that will last for many years. It appears to to them that they are just enjoying another innocent, fun night on a calm summer evening.

"We are now going to observe a youth group from Victory Now Church. Pastor Archer and Serenity Harper's two-story home mountain view with a huge game room and walk-out basement is proving to be the perfect setting for their Summer Slumber Party night."

As the omniciscreen opens, the youth pastors are sitting at their kitchen table discussing the fun-filled evening ahead while the volunteer adults welcome the incoming students and show the guys and girls their separate sleeping areas for the night.

"This is so exciting, dear," Serenity exclaims as the kids are being dropped off by their parents. "Your vision for this home is coming to pass right before our eyes! Some critical people thought your catchphrase from the popular movie, 'If you build it, they will come,' was just a pie-in-the-sky dream, even though God had given you: "'Go up to the mountain and bring wood and build the house, that I may take pleasure in it and be glorified," says the Lord,'[23] from Haggai 1:8 in prayer as a *Rhema* word to confirm it. But tonight sure proves them wrong!"

"Yes, sweetie," Archer replies, "and don't forget that group of God-blessed Christian business people from the Relators' Emporium who made large donations to help make this mountain home a reality. As they sought a word from God, many of them confirmed that this home for teenagers was indeed His vision. Let's also not forget all the volunteers who came from our church to help build it! Praise God! Our home is now functioning right before our eyes for the purpose He intended for it from before the foundation of the earth!"

"I know, I know. Praise God for praying people who know how to hear His heart and obey His leadings!"

"Serenity," one of the young girls interrupts, "where can we pile our sleeping bags: girls on the first floor, guys in the game room, right?"

"Yes, honey. Just please stay clear of Jared's band members who are bringing in their equipment for the worship time later tonight."

"I will, Serenity, but that drummer is pretty cute; I would not mind getting in his way!" At that, a group of girls start giggling.

Archer speaks up so that everyone can hear above the noise of all the people arriving. "Hey, everyone, it is almost eight o'clock, so let's start making our way to the game room. Find a hunk of floor to sit on for tonight's movie. Jared came early to help me set up the sixty-four-inch big-screen projection TV just put on the market by some new company out of Israel called Omniseecast!"

"Cool," several of the young teen boys shout.

"I wonder where they got the name for that company," Jack, one of the assistant youth leaders, asks Archer.

"I don't know, Jack, but I have heard that a group of Jewish businessmen, who are actually converted messianic Christians, founded this electronic startup company and are openly telling stories about how they pray over all of their designs and feel that God gives them product ideas."

"Okay, I need three girls to help me make a big batch of popcorn. Who's helping?" Serenity shouts out.

"Me, me, me!" several reply enthusiastically.

"Okay, Jodi, Aalyah, and Kali, you help me. The rest can set up a small table for snacks and soft drinks near the back of what will be the theater area downstairs in the game room so that people can easily serve themselves during the movie."

"Is everyone here?" Archer shouts out up and down the stairs to check with the other teens who knew pretty much who had planned to attend.

"Yes, the Bamford twins just got here after their dance class tonight. They were the ones we knew would be a little late," Jack shouts back.

"Okay, once everyone gets settled in and their stuff tucked away for later, let's start getting everyone seated for the movie," Archer affirms.

As Serenity passes Archer, she leans in and whispers in his ear, "Wow! Fifty-six teens in our home! This is so exciting!" With that, she gives him a gentle kiss on his earlobe and says, "Let's do this!"

"Okay, gang," Archer says. "Let's everyone grab a hunk of rug. For those of you who brought pillows and such, make yourself a comfortable space, as the movie is a little long. After it is over, we are going to have some discussion time to tie the movie in with the Bible studies we have been doing in youth group recently. I realize that this might not seem like the kind of movie that you would pick for a youth group sleepover; however, I have prayed a lot about this year's Summer Slumber, and I feel that there is a good reason why God wants us all to watch this particular movie tonight about the life of Jesus. At the end of the night, I promise you all that this evening's spiritual emphasis will have us all stirred up in our own hearts to be revived from whatever slumber we are in! Jack, start the movie, please!"

"Okay, Archer," Jack replies. "Three, two, one, showtime!"

As the made-for-Hollywood movie about the life of Jesus plays, Archer pauses the scenes from time to time to talk about different occurrences in the life of Jesus. "Someone, help me out here tonight," Archer says. "In what ways did Jesus suffer before and during the crucifixion?"

Chang Lee speaks up, "I am amazed at how many different ways he suffered, really. I mean, there are the obvious ways that we see depicted in the movie. We see Him being punched in the face, the crown of thorns being rammed down upon His head, the terrible thirty-nine lashes of the Roman whip, but I think also of the terrible emotional pain of the rejection of His own people! Isn't there a scripture somewhere, Archer, that talks specifically about that?"

"Yes, Chang, there is," Archer replies. "John 1:11 tells us that 'He came for His own, and His own did not receive Him!'" [24]

With that, several of the youth added a mixture of comments: "That is so sad." "Oh, wow!"

One of the girls says, "That just makes me want to cry!"

Another adds, "Just think about how we as young people get so offended if just a few of our friends don't think we are cool for one reason or another. It makes us freak out!"

Then many added other comments such as, "Yes, that's right," and "Wow, I can't imagine that kind of rejection!"

Leon then speaks out, uttering a very profound thought: "I think that Jesus actually suffered in many ways during His whole lifetime. Think about how He never had a girlfriend. He wasn't raised by His real Father, even though Joseph did a wonderful job as a stepfather. From a kid, Jesus was mocked by religious leaders as being a 'fatherless child.' Those are some of the reasons that I think Jesus knew the pain of rejection during His entire life!"

"Yet in spite of all of this suffering, He never sinned!" Serenity adds.

"So true, so very true," Archer affirms. "Now, let's continue to the best part of the movie!"

As the movie continues, the students gasp as they watch Jesus being nailed to the cross and see it being raised and dropped down hard in the pocket of the rock on Golgotha Hill.

Archer pauses momentarily to draw the teen's attention to the fact that Jesus hung on those three nails for six hours. "Yes, young people, please realize that through the years, the movies have been very well done; however, the time sequence of events is often skewed. One time, I wrote to a major Christian television network that had built a replication park featuring many areas of the Holy Land. In my early zeal as a Christian, I suggested to them that they create a 'healing room' where people could have the opportunity to come in and view a live reenactment of Jesus hanging on those three nails for six hours. I felt that it was possible that individuals' faith levels would be boosted by disciplining themselves to sit in a theater and feel a part of the six-hour time period as a professional actor acted out the scene of the suffering. The actor would not portray Jesus on the cross for the few minutes that pass in an average Jesus movie but for the actual six hours. Mark chapter 15 tells us in verse 25 that it was the third hour when they crucified Him, and then in verse 34, he says that He died in the ninth hour. I guess the park owners did not share my burden or vision, which I felt was from the Lord. They never wrote back or made that change in their theme park. To this day, I still feel that it would have a powerful impact."

"Oh, wow!" the teens shout out.

"Yes, yes..." another one says.

"But, Pastor Archer, do you really think that people would sit there for six hours, watching an actor portray that agony?" Isabella questions.

"That really was my exact point," Archer responds. "I wanted everyone to really grasp the huge price that Jesus paid for us. I thought it would be a dynamic experience. If people actually made themselves sit through the whole six hours, I believe that it would revolutionize their spiritual lives!

"Okay, kids," Archer shouts out again. "Let's get back to the movie because this next scene, to me, has the same mind-blowing effect I have experienced while watching several other Jesus movies through the years."

Some of the teens scramble to get more snacks and refills on their drinks, but they quickly return to their seats. As the movie continues, they are promptly mesmerized by what Archer has just been referring to.

As the resurrection scene had them oohing and awing, the teens were so focused that nothing could have distracted them. They noticed Jesus folding His bandages and laying them on the stone slab. Then, the awesome power of God suddenly rolled the giant stone away, and Christ exited the tomb.

The next scenes go quickly through the familiar Bible scenes featuring Mary Magdeline and Thomas. Next, Jesus waits at the seashore for Peter, cooking breakfast for His disciples, who have briefly resumed their former occupations as fishermen. Within a few minutes, the movie ends with Jesus miraculously ascending into heaven accompanied by two angels, whose famous words are quoted in Acts 1:11 (NKJV): "Men of Galilee, why do you stand gazing up unto heaven? This same Jesus, who was taken up from you into heaven, will so come in like manner as you saw Him go into heaven."

At this point, something happens to one of the souls, which has not happened to any of them since they began their sessions of unique training.

Isaiah-33 stands up in the middle of the 2001 youth video. Displaying unexpected enthusiasm, he interrupts the lesson, shouting out, "That is just what we heard about in the beginning of this session; we watched as Paul listened to Luke reading his account of what was then happening on the earth!"

With that comes a wave of laughter, which starts with Windrose and spreads throughout the arena. Then, Isaiah-33 himself begins to laugh because he realizes that he had let his own excitement get the best of him.

"It's okay, Isaiah," Windrose responds. "Let's get back to the year 2001 and see what exciting Bible story that Archer, the youth pastor, is going to highlight for his teens!"

Once again, they turn their attention to omniciscreen and find that Archer is talking to the group.

"Okay, young people from the coolest youth group in this entire state, let me ask you a question. We just witnessed Jesus's last days on the earth. What do you think the actual time period is from His resurrection to His ascension into heaven? The scripture actually tells us, but just from watching this movie, and many other similar movies about Jesus, what would you guess were the number of days that Jesus walked around on the earth as the resurrected Messiah of God before He left to go to heaven?"

Some of the teens hum and haw a bit as they talk among themselves. Some said, "Three days? Oh, no, that was how long He was in the tomb." Others guessed maybe five days, agreeing that it was hard to tell from the movie because He had to go and do all that stuff, including meeting with the men on the road to Emmaus.

Jack looks across at Pastor Archer and Serenity, who are both smiling.

"Okay, who brought their Bibles?" Archer asks. Several started digging through their stuff, but many had left their Bibles upstairs in their backpacks, not thinking about taking them downstairs to the movie. A few, however, take them out of their purses or sweatshirts.

"Those of you who do have your Bibles, turn with me to Acts chapters 1, 2, and 3 and then to 1 Corinthians chapter 15. Hold your spot in Corinthians because we are going there in a minute," Archer says. "Who wants to read Acts 1:2–3 to everyone tonight? I believe this is one of the most under-preached scriptures in the entire Bible for some reason. I'm sure only the devil himself knows the reason because he is good at hiding things and covering up truth!"

Chang shouts out, "I got it:

'Until the day in which He was taken up, after He through the Holy Spirit had given commandments to the apostles whom He had chosen, to whom He also presented Himself alive after His suffering by many infallible proofs, being seen by them during forty days and speaking of the things pertaining to the kingdom of God.'"[25]

"Wow, Pastor Archer! You are telling us that Jesus walked the earth as the resurrected Christ for forty days? That's almost a month and a half!" Isabella exclaims. "I don't know why I don't remember ever realizing that before!"

"Many people do not," Archer replies.

"Serenity adds, "You see, what my wonderful husband is trying to get us all to see tonight is that there are many, many nuggets of truth in the Bible. But like in a gold mine, you have to do some of your own digging to get them out!"

"Now, let's get to the good part of this clouded-over radically fantastic truth. Let's look at 1 Corinthians 15:3–8. Who wants to read that for us tonight and put the real meat sauce on the pizza to jump-start this youth group into some real action?"

With that statement, everyone starts laughing. "You are making us hungry, Pastor," Jack complains.

Rosie says, "I have it. You said chapter 15, verses 3 through 8, right?"

"Yes, Rosie."

"Okay, here goes:

'For I delivered to you first of all that which I also received: that Christ died for our sins according to the Scriptures, and that He was buried, and that He rose again the third day according to the Scriptures, and that He was seen by Cephas, then by the twelve. After that He was seen by over five hundred brethren at once, of whom the greater part remain to the present, but some have fallen asleep. After that He was seen by James, then by all the apostles. Then last of all, He was seen by me also, as by one born out of due time.'"[26]

"Okay," Archer says, "did everyone hear what Rosie just read to us? Shout with me, everyone: *He was seen by over five hundred people after He rose from the dead!* Some of whom Paul tells the Corinthian church were still alive during His day!"

"Hey, I got a cool idea!" Jack said. "Let's start a 500 collective! We can get bright red tee shirts printed up and have big white letters that say on the front: *'Did you know about the 500?'* Then, we can wear them when we are out witnessing in public. The tee shirts would be great conversation starters with unbelievers or people who are just religious but do not really know Jesus personally as their Lord and Savior."

At this point, all of the teens start getting excited and cheer at the idea! Then Isabella speaks up and says, "How about this: We just add the letters *'or'* on the front and then on the back write: *'Or that Jesus walked on the earth for over forty days after He had risen from the dead?'*"

"Yays" and "yeses" fill the room, along with praises to God. It is obvious that the teens can not wait until next week to get there so that they can start implementing this new idea.

With that, Jack speaks up, saying, "You are not going to believe this! I happened to make a quick call to one of the businessmen from the Reality Coalition. I told him about this new idea that just broke, and he immediately told me he wants to donate the first one thousand dollars to get our first batch of tee shirts printed!"

Serenity, with a huge, beautiful smile, walks clear across the room and hugs Archer. As she does so, she says in his ear, "God is up to something big, honey, really big!" This time, she kisses him right on the lips, which makes everyone in the room break out in laughter from the girls and groans from the boys!

At this point, the omnicisreen begins to go dark. Windrose, laughing out loud and shaking his head back and forth, starts saying over and over, "God is so good, our God, our Heavenly Father, is so good and has such good gifts for all of those who will reach out and receive them and put their trust solely in Him. Souls, do you remember what we were looking at before I took you to the year 2001 and allowed you to look into the future at that wonderful story?"

Kai-42 said, "Yes, we were starting to talk about the importance of the Day of Pentecost, and you were starting to teach us about two things: One being about the wonderful gifts God will one day pour out on His church. Then secondly, the sad truth is that the enemy of all souls, Lucifer, will be very active. He will go all out to try to cover up or deceive people about those gifts because he knows how powerful they can make the church!"

"Yes, Kai, that's true. Next, we are about to study some of those very strategies and how you, as souls, will one day effectively undermine and defeat his tactics. Just like in this trip to 2001, we can see how the Holy Spirit will use creative ideas and ordinary people to lead an unconverted and, sadly, sometimes even hostile world to a saving knowledge of Jesus Christ!"

At this, one of the souls shouts out, "Here I am, Heavenly Father. Please use me to do great things!"

Windrose responds, "As long as that is the lifelong cry of your heart, you will accomplish greater things for the kingdom and all of eternity than you can ever imagine!

"Let's now visibly travel back to the Day of Pentecost and watch even Mary, the mother of Jesus, be marvelously filled with God's Holy Spirit!"

CHAPTER 7

WHEN JESUS REVEALS HIS SECRET HERE, WILL IT BE YOURS?

indrose, smiling and saying over and over again, "Thank You, Father; thank You, Father," in a very worshipful way and laughing with heavenly joy, pauses for a moment while looking up towards heaven. He then voices a very profound prayer: "Thank You, Heavenly Father, for this wonderful and precious gift You will give to Your church. Thank You for the great honor of being able to teach Your souls. Thank You for allowing me to reveal to them through time travel the glorious event awaiting all of us in the future, an event which will take ordinary men and women and transform them into Holy Spirit-filled, effective, eternal, soul-winning soldiers of the cross of Jesus Christ!"

The souls in the arena begin to clap and praise God and celebrate loudly as they contemplate the wonderful day and date in coming history when God will come and dwell within His people, a day Windrose has been teaching them about. They have already learned that it will be a day when temples will be built without human hands, temples whose construction will bring glory to Him alone. Instead of great spires or steeples reaching towards the skies, there will be hands raised to the heavens in praise to the only true, all-powerful God. Then, in a likewise heavenly born harmony, instead of musical instruments made with carved wood, pottery, or dried gourds, the sounds of praise and adoration will come from voices expressing melodies stored and hidden from inside the hearts of those whom He so loved and has created! This praise will ascend from those who will have come to know Him, will have chosen to follow Him, and will have freely decided to receive and embrace the gifts of the Holy Spirit, which will enable them to truly worship Him as He desires to be worshiped.

At this point, Windrose turns once again to address the souls. "Stewards of the things of God!" he proclaims. Hearing him address them with this new title, the souls first respond with a moment of silence followed by some quiet interaction between the souls. Then Jasmine-21 speaks up and says, "Windrose, you have called us the 'children of God' and 'soldiers of God' but never the 'stewards of the things of God.' Why have you given us another title, and why now at this juncture?"

"Well, Jasmine," Windrose replies, "the Father knows it is the perfect time to begin to speak to you about a new level of responsibility, a responsibility that in time will be given to all of mankind who choose to follow Him. When an earthly father gives one of his children, say, for instance, a colt, as a gift, he understands that the colt will one day become a fully mature horse. Because of that, the earthly father knows that the full-grown horse will be capable of accomplishing a lot of good. However, he also knows it could be capable of doing a lot of damage, depending on the amount and type of training that the colt is given when it is young. This same principle applies to the spiritual gifts the Heavenly Father gives to His earthly children.

"That means that the earthly father also realizes the importance of working closely with his child regarding how to properly train that young colt in a way that is both loving and responsible," Harper-32 interjects as those around him, Billy-15, Peyton-29, and Akira-9, agree enthusiastically.

"Yes, Harper. And yes, yes, and yes to all of you," Windrose agrees. "Congruently with that wonderful assessment, you will see how God the Heavenly Father desires to work closely with those who are blessed with His wonderful gifts. These gifts are freely given to all of His children, that is, to all who desire to receive them. Because just like that adult horse that can one day be harnessed to a piece of farming equipment or harnessed to a carriage to carry people from place to place or even saddled for a single rider, it also, if not rightly trained, could wildly trample someone to death or throw a rider off of its back. Do you also know that as powerful and as helpful as a horse can be to a farmer, some farmers stubbornly reject owning a horse, insisting that they can do the work of their farm without one? So it is with the gifts of the Spirit. God's gifts are always good, but they also always need the instructions contained in His Word and the wisdom of His Spirit if they are to be used properly. In his sometimes stubborn, prideful, or ignorant way, man often rejects God's gifts, foolishly thinking that he can do everything himself. That is why today I am calling you His stewards! I call you 'stewards' because one day, you will have a part in the building of His Kingdom on earth, which means that you will all be managing the affairs of your Heavenly Father on earth! You will be called upon to be stewards of His gifts and also be charged with teaching others about them.

"In a short time, we are going to be journeying into the future once again, to a day we previously discussed, called the Day of Pentecost. As you will remember, the disciples had been in a troubled state of mind, having witnessed the loss of their beloved Jesus, who had been crucified on a cross just a short time ago. He had told them that He was going to leave, but they did not want to think about that and consequently did not believe it. He told them, as will one day be written in John's Gospel, 'I will not leave you comfortless: I will come to you.'[27] In another place, John will also write that Jesus said, 'And I will pray the Father, and He will give you another Comforter, that He may abide with you forever.'[28] Yet even with these promises, and so many others, the disciples find themselves feeling fearful and confused, even while they are all in total agreement that they will obey His commandment to go to Jerusalem and wait for the 'Promise of the Father.' So often, souls, you must understand that as future men and women of God, the best faith you will be able to aspire to is a 'wait and see' faith. A 'wait and see' faith, God's best, will allow you to always trust Him perfectly. It will allow you to know that He fully understands you, knowing your frame, knowing that you are but dust. You will be comforted, knowing that He understands man came out of the dust originally, and one day, he will return to the dust. You will be able to 'wait and see' because you will know that He loves you more than any of you can fathom and is merciful, gracious, and kind to you, even when you fail!

"Let's watch now as 120 of Jesus's disciples begin praying in the upper room. Souls, I would like to point out that Mary, Jesus's mother, is there. Can you tell me, anyone, why it is such a significant fact that Luke will one day record it in the letter he will write in the book, a letter that will later be called 'The Acts of the Apostles'?"

Mary-77 speaks up, saying, "I realize my name is Mary, but that is not why I am answering this question. I feel that just as God uses people to do certain tasks, He also wants us to know that even though Mary was a very committed, godly woman, she was nevertheless a woman in that room. She knew that she, too, needed every gift God would pour out upon the disciples or any of His followers. Although Mary was the birth mom of Jesus Christ Himself, she had just a few weeks earlier stood at the foot of the cross and heard Him utter His last words, 'It is finished!'[29] She fully understood that she was woman. If asked, her response would have been similar to that of the early disciples, as recorded by Luke in Acts:

> *'And Barnabas they called Zeus, and Paul, Hermes, because he was the chief speaker. Then the priest of Zeus, whose temple was in front of their city, brought oxen and garlands to the gates, intending to sacrifice with the multitudes. But when the apostles Barnabas and Paul heard this, they tore their clothes and ran in among the multitude, crying out and saying, "Men, why are you doing these things? We also are men with the same nature as you, and preach to you that you should turn from these useless things to the living God, who made the heaven, the earth, the sea, and all things that are in them."'[30]*

"Yes, Mary speaks up, and just as those early disciples acknowledged that they were men, Mary knew as a woman she also needed to be part of the outpouring of the Holy Spirit that day, so she, too, gathered in the upper room."

"Well-spoken, Mary," Windrose says, his response accompanied by a burst of delighted and loving laughter. "I really feel that God the Father has given you some insight here! May I call you 'Doctor Mary'?"

"*Whaaat*?" Mary replies. "Why did you call me 'doctor'?"

"I call you 'doctor' only for the sake of all the souls here in the arena, not to single you out for any personal honor or recognition at this point. However, Mary, yes, one day, you will be born into a human body and will eventually become a medical doctor. Just as the arena is filled with souls who will come from all different walks of life and professions in the future, you, Mary, will be a medical doctor. You will one day devote your whole life to medical missions. Remember, though, that in the future, you will have no memory of this day or this fact. The Father just wants to stir the hearts of the souls around you to help them realize that sitting to the right or the left of them may be a king of a foreign country or a plumber in a small country town. Only God the Father knows for sure where you will be placed in life, but know this: He will certainly be in the business of using ordinary men and women. He will fill them with the Holy Spirit. He will then multiply their work and talents for His glory and for the building of His kingdom on the earth. Mary, the day will come when you learn all about baptism in the Holy Spirit and all of the gifts the Holy Spirit will gift you with as you live out your days on the earth. Your life will be considered by yourself and by the many people who know you as fairly ordinary.

"In God's divine order of events, the day will come when, as a young teen, you will be asked the same question that Paul will one day be recorded asking. He will say to them, 'Have ye received the Holy Ghost since ye believed?'[31] On a future day, many years after Paul's death, a faithful soul will ask you this same question and will go on to explain this wonderful gift to you. You will say yes to it, and you will then be beautifully filled with the Holy Ghost. After that day, Mary," Windrose goes on to say, laughing with delight, 'your life will never be the same! The Word of God will come alive as you read it. Your heart will be filled with a burden to do whatever you can to reach the lost with the good news of the gospel. The love of God will fill your heart in such a magnificent way that it will compel you to tell others all about your wonderful new experience. Sadly, however, members of your own family will reject the truths of the gospel and even ostracize you from some of their family gatherings. In the midst of your heartache, Jesus's loving arms will pull you into His comfort, and He will be closer to you than you ever dreamed would be possible. A few years later, you will join a medical team, traveling to various remote areas of the earth and helping to heal the sick from their human sicknesses. In that process, your real ministry will be sharing with them the message that Jesus went to the cross for their sins so that they can spend eternity in heaven with Him!"

Windrose then draws everyone's attention back to the omniciscreen as he turns and points in that direction. He reminds them that they are now going to visibly travel to that upper room in Jerusalem where 120 people are gathered in obedience to Jesus's instruction to wait there for "the promise of the Father." He tells them to watch as they will now see into that space and time in history between BC and AD known as CI, a short time after Jesus had ascended into heaven.

The omniciscreen lights up, revealing a large empty room. It is indeed a large room, and nobody there knows for sure just how Jesus had known about it or had chosen it ahead of time. However, we do know now that a wealthy man in the town had the building built several years previously as a meeting place for local social gatherings, and so it is now working perfectly for the disciples to gather and pray. Large arch-shaped windows line the room, allowing natural light in during the day. In addition, oversized oil lamps, which someone said were removed from a dismantled old ship, hang on the wall in between each window. Mats woven from local reeds cover the entire floor, and dozens of wooden chairs form an arch-shaped arrangement around the central speaker's wooden book stand. The arched ceiling is composed of seven dome-shaped areas, which someone painted a blue sky color, adding puffy white clouds in various locations.

As the sun rises on the first day, many people begin to come and tie their donkeys and colts up at the street below, only bringing upstairs what they thought they might need for the day. Some bring prayer mats, and others small cushions to kneel on. The men all bring prayer shawls and tefillin, the little boxes containing scripture that are bound around the arms and forehead of Jewish men when they pray. It is obvious that everyone is looking forward and excitedly anticipating what is going to occur. They can be heard talking among themselves about what may happen while they wait in obedience in this Jesus-called prayer meeting.

Peter and John are quick to take the lead, helping everyone find a place and making sure that those attending know that this is to be a solemn assembly, so no unnecessary noise or needless talking is to go on while everyone prays.

"I hear a lot of you discussing among yourselves what we might expect to see here today," Peter says, raising his voice among the people. "We must remember that the ways of God are many times kept from us until they actually happen. As you come in, please just find a place to pray and begin to seek God earnestly as you would pray about any new undertaking, yet with an unprecedented level of confidence that this is a meeting that was preordained by Him. Please also know that we have no idea how long we are to wait, nor do we know exactly what He is going to do."

John then follows, lifting up his voice and saying, "Men and women of God, Jesus walked among us, teaching us the things of the Kingdom of God and instructing all of us concerning His righteousness and holiness for over three years. One of the last instructions He gave us was that we were not to depart from Jerusalem but wait for the promise of the Father, a promise that He had taught us about. He reminded us that John baptized us in water, but we will be baptized in the Holy Spirit not many days from now. Therefore, although we are gathered here to pray, we must realize that by the words of our Lord Jesus Himself, it could be days before God answers our prayer. This means that we must not be weary in praying. Sleep when you must. Fast if you can, eat as much as you need if you cannot, but please remember that this must not become a social gathering. We are here to do two things: pray and wait! The other apostles are here with Peter and me. Make no mistake; we will not hesitate to call you back to prayerful order if need be. God is going to do something awesome in this room, but He will do it in His way and in His time. Do not be afraid, and I repeat: do not get weary in waiting on God in prayer. Men and women… Pray on!"

At this point, the men and women conclude by greeting each other, understanding that their purpose there is not for fellowship but to follow the Lord's admonition to pray. Eleven of the men in that room had been admonished by Jesus in the Garden of Gethsemane the night before His crucifixion to watch and pray just a few weeks earlier, but instead, they had fallen asleep. While there would end up being some time in the next few days for sleep, those men were intent on praying faithfully this time, as their Lord had commanded. They would not repeat the same mistake twice.

In the course of this powerful prayer meeting in this upper room, a room preordained by God the Father for this special seeking and welcoming service of the third member of the Godhead, the Holy Spirit, some were praying quietly, but many were crying out with their whole hearts. No one knew how long they would be called on to pray or what was going to happen while they waited….

The omniciscreen permits a slow but consistent scan of the several days the 120 waited on the Lord in prayer. There was an amazing solemness to those days, with people only leaving the room for very short periods as life's physical necessities dictated, returning very soon to their chosen prayer posture, calling upon the Lord for *His will to be done on earth as it is in heaven*!

Rose-7 raises her hand to speak up. "Can I say something here, please?"

Windrose gently stops the omniciscreen and replies, "Yes, of course, Rose!"

"I can't help but notice that during this time of powerful prayer, the disciples are voicing the exact same words, 'Thy will be done,' which are on the banner that hangs across from the very throne of God. I remember you told us during an earlier lesson that God placed the banner in His throne room to remind the angels of God as they ascend and descend from heaven what 'the main focus' of every mission they were sent on would be."

"Rose, that is an excellent observation. Souls, please realize the following:

As time goes on, something very sad will occur in churches around the world. As the last days approach, the enemy, knowing that he has a very short time left, will succeed in dumbing down the importance of this truth, convincing spiritual leaders not to teach about the eternally important truth of the centrality of God's will and plan."

With that, you hear a groan of sadness, with several comments being interjected: "Oh, no! How could this ever be?" expressing the souls' deep shock over Windrose's latest revelation.

"Yes, you see, souls, you're calling on the earth, and the purpose for your training is to strategically position you in places of godly influence so that you will recognize and work to thwart these lies of darkness as you redirect the people around you back to the fundamental truths of God's word! In the future, you will not remember what we have discussed today; however, something will rise up in your hearts at just the right moment. At that point, you will be gently but unmistakably enabled to immediately recognize that, number one, what you will be witnessing is wrong, and number two, you will immediately seek, through prayer, effective ways to counter those lies with the truth. You will especially focus on the truth of the Father's will being done on earth even as it is in heaven."

Having interjected this brief but very important lesson, Windrose turns and restarts the omniciscreen projection of the events taking place in the upper room. After a few days of prayer, the souls witnessed Peter gathering the eleven apostles in a small room in the back right corner because he felt it was his responsibility and calling to do so. "Brothers in Christ, I believe that God is calling us to take some time today to attend to an important decision." As he begins to speak, he says, "Men and brethren, this Scripture had to be fulfilled, which the Holy Spirit spoke before by the mouth of David concerning Judas. This same Judas that David spoke about led those who arrested Jesus to him, in spite of the fact that Judas was numbered with us and had obtained a part in this ministry. Afterward, he purchased a field with the wages of iniquity, and falling headlong, he burst open in the middle, and all his entrails gushed out. As you well know, this has become known to all those dwelling in Jerusalem, so that field is called in our own language Aceldama, that is, Field of Blood.

"Of him, it was written in the book of Psalms: 'Let their [his] dwelling place be desolate; let no one live in their tents'[32] and 'Let another take his office.'[33] Therefore, of these men who have accompanied us all the time that the Lord Jesus went in and out among us, beginning from the baptism of John to that day when He was taken up from us, we must choose one of these to become a witness with us of His resurrection."

As the souls watch, the eleven disciples propose two candidates, namely, Joseph called Barsabbas, who was surnamed Justus, and Matthias. The souls take note as the disciples pray, saying, "You, O Lord, who know the hearts of all, show which of these two You have chosen to take part in this ministry and apostleship from which Judas by transgression fell, that he might go to his own place."[34] As the souls continue to watch, they see the disciples cast their lots and note that the lot falls on Matthias, which causes him to be numbered with the eleven apostles.

After a few more days of waiting and praying, the souls can see that a few are struggling a bit, wondering how much longer they are going to have to wait in prayer. Some are overheard whispering among themselves, saying, "Do you think that we have missed something?" Others are starting to focus more on speculating about just what is going to happen instead of continuing in fervent prayer.

At that point, John, sensing some of these questions, goes over to where Mary, Jesus's mother, is praying and speaks to her quietly, saying, "Mary, as you know, some are starting to doubt, yet I sense in my spirit that we are very close to seeing God answer our prayers in a very powerful and unprecedented manner."

"Yes, John," Mary quietly replies, "I can sense it too, but as we both know, God makes everything beautiful in His time. I well remember that when I was carrying our Lord as a baby, I went to visit Elizabeth because even though the angel Gabriel had appeared to me in all of his glory, telling me all that the Lord was going to do, I had started to doubt what he had promised me. I knew I was just a humble woman, so it was hard for me to understand why God had chosen me for such a great task. Elizabeth was a great encouragement to me, especially when she told me that her son, John, who would come to be known as John the Baptist, had leaped in her belly when I shared with her the news of me carrying Jesus. I ended up staying with Elizabeth for three months and was there for John's beautiful birth. I did not know all of the wonderful plans that God had for me, John, but as I waited, trusting in our Lord, all he had promised came to pass, and so much more that I wouldn't have even known to ask Him for."

"Yes, Mary, as the scripture says, 'So that no man can find out the work that God maketh from the beginning to the end.'[35] Thank you, Mary. Please forgive me for interrupting you for a minute. Let's just continue to seek the Lord. Tomorrow is the feast of Pentecost. Wouldn't it be wonderful if God did something on His special day?"

"Don't give it another thought, John. I'm so glad you came over to talk. Something wonderful is about to happen! I can feel it in my heart!"

At this point, Windrose slowly fades out of the omniciscreen in order to interject some additional thoughts regarding interesting future events, events that will coincide perfectly with each other. "Souls, one of the most important general lessons that you have been learning in a cumulative process is that God our Heavenly Father is sovereign over everything that happens on the earth. From before creation to now, everything has been done in divine order. As you have seen, there will be the divine order of the creation of the earth. There will be the divine order of the creation of man, the first Adam, and there will be the divine order of the coming of Jesus Christ, the Messiah, who will become known as the 'second Adam.' But long before Christ's appearing, the day will come when God's people will multiply on the earth, and as you witnessed on a trip in the omniciscreen, a man named Noah will build a huge boat called an ark. God will instruct him to build the ark because people eventually will become so corrupt that God will have to wash the earth clean of them. He will do this so that the righteous seed of Noah can replenish the earth.

"A day will come when God's children will multiply in a land called Egypt.

God will then raise up a prophet named Moses. Moses will be used mightily by God to deliver a nation within a nation from their Egyptian bondage. A great exodus of God's people, numbering in the millions, will suddenly pack their most necessary belongings and leave Egypt that same night. God will then work one of the most spectacular miracles on the earth of all time by parting, through the power of His Holy Spirit, the waters of the Red Sea, thus allowing millions of people to pass through safely on dry ground. This very special day will be marked in Jewish history and called 'Passover.' God allowed His people to both escape the wrath of and also destroy the army of the wicked Egyptian leader, Pharaoh, who will be following the Israelis in hot pursuit. Many who will leave Egypt in that time will become the forefathers of Hebrew leaders. They will be carried out still in their mothers' wombs, and some will still be in their fathers' seeds, but God will allow them to be born as seeds of promise and hope in the wilderness. They will have hearts to seek the Lord their God and to do all that He commands."

At this moment, the souls become so excited by Windrose's announcement that it is hard to discern which is louder: their clapping or their shouts of "amen" and declarations of praise to God! Once again, Windrose, while laughing and agreeing, "Yes, yes, praise God indeed!" must ask them to please quiet themselves so that he can continue teaching them about this all-important event foretelling the Jewish occurrences and celebrations.

"Please, please," Windrose exhorts them, "I know now that you are all starting to realize that some of you who will be there on that day are in the arena among us today! However, please let me continue to explain how, on exactly fifty days into their journey into the wilderness, Moses will come down from Mount Sinai and give to the children of Israel the Torah, as revealed by God, which are the first five books of the Bible. For years after that incredible day, the fiftieth day after Passover will be celebrated as the 'Shavuot.' Now, there will only be one date in all of time when God will undertake two major events on the same day! Fifty days after Passover will also be celebrated as 'Pentecost.' However, that, too, takes some explaining before we once again look into the future of that special day on the omniciscreen.

"What I am about to tell you will bring the greatest response of enthusiasm yet! However, knowing what I know about this, your response will be very understandable! You see, God will say, through the prophet Jeremiah, as will one day be written down in Jeremiah's book,

> 'Behold, the days are coming, says the LORD, when I will make a new covenant with the house of Israel and with the house of Judah, not according to the covenant that I made with their fathers in the day that I took them by the hand to lead them out of the land of Egypt, My covenant which they broke, though I was a husband to them, says the LORD. But this is the covenant that I will make with the house of Israel after those days, says the LORD: I will put My law in their minds, and write it on their hearts, and I will be their God, and they shall be My people. No more shall every man teach his neighbor, and every man his brother, saying, "Know the LORD," for they all shall know Me, from the least of them to the greatest of them, says the LORD. For I will forgive their iniquity, and their sin I will remember no more.' [36]

"God the Father understands that even though He will have spent over 2,000 years teaching them His ways and His laws, using many different prophets and teachers to continually instruct them in the way they should go, their human nature will repeatedly react the same way concerning sinful things. Mankind will always, left to themselves, trade a few minutes or even a few seconds of fleshly pleasure for the eternal things of God, which will last forever! That, souls, in itself, is the great evil of evil in God's eyes. The willful trade-off of the temporal for the eternal is always what separates the righteous from the wicked!

"God the Father, who fully understands that sad truth, will create a beautiful plan to pour out His Holy Spirit on all flesh who desire to come and receive Him. In so doing, by His power and through the transitional nature of being truly born again, His children will be enabled to become the children He always wanted to have. For His glory, they will become children of promise, children of obedience to His righteousness, children of holiness!

"Therefore, get ready, souls! Something beyond wonderful is going to happen on this Pentecost day. You see, throughout time, the number 'fifty' will have a special significance in the heart of the Father. As a matter of fact, the number 'fifty' will one day be used in the holy Scriptures in reference to something that God wants to highlight over 150 times. The reason that the number 'fifty' is precious to the Father is one of those secrets that only He understands. With some things, we must learn to simply trust God that something is so! The first fifty that will stand out in the writing of scripture will be when Moses writes down God's commandment, which specifies that every fiftieth year on the Day of Atonement, all debts must be cancelled in favor of the debtor. All slaves are to be set free and allowed to return home to their families. This is one of the key points to remember when using this sacred number!

"Now, listen carefully, souls, as I explain how the number 'fifty' will be entwined in a unique way around the special day of Pentecost.

"Over time, the Jewish people will begin to celebrate Shavuot, the anniversary of the giving of the law, as a festival of harvest. This will begin the first day after Passover each year. When an Israelite sees the first fruit of his various harvests, such as grapes, figs, wheat, barley, pomegranate dates, or olives, he will be instructed by the priests to tie a small rope around them to let the harvesters know that these portions of the harvest are set aside as his firstfruits. Eventually, during Shavuot, the people will come to enter Jerusalem, bringing their first fruit offerings to the temple. It will become a great celebration of music and thanksgiving to God for His provision in their lives! These offerings will be given to the priests, and afterward, there will be a great celebration of feasting and thanksgiving to God before they return home. This they will do every year. This day will also celebrate the fifty-day time period between the exodus out of Egypt and the day that Moses revealed the first five books of the Bible, called the Torah, to the children of Israel. This means that fifty days after the first day of Passover is the day of the original Pentecost!

"However, this Pentecost which you are about to observe, which will occur fifty days after the Passover of Jesus's crucifixion and resurrection, will be a celebration of the harvest of souls that are about to come into God's Kingdom! It will be a celebration of the giving of both the Law of God and the Torah, combined with forgiveness of the sin debt of mankind. It will be a celebration of the restoration of the relationship between God and man, which was lost in the garden. As God pours out His Spirit on "all flesh," as will be prophesied in Joel and the book of Acts, ordinary men and women will, for the first time in history, be able to obtain heavenly power, enabling them to live godly lives! That is why before He leaves the earth, Jesus will say to His disciples, 'It is necessary that I go away because if I do not go away, the Holy Spirit cannot come!' At that time, Jesus will have to shed His precious, sinless blood to cover the sins of mankind. The most precious substance that will ever touch planet Earth will be the sinless, perfectly righteous, perfectly holy blood of the Lord Jesus Christ! As John the Baptist will declare, 'Behold! The Lamb of God who takes away the sin of the world!'"[37]

Having shared this groundbreaking information, Windrose raises his voice, declaring with a shout, *"All praise be to the Father, who will choose the jubilee where all debts will be canceled every fifty years on the Day of Atonement, and all slaves will go free! Also, all praise be to God, who will teach us to observe the holiday of Shavuot, where we will recognize God for faithfully providing for us as we honor Him with the firstfruits of our yearly harvest and for giving us the firstfruits of His Word, including His Law. Genesis, Exodus, Numbers, Leviticus, and Deuteronomy will be the beginning in guiding us in pleasing Him. It will enable us by His strength to live righteous and holy lives before Him!*

"Then, foremost and above all things, let us thank Him for giving us His most precious possession, His only-begotten Son, to be crucified and rise from the dead for all of the sins of mankind. Then, on Passover, within the sacred year that He ordered, fifty days later on His chosen Pentecost, He will pour out His Holy Spirit to fulfill His own prediction through the prophet Jeremiah: 'I will put My law in their minds, and write it on their hearts; and I will be their God, and they shall be My people.'"[38]

With that, a thunderous praise starts from the souls, and in the midst of the clapping of hands, the stomping of feet, and the shouts of "praise the Lord!

Amen!" and "glory to God," an angelic company of a host of angels suddenly flies into the arena, some playing harps, some blowing golden trumpets, others blasting on rams horns, and all singing with the most beautiful angelic harmony, "All praise be to God who gives us all things freely to enjoy. All praise to Him who was and is and is to come! All glory and majesty to Him forever more."

Seeing this, Windrose dances with all his might, laughing and praising God, kicking his feet up high into the air and dancing in circles with great joy and abandonment. "Yes, yes, yes," he declares over and over again. He skips and jumps around with the childlike joy of a young boy, causing his white robe to flow like angels' wings behind his arms. After a while, he laughs and begins to calm the souls while cheerfully calming himself.

"All right, souls! Yes, this is indeed a great delight. Thank you for your participation in this celebration of God's goodness. Let's now quiet ourselves as we turn back to the omniciscreen and see what is about to happen in this upper room in Jerusalem."

With that, Windrose slowly brings up the ability by means of the omniciscreen to see far into the future, all the way to the day of Pentecost. "Once again, we are going to be seeing and hearing Luke and Paul discussing what Luke had written in the scrolls, recording what happened on God's chosen fifty days, counting forward from Passover Pentecost morning." As the scene opens, the souls see that Luke and Paul are sitting in the shade near a well. Women from the nearby city are coming and drawing out water to fill their clay pots for the morning.

Paul says to Luke, "Luke, I know that we have talked about what happened on Pentecost, and I know that you have been writing it all down. Let's talk about that again, can we?"

Luke then says, "Paul, I can do better than that; I can actually read my account of it to you if you would like. I have several scrolls with me today, and I know it's here somewhere. Let me look."

Luke peeks at the corner of each of the scrolls that he has on the chair beside where he is sitting. "Oh, yes, here it is. Do you have time now? I know you have to go and meet with one of the young disciples later."

"Oh, yes, gladly. I will definitely make the time for that!" Paul answers eagerly.

"Good. You can let me know if it sounds like the wording has a good flow."

"Sure, Luke, and thanks. I consider it a privilege!" Paul responds.

"Okay, well, I chose to start it like this:

> *When the Day of Pentecost had fully come, they were all with one accord in one place. And suddenly there came a sound from heaven, as of a rushing mighty wind, and it filled the whole house where they were sitting. Then there appeared to them divided tongues, as of fire, and one sat upon each of them. And they were all filled with the Holy Spirit and began to speak with other tongues, as the Spirit gave them utterance.*
>
> *And there were dwelling in Jerusalem Jews, devout men, from every nation under heaven. And when this sound occurred, the multitude came together, and were confused, because everyone heard them speak in his own language. Then they were all amazed and marveled, saying to one another, 'Look, are not all these who speak Galileans? And how is it that we hear, each in our own language in which we were born? Parthians and Medes and Elamites, those dwelling in Mesopotamia, Judea and Cappadocia, Pontus and Asia, Phrygia and Pamphylia, Egypt and the parts of Libya adjoining Cyrene, visitors from Rome, both Jews and proselytes, Cretans and Arabs—we hear them speaking in our own tongues the wonderful works of God.' So, they were all amazed and perplexed, saying to one another, 'Whatever could this mean?'*
>
> *Others, mocking, said, 'They are full of new wine.'"[39]*

Paul raises his finger for a minute, interrupting Luke, "Ha-ha! So they thought they were drunk! Huh, that is very funny!"

"Yes, Paul. Well, when God does something supernatural that man cannot explain, they are always desperate for answers. This, we have to realize, is a miracle that God had never done in all of Jewish history, so men being able to speak in languages that they had not learned was way out there for them to try to grasp."

"God did do the opposite when He confounded the languages of the people who tried to build the Tower of Babel!"

"Yes, Paul, and He did speak through a donkey once to redirect Balaam's plans to try to curse Israel!"

"Ha-ha, yes, it does seem that God has a sense of humor. He certainly also has the ability to use the human voice to do some extraordinary things!"

Luke agrees and then interjects, "You would think, though, that the fact that all of these people from this region of multiple countries and languages were able to hear and understand all that was being said through so many different speakers would convince them that this was unquestionably a move of God!"

"Well, God had to speak to me audibly, knock me to the ground, and blind me for three days to get my attention, even though I was one of the scholars who studied under the famous Gamaliel. I guess God's heart must often be broken over the fact that even His own spiritual leaders do not understand when He is obviously doing something miraculous! Please, Luke, continue reading; this is all so powerful!"

"Okay, Paul, let's focus on Peter's explanation:

> *But Peter, standing up with the eleven, raised his voice and said to them, "Men of Judea and all who dwell in Jerusalem, let this be known to you, and heed my words. For these are not drunk, as you suppose, since it is only the third hour of the day. But this is what was spoken by the prophet Joel:*
>
> *'And it shall come to pass in the last days, says God,*
> *That I will pour out of My Spirit on all flesh;*
> *Your sons and your daughters shall prophesy,*
> *Your young men shall see visions,*
> *Your old men shall dream dreams.*
>
> *And on My menservants and on My maidservants*

I will pour out My Spirit in those days;
And they shall prophesy.
I will show wonders in Heaven above
And signs in the earth beneath:
Blood and fire and vapor of smoke.
The sun shall be turned into darkness,
And the moon into blood,
Before the coming of the great and awesome day of the Lord.

And it shall come to pass
That whoever calls on the name of the Lord
Shall be saved.'

"Men of Israel, hear these words: Jesus of Nazareth, a Man attested by God to you by miracles, wonders, and signs which God did through Him in your midst, as you yourselves also know—Him, being delivered by the determined purpose and foreknowledge of God, you have taken by lawless hands, have crucified, and put to death; whom God raised up, having loosed the pains of death, because it was not possible that He should be held by it. For David says concerning Him:

'I foresaw the Lord always before my face,
For He is at my right hand, that I may not be shaken.
Therefore, my heart rejoiced, and my tongue was glad;
Moreover, my flesh also will rest in hope.

For You will not leave my soul in Hades,
Nor will You allow Your Holy One to see corruption.
You have made known to me the ways of life;
You will make me full of joy in Your presence.'

"Men and brethren, let me speak freely to you of the patriarch David, that he is both dead and buried, and his tomb is with us to this day. Therefore, being a prophet, and knowing that God had sworn with an oath to him that of the fruit of his body, according to the flesh, He would raise up the Christ to sit on his throne, he, foreseeing this, spoke concerning the resurrection of the Christ, that His soul was not left in Hades, nor did His flesh see corruption. This Jesus God has raised up, of which we are all witnesses. Therefore, being exalted to the right hand of God, and

having received from the Father the promise of the Holy Spirit, He poured out this which you now see and hear.

"For David did not ascend into the heavens, but he says himself:

'The LORD said to my Lord,

> *"Sit at My right hand,*
> *Till I make Your enemies Your footstool."'*

"Therefore, let all the house of Israel know assuredly that God has made this Jesus, whom you crucified, both Lord and Christ."

Now when they heard this, they were cut to the heart, and said to Peter and the rest of the apostles, "Men and brethren, what shall we do?"

Then Peter said to them, "Repent, and let every one of you be baptized in the name of Jesus Christ for the remission of sins; and you shall receive the gift of the Holy Spirit. For the promise is to you and to your children, and to all who are afar off, as many as the Lord our God will call."

And with many other words, he testified and exhorted them, saying, "Be saved from this perverse generation." Then those who gladly received his word were baptized; and that day about three thousand souls were added to them. And they continued steadfastly in the apostles' doctrine and fellowship, in the breaking of bread, and in prayers. Then fear came upon every soul, and many wonders and signs were done through the apostles. Now all who believed were together, and had all things in common, and sold their possessions and goods, and divided them among all, as anyone had need.

So, continuing daily with one accord in the temple, and breaking bread from house to house, they ate their food with gladness and simplicity of heart, praising God and having favor with all the people. And the Lord added to the church daily those who were being saved.[40]

"Paul, that is where I chose to end that section. In the next scroll, I begin to talk about Peter and John starting out to evangelize together."

"Luke, your letter recounting the events of that day is very nicely done," Paul responds.

"Paul, I know God is using you to write letters to the church. It's really hard to explain, isn't it? Somehow, you feel a stirring in your heart and mind about what to write, and with that also comes an uncanny ability to remember events in great detail just exactly as they happened."

"Yes, Luke, I know that exact feeling and, with it, the awesome responsibility to seek God with my whole heart continually to be able to hear and know His voice for every direction that I am to take."

With that, Windrose turns off the omniciscreen and says to the souls, "You just witnessed one of the most amazing collections of God working His sovereign and unique miracles. However, sadly, on our next journey into the distant future, you will bear witness to the fact that not everyone is receptive to what God chooses to do! Even though God *soooooooo* loved the world that He gave His only-begotten Son, the most precious gift that He could give you will have the sad experience of witnessing what can happen when people say 'no' to God!"

CHAPTER 8

FROM FLYING LIKE ANGELS, TO FIRE ON THE FLOOR, TO NO FIRE AT ALL

Windrose next draws the souls' attention to the omniciscreen, which once again lights up, revealing the entire world rotating on its axis as all of the continents slowly pass by. While he uses a long-pointed staff to point around to different areas, he asks them a question: "Souls, where in this entire world do you think that God might choose to pour out another type of Pentecostal outpouring? By the way, I will tell you that the year we are looking at here in the future is 1832."

Anastasia-44 speaks up and asks, "Windrose, why are there little specks of light in some areas on the earth, other areas with somewhat larger specks of light, while some areas seem to have large blotches of light coming from them?"

"Anastasia, what a wonderful question! You see, when you look down from heaven, everywhere that you see, even small specks of light, shows you that someone there is praying right then."

"And the somewhat larger specks of light mean that even more people are praying?" she asks.

"Yes, Anastasia, the large blotches of lights are areas in the world where hundreds and sometimes thousands of people are praying, all at the same time."

Hearing that, the souls all began to respond with *ohs*, *awes*, *amens*, *praises*, and *thanksgiving* to God.

Then, the omniciscreen begins to reveal another dimension of the prayer lights. The souls watch in awe as, all over the earth, the lights begin to shoot beams of golden tracer light up towards heaven. Following the paths of the lights upward, the souls are stunned to see people in heaven darting out to catch the lights in golden globe-like vases with long funnel-like spouts. Once the vases are full, the heavenly inhabitants put their hands over the tops of their vases and fly them up back into heaven.

"What's that, Windrose?" soul after soul begins to ask, all talking over top of each other, rhapsodical over what they were seeing!

Windrose responds, saying, "Remember when we learned about the many supernatural things that you will be able to do when you get to heaven? Have you forgotten that I told you that one of the things you will be able to do will be that you will be able to fly like the angels? God has so designed that your loved ones in heaven, now having their glorified bodies, are, by God's selective choice, able to fly up and catch your prayers and carry them to the Father Himself through the grace of our Lord Jesus Christ! God does understand that some prayers are very private and personal, so those He allows to come straight to His heart. Amazingly, in His infinite wisdom, in a way only He can do, He has somehow designed it so that no prayer is ever slowed by your loved one or hastened by His direct reception. There is a lot to do in heaven. Souls, heaven is no boring place!

"Throughout history, souls, mankind will succumb to misunderstandings about many things, misunderstandings often perpetrated through thoughts seeded in their minds by Lucifer. Sadly, God's special outpourings of His Spirit on different regions of the world in different times and in different places will provoke more attacks and more misunderstandings than almost anything else He will do. Do you see the areas with the brightest concentrations of light? Those believers' prayers are not only for their loved ones, which God perfectly understands. Those prayers are lighting up the brightest because they are also praying very unselfish prayers, prayers for all of the souls all around their towns and cities to find Christ as their Savior! In essence, they are praying diligently for revival! One day, Paul, the writer of the book of Hebrews, will say, 'But without faith it is impossible to please Him, for he who comes to God must believe that He is, and that He is a rewarder of those who diligently seek Him.'[41] Does anyone care to guess what 'diligently seek Him' means?"

Once again, several souls begin to answer at once, so this time Windrose says, "How about everyone who thinks that they know the answer put both hands up where I can see them. Okay, Vadim-19, I see you seemed to shoot your hands up the fastest. Vadim, what do you think 'diligently seek Him' means?"

"Windrose, does it mean to seek Him in prayer a lot?

"Yes, Vadim, and you could almost say more than even a lot. Very well done, Vadim. I'm sure many of you had similar answers. In Paul's writings, one day, he will use two of the same words, words that mean 'seek-seek' Him. Paul understood that God designed prayer to be, as I taught you in the garden lessons, an act of humility and submission. Prayer is the very opposite of mankind's fall from grace due to the original sin of pride and rebellion. Prayer must start with an ongoing attitude of repentance and contrition. Prayer causes a person to completely surrender their life to God. Due to the fact that any believer will be able to pray both silently and out loud, it gives them the ability to, as Paul will write in another book, 'pray without ceasing.'"

"*Wooaaah*," the souls groan in unison, completely amazed at the multiple opportunities to pray. They suddenly realize that through what Jesus will do on the cross, and because He will rise from the dead, the ongoing communion that was once lost in the garden can, in many ways, be restored to believers in the future.

Windrose once again asks a question that is very similar to the one he asked before. "Who then will He send other outpourings to, outpourings that will resemble that first outpouring of His Spirit on Pentecost?"

For the first time, not a single soul seems to be able to answer Windrose's question! They all talk with each other, shaking their heads back and forth, indicating that out of the thousands of souls there in the arena, nobody seems to have the answer.

"Well," Windrose responds, "we are about to look back to the omniciscreen to the year 1832, to a place in the world called Armenia. What you are going to see will amaze you!"

As the omniciscreen lights up again, the souls see a large landmass on which God has superimposed the words: "*Armenia, a land with thousands of people who want My presence to fill their country.*" In certain areas of that country, large blotches of bright lights can be seen, signifying the thousands of people who are praying. There are so many beams of lights shooting up to heaven, and they come from so many different places that it is hard to distinguish which prayers are coming from which areas of the county.

Windrose explains, "You see, if God were to pour out His Spirit randomly or sovereignly or by His will, and thousands of people were then saved in that time period, how then would God be just? How would He be fair and just to those people groups in times and places where God does not pour out His Spirit, and as a result, thousands are lost during those generations? However, if God, as we will see here, is not choosing Albania, but instead, Albania is choosing Him, then God is indeed fair and righteous. This means that the responsibility for when revival falls rests on man and on what man does! Indeed, God's Word will one day say, 'Ye have not, because ye ask not.'[42]

"Souls, do you remember what Cain asked God about his brother when God confronted him about killing him?"

Numerous souls can again be heard, all answering at once, many answering over top of each other. "Am I by brothers' keeper?"

"Yes," Windrose answers, "you are all correct, and in truth, by God's loving, righteous design for mankind, you are all called to be your brothers' keeper. Revival outpourings happen when a growing number of people begin to pray, often just a few, sometimes even a few teenagers or even a couple of elderly ladies, but as that prayer spreads, more and more people pray until sometimes hundreds, even thousands, are inviting God to visit their church or town, and guess what?"

All the souls shout out, "What?"

"God the Father loves to show up where He is invited! I can hear the Father telling the angels right now, "I did not choose Armenia; Armenia chose Me!"

With this thought, once again, the souls shout out in simultaneous praise to God!

Windrose points to the omniciscreen. "Let's take that trip to 1832."

With that, the screen lights up, revealing a dimly lit room. A few oil lamps sitting on small tables placed strategically around the room provide minimal light. A small woodstove in the back of the room supplies heat on that early winter night. Small flickers of light reflect on the wall from a somewhat large crack in the stove door. Every once in a while, a hot spark pops out, landing on the old piece of tin nailed to the floor. Whoever is nearby quietly walks over and steps on the spark at once to extinguish it. Pastor Avakian frequently jokes in his sermons that those sparks remind him of the spiritually dead churches in the region that always try to stomp out the Holy Spirit's fire to keep it from spreading to other places.

A group of warmly dressed Albanian men and women can be seen in the front of the church, loudly praising God with their hands held high. The pastor sits on the front bench with his Bible cradled in his arms, rocking back and forth, praying in preparation for his preaching later that night. From time to time, he raises one hand to praise God as he feels the Holy Spirit's presence in their midst. A number of young women sit quietly in the back corner with blankets thrown over their shoulders, nursing their babies. Their heads are lifted slightly towards heaven; they sing along with those who are quietly worshipping.

When Pastor Avakian feels in his spirit that it is time for him to begin his evening message, he approaches the crude pulpit made from a spare fence post one of the farmers brought in. It is propped up between two big stones somebody carried in from a nearby stream. An old wooden church sign is nailed horizontally to the top, and two boards have been attached on the bottom in a crisscross pattern. It is not a Russian Orthodox church anymore, so that old piece of pine makes a fine Bible holder, as elegance and formality are no longer needed. The pastor also often jokes about formality being something that they do not need anymore and says that besides that, they aren't throwing out the Bible that the Orthodox taught from. They were just adding more Bible to it! Everyone always chuckles in response.

As the pastor approaches the primitive pulpit, everyone immediately becomes very quiet. Everyone there feels the Holy Spirit's presence clearly, except Brother Jamgochian, who is battling bitterness against his brother and, as a result, is always complaining about something. Nevertheless, everyone is glad he has come to church. All are praying that he will have a revelation of the implication of the fact that Jesus died on the cross for both his sins and also for the sins of his brother. Those present understand how gentle the Holy Spirit is and how easily someone can grieve Him. They know that one day, this brother will drop to his knees in prayer, break out in tears with his hands raised, praise God, and cry out, "Forgive him, Father, for he knows not what he did!"

All of a sudden, from the back corner of the room, the souls hear, "*Coomdulababa Coomdulababba la chamma ooh do la ba ba Coomdulababa Coomdulababba la chamma ooh do la ba ba.* Thus says the Lord: 'My presence is among you this night to bless you and draw you closer unto Me. Do not be afraid; only believe. Do not let your heart be troubled about what is going on around you. Only trust in Me, and I will work all things together for your good,' says God!"

The congregation begins to respond with shouts of praise and adoration to God, which leads to about fifteen minutes of spontaneous worship. As the Spirit often does, He gradually begins to quiet the people, and the pastor once again approaches the pulpit.

"Brothers and sisters, God is moving all over Armenia through His Spirit, touching many lives with this fresh outpouring, similarly to what He did at Pentecost and also on Cornelius and on all who were with Cornelius through the Apostle Peter. Let's be so thankful tonight for this wonderful experience, an experience that so few people worldwide even know about. I believe that

God has shown me in prayer that out of our country, this message will one day reach the entire world!"

The pastor goes on to quietly exhort everyone to continue praising and worshiping the Lord. Many people begin to sing in their heavenly prayer languages, and others in their known tongue.

He then begins to solemnly discuss a crucial topic. "I know a lot of you are having to endure being persecuted by your family, friends, and neighbors because you believe in this marvelous gift of the Holy Spirit. We must ask God for His love and compassion, and as we are being mocked, we must have this prayer continually in our hearts, 'Father, forgive them, for they know not what they do!'[43] You see, people tend to fear what they do not understand, and unfortunately, when it comes to the spiritual realm especially, they have had more exposure to the evil things that Satan does than any good thing that God does. Some have been taught in their own churches since they were children that the age of the miraculous ceased after the writing of John and the book of Revelation. However, the prophet Malachi declared, 'For I am the LORD, I change not.'[44] It is very difficult to convince those people that their teachers were wrong. Just consider the fact that we are in the 1800s and that no matter how much of a witness we have that this is a work of God, it is true that it has been centuries since any recorded Holy Spirit outpouring that we know of has occurred. May God give us all the grace to have mercy, realizing that because these good folk have never received this beautiful gift by faith, they just simply do not know how wonderful an experience it is. I recently was talking with a man who attends an Orthodox church. He was making fun of our church and of our wonderful shouts of praise, which we know bless the very heart of God. I asked him, 'Brother, do you believe in the baptism in the Holy Spirit with the experience of speaking in other tongues?' He replied by flipping his head back and forth 'no' so violently that it looked as if his lips were flapping back and forth! I then exhorted him, saying, 'Then, brother, you will never ever have to worry about speaking in tongues because Jesus said in Mark 16:17, 'And these signs shall follow them that believe; in my name they shall cast out devils; they shall speak with new tongues.'[45] Therefore, if you do not believe in speaking in new tongues, you will never ever speak in new tongues! I must say, brothers and sisters, he walked away mumbling something, but I do not believe it was in any heavenly tongue!"

At that moment, Sister Papazian shouts out, "Pastor, let them come and taste and see that the Lord is good!"

With that, several other people shout out, "Yes, amen! Praise the Lord, and thank You, Jesus!"

Pastor Avakian then continues, "In the fourth century, Augustine wrote, 'We still do what the apostles did in when they laid hands on the Samaritans and called down the Holy Spirit on them the laying on of hands. It is expected that converts should speak with new tongues.' Also, the very well-known archbishop of Constantinople, John Chrysostom, who lived during part of both the fourth and the fifth centuries, wrote: 'Whoever was baptized with tongues,' acknowledging that people from his day were receiving the baptism in the Holy Spirit in conjunction with the experience of speaking in tongues. Brothers and sisters, the scripture teaches in Hebrews, 'Jesus Christ the same yesterday, and to day, and for ever.'[46] This same Jesus who shed His blood and died on the cross all those years ago so that our sins could be forgiven and so that we might receive and be filled with the Holy Ghost has not only worked as He is working now in Armenia but ever since in Jerusalem on the day of Pentecost.

"Few know that it is well recorded that He poured the baptism in the Spirit out in Constantinople and North Africa in the fourth century! I know in my heart that He is also going to pour out His Spirit again and again in other countries and regions in the years to come. Praise God! For now, let's all be asking God to give us creative ways to tell others about this wonderful experience. May God help us to be wise as serpents and harmless as doves. Let's all remember how we felt when we first heard the news about a church where you could 'feel God's presence!' It sounded very odd to us, so we must understand that it sounds odd to others. I know personally, as your pastor, I got excited when I realized that Paul wrote to the Corinthian church and said,

'Therefore tongues are for a sign, not to those who believe but to unbelievers.'"[47]

Once again, amens began to ring out throughout the church.

Just then, another of those hot sparks jumps out of the stove, going so far that it hits the edge of the piece of tin and rolls onto the wooden floor, where it immediately begins to burn the wood and make some smoke. The pastor starts laughing in his jolly fashion, runs back, and quickly stomps it out, saying, "Well, you can't keep the fire of God contained, can you?"

Everyone starts laughing with him, sharing more amens with one brother who always just says a simple "glory" when he gets blessed.

With that, Pastor Avakian says, "Let's all come and gather around the altar and close out our service with some fervent prayer."

As the omniciscreen begins to close out, the souls see the Armenian church's people moving towards the front of the church to pray.

Windrose, with his head down and his right thumb in under his chin, moving his four fingers up and down, longest to shortest, over and over, begins to pace back and forth for a few minutes, seemingly trying to decide how he can explain what he has to say next. He then turns his head up as if he were looking towards heaven and says, "Yes, Heavenly Father. Yes, I believe that will help explain it well!

"Souls, remember how you learned that Jesus drew a lot of criticism from the scribes and Pharisees, who, although they were supposed to be the religious leaders of their day, could not even recognize God in the flesh as the form of the very Son of God?"

Several yeses and amens arise from the souls in the arena, acknowledging that what Windrose is saying is true!

He goes on to say, "To reiterate, John will one day record in his gospel that a Pharisee named Nicodemus will come to Jesus by night, so to keep his meeting secret. He will ask Jesus what He means by His statement, 'Except a man be born again he cannot enter the Kingdom of Heaven.'[48] Nicodemus will then follow up with another question: 'Can a man once again enter into his mother's womb and be born a second time?'[49]

"Jesus will reply, saying, 'That which is born of flesh is flesh and that which is born of spirit is spirit, but unless a man is born again spiritually, he will never see the kingdom of God!'"[50]

"You see, Jesus knows that throughout the passing of time, there will be people who will be very fleshly-minded and likewise those who will be very earthly-minded. A person's spirit will have to be reborn through that person repenting of all their sins up until that time period of their life. They then receive forgiveness of those sins. This forgiveness is made possible through Jesus's death on the cross. They will be born again when they receive by faith what Jesus will do for all of mankind by dying on the cross and through His resurrection from the dead three days later! This allows the door to a person's heart to be opened so that it can then be filled with the very Spirit of Christ and begin to have 'Christlikeness' within it! That is where the term 'Christian' will come from, as will be recorded by Luke in what will one day be called the book of Acts.[51] The people of the city of Antioch will one day identify these followers of Jesus, previously called 'saints,' by calling them 'Christians.'

"Jesus's first cousin, John the Baptist, will set the pattern for being baptized in water as a sign of repentance. Baptism will be a picture of a 'born-again' person, testifying to their family and friends that when they go down under the water, it symbolizes their old nature, as a type of dying to themselves, and then come up out of the water as a picture of the new person rising up from the dead, victorious with Christ in His resurrection!"

"Wows" fill the arena! The souls begin cheering and shouting amens again, praising God for His beautiful plan of salvation, which will restore man's relationship with God back to what mankind lost in the garden.

"Souls, always remember the mountaintops, meaning the high experiences of praise and worship of God in the good times and following the good reports; those memories will help you through the low experiences or the valleys of life. I am telling you this because I am about to share with you now, which will be very sad but necessary information."

At that point, a somber yet recognizable "hmm" and mumbling between the souls roll through the arena. It is obvious they are trying to brace themselves for whatever they are going to hear next.

"Souls, you are soldiers, so pay close attention to what I am about to teach you because this will be the foundation of every battle you will ever fight for the Lord Jesus Christ and the eternal Kingdom of God. This next lesson will furthermore be especially true as it pertains to the Father's will be done on earth as it is in heaven! You see, the abovementioned individuals, who prefer their fleshly or worldly ways, will always be part of the human race from the very first Adam and Eve all the way through time until the last humans leave planet Earth. Because this is true, although millions will be genuinely saved by being born again, millions also will not. They will not be saved for what some will believe are three reasons, but in reality, there are only two."

At this point, Windrose does something that he has never done before, but he does it to aid in teaching the souls what he is about to say. He takes his right pointer finger and draws a big rectangle in the air, as far as his arm will reach. What he does next is done by the power that God the Father has given him, which only the mysteries of God's miraculous power understand at that moment. He takes his right hand, spreads it out wide, and starts waving it back and forth over the rectangular area, filling it in with something white, creating a large drawing board-like area. Then he turns and smiles at the souls as they all start laughing at his creation. Having done that, he proceeds to blow a little puff of air on the tip of his right pointer finger. When it immediately becomes blue, he uses his finger to draw a big blue smiley face on the white area, making everyone laugh. Then, smiling, he turns back to the souls, rolls his hand three times, and takes a bow. Once again, they all start laughing, and he joins them in an empathetic chuckle. Windrose, knowing how intense the next lesson is going to be, wants to add a lightness in the air to help balance their upcoming sadness. Having added some levity, he then quickly opens his hand wide, erases the smiling face, and, returning to the subject at hand, writes the number "one" at the top with a period after it and a parenthesis around it.

"Souls, the most important of all reasons for all of the time will be that certain people on earth will pass away into the next life and never will have heard the soul-saving message of the Gospel of Jesus Christ. Tens of thousands through the years will hear the call of God and say 'yes' and leave everything and everyone behind to carry the message of salvation to the lost. Millions, therefore, will spend all of eternity in heaven! However, sadly, many will also hear the call of God, will resist that calling, and say 'no' to God. Because of that, other millions will perish without ever learning about being able to have a personal relationship with God through Jesus Christ our Lord. King David, who will one day hold the three ministries of prophet, priest, and king, will write in Psalms that the fool has said in his heart there is no God! Over time, humanity will add words to that scripture to try to cover its true meaning, but the Holy Spirit of God, who will inspire David to write those words, will know what is to be written."

The souls began to groan in mumblings of awful sadness and sorrow over the thought that millions might end up in the lake of fire, which had been prepared for the devil and his angels for all of eternity, all because of the selfish wills and desires of some men and women.

Dierdre-27 speaks up loudly and says, "Windrose, how can this be fair? I mean, if they never heard about Jesus and what He did for them on the cross, then how can they one day be held accountable?"

Windrose answers with tears running down both of his cheeks, "Dierdre, remember when we learned that it will one day be written in the gospel of John: 'For God so loved the world that He gave His only begotten Son, that whoever believes in Him should not perish but have everlasting life'?"[52]

"Yes," Dierdre replies.

"John will one day write, just two verses later: 'He who believes in Him is not condemned; but he who does not believe is condemned already, because he has not believed in the name of the only begotten Son of God.'[53] You see, all mankind, by God's righteous standards, have been born into sin because of the fall of man in the Garden of Eden. 'The Way' that God made for mankind to be forgiven for their sin is by being born again through the shed righteous blood of His Son!

"Dierdre, do you remember one of our very first lessons? We have revisited it before because it is one of the most central and important truths of all the wisdom of mankind as it relates to God. Do you remember the story of the two brothers, Cain and Abel? Remember, after Cain killed Abel, God asked him where his brother was. What was his response?"

"Am I my brother's keeper?" Dierdre replies.

"Excellent, excellent. Yes, and that is the essence of the righteousness of God in His responsibility to all of the lost souls who ever end up missing heaven because somebody never told them. Somebody said no to a calling of God. Somebody had the perfect chance to tell somebody about what Jesus did for them on the cross and did not do it. Dierdre, all of the responsibility of the souls of all of mankind falls on mankind itself, who *is its brother's keeper*! The saving of souls is not God's responsibility. It is man's responsibility. God has already done all that He can do by giving His most precious gift, the death of His only-begotten Son, as the perfect sacrifice for their sins. Now, Dierdre and souls, the question will one day be: *What are you going to do about that fact?*"

The souls' discussion starts out as a low mumbling and discussion between themselves, and then as their understanding becomes more and more enlightened, they begin to sing and shout and declare praises to God for His good and perfect gifts to mankind and to the world.

Windrose is once again smiling and humming a melody unfamiliar to the souls, but it is obviously something heavenly, as his head moves back and forth and his long hair sways. He continues to worship in a way that is obviously delightful to him.

He approaches the whiteboard once again. As he blows a puff of air on his pointer finger, it once again turns blue. He then writes the number "two" with a period following it and a parenthesis before and after it. He then begins to write out the next reason with his finger in blue letters.

"Reason number two is that they hear the gospel preached but, for one reason or another, reject God's plan of salvation. This is where we must understand that the 'free will' of mankind enters the picture. The prophet

Jeremiah will one day pen these words, "The heart is deceitful above all things, and desperately wicked; who can know it?"[54] The sad truth is, souls, that there are some people, and actually you could rightly say many people, who love their sin so much they will not let go of it to serve God! Think for a minute of Lucifer himself, who was once one of three archangels. Scripture declares that wickedness was found in him, and he was lifted up with pride because of his beauty. He foolishly thinks that since he took one-third of the other angels, he can overthrow God. He is wicked at heart, and so will be all those who will one day reject the righteous plan of God for salvation. It will be written by Matthew in Matthew 25:41: 'Then He will also say to those on the left hand, "Depart from Me, you cursed, into the everlasting fire prepared for the devil and his angels."' Those who have rejected God will join the devil and his angels there."

With that, the souls just sit there, staring straight ahead, saying nothing, realizing a somber possibility. This possibility was that some of the souls sitting there at that time had the potential of failing God and ending up in that lake of fire themselves!

"Yes," Windrose responds, "I know what you are thinking, and to be completely fair and understanding the righteous love of God, you, too, will one day all be given a free will so that you will not be like automatons. You, too, in your human form, will one day have the ability to choose between good and evil."

Then Windrose, for the last time in this session, blows on his pointer finger. This time, it becomes red. As he begins to speak, he says, "Souls, the reason I am writing this one in red is to get it to stand out above the others. It is a common reason people give, but it is really based on a hidden lie. We are going to discuss this given reason and then the basis for the lies surrounding it." He then writes on the bottom of the white screen the number "three" with a period after it and a parenthesis around it.

"The third reason why some people do not become 'born again' is because they want to claim that they did not really understand all that this conversion to Christ really entailed.

"In reality, souls, just as we previously mentioned concerning the human heart, Jeremiah will say that it is 'deceitfully wicked above all things, who can know it?'[55] Well, souls, the truth is that the Spirit of God, also known as the Spirit of Truth, does know the human heart. That passage refers to what humans can know, but God sees all, hears all, and knows all. The greatest battle of the human heart is to submit itself fully to God's will. The human heart always wants its own way when it wants it and how it wants it. The most effective deception that man will ever attempt to accomplish is to pretend to be religious through doing certain works. He will believe that he is always the author of correct thinking, and he will continually deceive himself into thinking that what he does and thinks is pleasing to God. True believers are called to be 'rich in good works,' as will be one day written by Paul to Timothy. But allow me to tell you a little story to help you understand the difference between God's desire for 'good works,' which believers will be called to do 'with God,' and the works of the flesh that people try to do for God.

"There once was a carpenter whose business was going well. He did really good work for everyone, and it was not long before he needed to hire a second carpenter. So, he posted a note in the town square and began to put the word out wherever he could that he wanted to hire some help. One day, a man carrying a wooden toolbox full of carpenter tools approached him. He said, 'I understand you want to hire a carpenter, so here I am.' The man looking for a new employee was interested in talking to this candidate some more but had to turn around for a minute to talk to a potential customer. When he turned back, the man who had approached him was gone. Assuming he must have had to go to the bathroom and would be back, the businessman walked across the street and purchased some supplies. However, when he finished, the toolbox-toting man appeared to have left, so the businessman assumed that perhaps the man who had approached him decided that he did not want to work for him. So, he left and went on to his next job. It was customary in that land to pay your help on a certain day of the week, and, to the businessman's surprise, on payday, here came the new carpenter walking up to him with a big smile on his face.

'Hello,' he said, 'I am here to get paid!'

'Get paid?' the businessman asked. 'Get paid for what?'

'Well, I built you a very nice little stable for your donkey to sleep in at night,' the new carpenter said.

'I never asked you to build me a stable for my donkey! What are you talking about?'

'Well, you said you needed another carpenter, so I built you a nice stable down on the edge of town. I purchased the materials at the supply store and built a very nice stable. Now, I would like to get paid!'

'I'm not paying you for anything; get out of here, you foolish man!' the businessman shouted."

By this time, the souls were all looking at each other and laughing and saying among themselves, "What a ridiculous story."

Hearing them, Windrose chimed in. "Yes, souls, and it is also ridiculous for any man or woman to feel that God is interested in blessing people for doing things 'for Him' instead of with Him. As the God of the universe, does He need any instructions from man or angels? Is He ignorant of what kingdom priorities need to be? Shouldn't He be the one in charge? Shouldn't He be the one calling us to do His work, not us picking and choosing things to do for Him? That is why God will one day say, through the prophet Isaiah, 'But we are all like an unclean thing, and all our righteousnesses are like filthy rags.'[56]

"However, souls, it is because the human heart is so evil it feels that it can manipulate others. Believe it or not, mankind will think that they can manipulate God. They will believe that one day they can stand before Him in judgment and say, 'Oh, I did not know,' 'I misunderstood,' or perhaps 'I was mistaught.' No, souls, they knew exactly what they were doing in choosing the church they went to, in deciding how much they needed to pray, how much they needed to study God's Word to keep their lives doctrinally correct, and if they needed to follow the admonition, 'seek first the kingdom of God and its righteousness, and all the things you have need of will be added unto you!'[57] That is exactly why I wrote this third reason in red. This explanation of why people are not 'born again' is not a reason. It's just an excuse. It is an excuse that will not hold up when they arrive at what will one day be called 'the judgment seat of Christ'!"

Now Windrose looks all around the arena and says, "Souls, all that we have been talking about in this lesson is going to lead us to a sad conclusion, a conclusion that you are about to see highlighted on the omniciscreen. Just as human nature will wrestle with God in areas such as being religious versus being truly born again, human nature will also resist the deeper things of God. They will rebel if required to enter into a deeper consecration to God or if called to do things 'with' Him, if prayer is presented not just as a suggestion but a requirement. In the same way, humans also will resist the Holy Spirit. This will be recorded over and over again in God's Word over thousands of years. Over and over again, the Word will record that it usually gets down to 'man's will' versus 'God's will.' The Word will demonstrate that if it involves the Holy Spirit, God will not argue with man, nor will He submit to their manipulations. The last sermon of Stephen, the first of the twelve apostles to be martyred for Christ, will be recorded by Luke in the book of Acts. 'You stiff-necked and uncircumcised in heart and ears! You always resist the Holy Spirit; as your fathers did, so do you.'[58] Steven was stoned to death by the same men to whom he was preaching his last sermon.

"Souls, you must realize as well that Satan is the enemy of all souls and exists in a constant state of hateful revenge towards God. He is eternally bitter towards God and all of His creation ever since God cast him and his evil angels out of heaven down to earth. Satan is always at work, looking for people whose evil hearts he can fill with his same hatred. Satan also realizes that his greatest enemy is people who are full of the Spirit of God. Notice, souls, that I did not say 'filled' with the Spirit of God, but I said 'full' of the Spirit of God! One day, Luke will also record the joint counsel of all eleven of the original apostles and Matthew, who has just decided to take Judas' place concerning the special needs of the early church. They will jointly decide: 'Therefore, brethren, seek out from among you seven men of good reputation, full of the Holy Spirit and wisdom, whom you may appoint over this business' (Acts 6:3, NKJV). Souls, please notice that even in regard to the smaller duties of the early church, the apostles will want to be sure they are handled by men 'full' of the Holy Spirit! The New Testament will be written in Greek because it will be the most common language of that day. Luke will use the same Greek word for 'full' as Mark used to describe the 'full' baskets in chapter 8 of his writings. Quite simply put, souls, 'full' means 'full.'" With that, Windrose breaks out in winsome laughter.

As he continues to chuckle, his countenance starts to change. "So, souls, as we are about to take a brief journey via the omniciscreen, and after everything that we have just learned, please consider why the following situation will one day occur."

As the omniciscreen begins to light up, Windrose introduces the time and place that they are about to see.

"Souls, we are going to join a Midwestern conference of a large denomination in America in 1987. There are about 3,000 ministers and their wives present from all over the country. They have invited speakers to address a problem they have been having in certain churches in their districts. Some of the people speaking have had direct encounters with what they believe to be demonic deceptions occurring in their churches. In addition to pastors, several congregants are also present to discuss this present crisis. Dr. Hopstedder, Dr. Smalley, Dr. Kildare, and Dr. Ripstadt from the National Council area are also here. These are all men of respected experience in theology, doctrine, and ministerial experience within their denomination. Please pay close attention as Rev. Lipstoph, a former evangelist from within their ranks, begins to speak."

"Brothers and sisters in Christ, it is my great privilege to be here today to express my concerns over these outbreaks of 'speaking in tongues' and fanatical behavior that have been happening in our churches. In the past, our services have always been very orderly and dignified. Our congregants have always been respected and have been outstanding citizens in their communities. While it is true that our numbers may be dropping in some areas of the country, we only closed seventy-two churches last year. That number is down from the ninety-one we had to close last year due to a lack of young ministers willing to pastor in some of these rural communities. To tell you the truth,

brethren, I have paid a dear price in my lifetime as many of you who are here today have to minister in some less-than-desirable conditions. But the times are changing, and people are changing, and the last thing we need is some Pentecostal fanatics coming into our churches and getting people all stirred up about things that do not really matter!

"Brothers and sisters, we see in part, and we preach in part, but when that which is perfect is come... Well, we know that He has already come. His name is Jesus!"

The ministers and their wives start saying "amen, amen" and gently clapping their hands.

"I have one message for our Pentecostal fanatics: tongues shall cease!"

With that slightly louder proclamation, there is an increase in head nodding, and the clapping of the hands becomes a little more enthusiastic.

"As an evangelist, I traveled through our districts. Pastors knew that if they had a problem with 'tongues' in their churches, they could call me, and I would be there the very next week. I would always recommend two weeks of nightly services, during which I would take the confused congregants through the Word of God, showing them that Jesus is all we need. I heard plenty of testimonies of this wild fanaticism, of people in the country churches falling down when they got prayed for and rolling around and speaking in a strange tongue. Brothers and sisters, that stuff just ain't from God! By the time I got done being there for two weeks, anybody who believed that stuff had either left the church or got convinced that they were off base! All that talk of miracles and healing and stuff, I am telling you, when John wrote his last words on that island of Patmos, we know that Jesus was all the New Testament church needed. When we got Him, we got it all! We need no miracles. We don't need to raise our hands or roll on the floor or anything else! I don't know about you, but I like a dignified Jesus! Our people also like a dignified Jesus, and it's a fact that that's all we need! So, fellow ministers, feel free to call me if you like. If you have that tongues problem in your church, I will be there just as soon as I can, and when I get done, I promise you there will be no more of this Holy Ghost talk! We got Jesus, and He's all we need!"

With that, Dr. Hopstedder, Dr. Smallwood, Dr. Kildare, and Dr. Ripstadt all stand to their feet and quietly and calmly clap their hands as Rev. Lipstoph turns and walks back to where they were, sitting down beside them in a very dignified manner.

Dr. Smallwood then approaches the microphone and closes with prayer. "I thank Thee, oh God, that Thou art a holy God and a God of order and structure. I thank Thee, oh God, for Thy Son, Jesus, and that we have Jesus, and that is all we need. Please bless Evangelist Lipstoph for all his hard work, and please give his wife strength as she battles cancer and his son as he is in rehab. Lord, please also provide them with a new van as the engine blew in theirs last week. In Jesus's name, amen."

With that, the ministers and their wives scurry to tables set up in the back that provide discount coupons for local restaurants and free boxes of used hymnals, communion sets, and offering plates left over from the churches that had to close.

Once again, Windrose is standing with his forehead cupped in his hands, and the omniciscreen is shutting down. Tears are dripping down between his fingers and landing on the leather bindings of his sandals.

"We know, Windrose, we know," the souls start expressing their concern in different ways as they respond to what they have just heard and seen. "We, too, are so sad! It seemed just like during Jesus's day when the scribes and Pharisees could not even see that God in the flesh was standing right in front of them."

"I know," Windrose responds, "and what I could have done was show you so many places during the same time period where the Holy Spirit was being prayed for, wanted, welcomed, embraced, and received in every way. However, there are always those who embrace traditional religious practice over the supernatural power of God! Don't worry, souls; God never loses a battle. His best is yet to come! Hang on to your robe ropes. Revival is coming! God always has a remnant!"

When the souls suddenly begin to sing "Hallelujah" together in unison, Windrose says, "Wait a minute! That is singing in the Spirit! It's so beautiful! Thank you, thank you! You just made my day! Fantastic! Now I can't wait till the next lesson and our next trip into the future!"

CHAPTER 9

A SOLDIER FINDS LIGHT, DARKNESS ATTACKS LIGHT, ANGELS OF LIGHT

Windrose once again draws the souls' attention to the omniciscreen as he begins to tell them who they are about to see. "For this lesson, it's time to once again visit John the Apostle on the isle of Patmos. Because of his good behavior as a prisoner, he has been given the liberty to be alone on a somewhat remote part of the island. A lone guard has been given the duty to stand watch at a distance to make sure that John is not harassed by other prisoners."

The omniciscreen lights up, revealing a hot summer day. John is seen wrapped in a linen robe and leaning over what appears to be a piece of dried-out driftwood plank, writing on parchment paper. A propped-up Y-shaped tree branch with a piece of a cotton tarp provides him some shade. From time to time, John is heard exclaiming, "Yes! Amen! Praise the Lord!" Then, all at once, he leans back from where he is sitting, sighs deeply, and says, "Now for my read-through!" followed by a brief prayer. "Lord, these are some strong words. Although your heart is totally pure, sometimes it seems as if You alone understand the depth of the wickedness of all evil." With that statement, he begins to read out loud into the salty sea air, even though the only living beings within the sound of his voice are a few seagulls soaring about above him.

"To the angel of the church of Ephesus write,

'These things says He who holds the seven stars in His right hand, who walks in the midst of the seven golden lampstands: "I know your works, your labor, your patience, and that you cannot bear those who are evil. And you have tested those who say they are apostles and are not and have found them liars; and you have persevered and have patience and have labored for My name's sake and have not become weary. Nevertheless, I have this against you, that you have left your first love. Remember therefore from where you have fallen; repent and do the first works, or else I will come to you quickly and remove your lampstand from its place—unless you repent. But this you have, that you hate the deeds of the Nicolaitans, which I also hate.

"He who has an ear, let him hear what the Spirit says to the churches. To him who overcomes I will give to eat from the tree of life, which is in the midst of the Paradise of God.

"And to the angel of the church in Smyrna write,

'These things says the First and the Last, who was dead, and came to life: "I know your works, tribulation, and poverty (but you are rich); and I know the blasphemy of those who say they are Jews and are not but are a synagogue of Satan. Do not fear any of those things which you are about to suffer. Indeed, the devil is about to throw some of you into prison, that you may be tested, and you will have tribulation ten days. Be faithful until death, and I will give you the crown of life.

"He who has an ear, let him hear what the Spirit says to the churches. He who overcomes shall not be hurt by the second death."'

"And to the angel of the church in Pergamos write,

'These things says He who has the sharp two-edged sword: "I know your works, and where you dwell, where Satan's throne is. And you hold fast to My name and did not deny My faith even in the days in which Antipas was My faithful martyr, who was killed among you, where Satan dwells. But I have a few things against you because you have there those who hold the doctrine of Balaam, who taught Balak to put a stumbling block before the children of Israel, to eat

things sacrificed to idols, and to commit sexual immorality. Thus, you also have those who hold the doctrine of the Nicolaitans, which thing I hate. Repent, or else I will come to you quickly and will fight against them with the sword of My mouth.

"He who has an ear, let him hear what the Spirit says to the churches. To him who overcomes I will give some of the hidden manna to eat. And I will give him a white stone, and on the stone a new name written which no one knows except him who receives it."'

"And to the angel of the church in Thyatira write,

'These things says the Son of God, who has eyes like a flame of fire, and His feet like fine brass: "I know your works, love, service, faith, and your patience; and as for your works, the last are more than the first. Nevertheless, I have a few things against you, because you allow that woman Jezebel, who calls herself a prophetess, to teach and seduce My servants to commit sexual immorality and eat things sacrificed to idols. And I gave her time to repent of her sexual immorality, and she did not repent. Indeed, I will cast her into a sickbed, and those who commit adultery with her into great tribulation, unless they repent of their deeds. I will kill her children with death, and all the churches shall know that I am He who searches the minds and hearts. And I will give to each one of you according to your works.

"Now to you I say, and to the rest in Thyatira, as many as do not have this doctrine, who have not known the depths of Satan, as they say, I will put on you no other burden. But hold fast what you have till I come. And he who overcomes, and keeps My works until the end, to him I will give power over the nations—

> *'He shall rule them with a rod of iron;*
> *They shall be dashed to pieces like the potter's vessels'—*
> *as I also have received from My Father; and I will give him the morning star.*
> *"He who has an ear, let him hear what the Spirit says to the churches."'*[59]

With that, John rolls up the parchment, lays it in his lap, leans back again, and looking up, he says, "Oh, Father, grant that all men and women everywhere will come to know *the true Jesus*! He then bows his head and starts weeping and praying for the state of the church.

"John, are you okay?" a Roman guard, hearing him crying and praying, shouts from a distance as he walks towards him to ascertain what is going on.

"Yes, Markus!" John says. "I am not praying for myself. I am praying for the condition of Christ's church. It has been such a short time since He left us. He gifted us all with the power of the Holy Spirit. If only we would just seek His power! Do you remember, Markus, that night that you and I sat up late by a campfire? I explained to you then the whole reason that Jesus, the very Son of God, had to leave the spectacular beauty and perfectness of heaven. I explained that it was part of the Heavenly Father's plan for Christ to come in the form of a baby and to grow up as a normal human in the middle of the very type of people that He would one day be called to save."

"Yes, I remember it well," Markus replied. "You know, John, I have thought about what you told me over and over again since that night. It really makes sense to me."

"That's great, Markus! I prayed that somehow God would give you understanding about what some may think is a very complex plan. However, it breaks my heart that after all that God did by sending His only-begotten Son, the only Heavenly Son that He ever has had or ever will have, mankind is still treating God's love in a trite fashion. They are constantly trying to manipulate their way around His truths, even though it has only been ninety-five years since His resurrection from the dead! Markus, I knew Him personally! I traveled with Him everywhere He went and saw almost everything He did for over three years. I saw Him heal people without number. I was there that night in that fishing boat when He came walking on the water to us in the middle of that storm. I was there when He raised Lazarus from the dead. I was there when He fed thousands of people, miraculously multiplying one time a little boy's lunch. I saw Him cast the legion of devils out of the demoniac of Gadara and watched a raving lunatic who lived among the tombs, a man so strong that he could break chains of steal with his bare demonic empowered hands, be instantly transformed into a man rightly clothed and in his right mind! Markus, I wish you could have seen how beautiful He was on the Mount of Transfiguration and had been with me to be able to see Moses and Elijah, two men whom God used in centuries back to guide us Israelites!"

"Really?" Markus answered excitedly, his demeanor changing from that of a stoic Roman prison guard to that of an enthusiastic schoolboy! "Our scholars and mystics describe our Roman gods in their stories, but I do not know of any provable miracles that any of them ever did. The accounts of our gods are always just stories; however, John, I can tell by your fervor that you truly have seen the things that you describe. You actually did know Jesus of Nazareth personally! You were an eyewitness!"

"Markus," John replied, "if I can be more specific, I *do* still know Him. He is still alive. By His Spirit, He is inspiring me to write these letters to seven of the churches, churches that He Himself instructed various apostles to start. As I wrote in my account of the life of Jesus, He once met with a Samaritan woman at a well. As He talked with her, He said these important words to explain to her who God is: 'God is a Spirit: and they that worship him must worship him in spirit and in truth.'⁶⁰ You see, Markus, as you and I stand on this island, not too far from the landmass in Asia where these churches are, God, as a Spirit, can both see everything that is going on in those churches there and, at the same time, He can also speak to me here and tell me what to write. I know it may be hard for you to believe this, but He has shown me that I will eventually leave this island. When I leave, I will be able to take these scrolls back to the mainland and have them copied and distributed to the churches they are written to!"

"John, although I admit that I have a hard time believing a lot of what you tell me, there is one thing that I am certain of. As I observe and listen to you, I know, without any doubt, that you are a man of God. In addition, we do know from your records that you did travel with Jesus as one of His disciples when He was alive."

"Sir Markus, He is still alive!"

"Yes, John, I know you believe that, and hopefully, one day, I will believe that as well. If He is who you say He is, then everyone should believe in Him!"

"Markus, the problem is that many people initially say that they believe in Him. Many even take the next step and say that they want to follow Him. However, sadly, many, many people either ignore the things He taught or twist what He said to mean something totally different. Also, Markus, just as much as there is a very real God and Jesus is His Son, there is also another spiritual force at work in the heavenlies. His name is Satan. He was one of three archangels in heaven, and he was originally called Lucifer. Because of his God-given beauty, he became lifted up with pride. Then, his heart was filled with the sinful delusion that he could become God. When he convinced one-third of the angels to try to overthrow God's kingdom, God cast him and the rebellious angels down to the earth. You see, due to his bitterness and unremitting vengefulness, Satan is always at work trying to destroy both God's creation and Christ's church.

"As a result of his subtle influence, these churches that I just finished writing to have followed Satan's false doctrines. Satan's teachings are always designed to appeal to a person's sinful nature. You should always try to remember that God would never deceive anyone for any reason. Nor will He ever use any disguise to try to mislead people into thinking that He is evil. However, Satan, on the other hand, often comes as a deceiver in a godlike disguise to trick people into thinking that he is God! That is what I mean, Markus, by Satan's false doctrines. Using a false teacher, a false prophet, or a false apostle, Satan tricks them into thinking certain sins are acceptable to God."

"Yes, John. You probably did not realize it, but I was within earshot when you were reading what you had written earlier out loud. I must say that while I had heard about your Jesus being meek, I had also heard He was authoritative! I guess if you are the son of the One True God, you do have that authority. It certainly sounded to me that the letter you wrote to the church at Ephesus establishes that fact!"

"That is so true, Markus. To know Jesus as I knew Him is to recognize all sides of His heavenly personality. Yes, He was by far the most compassionate, loving person I have ever known. However, when it came to dealing with the hard-hearted religious leaders of our day, He was very stern and corrective. He pulled no punches verbally when He dealt with them. For example, He once told them they were a generation of vipers and snakes! He also told them, in regard to their harsh, unloving judgments and their own additions to God's law, 'Ye are of your father the devil, and the lusts of your father ye will do.'[61] So, yes, Markus, He was both tender and tough! But, Markus, please understand that although I speak in the past tense as I knew Him, I could also be speaking in the present tense as I know Him still, as He is the one inspiring me to write these seven letters to the churches in Asia!"

"John, I didn't understand what I heard you say to the church at Ephesus about the doctrine of the 'Nicolaitans'?"

"Oh, yes, Markus, the doctrine of the Nicolaitans! I am so glad you heard that because that is exactly what I was talking about when I was describing to you how Satan likes to create false doctrines, doctrines that usually have a little bit of truth in them just so they will deceive people. However, as it has been said, 'It is not the glass of wine that killed the emperor but the little drop of poison that was in it!'"

"Oh, yes, so true!" Markus replies.

"The doctrine of the Nicolaitans teaches many minor false things, again mixing a lot of wine with a little bit of poison. However, the most evil deception they teach is that the body can be sinful as long as the spirit is holy. This always leads to people practicing sexual immorality and believing that their practices are either acceptable to God or that as long as their spirit man is cleansed, their fleshly body can do as it pleases. The whole reason, Markus, that Jesus endured the pain of the cross and died for our sins is so that the power of sin can be broken through His shed blood and the power of the Holy Spirit. For the Ephesian church to teach that people could do whatever they wanted with their bodies as long as their spirits were washed clean by some ritual defies the very reason for the need for salvation and the cross of Christ! That is why Jesus is saying to their church that He *hates* this false doctrine! He then goes on to speak in even stronger language to the other churches about a woman in their church who was teaching young men that it was okay to commit fornication. Jesus probably further knows that she is teaching them to commit this fornication with her; however, He does not say that!"

"John, it sounds like God's standards of holiness are certainly stricter than many people want to believe. Maybe that is why Jesus felt the need to speak so strongly about those things."

"Yes, Markus, and above all things, Jesus knows that God intended sexual pleasure to be between one man and one woman after they are married. His purpose is to further bond their hearts together as a couple. Sex within the bonds of marriage is a precious gift and a wonderful design for the human body. Not only is it the means by which babies, which the Bible tells us are gifts from God, are created, but it also provides a closeness between a husband and a wife that is sort of an oasis in the middle of the deserts of life's trials. Sexual relations give them something wonderful to look forward to at some time in their day, as it brings great pleasure. However, when used without restraint between people who are not married to each other, it disrupts God's plan for fidelity. The truth is that most of the false doctrines that Satan sows within churches have sexual immorality tied into them somehow. What God strictly restricts, Satan glibly liberates. While God's instructions solidify relationships, Satan's permissions tear them down. While God's plans lead to eternal life with Him in heaven, Satan's plans lead to unconfessed sin and eternity with him in hell, which Jesus said was prepared for the devil and his angels."

Markus responds with a deep sigh and then says, "John, among the fighting men in Roman wars, I was awarded many times for my bravery in battle and the many wounds I endured in those conflicts. However, those who know me best, including my wife and children, know that underneath this tough exterior is a tender heart that loves music, poetry, and the arts. I also often feel touched by the struggles of others, although for years, I felt it was my manly duty to keep those thoughts hidden. It sounds to me like Jesus was, in some ways, a strong man among men yet held a tender heart underneath His thick skin. I can see He truly cared about others, a trait that I can also see in you, John."

"Thank you, Markus, but do you know what amazes me the most about what you just said? I once heard Jesus, in describing Himself to others, say, 'If you have seen the Father [meaning God], then you have seen Me.'[62] He was trying to explain to the self-righteous scribes and Pharisees that all of their self-prescribed, humanly created sub-laws showed that they were so blinded to who God really was they could not recognize that the Son of God was standing right in front of them. So, Markus, all of the very masculine, courageous, tough character traits that you see in Jesus, combined with His compassionate, patient, kind, loving side, are really a perfect representation of who God is! Personally, Markus, because I have become born again and have asked the Spirit of Christ to live in my heart through the years, I have become more like Him too! The small different pieces of your own person, Markus, that you recognize as seemingly odd for a man and indeed rare for a Roman soldier are actually a vague outline of who God is!

"Markus, I have another thought for you to ponder. In the book of Genesis, in God's Word, scripture teaches us that God first created a man and named him Adam. It states that the three members of the Godhead, the Father, the Son, and the Holy Spirit, conversed and said, 'Let Us make man in Our image, according to Our likeness.'[63] As a matter of fact, I have been told this story since I was a child, and I can quote it word for word:

> *'And the Lord God caused a deep sleep to fall on Adam, and he slept; and He took one of his ribs, and closed up the flesh in its place. Then the rib which the LORD God had taken from man He made into a woman, and He brought her to the man. And Adam said: "This is now bone of my bones and flesh of my flesh; she shall be called Woman because she was taken out of Man."'[64]*

"John, I have to be honest; your Hebrew beliefs seem so much simpler and easier to understand than those taught to me by my Roman forefathers. We have been led to believe that there were many gods involved in creation but that none of them ever came back to become a man, and none of them ever worked thousands of miracles among our people as Jesus did! Now you are telling me these amazing truths about creation and that God is still alive, looking from heaven and seeing the good, the bad, and any evil that is going on in His churches!"

"Yes, Markus, but think about this one powerful truth out of all that I have told you! First, God made man after His image and likeness, and then He took from man one of his ribs and made woman. What does that tell you about the fullness of the character of God?"

"Oh, I see what you are saying. God's character and nature cannot just be seen in man as we know him. Neither can it be seen only in women. For us to understand more fully what God is like, we have to understand that parts of Him were formed in man, and then out of man, He formed woman! So this means God is more like man and woman together, right? Someone could go as far as to say that a married couple together, fusing their strengths together to form 'one flesh,' is the most complete image we have of God, right?"

"Yes! Yes! Markus, I feel that the Spirit of God could be here tonight with us, giving you these understandings. That is exactly what I feel that God wanted people to see when He created man and woman and joined them together! So then Jesus, whom the scripture refers to as the second Adam, has both the masculine character traits of a man and the more compassionate loving traits of a woman!"

"Oh, ha-ha-ha! My wife would love to hear this one, John! But, yes, I can see from what you are saying that is how God, as the One True God, could have created all of life! Tell me, John, what must I do to become a follower of Jesus?"

"Markus, if you confess with your mouth that you believe that Jesus is the Messiah sent from God and believe in your heart that God raised Jesus from the dead, you will be saved and become a Christian!"

"Yes, John! Let's pray!" And with that, Markus takes off his Roman cape and sets it on the ground. Next, he unbuckles his sword belt and places it on top of his cape. He then unstraps his knee-high sandals and lays them on top of the pile.

John inquires, "Markus, why did you remove your Roman soldier uniform and weapons? Why are you now standing barefoot before me?"

"Because now I want to show that I am coming before Jesus as a simple man, humbly admitting of my sinful life and asking for forgiveness for all the innocent blood that I have shed in battle!" With that, he drops to his knees, cups his head in his hands, and begins to weep and sob uncontrollably in prayer. "Dear Jesus, I thank You for giving me the honor of watching over Your disciple, John. I believe his words. Please forgive me for being a very sinful man. I admit that I have committed horrible sins in my life that are too ugly to describe in detail. I plead for Your forgiveness. I believe Your Son died for me and was raised from the dead. John has testified that Your Spirit has changed his life, so I ask You to also send Your Spirit to fill my heart with You!"

At this point, it becomes obvious to the watching souls that Markus has been immediately flooded with a heavenly peace. His hardened, haggard, and bitter countenance is transformed right before their eyes. He raises his hands and starts praising God. In this life-changing moment, he starts addressing God in a brand-new way. No specific instruction is needed by John as Markus utters the most beautiful words that a new Christian can say: "Heavenly Father, I ask that as soon as you bid me leave of my current weeks of duty on this island, I will be allowed to travel home to my wife and family and share with them the wonderful experience of becoming a new person in Jesus Christ!"

"Soldier, you can put your uniform back on now, but you will find that the soldier, the guard, the Roman named Markus, will begin to see and feel life in a brand-new way." With that, John starts laughing and praising God. He first shakes Markus's hand but then quickly envelopes him in a godly embrace as they both praise God together for another soul that has entered the Kingdom of God!

As the omniciscreen began to fade back to white, Windrose turned his head back and forth to discern the reactions of the souls in the arena to what they had just seen. "Soldiers, stewards, future children of God, now I call you 'defenders'! Defenders of the faith and defenders of the true gospel of Jesus Christ!"

Katrina-83 speaks out and asks, "Windrose, after all that God will do in sending His Son to this world, and after all that Jesus will do, why would we ever have to defend that message?" Several of the other souls who had raised their hands nodded in agreement with Katrina. It is obvious that they do not understand either.

"Katrina and all of you who are likewise concerned, you surely speak from pure motives. I understand completely why you cannot see the need for what you are being asked to do. When the Apostle Paul says goodbye to the elders in Ephesus, he will declare powerful words of explanation, words that will one day be recorded by Luke in the book of Acts. For now, I am going to open up the whiteboard once again. This time, you will be able to read for yourself what Paul says in his tearful departure, knowing that he will not see them again until they are all in heaven together."

Once again, Windrose uses his right index finger to outline the large whiteboard, but this time, they see that the following passage of scripture has already been very beautifully handwritten in dark purple ink:

> *Therefore, I testify to you this day that I am innocent of the blood of all men. For I have not shunned to declare to you the whole counsel of God. Therefore, take heed to yourselves and to all the flock, among which the Holy Spirit has made you overseers, to shepherd the church of God which He purchased with His own blood. For I know this, that after my departure savage wolves will come in among you, not sparing the flock. Also, from among yourselves, men will rise up, speaking perverse things, to draw away the disciples after themselves. Therefore, watch and remember that for three years I did not cease to warn everyone night and day with tears.*
>
> *"So now, brethren, I commend you to God and to the word of His grace, which is able to build you up and give you an inheritance among all those who are sanctified. I have coveted no one's silver or gold or apparel. Yes, you yourselves know that these hands have provided for my necessities, and for those who were with me. I have shown you in every way, by laboring like this, that you must support the weak. And remember the words of the Lord Jesus, that He said, 'It is more blessed to give than to receive.'"*
>
> *And when he had said these things, he knelt down and prayed with*

them all. Then they all wept freely, and fell on Paul's neck and kissed him, sorrowing most of all for the words which he spoke, that they would see his face no more. And they accompanied him to the ship.[65]

Roberto-37 shouts out to Windrose, "Paul here is very passionate in his writing to warn the early church about some sort of evil people. What could be so evil that Paul would be so emphatic, so passionate, so determined to not only preach the truth but to demonstrate how to live it in such a selfless way?"

"Roberto, you are very astute to recognize this. Do you know what one of Satan's most effective tools is as he tries to deceive both the unconverted world and those who are professing believers in the Lord Jesus Christ?"

"What?" Roberto answers.

"Twisting the truth to mean something different than God the Holy Spirit originally inspired it to say. As a matter of fact, one of his spiritual nicknames is 'the Twister'! As you saw in the last trip to the isle of Patmos, John explained to Markus that man's heart is evil to its very core. Jeremiah, the prophet, will one day write, 'The heart is deceitful above all things, and desperately wicked; who can know it?'[66] Satan looks for men's and women's greatest weaknesses and tempts them right in that very area of their lives." Windrose then shouts, "*Souls! Do you know what one of the greatest weaknesses that mankind will ever display is?*"

Having gained their full attention, he lowers his voice back to a normal tone. He once again raises his finger and draws the whiteboard, which once again appears in thin air, and he blows on his finger again, making it glow in bright red. He then proceeds to write the following words in big letters so that everyone can clearly see what he is trying to teach them.

"*From the very beginning, mankind has had the tendency to rebel against God's words, hiding the wickedness in their own hearts and trying to justify their sins by reinterpreting them to say or mean something that God has not said or did not intend!*

"Souls, we are going to now take a trip via the omniciscreen into the future to a planning meeting into the realms of darkness. Do not let your heart be troubled. Remember, Satan was Lucifer, a former archangel. Yes, he had a limited amount of power, but nowhere near the omniscient, omnipresent, omnipotent power of the Almighty God who is bringing you into the kingdom for such a time as this. This One True God will be equipping you at different times in your life with the fullness of the Holy Spirit of God. Never forget that this is the Spirit whose power is so great that in creation, He lifted up the continents, separating the waters from the dry ground. Remember also that Jesus will take back from Satan the keys of death, hell, and the grave through the power of His perfect, sinless, spotless, righteous, holy blood! Neither Satan nor any of his demonic fallen angels are ever to be feared, no matter what war they may one day wage against you!"

With that, Windrose points to the omniciscreen, and this time, something very unusual happens. The screen is obviously energized, but instead of lighting up brightly as it usually does, all that can be seen are very dark caverns and coves. Shadows seem to move about with manlike forms, but no distinctive characteristics can be recognized. All at once, in what appear to be rolling clouds of thin, foul-smelling smoke, a pair of luminescent green eyes with flashing black pupils recognizable as something from some sort of creature begin to move about. Then another set of grey eyes emerges, and another, and raspy voices are heard, which seem to be mumbling something, but at that point, it is not clear what these creatures are saying to each other. Whatever is being said sounds like words frequently interrupted by coughing-like sounds, as if these beings have to keep clearing their throats to talk due to the smokey atmosphere.

Windrose begins to explain to the souls that they are being allowed to see inside the spiritual realm of darkness as demonic forces discuss their strategy for attacking what sounds like "Gis gride."

"Gis gride buz zee glopped, Gis gride buz zee glopped, Gis gride buz zee glopped," the twisted spirit keeps saying, having to clear its drooling throat frequently, speaking in what seems like garbled words that the souls understand but seem to not quite be able to figure out. After Windrose allows the souls to view into the dark realm and listen to the demons' garbled talk for a short period of time, he interrupts them to say, "God the Father, in His wonderfully creative way, has provided another amazing tool for this class. The 'demonitrac' device translates their evil language into intelligible languages for your understanding. As God has designed, I can synchronize the demonitrac to the omniciscreen so that their words can be understood."

All of a sudden, as Windrose connects the two devices, the demonic rambling "Gis gride buz zee glopped, Gis gride buz zee glopped, Gis gride buz zee glopped" becomes more understandable: "His bride must be stopped, His bride must be stopped, His bride must be stopped!" comes through loud and clear! The souls gasp and utter other vocalizations, revealing that they are shocked by what they hear!

"Future children of God, soldiers, stewards, and now defenders of the faith, do you now see how important your mission on the earth will be? Jeremiah, who will be one of the most well-known Old Testament prophets, will one day proclaim, 'O earth, earth, earth, hear the Word of the LORD!'[67] Jeremiah will be known as the prophet who could easily recognize false prophesies and the character traits of the people who became false prophets. He will be called to reprove the worship of Baal, a false god who basically taught humans to worship earthly wealth or gain and to not deny oneself the things of this world, as the apostle who will pen the letter to the Hebrews that, for instance, those who are martyred for Christ might obtain a better resurrection. The greatest conflict in the history of all of creation will repeatedly be ongoing battles in which the forces of darkness will constantly wrestle against God's instruments of light! The darkness will continually try to shroud the light, but the true light's brilliance will continuously and spectacularly dispel the darkness! False teachings promoted by false teachers aimed at hearts weakened by the lusts of the world will be the primary offensive tools used by the evil one in the battles. Souls, you will each find yourselves in different places and times in the future. These lessons that I am giving you will cause sparks of zealous truth to rise up from within you at just the right time and place. Again, you will not specifically remember these classes, but sown in seed form, they will suddenly sprout up at your predesignated times in the future, foreordained times only the Father knows! Now, let's return to the omnicrescreen once again. Listen in on the demonic strategy meeting once more to see what some of Satan's future plans are."

Once again, the screen displays the dark figures moving about and speaking to one another. However, this time, with the demonitrac in place, what they were saying was coming through loud and clear.

"Yes," Sparchek says, "His bride must be stopped, but how can we hope to stop the church of the very Son of God from growing? People everywhere are hearing of God's plan of salvation and accepting it by the thousands!"

"Ah, yes, this is true, Sparchek. However, if we give them a deception, a kind of close copy of the real thing, then they will not be truly born again, will they? Ha-ha-ha....." Tryovor declares.

"Tryovor, I know that you are one of the principalities, but you are still only a captain in Satan's leadership. In spite of not being very high up in the hierarchy, you always amaze me because, over and over again, you seem to be able to come up with a new evil plan to try to stop, disrupt, slow down, or confuse God's people!"

"That's what I glean from spending time with pure evil himself! Ha-ha-ha!"

"Sparchek, what was the number one thing Satan always taught us that we should know well if we were going to be able to keep God's children in a defeated state of mind?"

"The Bible, sir. Knowing as we do that, their *alllllmiiiighty* so *grrrrrreat.* God can do nothing apart from His Word; our motivating motto is, 'My people fail for lack of knowledge!'"

"Yes, yes, yes. We have to keep them weak and unlearned, and we have to understand what God really said through His servants if we are going to be able to effectively twist His Word or take important parts out. We have to give them just enough truth to not be able to recognize the poison that we mix in it! Isn't it great where the *Soooooon* of *Gooooood* says, 'Till heaven and earth pass away, one jot or one tittle will by no means pass from the law till all is fulfilled.'

[68]People really do have to love God with all of their hearts and fully appreciate heaven's gift to want to know His Word that closely. Their weak love of Him and their superficial knowledge of His Word make our job of sending false teachers and prophets to lead them away from the truth very easy. Ha-ha-ha!"

At this point, Sparchek and Tryovor join in insane-sounding laughter, which stirs up the other evil entities, causing them all to point their long arms and pointy fingers down towards the ground in a jerking-like motion, once again praising Lucifer, the chief of all sinful failures in the history of the universe.

"Okay, listen up, demons. We are all going to gather in the instruction cavern now, as Satan will soon be teaching us how to use another one of our chief strategies in stealing people right out of what they 'think' is a true born-again experience. When that phrase is heard, there is a concerted expression of gasps and nos as the slimy creatures use their long, bony hands to cover up their filthy and ragged ears. It is evident to the watching souls that 'born again' is the one phrase the demons hate to hear more than any other. The demons know that the angels of God rejoice every time one sinner comes to God, so even the phrase itself sends chills up their crooked and bony spines."

As the noise settles down, Tryovor continues his instruction. "Fellow demons, Satan created this dome-shaped mega theater with a projection system built into the ceiling for his teaching sessions. Because hell will always be looking up at earth, he prefers his teachings be projected on the ceiling over our heads, requiring us to look up at him and up to what he is designing in his deceptions." As shrill whining erupts from his ragged and furtive crowd of listeners, he responds, "I know, I know. This is difficult for your necks. Tough. It is what it is. Deal with it."

With that piece of information, thousands of pairs of evil eyes moving in the heads of darkly shrouded humanlike figures begin to move reluctantly towards the "deception center." As the souls watch intensely, the omniciscreen begins to fade back to total black.

Windrose, in preparation for the next lesson, drops down to his knees before the gathered souls and prays silently. He knows that he wants all the souls to have a moment to reflect on what they have just witnessed. He also knows that this next trip into the future will be the most troubling one that they have experienced so far. He understands how difficult it will be for them. When he finishes praying, he says a sharp "amen" and stands up.

"The Father just told me that you are ready for the next lesson, so tighten up your robe ropes once again. In addition, this time, I want you to tighten your sandal straps, too, because you are about to witness demonic influence at work in its most seductive form. Jesus will one day refer to the tricks and traps of the devil as He speaks to the church in Thyatira: 'But I say to you, to the rest of those who do not have this teaching, who have not known the depths of Satan, as they say: I will not cast upon you any other burden.'"[69]

"*Woah!*" the souls seemed to speak out in unison. Their vocal response is paired with similar body language, expressing sorrowful surprise. Hands then shoot up all over the arena as souls blurt out parts of questions.

Windrose raises his voice, saying, "Not everyone at once, please. Makawee-9, please state your question again."

Makawee responds, saying, "How could some people know the depths of Satan's evil, but others don't?"

Yeses, amens, and other similarly affirming comments are heard all around the arena, indicating that many are wondering the same thing.

"Remember when we heard some of John's writings on the isle of Patmos? John had recorded Jesus's words to the church in Pergamos. He addressed many topics in His letter to them, but He also promised that to those who overcome, He will give some of the hidden manna to eat. Do you remember that?"

In response, the air in the arena is immediately filled with multitudes of "yeses" and "amens."

Windrose drops his head in his hands and starts to cry tears of joy, saying, "Thank You, Father, thank You, Father," over and over again as he raises his hands in praise to the Father.

His voice cracked slightly with emotion, and he went on to teach the souls.

"You see, there are added blessings for those saints who will one day press on determinedly through great hardships to serve their God with unflagging fervency. These 'overcomers' will have spiritual privileges that other believers just will not have, not just here but also in heaven. Here, they will be granted heightened levels of discernment regarding good and evil. Open doors of opportunity to share the gospel will only be awarded to those who have been proven faithful. Sadly, though, the day will come when many will try to take advantage of the gift of grace of their salvation, never realizing the special blessings that come from walking very closely with their Lord each day. Always remember that the Father's goal is for close personal communion between Himself and His creation, a communion that was lost in the Garden of Eden. That is why Jesus will one day say that the most important commandment is this: 'And you shall love the LORD your God with all your heart, with all your soul, with all your mind, and with all your strength.'[70] However, the very evil side of human nature is to try to always manipulate themselves into an easier way of doing things.

"Now, souls, look once again at the omniciscreen as we visibly travel in the year 2023 to what is being called '*Reaching the AI Generation Church Growth Conference.*'" As the screen lights up this time, the focus is on the sports press box, where two gentlemen are seen speaking.

"Frank Crawford, what a delight it is to join you tonight at Madison Square Garden for a nearly full house of ministers from all over the world!"

"Thank you! Bill Bestley, you are well-known in the financial world for having built multiple real estate projects totaling billions of dollars worldwide over the last twenty years. I understand that it was your connections in the business world that enabled us to secure this marvelous facility for this special three-day event."

"Yes, Frank, I am totally unashamed to say that I am a believer in the Lord Jesus Christ and a proud sponsor of this event. Vendors and booksellers will be here lining the walkways, selling everything from Christian-themed clothing to Bibles and how-to books, including books written by our featured speakers here this week, speakers who, as we like to say, are like the 'sons of Issachar' in the Chronicles, men who had an understanding of the times to know what Israel ought to do!"

"Yes, amen, Bill. These are certainly challenging times. We need to deal with the fact that this generation sees things and thinks about things much differently than you and I do. I also see we have some protesters outside who are not too happy with this conference. Let's take our video connection out there for a minute and see if we can tell just what these people are so unhappy about."

Outside, they encounter crowds of professing believers who have also traveled long distances to get there. They have large posters and banners with scriptures and biblical quotes on them. One sweet-looking little old lady is leaning on a cane with one hand and holding up a sign in the other that says in big letters, *"PAUL SAID TO RIGHTLY DIVIDE THE WORD OF TRUTH!"* Others are chanting things like, "Preach the truth. Preach the whole truth!" A man wearing a bright blue suit has a poster that says, "Without holiness shall no man see the Lord." A lady holding a little baby is standing beside a tripod sign that says, *"James, the half brother of Jesus, wrote, 'Show me your faith by your works'"* (James 2:18b; paraphrased). A school bus that brought a load of protesters from Texas has the words: *"The hyper-grace message needs biblical balance!"* spray-painted on its side. Several hundred people have come from all over the country to strongly voice their concerns about this modern movement, which seems to appeal to a lot of people.

"Bill, it seems like these people are very determined to get their message across. I believe they actually feel that in their attempt to reach this younger generation, the teachers at this conference this week are teaching false doctrine."

"Well, Frank, to be quite frank with you, no pun intended, ha-ha-ha, the 20,000 people who have come from all around the world do not feel our teachers are wrong. Book sales from the teachers at this conference last year were in the millions of dollars. It sounds to me like the attendees' ears do want to hear what these teachers are saying to today's church."

"Yes, Bill. Well, since you footed the 'bill' for reserving the garden for tonight, ha-ha-ha, I will let you introduce the worship band as they come on stage tonight and help us all enter into God's presence."

"Thanks, Frank. I hear that tonight's worship band has been busy traveling all over the world, playing for various events. They are also well-known in secular venues because they like to mix up their music with famous secular songs of the past. Let's take the cameras to center stage now and welcome Robby Jerkins and his band, X Sinners Rock on God."

With that, Madison Square Garden is filled with the music of screaming guitars mixed with the radical drumbeats of three different drummers, each on an individual rotating platform. Fireworks shoot off from the front of the stage, showering sparks down on the band. The crowd cheers with raucous delight as six dancers, dressed in pure white with angel-type wings attached to their costumes and long shining streamers flowing from their arms, jump and dance in choreographed precision. With that, a light show starts with a simulated rainbow effect, which shoots up from the back of the stage, hitting mirrors on the ceiling, which reflect the colors back down towards the main floor where the crowd is seated.

The lyrics are quite simple, and everyone seems to join in and sing along: "I'm an ex-sinner but rock on God, / I'm an ex-sinner but rock on God. / I once was lost, but now I'm found. / Rock on, I say, rock on God! / Yayyyyyy!"

After that song finishes, the band plays a few more of their well-known praise songs, and then one of the conference speakers comes out to speak. Bobby Jerkins, in a well-rehearsed move, drop-kicks his mic to Dr Willy DeNaldo, who reaches out and suavely catches it with one hand. With that move, the crowd once again goes wild with enthusiastic cheering. Dr. Willy then proceeds to somehow twirl the microphone like a baton between his fingers, shouting, "*The old school of religion is dead. We now serve a living God who loves us just the way we are!*" As he says this, the multicolored rainbow lights can be seen reflecting off of his white suit.

Once again, the crowd goes wild, shouting and saying, "Praise be to God who is good!" Then everyone yells back, "All the time!"

Dr. Willy then yells out, *"Hello, Madison Square Garden and the believers here from all over the world!"*

Everyone responds by clapping and shouting "amens." Some can be heard yelling, "We love you, Dr. Willy!"

"I love you all too," Dr. Willy responds. "Do you know I feel like I have spent my whole life compiling the teachings I bring out in my new book series? These titles are available for purchase here tonight: at bookstores everywhere and online at multiple locations, by the way. The first one is *Better God, Better Life*. The second one is *Jesus Loves You More than You Have Been Taught*. The third title is *Everyone Gets Caught with Their Hand in the Cookie Jar Sometimes*. Then there is the one I am working on now, which is getting a lot of people upset with me—'Every Part of the Bible Is Not for Everyone All the Time!'"

The crowd cheers wildly, but as the noise dies down, suddenly, there is a commotion on the main floor. A white-haired man jumps up on his chair and starts yelling. "This man is a false prophet! He is one of the ones Jesus tried to warn us about in the last days. Repent, repent, you people pleaser; you are not from God. Paul warned Timothy that there would be those who would teach that to gain is godliness, from such withdraw yourself."

It only takes the event security a few seconds to get to the elderly man and restrain him, taking him down to the floor. Dr. Willy is immediately escorted off the platform for his safety as the band quickly rushes back onto the platform.

Billy Jerkins quickly adlibs and starts jamming on his guitar as the other band members hustle into place. They once again start playing: "I was once a sinner but rock on God. / Rock on God."

The crowd resumes their loud cheering. It seems as if everyone ignores the words of the white-haired man.

With that, the omniciscreen begins to darken, and Windrose turns to address the souls again.

"Over our next few sessions, we will begin more and more to approach the end of the age of man on the earth. The scenes you will witness will be, as this was, sometimes shocking and hard to comprehend. Always remember that the battles you will be in, souls, will be for the 'souls of men.' Always be aware that the decisions you make and the decisions that are made by your fellow man, as they relate to the will of God being done on earth even as it is in heaven, will have a direct impact on millions and millions in regard to eternity.

"Our next journey into the future will help you to see more clearly the need for you to become defenders."

CHAPTER 10

GOOD EXPOSES EVIL, SOULS SEE JESUS, AND ONE PRAYING MAN

Windrose, realizing that the souls have been given a lot of heavy-duty resistance training, chooses to open up this new learning session with a follow-up question-and-answer time.

"Souls, as you have been given a little time to think about what you have just learned visually through the omnisciscreen during the last trip into the future, have any new questions come to you?"

Mylon-7 raises his hand and asks, "Windrose, why would God even allow such false teachings and false prophets to exist under the New Covenant of God's grace? Won't it be enough for Jesus to leave the riches and splendor of heaven and come down to this world? Why would the Father tolerate such evil deception concerning His perfect act of love?"

"That is such a good question, Mylon. However, you all do know that the Holy Spirit is present here among us, and He is helping to bring to your understanding what the big picture in these accounts is really portraying. This work of the Holy Spirit is what is prompting these great questions. The Apostle Paul, answering a similar concern to the Corinthian church, will one day write, 'For there also must be factions among you, that those who are approved may be recognized among you'!"[71]

Mylon responds with another question, "What should our response be to factions and heresies in the future when we are on the earth in our human bodies? If God allows them, should we try to prevent them or stop them?"

"Mylon, that is when you will be led by the Holy Spirit, who will use God's Word to guide your life. King Solomon, King David's son, will become to be known as the wisest earthly king who ever lived. Ironically, he will learn much of his wisdom through unwise mistakes he will make during his own life. He will write the following words in a book called Ecclesiastes, which will be included in the Bible: 'There is a time to be silent and a time to speak.'[72] Notice that he says there is a time to be silent first! This statement contains great wisdom, and it answers your question.

"The best way to handle factions or heresies will be to bring your concerns to either your spiritual mentor or to a church elder. They will be able to recognize just how dangerous the error that is being taught is and also will recognize just how dangerous the person who is teaching it is. Jesus will one day say,

'Either make the tree good and its fruit good, or else make the tree bad and its fruit bad; for a tree is known by its fruit. Brood of vipers! How can you, being evil, speak good things? For out of the abundance of the heart the mouth speaks. A good man out of the good treasure of his heart brings forth good things, and an evil man out of the evil treasure brings forth evil things. But I say to you that for every idle word men may speak, they will give an account of it in the day of judgment. For by your words, you will be justified, and by your words you will be condemned.'[73]

"So, Mylon, always remember the vital importance of your individual prayer life and your daily moment-by-moment walk with God. He is as close as a prayer breath away. The Holy Spirit is your 'Wonderful Counselor,' but then, depending upon your own spiritual maturity, if there is that tiniest little question mark down in your spirit, remember Solomon's wisdom. It may be that this will be the time to be silent first! Remember what I just told you; if you are unsure, seek the counsel of someone who has walked with God for many years. Make no mistake; however, there will be times when you should speak up. You will learn that human nature often leans towards the path of least resistance. Far too many will allow evil teaching to go unchecked. However, with that being said, we must remember the second half of what Paul will one day write to the Corinthians, baby believers who will need a lot of teaching. There will be a large number of new converts in the city of Corinth who will become Christians out of the very immoral environment in their city. Paul's Holy Spirit-inspired wisdom will say that the false doctrines will be allowed so that those who are approved will be recognized!

"Even people who will not yet be converted will have an inherent nature that will allow them to tell the difference between something that is fake and something that is genuine. Those who may appear and sound genuine on the surface will often exhibit character flaws that are obviously not Christlike. Most of what they will teach will sound biblical, but there will be a small amount that will be like a fly in a bowl of ointment. In a very short time, that oil will start to stink simply because of that one tiny little fly!

"On the other hand, those whose God's hand is on, those who are truly called by Him, will shine brightly in the glory of God, and as Jesus will one day teach, they will be known by their good fruit! They will produce converts from the witness of their own lives, and those that they have won to Christ will be likewise fruitful, producing a constant stream of new believers.

"You see, Mylon, a real diamond is obviously proven real if it is sitting next to a false one. Real gold is obviously real when it is set next to the crystal ore, which will one day be called pyrite. In answer to your original question, God will allow false doctrines to exist in order to prove to all those who look on and to all those who are prayerful what is real and to also reveal which doctrines and people are from Him.

"Jesus will also one day teach a parable about the wheat and the tares. As a matter of fact, as a special treat, we are going to take a trip by way of the omniciscreen to a place where Jesus will be teaching. He actually will teach many parables that day; however, in a short time, He will explain this one in great detail to His disciples in a secret place."

The souls at once all shout amens, cheering the fact that this time, they were going to actually be seeing Jesus Himself teach. One of the souls shouts out, "Windrose, you seem like Jesus yourself!"

Windrose chuckles, responding, "All praise and glory be to my Father! We all are expected by the Father to be like Jesus! Isn't that, under the powerful anointing of the Holy Spirit, what we are all supposed to be doing, continually becoming more 'Christlike'?"

As Windrose begins to illuminate the omniciscreen, he says, "I'm going to really enjoy this trip into the future myself! We will be seeing into the time period when Jesus walked on the earth.

"Jesus will have just spent some time teaching in one of the neighborhood houses after having been recently once again confronted by area Jewish religious leaders. He will teach using several different parables that day, but for today's lesson, we will see Him recount the parable of the wheat and the tares. The omniciscreen will then jump ahead a short period in time to later that day when He will unpack the true meaning in a private session back at the house, speaking only to the disciples."

As the omniciscreen opens up, the souls see Jesus walk away from the house where He had been speaking, headed down to the seashore. They see that He is a very ordinary-looking man with olive skin, dark brown eyes, and dark flowing hair.

The souls began commenting to each other that He looked different than they thought He might. Windrose, overhearing what some of them were saying among themselves, pauses the motion on the omniciscreen for a moment, allowing them to focus on a still image of Jesus as He walks down the hill towards the sea of Galilee.

"Souls, God, in His infinite wisdom, knew that it was important that Jesus's physical appearance when He lived on the earth be that of a common man. The prophet Isaiah will one day write a prophecy describing this fact, saying, 'For He shall grow up before Him as a tender plant, and as a root out of dry ground. He has no form or comeliness; and when we see Him, there is no beauty that we should desire Him.'"[74]

Souls Susan-13, Susan-28, and Susan-33 happened to be all sitting near each other and discussing their mindsets about how they had thought that Jesus would look. They all agree, so Susan-33 speaks up loudly to Windrose, asking, "Why wouldn't God make His Son be the most handsome of all men ever born so that people would be drawn to Him, Windrose?"

This question tickles Windrose's thought process, causing him to tilt his head back and start laughing so hard that he puts his hand on his stomach, leans back, and laughs some more. "I'm not laughing at your question, ladies. It just amused me, Sues, that the three of you found each other and that you all had the same question at the same time. Oh, may one day such unity fill all the churches of the earth! Well, souls, you all must understand that the entirety of the kingdom of God and its complexity exists in the spiritual world, a world which, in many ways, is more real than the natural world in which men will grow up. God the Father Himself is a Spirit, and it is widely understood that the Holy 'Spirit' obviously is also a Spirit. However, you must understand that Jesus is in His God-most perfect form a Spirit as well, a spirit who will one day take the form of a baby and grow up as a natural man on the earth. The Father does not want anyone worshipping any earthly created thing, any being, any natural person, any form of nature, or any individual. Simply put, God does not want people to be drawn to His Son because He is physically beautiful. He wants people to be drawn to His Son because He is *Jesus*, the Son of God, as God, very God, taking the form of a man who will eventually be baptized in the Holy Spirit. This will set the perfect example for all of mankind who fully surrender their lives to Christ. They will then allow *their ordinary selves* to become beautifully baptized in God's Holy Spirit, permitting that spiritual beauty to reflect the glory of God in ordinary lives."

As Windrose restarts the omniciscreen, the souls see that the many people who are following Jesus as He leaves the house are shouting to those in the streets, drawing attention to the fact that Jesus of Nazareth is among them. This causes many others to come running in order to catch up to the group. The souls see that Jesus is dressed in a plain white linen robe and camel leather sandals. He begins teaching from a borrowed fishing boat, which He

Himself had pushed out a short distance using an oar on the sea bottom. He had then dropped an onboard anchor over the side to keep the boat stabilized. This kept the people from pressing in too close. In addition, the water surface helped amplify His voice so that all could hear Him perfectly. As He teaches, the souls see that people are listening attentively to everything that He is saying. Having just finished another parable, He goes on to say,

> *"The kingdom of heaven is like a man who sowed good seed in his field; but while men slept, his enemy came and sowed tares among the wheat and went his way. But when the grain had sprouted and produced a crop, then the tares also appeared. So the servants of the owner came and said to him, 'Sir, did you not sow good seed in your field? How then does it have tares?' He said to them, 'An enemy has done this.' The servants said to him, 'Do you want us then to go and gather them up?' But he said, 'No, lest while you gather up the tares you also uproot the wheat with them. Let both grow together until the harvest, and at the time of harvest, I will say to the reapers, "First gather together the tares and bind them in bundles to burn them, but gather the wheat into my barn."'"*[75]

"His disciple Matthew will one day record the other parables that He taught that day…"

> *Then Jesus sent the multitude away and went into the house. And His disciples came to Him, saying, "Explain to us the parable of the tares of the field."*
>
> *He answered and said to them: "He who sows the good seed is the Son of Man. The field is the world, the good seeds are the sons of the kingdom, but the tares are the sons of the wicked one. The enemy who sowed them is the devil, the harvest is the end of the age, and the reapers are the angels. Therefore as the tares are gathered and burned in the fire, so it will be at the end of this age. The Son of Man will send out His angels, and they will gather out of His kingdom all things that offend, and those who practice lawlessness, and will cast them into the furnace of fire. There will*

be wailing and gnashing of teeth. Then the righteous will shine forth as the sun in the kingdom of their Father. He who has ears to hear, let him hear!"[76]

The souls are awestruck by the trifold complexity of the moment. This was the first time they had actually been able to see Jesus Himself teaching the people of Galilee. The souls are silent, absorbing His intense teaching regarding discerning between those who are good and evil. The arena is then immediately filled with "wows" and phrases such as, "Oh my," some "amens," and many simple gasps from those who are wordless at the thought of some humans ending up being like tares, to one day be bound up and cast into the fires of obvious hell! They are overwhelmed by this long-awaited opportunity to hear Jesus teach a parable and hear Him explain that parable, using it to develop a tricomplexium declaration! The Father made sure that the souls' emotilliance could not retain Jesus's visage so as not to reveal too much too soon!

Windrose raises and lowers his hands once again in an attempt to calm the souls. "Be assured, souls, that yes, many of you here will have the potential to someday do great things for the Father. Others of you, sadly, may choose to rebel against the things that God has taught you and follow the fleshly nature that you will one day have. It is very hard for you to grasp this concept now, still being souls, not yet having received your human bodies through your future births on the Earth. However, remember God, being a just God, must honor your free wills, or it will not be love, will it?"

As the souls answer, resounding "nos" are heard all through the arena, yet it is plain that they are still awestruck by the enormity of their future responsibilities.

"Souls!" Windrose shouts abruptly! "This evil that we have just learned of, however, is not the most dangerous form of evil! This evil that we have just discussed will be recognizable by most people, but the evil that we are about to visibly travel in time to witness is far more subtle. However, in the end, it is just as potentially damming. We could easily label the next evil as 'Satan's favorite tool' because it is a 'slow burner.' It is sown over a lifetime and bears fruit in its complexity after many years of have passed. Its unnoticeable deceptions will be sown in hearts in the name of everyone's favorite word, '*love*'! Then, because it comes introduced in the deceptive wrapper of love, those who tend to be people pleasers will be exceptionally prone to fall for its multiple lures. Let's take a trip in a few minutes to 1985, where we will observe the Dawkins family, who will be very seriously motivated to raise their children properly. We will see that they have a six-year-old son named Isaac, Sarah, who is four, and a little baby named Rachael. As we look at the omniciscreen again, we will see that Evangelist Blangdon and his wife, Rosie, are getting their children ready to go to church. As in previous time travel, the Father is supernaturally giving you the ability to have a one-time understanding of the culture that you are viewing. If He did not, it would all be very foreign to you! However, before we go there, we are going to take a sneak peek into the realms of darkness and listen in on the demonic plans to destroy this family over time."

The omniciscreen opens again to the dark regions of the demonic caverns. The souls witness the dark, shadowy creatures again, moving slowly towards the "deception center." This time, however, the sinister figures are looking up and observing a particular family that is involved in Christian leadership. The souls see, in flickering green light, the words "*The Deception and Destruction Board*" flashing on and off at the top of a dark-colored light board. Under that heading, they see a subheading that says "*Targeted Individuals.*" Then, to the souls' amazement, they see written in smaller flashing red letters, "the Dawkins family," followed by all of their names: "Rev. Blangdon, Father" is doubly highlighted with purple light because he is a minister. Then they see "Rosie" with flashing red capital letters "MINISTER'S WIFE" next to her name. Underneath is a listing of their children: "Isaac" with flashing "*firstborn son,*" "Sarah, *middle child,*" and "Rachael, *baby of the family,*" all flashing in red to help the demons know each child's potential strengths and weaknesses.

Once again, the souls hear the demons emitting unintelligible and garbled words. This time, they are chanting, "*Disawkins famisky buz zee glopped! Disawkins famisky buz zee glopped!*" However, Windrose once again synchronizes the demonitrac with the omniciscreen, and the demonic chanting immediately becomes understandable once again: "The Dawkins family must be stopped! The Dawkins family must be stopped!" produces instant understanding in the minds of the souls, as Satan's focused efforts to destroy not just this family but all families, especially those of believers who are in Christian leadership are revealed! As the souls begin to react in horror to what they are seeing, Windrose once again approaches the omniciscreen, dimming it down to the off position for a moment to allow him to make a momentous announcement.

"Souls, I know that you have made many journeys into the future and that many have revealed troubling realities about the impact that evil will one day have on God's creation. However, what you are about to see will help calm any fears that you have and will help you to realize that in your future battles against Satan, there will be more that are for you than are against you! This will be especially true after Jesus completes His most important mission by dying on the cross for the sins of the world! Before we take a trip to 1985 and the Dawkins family, the Father has shown me *that He wants you to see what is going to happen next! Let's look at what stands ready to fight and defend behind the scenes in 1985!"*

Then, with a sudden explosion of bright light, the omniciscreen lights up to reveal a gigantic arena in 1985, where everything is either pure gold or brilliant white. Tens of thousands of angels stand at attention, shoulder to shoulder, holding their golden shields, valiantly wearing helmets of pure gold, each face fixed straight forward. The angels are of giant manly stature and strikingly muscular, exhibiting battle-ready perfection. Every angelic soldier is focused straight forward as Windrose speaks into this arena, declaring,

"Angels of the Most High God, are you ready to go forth?"

To this question comes an answer in the form of a *loud roar*!

"We are ready to do the Father's will, whatever He calls us to do, and whenever He calls us to do it!" They then, in perfect unison, take their golden swords and swing them around in order to tap their shields up against their golden armor. They next bring their swords back to their sides, making a "phut" sound as they penetrate the platforms under their feet. With that, the angels'

eyes begin to sparkle in anticipation, and their faces shine with confident and contented smiles.

The angels then further reply, *"God's will be done on earth as it is in heaven!"* Once again, the souls began to comment to each other about the fact that when the angels spoke in unison, it was amplified with such great power that the sound was almost as if it had thundered, but they saw no clouds or lightning.

Windrose then chooses to ask the angels one last question: "Angels, how ready are you to go and do whatever it is that the Father commands you?"

With that question, the countless numbers of angels standing on the tiers of the arena began to spread exquisitely beautiful white feathered wings, which had been tucked behind them until now, in preparation for their eminent mission.

Suddenly, two angelic beings of superior size and power step onto the main platform of the angelic arena. A golden aura of God's presence, resembling a transparent cloud, immediately engulfs them. Little flashes of light, almost like sparks, begin to flicker from their golden armor. The notable dings, scratches, and scrapes on their swords and shields do not dim their glory. It is plain to see that they are military badges of courage and that they have not been removed in order that they can serve as constant reminders to the other angels of the faithfulness of the many years of battle of these two who have ascended the main platform.

Windrose speaks up, stating, "Give a grand welcome to Michael and Gabriel, the two remaining archangels under the Father's command!" Then, as Windrose senses the souls' enthusiasm and their eagerness to applaud the beauty of Michael and Gabriel, he immediately raises his voice, speaking loudly and quickly to the souls before they can react, saying, *"Souls, souls, please remember all glory and honor and praise belongs to the God the Father, God the Son, and God the Holy Ghost.* These angels desire no praise or applause for having become who the Father has created them to be. They are simply holy servants of the Father, created by Him, created for His service to battle the forces of evil in order to protect His children because He knows that they need strong protection!"

In a split second, one after another, then another of the assembled angels launch out, vanishing in different directions, creating "whooshing" sounds and leaving trails of golden glory as they are each sent on multiple missions either in the moment or in order to prepare them for Earth's future battles.

"Now it's all right to cheer, souls!" Windrose says, to which the souls shout out thunderous praise and adoration to God for creating such a magnificent angelic army! The souls' praise is greatly amplified as they consider the contrast between the pure beauty and power of God's angel army with the ugliness and evil nature of the satanic creatures that the souls had earlier observed in the evil one's unholy lair as they planned the destruction of the Dawkins family.

Windrose once again momentarily shuts off the omniciscreen in order to quickly prepare the souls for their next trip. "Are there any questions, souls, about the magnificent angel soldiers of God?" Windrose chuckles as thousands of pairs of eyes, looking stunned, move their heads back and forth, indicating, "No!" One finally speaks up from the crowd, saying, "No questions, sir, no questions at all!"

"Okay, souls, now it's time to take the trip to the year 1985 and look in on the Dawkins family as they are getting ready to go to midweek service. The church they attend had experienced a decline in membership a few years earlier, so a former pastor had eliminated the Wednesday night service. However, under this new pastor, whose father had been a pastor, Wednesday night services have been started once again. As the omniciscreen opens, souls, you will see that Rosie is having a private conversation with Blangdon while she hurriedly gets the children ready for church, having just cooked dinner and fed the family. Blangdon is helping with the dishes and runs the vacuum cleaner quickly, where baby Rachael spills her food all over the kitchen floor."

"Blangdon, why does the church feel the need for a Wednesday night service anyway?" Rosie asks, obviously feeling a bit overwhelmed as she rushes to get the kids ready to head out the door.

"Rosie, Wednesday night services give the church the opportunity to conduct a variety of children's ministries. Also, those who have just found Jesus as their Savior really need the middle-of-the-week dose of teaching and, in addition, greatly benefit from being touched by the presence of the Lord in the worship service. We are starting to see a decline in the number of churches in our denomination that are holding extended evangelistic meetings. Those churches that still have Sunday evening and Wednesday night services seem to be more prone to have an evangelist like me come in and preach nightly, Sunday through Wednesday, or Wednesday through Sunday! Don't you see how the enemy loves it when churches start cutting out the midweek services? It's the stepping stone to spiritual decline in those churches."

Rosie just grumbles something under her breath. Rachel starts crying, and at the same time, Isaac and Sarah start arguing about what TV show they are going to watch when they get home from church.

"Let's just get them loaded in the car, Rosie," Blangdon encourages. The family rushes hurriedly towards the door as they are running a little bit late.

"Did you put Snickerdoodle in his cage, Isaac?" Sarah asks.

"Yes, I did, Sarah, and I filled his bowl with water." At about that time, Snickerdoodle starts barking and whimpering, which is always his signal that he is hoping that he can go along in the car with the family.

"You'll be fine, Snickerdoodle," Blangdon shouts as he shuts the door, and they all head towards the minivan. After buckling Rachel in the car seat, Blangdon jumps in the car and starts the engine as they head towards the church.

Everyone is subdued during the short ride to church. To Blangdon, quiet seems like a calm oasis compared to the children's bickering and the stressful activities going on at home. The omniciscreen allows the souls to listen in as Blangdon whispers a silent prayer on the way, saying, "Lord, it seems as if Satan is attacking our family. I pray in Jesus's name that the evil one be bound from causing us any more trouble. You know how hard this all is for Rosie because she was saved right out of the world and, growing up, never knew what it was to attend church. Please also bless the pastor's message tonight, and may many lives be ministered to. Amen!"

About that time, they pull into the church parking lot. Rosie takes Rachel and Sarah and heads to the nursery, while Blangdon and Isaac go into the sanctuary. A short time later, after worship and after Pastor Bloom finishes his announcements, the pastor opens his Bible to begin his evening message. "Brothers and sisters, turn in your Bibles to 2 Corinthians 10:4–5 and read with me tonight." After pausing briefly to allow his congregation time to find the verse, Pastor Bloom begins to read, "'For the weapons of our warfare are not carnal but mighty in God for pulling down strongholds, casting down arguments and every high thing that exalts itself against the knowledge of God, bringing every thought into captivity to the obedience of Christ.'[77]

"Church, tonight we must realize we are in a spiritual battle. We are being attacked by demonic forces. Although we cannot see with our physical eyes, we can still sense their attacks all around us! In this passage, Paul reminds us of this fact and teaches us what to do when we know we are in a battle!

"Just last week, for example, I was asked to speak at our sectional ministers' meeting. The day before, it seemed as if all hell had been loosed against me. Fortunately, I had been praying and had felt called to do some fasting during the week, which enabled me to recognize what I was up against. First of all, I had great sleep disturbances the night before I was going to prepare my message. I was plagued by crazy dreams that left me feeling confused inside, full of unexplained feelings of inferiority and guilt. Yes, I knew to rebuke them in Jesus's name, but then my wife got very sick with some kind of flu, and then after that, our newer car that she usually drives started running so rough we did not dare drive it. She usually asks me to take her car whenever I am called to do something special, but we decided instead that I had better take my old Ford truck, or 'Old Bessy,' as I like to call it. My kids then came home from school, telling of a fight in the schoolyard after school. And to top it all off, when we went down in the basement to get meat out for dinner, we discovered, to our dismay, that the freezer had quit working! Thankfully, nothing was ruined, and our wonderful neighbors had space in their freezer, so they stored everything for us until we could get our freezer repaired.

"I ask you, church, were all these things just coincidences?" The souls listen attentively as the congregation responds with many "nos." Some congregants shout out, "That was just the devil, Pastor," and other similar comments. The pastor continues on, reminding the congregation of many biblical accounts of Satan's attacks, directing their attention to a statement of Paul, which is sometimes forgotten. "Brothers and sisters, I believe Paul described spiritual warfare best in 2 Corinthians. Allow me to finish up tonight by reading his words to you:

> *"'For we do not want you to be ignorant, brethren, of our trouble which came to us in Asia: that we were burdened beyond measure, above strength, so that we despaired even of life. Yes, we had the sentence of death in ourselves, that we should not trust in ourselves but in God who raises the dead, who delivered us from so great a death, and does deliver us; in whom we trust that He will still deliver us, you also helping together in prayer for us, that thanks may be given by many persons on our behalf for the gift granted to us through many.'"[78]*

The souls realize from the expression on his face that Blangdon is sitting in awe, thinking how appropriate tonight's message is for him and his family, realizing at the same time that Rosie would have also heard it as she watched the midweek meeting on the nursery video screen. "Thank You, Lord," Blangdon says as he gets up, telling Isaac, "Let's go get your mother and sisters and head home."

Rosie breaks the silence on the way home, saying, "Blangdon, I know that you have told me there have been ministers in your family going back several generations. Do you think that maybe God has a uniquely special calling on your life because of your spiritual heritage?"

Blangdon responds, "Rosie, I know that this may all be very hard for you to understand because you were not raised in a Christian family and did not attend church when you were growing up but, yes, ever since I was a child, I felt that there was some unique purpose for me being born. I have never been sure what it is. I do know that according to the scripture, all of our righteousness is like filthy rags in the eyes of God and that the whole reason that Jesus went to the cross was to die for our sins and purchase our salvation. Therefore, no matter who my fathers or grandfathers were, some were pastors, some were evangelists, and some were missionaries, it is not their righteousness that has earned anything for me or the ministry that God has called 'us' to, honey; we have been called and enabled by God's grace alone!"

With that statement, Blangdon reaches his hand over and lays it gently on Rosie's shoulder, then moves it down, taking her hand and holding it for the remainder of the trip home. As they walk in the door, they hear the phone ringing. Blangdon says, "I'll get it!" as he puts Rachel in her playpen.

"I'm gonna get Sarah ready for her bath," Rosie says, convincing Sarah to put her toys down so that she can focus on getting ready for bed.

"Hello," Blangdon answers. "Yes, Pastor Bloom; no, no, not at all. It's not too late. As a matter of fact, we just now walked in the door. Yes. Of course, yes, I would be glad to come in and meet with you tomorrow. I have a few lawns to do with my side job that helps with the expenses of evangelistic travel, but yes, 11:00 a.m. will be fine. Yes, okay, I will see you then!"

Rosie pokes her head around the corner and, smiling, says, "Hmm, I wonder what he wants to see you about?"

"I don't know, but he sounded sort of excited about something. I guess we will find out tomorrow."

The next day, as Blangdon is driving to the church, the souls hear his prayer. "Lord, whatever it is, help me be Your willing servant. Not my will, but Thine, be done, as Jesus prayed. You know, Lord, that I love getting out to preach as an evangelist, but the meetings have not been too frequent lately. Nevertheless, whatever You want, Lord, I am Yours!"

Pastor Bloom greets Blangdon at the door and, with a big smile, says, "Come in, Blangdon, come right in." Once they are seated in his office, he goes on to say, "I want you to know that I have been praying and have really been seeking the Lord about what we can do for our teens here at the church. I know you travel out every few weeks to preach in churches, but I would like you to also consider being our youth pastor. We want Rosie to feel welcome to help alongside of you as she can but understand that she already has a lot on her plate with your three young children. Although we can't afford a salary, we will give you a little bit each week to help with gas money."

"Pastor, thank you so much. My first response is that I feel strongly that this is God's will, but I must, of course, be responsible and go home and discuss it with Rosie before I say yes. We will naturally want to pray about it as a couple first. Is that okay?"

"Absolutely, Blangdon, and to be honest, I am so glad to hear you say that. It speaks volumes about your character and shows me that you have the right priorities."

The souls, wondering what will happen next, watch as Blangdon goes home and discusses it with Rosie. The souls listen in as both Blangdon and Rosie say that they sense God's presence as they talk about what the pastor has proposed but agree to ask God for a confirmation by praying about it for a couple of days, as saying yes would be a big commitment.

Windrose approaches the omniciscreen, pausing it on a fixed frame setting so that the souls can all see Blangdon with his family sitting around the kitchen table. At that point, Windrose says, "Please allow me to take more time than I usually do off-screen in order to tell you in some detail the story of the future of the Dawkins family.

"Blangdon will accept the position of youth pastor of that church while continuing his landscaping business in order to provide for his family. He will also continue to travel and speak as an evangelist as the doors are opened. I will tell you that his life had been radically transformed when he was baptized in the Holy Spirit as a young adult. Having come from a non-Pentecostal background, Blangdon became very zealous in helping others in the large Pentecostal denomination, which had credentialed him to find this wonderful life-changing experience. The years will pass quickly as Blangdon and his wife watch both their family and their ministry grow up. Each time that they are led to attend a different church, it seems the new church always also needs a youth pastor. Blangdon was a man of much prayer, and God kept burdening him to 'preach revival' to the Congregation of God in the Pentecostal denomination that he was a part of. As a couple, they eventually purchased an older motor home for Blangdon to stay in while he traveled to conduct evangelistic meetings. Although the motor home was older, fortunately, it had low mileage, so it was very serviceable. Most of the churches he spoke at were smaller and could not afford to put him up in a motel, making the motor home the ideal solution for both him and the churches.

"As their children grew older, Rosie began to pick up work as a schoolteacher, which is what she went to college for. Life was hard for the Dawkins family, but both Blangdon and Rosie agreed, at least at that time, that they were doing what God was calling them to do. However, something began to surface in Rosie's life that she had kept hidden for years. It began to take its toll on their relationship with each other.

"Since Blangdon always prioritized his family, the few days a week that he was home, he always spent quality time with them and made sure that they had a vacation away together each summer. At one point, Blangdon started getting reports of the terrible rate of depression among America's youth, hearing that in America, one teenager was committing suicide every ninety minutes and that one to two thousand a day were attempting and failing! While in prayer one morning, Blangdon felt the burden of going to the streets in the city where they were living. Blangdon shared his burden with the senior pastor. The next Sunday morning, the pastor announced to the congregation that 'Brother Blangdon,' who had been working with their teens building a drama team, wanted to go to the streets on Saturday night and talk to teenagers about God. He said, 'Blangdon will be waiting in the foyer after service to talk to anyone interested.' At that time, Blangdon and his family were part of a larger church. This church had a large and very active bus ministry and brought many young children from the impoverished parts of the city into a specially designed Sunday school each week. However, to Blangdon's shock, not one single person approached him that Sunday to join him in his outreach to teens.

"Blangdon decided to make it a matter of fasting and diligent prayer, and eventually, two brothers approached him, Paul and Mark, both of whom were still teenagers themselves, saying that they felt called to work with him. Blangdon would continue in this ministry with those two youthful volunteers for over three years, and they would see many teens come to Christ. Still, the difficulty he encountered was that the churches in his area did not have a ministry that was accepting of those teens who were coming in off of the street. Blangdon was not the youth pastor in his church and only helped with a drama team. Therefore, Blangdon, seeking counsel from a nearby community pastor, ended up leaving that church and joining the community church with plans to develop a youth group more conducive to the culture at hand.

"God's hand was mightily on Blangdon, as he and Rosie had once discussed. God had a larger plan for him than anyone realized, and subsequently, Blangdon faced a lot of 'in-house' persecution and rejection because of his zeal for the baptism in the Holy Spirit and his radical understanding of the needs of America's teens.

"During this process, Blangdon was still traveling and was observing that the Congregation of God churches was following the same path to lukewarmness that other denominations in American history had followed, so he began preaching regarding the need for revival of the denomination. He also began to write articles, which he printed out and passed out at denominational ministerial functions, sadly, often to blind eyes.

"He then felt God lead him to take an inexpensive local electronic store microphone and a stereo cassette recorder and begin to record a broadcast or two aimed at teens, mixing in contemporary Christian music. He had heard of a small Christian AM station starting up in the area, so he set up a meeting with the owners. Although they were a commercial operation, they agreed to let him try to find sponsors and said that he could go on the radio for only fifteen dollars a week. He knew this would be an additional burden on his family if the funds did not come through. However, he sensed God was leading him, and with Rosie's blessing, he started producing weekly programs, convinced that God wanted him to start a weekly radio show for teens, which he called 'Teens for Life.'

"Over the years, as the radio broadcast began to grow, Blangdon came under increasing attacks from the forces of darkness. During this time, Blangdon worked with a man named Don. Don had lost his wife due to her having an affair with another man. Don had been talking about suicide. A neighbor lady friend, whom he was not romantically involved with but who knew that he was in deep anguish, had been trying to help him. Blangdon had also spent hours with Don on the phone and in person, trying unsuccessfully to convince him to come to the new church that Blangdon and his family were attending. One night, Blangdon received a call from a woman in his community to come to Don's home. The woman who called seemed frantic. 'Blangdon, he has a gun, and he is talking weird stuff like I told you about before.'

"Blangdon grabbed his coat, telling Rosie where he was going, and drove quickly to Don's home. Blangdon had experienced many spiritual crises during his many years of walking in the Holy Ghost, but this was to be only his second encounter dealing directly with demons manifesting in a person who was possessed.

"As Blangdon walked in the door, the neighbor lady met him and said, 'He is lying on the couch.' When Don rolled over and caught sight of Blangdon, the demons in Don began to growl and speak out. The neighbor lady's eyes almost popped out of her head, and she ran out of the door screaming and fled back to her house. Meanwhile, Blangdon began to address the demons, using the authority that he knew all believers have in Christ:

'Satan, I command you in Jesus's name to leave Don.'

In response, one of the demons replied, 'He wants us here.'

Blangdon replied, 'No, he does not. I once again command you to go in Jesus's name!'

The demon then replied, 'We try to do good in the world!'

"Blangdon then remembered that during his study of deliverance, he had learned that many of the spirits often resist leaving and try to engage their host's deliverer in distractions, so he then began praying hard under his breath for a powerful anointing and once again commanded the evil spirits to come out of Don immediately.

"With that, Don rose from his prone position, and out of Don's voice came the very raspy response of the chief demon: 'We are going to destroy you, Blangdon!'

'No, you are not because greater is He that is in me than he that is in the world. In the name of Jesus, leave Don immediately!'

"At that point, the neighbor lady had come back and was peeking in the door. She said, 'Blangdon, look! There he goes! Don is headed towards the bedroom! He is going to get the gun!'

"Blangdon immediately started praying in his heavenly prayer language and, waiting just a few moments, followed Don into the bedroom. He immediately saw that Don was lying on his bed with a chrome 357 magnum cocked and pointed at his chest. Blangdon, at this point full of the power of the Holy Spirit, said, *You spirit of suicide, in the name of Jesus, I command you to loose him and let him go!*'

"With that, the evil spirits left, and Don became limp. The gun rolled off the bed, toppling harmlessly onto the floor.

"Blangdon immediately began praising God. At this point, Don began to mumble some words and come back to his conscious self. Blangdon immediately asked, 'Don, Don, are you all right?'

Don said, 'Yeah, ugh, I don't know. I guess so. Agh! What just happened?'

Blangdon replied, 'Don, don't you remember what just happened to you? You have just been set free from demonic spirits that almost killed you!'

'Oh, no!' Don said, 'Thank you, Blangdon, thank you so much. Did my neighbor call you?'

'Yes, Don, she called me. Thank God that you are all right.'"

At this point, Windrose concluded his rather lengthy account of the early years of Blangdon's story and then allowed the omniciscreen to turn off.

"You see, souls, Blangdon went on to find out that Don had made the mistake of growing bitter at the Father because he felt that He had let him down by not stopping his wife's affair. Then, when he further prayed that God would bring her back and realized that God would not override her rebellious will, Don foolishly began to tell God that if He would not help, then maybe someone else out there would. Don confessed to Blangdon that, at that point, a spirit calling himself 'Lou' began to feed him accurate information about where his wife was and what she was doing. Ominously, Don did not realize that by communicating with 'Lou,' he was opening himself up to demon possession. Souls, many people play with the spirits of darkness and do not realize that in doing so, they can open themselves up to major spiritual trouble."

Windrose then goes on to tell the souls that Don also told Blangdon that the spirit told him that if he committed suicide by holding the pistol at just the right spot on his chest, he would be reincarnated and come back as a famous, wealthy world leader.

"Oh," Windrose then exclaimed, "souls, it must be your lifelong mission to reach as many people as you can with the truths of the Word of God because one day, it will be written: 'My people fail for lack of knowledge.'[79]

"Souls, there is one other thing that we are now going to do. Blangdon's life story and the most deceptive form of Satan's strategy are yet to unfold in his long life on the earth. Therefore, we are going to take a whole other trip next on the omniciscreen to the second half of his life. You will witness his sad heartaches and what will seem like Satan's successes, but we will also witness the most exciting part of his ministry. When you see how God will use him because of the humility he gains through his many heartaches, I know that you will bring this arena alive with praise and thanksgiving to God! So, hold on! Victory day is coming for both God's church and for the many earthly souls that will yet come into the kingdom before the end of time on earth."

CHAPTER 11

BATTLES FOR THE SOULS OF MEN, DEMONIC STRATEGIES, WORSHIP LEADER GETS PROMOTED

Before Windrose starts up the omnicscreen again for another trip into evangelist Blangdon's life, he decides to share some basic teaching with the assembled souls to help them further understand the multiple struggles and painful battles of his life. So once again, Windrose takes his pointer finger and draws the whiteboard in the air. However, this time, the ink he uses is deep red, the color of blood, representing the suffering that eternally important missions always require.

As he writes the number one on the board, Windrose starts out by saying, "Souls, there are three things that every ministry soldier of God must understand." He then begins to share a very powerful teaching, one which will one day be shared by Jesus at what will come to be called "the Last Supper," the last meal that He will have with the disciples before He is crucified.

"Souls, Jesus will know that His disciples still do not understand the true mission of the Messiah of God. They are still thinking very militarily. They were looking for a great military leader like Joshua of the Old Testament, and even one possibly who had supernatural strength like Sampson or supernatural wisdom like Solomon. Jesus understands that as they watch Him do miracle after miracle during the past three and a half years, they become convinced that since He has such astounding powers, then surely Jesus could defeat the

Roman government, allowing Israel to rule and reign again! Let me read to you the words that will one day later be recorded by Luke as he shares some of Jesus's words at the Last Supper:

> *Now there was also a dispute among them, as to which of them should be considered the greatest. And He said to them, "The kings of the Gentiles exercise lordship over them, and those who exercise authority over them are called 'benefactors.' But not so among you; on the contrary, he who is greatest among you, let him be as the younger, and he who governs as he who serves. For who is greater, he who sits at the table, or he who serves? Is it not he who sits at the table? Yet I am among you as the One who serves."*[80]

"Jesus is very aware of the fact that the disciples will need to know that their mission will not be an easy one and that He is not setting the scene for them to be political leaders in a new regime! He is setting them up to be exactly what He was, namely, a servant to those around Him. What He says next is the perfect lead into the three things you need to know, so I am going to write His words on the whiteboard."

Windrose then proceeds to write the following words, his index finger creating letters in deep blood-red ink:

1) "BUT YOU ARE THOSE WHO HAVE CONTINUED WITH ME IN MY TRIALS."[81]

"You see, souls, there will be countless battles and wars on the Earth throughout the years, but the greatest battle that will ever be fought will be the '*battle for the souls of men*'! Because that battle is so great and the reward of eternal souls precious beyond measure, followers who possess a right understanding do not complain when trials come but instead anticipate them.

"Jesus will want them to have a basic understanding that, piece by piece, everything that He tells them will eventually make sense to them following the resurrection. Like the disciples after the resurrection, you also must remain faithful to the Lord regardless of whatever trials may come your way."

Then Windrose writes on the whiteboard after the number two the words:

"THERE IS A PRICE TO PAY FOR THOSE IN THE MINISTRY."

Windrose goes on to explain: "Souls, during the battles between light and darkness, and the battles between your flesh and your spirit man, you will feel a great ebb and flow in your person who will often lead you to very uncomfortable situations. You will be continually tempted to compare yourselves to others, even though you know they are not called to either the same ministry you are called to or to the same level of ministry sacrifice. This is known as your personal cost or the price that you can expect to pay in ministry. Always compare your cost not to the costs others pay but to the cost of Jesus, who will die on the cross for the sins of the world!

"Number three is by far the most important!" Windrose says as he begins to write on the floating whiteboard.

3) "BE WILLING TO OVERCOME ALL STUMBLING BLOCKS. SOMETIMES, SUCH HUGE THINGS WILL HAPPEN IN YOUR LIFE THAT YOU WILL NOT UNDERSTAND HOW A GOD, WHO IS LOVE, COULD ALLOW THEM."

"Souls, because this is so very important, God the Father is going to allow you to have reoccurring remembrance of the lessons I am teaching you today. With the other lessons, you will be programmed to have a recall at just the right moment so that you can, in silent acquiescence, prayerfully respond to these difficult situations. These are the dark times in life that only the Father understands why He has to allow. The keyword here is '*has*' to allow! Learn to decide with your mind that you are going to choose to trust God in these places and wait for whatever answers may come or may not come until you get to heaven one day. This is the place of great testing. Smaller tests of faith will come into your life, which will be easier to overcome. However, most people who serve God for a lifetime have one or two situations in their whole life, which usually involve great personal loss. These situations will always leave a huge '*why*' in your heart! Learning the secret of making it past these often catastrophic situations can have a huge impact on where you spend eternity!"

Windrose then reactivates the omniciscreen, taking the souls to revisit the Dawkins family in the late twentieth century.

"Souls, we are going to return to the Dawkins family and Blangdon's story, but we are fast-forwarding from the 1980s to 1996. At this point, Blangdon's 'almost live' broadcasts, being recorded in a studio that he had built in his home, will have been picked up by multiple radio stations and are now on over twenty radio stations, covering a large percentage of the populated northeastern United States. Each year, he goes to a large Christian music festival and gives away twelve dozen tee shirts with the show's name on them. He also gives away a free mountain bike each year, and although his requests for support go out over the air to thousands of listeners, he usually just has to buy the bikes out of his own earnings. Every year, without fail, the teen who wins the bike has an amazing testimony of how much they needed one. Blangdon gradually came to understand that people were not supporting his ministry because they just did not share his deep sense of responsibility to try to save teenagers from self-destruction. Plus, he knows that he has a calling on his life from God. He knows that two key spiritual points are the foundation of his life and ministry. The first is to prayerfully endeavor to love the Lord his God with all of his heart, soul, mind, and strength, seeking first the Kingdom of God and its righteousness, knowing that all the things that he needed would be added unto him. Secondly, he knows he must always diligently seek God's will regarding every new ministry step. The section of the pattern of prayer that Jesus laid out for His disciples, 'Thy will be done on earth as it is in heaven,'[82] always stands out to him as a centerpiece of importance in everyone's walk with God.

"As time goes on, however, he notices that no matter how excited he is, praising God, Rosie does not share his enthusiasm. He also notices that Rosie does not have any routine to her prayer life, mostly praying on the run. Whenever he senses that she is troubled, he knows that God would show her what He had shown him if only she would just seek Him diligently! Without fail, he asks her, 'Rosie, did you spend quality time in prayer today?'

She invariably responds, saying, 'Not like I should have.'

"Blangdon lovingly assures Rosie that he understands how busy she is with the children and her job responsibilities but reminds her that other mothers whom they know, with similar responsibilities, are fitting prayer time into their days. He also kindly reminds her that they had been called into a ministry that Satan would fight against because what God loves the most, Satan hates the most, and God for sure loves teenagers! She always seems to listen to the challenge but still seldom goes on to have any prayer or devotional time in her life.

'I know, Blangdon, I need to do better, and I will... I will," she invariably replies.

"This leaves him greatly concerned. When asked, she always says that she is fine. However, he knows through both his spiritual gifting and through the distance in her eyes that her initial love for him is waning and that the costs of the ministry are taking their toll.

"Blangdon does a lot of praying and fasting during this time because he wants to make sure that what he is doing is indeed at the center of God's will for his life.

"During this time period, Blangdon has the opportunity to visit a Teen Challenge Center in a northern city. Whenever he preaches in that area, the assistant director brings a load of their men into his meetings, so Blangdon knows them well. On the day that he visits, as he is pulling in, the director, Dave, arrives in his personal family station wagon with a bunch of the guys. Blangdon hears 'kerplunk' as the station wagon bottoms out because it is loaded up with logs from the local state forest, which people were allowed to cut up. Dave and the men are laughing because logs are sticking out of every window in the car. Dave and his cheerful wife have spent their entire adult lives subsisting on a meager stipend salary, making personal sacrifices while rejoicing in the fact that dozens of men through the years have been set free from drug addiction and other life-controlling problems through the ministry of Teen Challenge.

"Blangdon's heart is saddened by Dave's response to his question: 'Dave, I didn't know you supplemented your heat at the center with wood!'

'Oh, Blangdon, great to see you. Praise the Lord; God's presence sure was awesome at the meeting last night, wasn't it? As to your question, how I wish firewood was supplemental, but actually, it is our only source of heat. Have you seen our stove, though? It's an old potbelly type, and man, it really puts out the heat.'

'Is your furnace broken, Dave?'

'No, it works fine. It's just that giving has been way down, so we just have to cut expenses everywhere we can. Billy Jenkins comes from a rural community, and this is a stove that sat unused in his barn for many years. It was his grandfather's. It's made of cast iron, so that thing will last until Jesus comes back!'

"Blangdon hears God speak to his heart at that moment. *If an internationally recognized ministry focused on youth has to heat its residential facility with wood because they cannot raise enough support, then you should not feel condemned because you and Rosie struggle financially to fund your syndicated broadcasts to teenagers.*

'Thank You, Lord,' Blangdon says as he shakes a few hands and heads inside to have lunch with the men."

"Souls, you will be pleased to hear that as time goes on, God continues to use Blangdon in evangelistic ministry."

Having filled the souls on about what is going on during that period of Blangdon's life, Windrose then says to the souls, "Now let's take a peek into the lair of darkness. There has been trouble brewing in Blangdon's life. I want to show you who the culprit is behind this ongoing plot to cause mayhem and destruction."

He turns on the omnicscreen, revealing a large number of demonic creatures in their dark, slimy arena of demonic planning. As the scene opens, the souls see that the demons are receiving instruction from one of Satan's colonels, Extarzor, an expert in ministry destruction. As the screen opens, the hazy darkness makes it hard to sort out specific movement, but shifty green eyes can be seen, revealing that there are dozens of evil beings listening intently to the crafty speaker.

"Itzzzzzst zoooooo zzzimportant that you move subtly"; the demonitrac quickly begins to kick in so the souls can understand what is being said. "You must learn to use subtle forms of temptations, like feelings of laziness or lethargy, to attack them whenever you see that they plan to set aside times for prayer and Bible study. Attack them with bouts of anxiousness, such as feeling that this or that thing needs to get done right now. Also, to keep them from praying, stir these same feelings in their children's parents or other family members, making them feel like 'they have to call them now'!

"Praying people are your worst nightmare. Praying pastors are whole evil armies' worst nightmare. Praying churches are the whole kingdom of darkness's worst nightmare."

Condigctin, a foot soldier, asks Extarzor, "Why is it that pastors' prayers are more powerful than anyone else? They are always yacking on about the fact that all of their righteousness is in Jesus. So being a pastor shouldn't mean squat!"

Extarazoar lets out a long, subtle growling sound and says, "Condigctin, how long have you been under my command, and you do not know this one yet? You idiot, do I have more demonic power than you do, you little snit?"

"Yes, sir. Oh, yes, sir. You do!" Condigctin hastily replies.

"Why, you stupid demon, tell me! Why do I have more power?"

"Because you are a captain, sir! You have more authority because you have a higher rank, sir!"

"So what's the answer, you idiot?"

"*Aaaaah*, a pastor has more prayer power because he has a higher level of position in God's Kingdom? Is that right?"

Exactor, spying a rock hanging down above them from the grimy ceiling, reaches up and breaks off a piece of it, throwing it at Condigctin and hitting him right in the side of the head. "Let that help you to remember simple things like this next time! Now go and stir up a nightmare in the little girl's sleep and make it a good one. I want to hear her crying out to mama, disturbing her parents' rest!"

With that, Windrose turns the omniciscreen off and begins to address the souls once again.

"One day, souls, a scripture will be penned by James, the half brother of Jesus, which will state, 'You believe that there is one God. You do well. Even the demons believe—and tremble.'[83] Allow me to remind you, souls, that on one of our earlier trips through time, we heard the demons say that one of their most effective tools was knowing the Bible well. Yes, Satan does know the Bible from cover to cover, and he is constantly working to try to deceive people by using partial truth to cover up the pure truth of God's Word. We just witnessed this angry exchange between two fallen angels as they discussed their plot against Blangdon's ministry. Did you notice how they recognized Bible truth in their teaching of how to attack someone's ministry? This, souls, is no small thing! It is the major axle that all of their lies twist off of and spin from. They take out keywords and then add deceptive sidetracks to make it sound like the original text. Far in the future, the day will also come when there will be so many English Bible translations that, although many will be accurate, new believers will need their proven spiritual elders to help them confirm the truth from the language of the original text.

"Now, souls, let's look back into Blangdon's life a few years later to view some further developments in his life and ministry." As the omniciscreen opens again, the souls see that Blangdon has taken Rosie out to dinner in an upscale restaurant along a canal. Sailboats are gradually making their way to docks for the night, and their owners can be seen onboard rolling up their sails and tying everything down. A beautiful bright orange sunset of purple and blue hues can be seen from the window next to Blangdon and Rosie's table. For a moment, they both are caught up in deep thought as they take in all of the beauty of God's artistry.

"Thank you, Rosie, for taking some time out with me tonight. Wasn't it nice of the Jamesons to give us this gift certificate? I know it wasn't easy finding a sitter and getting so much work done so that you felt we had time to do this."

"No problem, Blangdon. My goodness, you are so busy between your job and your ministry responsibilities that it sometimes feels like we are strangers passing in the doorway."

At that moment, the waitress walks up, suggesting that they look at the drink menu.

"Just ice water for me," Rosie replies.

"The same for me, but no lemon, please," Blangdon adds.

"Are you ready to order or...?" the waitress adds.

"No, I think we need a few more minutes. Is that okay?" Rosie asks politely, just wanting the waitress to scoot as she and Blangdon are in the middle of an important discussion!

At that point, a large barge-like boat going up the canal blows a loud horn as it goes by, signaling the small boats that it needs them to move aside so that it can pass through. Both Blangdon and Rosie watch in curiosity as people on the boats who are already docked scurry about, tending to tie their boats up and rolling out their canvas covers in order to prepare for an incoming storm, visible as it slowly approaches in the distance!

"I'm so sorry for that, honey, but we both knew that God was calling us into the ministry and were aware of the many hours it would require. One thing is that we are seeing a lot of lives touched by the messages that He gives me, and the radio broadcast has opened a lot of doors for me to go out and preach His burden to teens in churches. We are on over twenty-seven stations now, and part of our broadcast reaches all the way up the northern parts of New York City and even to southern New England. I have been getting mail from teens and parents telling me that the show is helping them, and a Westchester County sheriff wrote to me last week for more information about the animal sacrifices of teens being conducted by teens who are getting caught up practicing witchcraft with young adults! This is all so much of what God showed me in prayer would one day happen, and it's so exciting, don't you think?"

"Yes, honey, and you sound so professional on the radio," Rosie replies. "I do trust that God shows you things when you pray, so you just keep doing whatever He is showing you, okay?"

"I do not want to sound like a broken record, but honey, God would show you those same things if you could just decide to seek Him with all of your heart. It would be of such a huge help to me knowing that we both were hearing the same things."

"I know I need to, Blangdon, but let's face it, you pray enough for both of us! I have seen God's answers over and over, and I'm okay!"

"Well, you know that's a bit exaggerated, but I just want to make sure things are good between us. We both need to pray for reasons that God teaches. I know you have a good friend from your work at the school in Judy! The two of you spend a lot of time together when you are not busy with the kids. It is a bit difficult when you go with her on her overnight business trips, but we always work that out. Maybe you could go with me the next time I am asked to preach out of town?"

"Blangdon, you know that could rarely happen as the kids have so much going on with school activities and such that it would be hard because one of us always has to be here."

"Well, I'm going to take some of that prayer time I have and start praying for God to make that possible," Blangdon says with a big smile on his face.

"Knowing you, you will get it," Rosie replies with a grin, but she is not smiling on the inside. All that she could think about that night was getting back home to the kids and getting on with life as usual.

As the waitress approaches, she asks, "Have you had time to look at our menu? The chef recommends our fresh Maine lobster that comes in every day or our Angus sirloin."

"I'll have the lobster," Rosie states.

With that, Windrose turns off the omniciscreen. He puts his chin in his hand and begins to walk back and forth, thinking and praying about what to say next. Then he stops, pivots, and turns and faces the crowd. He lifts his pointer finger and says, "Souls, we did not listen to the specific planning of the demons when we visited their lair again, but can you recognize some areas of concern from our trip into this couple's life? From what you have learned already about demonic tactics, does anything jump out from the visit to the restaurant?"

Lawrence-27 raises his hand and asks, "Windrose, what is a lobster?"

Windrose starts laughing and laughing and says, "Lawrence, I so apologize. Your cultural recognition part of your emotilliance needs to be adjusted a bit." Then Windrose turns and seems to push a button in the air. "Now, do you have it?"

"Oh, yes, yes, I understand now; no more explanation needed," Lawrence replies.

There is a bit of a long pause from the souls as no one seems to know how to answer the question about the demon's strategies, so Windrose speaks up a second time and adds something to help jog their perception of the situation.

"Souls, do you remember when we viewed the demons learning about tactics to undermine families and their ministries? What did Tryovor, one of the demonic leaders, say to the other demons?"

Gerard-22 speaks up and says, "They were being taught to use subtle things that would not be recognized as evil. Is that right, Windrose?"

"Yes, Gerard, and to the rest of the souls, what subtle things do you see going on in Blangdon's life that indicate that the enemy is at work trying to destroy his marriage and his ministry?"

Blangdon-34 speaks up, "Well, first of all, Windrose, because his name is Blangdon, this has my full attention! That could, in theory, be me someday, correct?"

"Ha-ha-ha!" Windrose leans back and laughs because he knows that every time one of the souls hears their names in a journey into the future, they are asking themselves the same question. "Yes, Blangdon, yes, that could be you someday, but the Father knows the importance of keeping that information hidden in all of your training so as not to cloud your understanding with worries."

Blangdon responds, "It does seem as if hints are being given that Rosie is not happy in her marriage and that there could already be some reason for concern."

"Excellent observation, Blangdon," Windrose replies. "Marriage is a wonderful gift from the Father. When a man and a woman exchange their vows in marriage, they are not just traditional words they recite in front of the invited guests. Marriage is a holy covenant, a covenant that they make with each other and, most importantly, with God. In fact, it is also the second most important covenant they will ever enter into with the Creator of the universe. The only other covenant that is of higher responsibility is when they agree to take Jesus Christ as their personal Savior, to accept Him into their hearts and lives, agreeing to put Him first in all that they do from that point forward."

With that statement, Windrose leans his head back, and the souls all clearly see his lips whisper a prayer to the Father, "Thank You, Father." At that moment, two big tears come out, one from each eye. He catches them in his cupped hands, then, as if offering those tears up to heaven, he raises his cupped hands up, tilting his head back, his face engulfed in a most wonderful smile, saying, "One for every her and one for every him," and says amen.

There is a moment of awed silence throughout the arena of souls as they all sit motionless, contemplating the complexity of the simple expression of love they have just witnessed, wondering just who this person called "Windrose" really is....

Windrose then goes on to address the souls, "Because marriage is so key to those who are married and are in ministry, Satan will throw everything that he can at those marriages. He also plays on the sometimes narrow-mindedness of church people who have the mistaken idea that when the marriage of those who are in the ministry fails, neither of the wounded spouses can ever be qualified for ministry in the future. While it is true that sometimes, for some ministries in a good, better, best scenario, it is best for such people, after much prayer, to consider that their days in certain types of ministry on the earth for them is over, it will in the future be written in the sacred scriptures that the gifts and callings of God are without repentance.

"Now, let's take another trip through the omnisciscreen to a time when the new church is just getting started after Jesus's resurrection from the dead." All of a sudden, the souls notice that the earth underneath them is beginning to shake. They all grab ahold of their seats as they are not sure what is happening. Then, it seems as if a sound like thunder begins to rumble around them. A booming voice whose deep vibrations seem to shake the souls fills the whole arena, but with it comes a reassuring peace.

"Pay very close attention, souls, to what you are about to see. Your journey into the future will allow you to see one of my greatest works of grace that I will ever perform through My only-begotten Son, transforming evil into My eternal love."

The souls all began to clap and praise with exuberant expressions of awe and eager anticipation: "That was God Himself! That was the Father speaking directly to us! Thank You, Father! Thank You, God!" And countless numbers of such statements are heard among them. After the souls composed themselves, they realized that Windrose had simply "sat down" after the Father was finished speaking directly to them.

Windrose then stands up and points to the omniciscreen, informing the souls that they are now going to be traveling to a small area in a corner of Jerusalem in the year AD 1, soon after the Holy Spirit's outpouring. The souls see that people are running in every direction, knocking on doors, some shouting and running, while others are going up to people and whispering in their ears, "He's here; run and hide! And gather your Christian parchments, small wooden crosses, and anything that shows you have held a prayer gathering in your home. Saul of Tarsus just arrived outside of town! He has captured and sent many to be imprisoned and has even overseen the execution of some. So quick, hide yourselves and hide any evidence that you are a Christ follower! Make it appear as if you are only good religious Jews. Saul loves religious people who he thinks believe as he does."

With all the people scurrying about, the dogs barking, camels that had been lying down standing up, and donkeys, startled by all of the commotion, braying their loud *"eeyores."* In all the commotion, even the small sparrows and swallows are spooked off of their perches and start flying about in every direction. Instead of a typically calm day in that part of the city, it is clear to everyone that something very evil is amiss.

A religious, self-satisfied, and evil grin covers Saul's face as he and his companions arrive. He knows full well that the Jewish Christians know that he is there. He completely understands the threat that his presence and influence bring with him. In the perception of his sect of Jews, he is and was a hero; he is very proud of that fact. He knows that he cannot find all of Christ's followers, but his just presence will be enough to strike fear into the hearts of the rest. To him, that alone will make his mission a success!

"Saul, Saul, there are some in here. There are six men and two women. I heard one of them praying to Yeshua. They were very frightened when we forced our way in. I just found some small nail necklaces hidden in a drawer and some small pieces of parchment from the former tabernacle that have the promises of the coming of the Messiah underlined. Surely, these are followers of 'the Way.' Look, look! I also found some small challises, a partial flask of wine hanging on the chair, and breadcrumbs on the table. Evidence, Saul, of their practice of communion that the weak ones had told us about when we tortured for the truth about their 'Way'!"

"Excellent work, Amias," Saul responds. "Tie their arms behind their back and their legs with short ropes to keep them from running and bring them with us."

Some of the Jewish believers begin to talk among themselves, saying, "We should go and secretly begin to pray that Saul does not hear that Apostle Steven is in the area and that the Jewish leaders have been chiding him about preaching concerning Christ in the public square!"

As Windrose steps up to address the souls, he pauses the omniciscreen and says, "When the early Christians go off to secretly pray for Stephen's safety, they have no idea that God has a much greater plan in mind for that same day, a plan that will place Stephen in a huge confrontation with the Jewish leaders. Stephens's time on earth is almost finished, and God, like He did with His own Son, Jesus, is about to allow him to be sacrificed for the greater cause of the spreading of the gospel. Luke will one day tell about this day in the book called *The Acts of the Apostles*. Notice first the way and the reason that Stephen was chosen for a specific task."

Now, in those days, when the number of the disciples was multiplying, there arose a complaint against the Hebrews by the Hellenists, because their widows were neglected in the daily distribution. Then the twelve summoned the multitude of the disciples and said, "It is not desirable that we should leave the word of God and serve tables. Therefore, brethren, seek out from among you seven men of good reputation, full of the Holy Spirit and wisdom, whom we may appoint over this business; but we will give ourselves continually to prayer and to the ministry of the word."

And the saying pleased the whole multitude. And they chose Stephen, a man full of faith and the Holy Spirit, and Philip, Prochorus, Nicanor, Timon, Parmenas, and Nicolas, a proselyte from Antioch, whom they set before the apostles; and when they had prayed, they laid hands on them.

Then the word of God spread, and the number of the disciples multiplied greatly in Jerusalem, and a great many of the priests were obedient to the faith.

And Stephen, full of faith and power, did great wonders and signs among the people.[84]

"Souls," Windrose asks, "what stands out to you as the main reason that Stephen will be chosen as one of the seven to watch over the practical needs of the widows of that day? We discussed this in part at one of our earlier lessons. I want to see if you remember."

Blangdon-53 calls out his answer abruptly. "It was because he was a man *full* of the Holy Spirit, as were the other six chosen!"

"Ahhh, Blangdon, very good. For the sake of everyone in the arena today, how many 'Nathans,' for instance, do we have present as souls in training for future spiritual interventions against the enemy's attacks and strategies? All the Nathans, speak up and say 'I.'"

Hands shoot up all over the arena. "I, I, I" seems to come from everywhere.

"Ah, yes," Windrose responds, "it's a common name, that of an Old

Testament prophet. Yes, and because of time and space, souls, you would have no way of knowing or perhaps perceiving this, but as a soul who has not yet received a body, you do not take up a physical space. There are actually many thousands here for each teaching. The spiritual realm, by God's design, is multidimensional. The all-knowing Heavenly Father has altered time and space to equip more souls than you can see or perceive to serve Him during the thousands of years of human existence. He has reduced the exposure of unique names of foreign lands by filtering them into the common names that everyone can be familiar with. The Blangdon in our story, starting in the 1980s, could be representing many others here right now, even though his name is unique. You do not need to have an awareness of all of that now. Just know that God knows best. This is His training designed to span thousands of years of time, reaching all the Sues and the Nathans as well as the Abdalalims, Tilos, the Thiagos, and other rare names of the future world."

With that statement, different reactions echo throughout the arena—whoas, wows, and amens.

At that point, Windrose looks up, and as he communicates with the Heavenly Father, he says, "Yes, amen, Father. I think they would enjoy that, and it would be enlightening as well."

Immediately, the thunderous noise of the whoas, wows, and amens of the thousands of souls, both seen and unseen, can be heard in the arena as the Father lets everyone hear all the comments of everyone revealed and also those unseen, joining in together at one time. This sends joy and laughter and a new level of confidence to all the souls. Then, in a split second, as if God the Father wants to seal this moment in time for all, the omniciscreen comes on again, and the souls see inside the arena of angels. The souls realize that the angels are all standing and applauding the soldiers, the servants, and the commanders who will participate in the future in God's many interventions on the earth. This is what the Father has told Windrose to reveal to the souls.

"Now back to my question, and yes, Blangdon-53, it was because Stephen was a man who not only had been filled with the Holy Spirit, as Luke will refer to many different scenarios of individuals in his book *The Acts of the*

Apostles, but Stephen was a man *'full'* of the Spirit of God, a conditional qualifier. You see, all believers who seek God often have Him fill them to run over with God's great Spirit. These are the believers whom God will be able to one day use to do amazing things on the earth in the name of His precious Son, Jesus!

"Now, let's look back at the omniciscreen, where we are fast-forwarding to the very place where Stephen is preaching, presenting the scribes and Pharisees with a glorious outline of the events in Jewish history. You see Stephen standing there in a synagogue in Jerusalem, facing a large group of hostile religious Jewish leaders. Because so many Jewish leaders are being converted to faith in Jesus Christ, these enraged leaders have resorted to hiring false witnesses against Stephen. You are seeing Stephen's reaction to having just been accused of speaking blasphemous words against the holy place and the law. Observe as the Holy Spirit's joy fills his heart; you will see that his face is shining like the face of an angel."

Highly frustrated that these accusations were not at all bothering Stephen, the high priest confronts him with the words:

"Are these things so?"

And he said, "Brethren and fathers, listen: The God of glory appeared to our father Abraham when he was in Mesopotamia, before he dwelt in Haran, and said to him, 'Get out of your country and from your relatives, and come to a land that I will show you.' Then he came out of the land of the Chaldeans and dwelt in Haran. And from there, when his father was dead, He moved him to this land in which you now dwell. And God gave him no inheritance in it, not even enough to set his foot on. But even when Abraham had no child, He promised to give it to him for a possession, and to his descendants after him. But God spoke in this way: that his descendants would dwell in a foreign land, and that they would bring them into bondage and oppress them four hundred years. 'And the nation to whom they will be in bondage I will judge,' said God, 'and after that they shall come out and serve Me in this place.' Then He gave him the covenant of circumcision;

and so Abraham begot Isaac and circumcised him on the eighth day; and Isaac begot Jacob, and Jacob begot the twelve patriarchs.

"And the patriarchs, becoming envious, sold Joseph into Egypt. But God was with him and delivered him out of all his troubles and gave him favor and wisdom in the presence of Pharaoh, king of Egypt; and he made him governor over Egypt and all his house. Now a famine and great trouble came over all the land of Egypt and Canaan, and our fathers found no sustenance. But when Jacob heard that there was grain in Egypt, he sent out our fathers first. And the second time Joseph was made known to his brothers, and Joseph's family became known to the Pharaoh. Then Joseph sent and called his father Jacob and all his relatives to him, seventy-five people. So, Jacob went down to Egypt; and he died, he and our fathers. And they were carried back to Shechem and laid in the tomb that Abraham bought for a sum of money from the sons of Hamor, the father of Shechem.

"But when the time of the promise drew near which God had sworn to Abraham, the people grew and multiplied in Egypt till another king arose who did not know Joseph. This man dealt treacherously with our people, and oppressed our forefathers, making them expose their babies, so that they might not live. At this time Moses was born and was well pleasing to God; and he was brought up in his father's house for three months. But when he was set out, Pharaoh's daughter took him away and brought him up as her own son. And Moses was learned in all the wisdom of the Egyptians and was mighty in words and deeds.

"Now when he was forty years old, it came into his heart to visit his brethren, the children of Israel. And seeing one of them suffer wrong, he defended and avenged him who was oppressed, and struck down the Egyptian. For he supposed that his brethren would have understood that God would deliver them by his hand, but they did not understand. And the next day he appeared to two of them as they were fighting, and tried to reconcile them, saying, 'Men, you are brethren; why do you wrong one another?' But he who did his neighbor wrong pushed him away, saying, 'Who made you a ruler and a judge over us? Do you want to kill me as you

did the Egyptian yesterday?' Then, at this saying, Moses fled and became a dweller in the land of Midian, where he had two sons.

"And when forty years had passed, an Angel of the Lord appeared to him in a flame of fire in a bush, in the wilderness of Mount Sinai. When Moses saw it, he marveled at the sight; and as he drew near to observe, the voice of the Lord came to him, saying, 'I am the God of your fathers—the God of Abraham, the God of Isaac, and the God of Jacob.' And Moses trembled and dared not look. 'Then the LORD said to him, "Take your sandals off your feet, for the place where you stand is holy ground. I have surely seen the oppression of My people who are in Egypt; I have heard their groaning and have come down to deliver them. And now come, I will send you to Egypt."'

"This Moses whom they rejected, saying, 'Who made you a ruler and a judge?' is the one God sent to be a ruler and a deliverer by the hand of the Angel who appeared to him in the bush. He brought them out, after he had shown wonders and signs in the land of Egypt, and in the Red Sea, and in the wilderness forty years.

"This is that Moses who said to the children of Israel, 'The LORD your God will raise up for you a prophet like me from your brethren. Him you shall hear.'

"This is he who was in the congregation in the wilderness with the Angel who spoke to him on Mount Sinai, and with our fathers, the one who received the living oracle to give to us, whom our fathers would not obey, but rejected. And in their hearts, they turned back to Egypt, saying to Aaron, 'Make us gods to go before us; as for this Moses who brought us out of the land of Egypt, we do not know what has become of him.' And they made a calf in those days, offered sacrifices to the idol, and rejoiced in the works of their own hands. Then God turned and gave them up to worship the host of heaven, as it is written in the book of the Prophets:

'Did you offer Me slaughtered animals and sacrifices during forty years in the wilderness,
O house of Israel?
You also took up the tabernacle of Moloch,

And the star of your god Remphan,
Images which you made to worship;
And I will carry you away beyond Babylon.'

"Our fathers had the tabernacle of witness in the wilderness, as He appointed, instructing Moses to make it according to the pattern that he had seen, which our fathers, having received it in turn, also brought with Joshua into the land possessed by the Gentiles, whom God drove out before the face of our fathers until the days of David, who found favor before God and asked to find a dwelling for the God of Jacob. But Solomon built Him a house.

"However, the Most High does not dwell in temples made with hands, as the prophet says:

'Heaven is My throne,
And earth is My footstool.
What house will you build for Me? says the Lord,
Or what is the place of My rest?
Has My hand not made all these things?'

"You stiff-necked and uncircumcised in heart and ears! You always resist the Holy Spirit; as your fathers did, so do you. Which of the prophets did your fathers not persecute? And they killed those who foretold the coming of the Just One, of whom you now have become the betrayers and murderers, who have received the law by the direction of angels and have not kept it."[85]

The souls are shocked by the confrontational declarations of Stephen, yet they understand, as Windrose had been teaching them, that godless religious practice had hardened these religious leaders' hearts and that, because of that, those hard hearts had to be challenged by and confronted with hard truth! As Windrose once again reveals his deep compassion, this time for what Stephen is about to endure, tears run down both cheeks. He cups his hands together in a prayerful position in front of his face and says, "Souls, one day, these words will be written in sacred scripture: *'Precious in the sight of the LORD is the death of His saints.'*[86]

"Yes, souls, Saul of Tarsus has arrived with his entourage and is listening to them condemn Stephen. The incensed leaders are about to stone Stephen to death. Saul is actually guarding the robes of these men and is cheering them on to stone Stephen as the leaders take off their traditional public priestly robes and lay them at his feet! Souls, this is how evil a religious-spirited person can become when their doctrine is based on the doctrine of men and not on the Word and the heart of God! Think if you can for a moment how filthy their own souls must have been for them to reject the very Son of God and then also reject Stephen, hating him, even stoning him to death for trying to reach them with the truth of who their own Messiah was and is and is to come."

As they sadly consider what they had just learned about man and his capacity to do evil, all the time while wearing a mask of good, a somber attitude of silence fills the souls of each in the srena.

"This," Windrose states, "is the most important lesson that you will ever learn. You must grasp the fact that although man-made religion represents itself as being good and kind and loving, at its heart, even at the very core of its being, are evil forces at work laboring to destroy what is truly good and what is truly sent from God!

"Souls, listen now as I read to you the words that Luke will write in the book *The Acts of the Apostles* concerning what the religious leaders did next to Stephen. I am also going to have those words written in the dark red color on the whiteboard so that you can read along as I read them aloud to you:

"When they heard these things, they were cut to the heart, and they gnashed at him with their teeth. But he, being full of the Holy Spirit, gazed into heaven and saw the glory of God, and Jesus standing at the right hand of God, and said, 'Look! I see the heavens opened and the Son of Man standing at the right hand of God!'

Then they cried out with a loud voice, stopped their ears, and ran at him with one accord; and they cast him out of the city and stoned him. And the witnesses laid down their clothes at the feet of a young man named Saul. And they stoned Stephen as he was calling on God and saying, 'Lord Jesus, receive my spirit.' Then he knelt down and cried out with a loud voice, 'Lord, do not charge them with this sin.' And when he had said this, he fell asleep.[87]

"Stephen knows in that moment," Windrose said, "just as Jesus will know as He dies on the cross that the sin being committed there that day is so evil that unless they each will pray, 'Father, forgive them; for they know not what they do,'[88] or as Stephen will pray, 'Lay not this sin to their charge,'[89] the Father's wrath could have instantly destroyed them all and been fully justified in doing so! However, with those two prayers of the purest love that could ever have been displayed on the planet, God's wrath was averted. Once converted, the Apostle Paul will one day write to the Thessalonian church, 'Since it is a righteous thing with God to repay with tribulation those who trouble you.'

[90]"Therefore, souls, before we move on back into the future of Blangdon's story through the omniciscreen, do you have any ideas about why the scribes and Pharisees, the religious leaders of that day, became so enraged by what Stephen preached to them?"

The souls seem to respond corporately, as they have done with other questions, with resounding "nos" heard throughout the arena.

Windrose then goes on to say, "Note that Stephen starts by reminding them that Abraham came from nothing, which was designed to humble them in their spiritual and generational pride. Then he rolls into the story of Joseph and how he was *rejected* by his brother's jealousy and sold into slavery!"

He then reminds them that Moses also came from a nothing beginning, but God raised him to be a prophet they would hear. Stephen once again refers to how their forefathers rejected Moses! Then Stephen takes them to the story of David and how David wanted to build a temple, pointing to a time when David was wrong because it was Solomon who built the temple. He reminds them that God Himself once spoke and said, "What house will you build for Me?"[91] Stephen then concludes his message by saying, "You stiff-necked and circumcised in heart and ears, you do always resist the Holy Ghost just as your fathers did! Which of the prophets have your fathers not persecuted and have slain?"[92] And he concludes by stating, "You have been betrayers and murderers of the Just One."[93]

"You see, Stephen brought on the wrath of man when he declared to them not only their crime but their self-righteously wicked man-made religious heritage." Windrose next bows his head in sadness. His long, pure white hair hangs down over his arms, and for a moment, he succeeds in hiding the expression of sorrow that he has on his face. In a shocking change of demeanor, however, his hands suddenly shoot straight up into the air, and he begins to sing praises to God the Father: "One, one, one—we are one; / one, one, one, one, one—we are one, one, one… / Father Spirit and the Son, Son, Son, / one, one, one—we are one, one, one!" As he repeats that simple worshipful song several times, the souls once again begin to wonder just who Windrose is. He certainly is no ordinary teacher, no ordinary person, no ordinary anything. He is, instead, extremely godly, loving, and humble. Once again, they just decide that if it is meant to be that they should know, then they would know, so let the thought be for now.

Then Windrose turns once again to the omniciscreen and says, "Now, let's look at Blangdon's life and ministry again and see how the Father is using him in the unique calling that he has grown up in."

CHAPTER 12

A BRACE-YOURSELF PROPHECY, AN OLD ENGLISH WORD, AND BLANGDON'S GREATEST CONVERT STRATEGIES

As Windrose turns on the omniciscreen once again, he says, "Souls, we are now jumping ahead to the year 2001. In this time period, a huge attack from an anti-Christian nation had just hit the United States of America in the month of September. Blangdon will be used by God in his church to give a prophetic word the Sunday before it happened, telling of a great darkness that was coming over the land and encouraging the people there that day that God was the Light of the World. Thousands will be killed on September 11th of this year, and it will prompt a spontaneous but short-lived spiritual revival in the country.

"Blangdon has been praying for a great awakening in his country for years in this time period we are about to enter. As he has been traveling and preaching as an evangelist, he is realizing more and more that people were not accustomed to the strong messages that God the Holy Spirit has been giving him. He continues to pour out his heart to God for an understanding while spending time studying both the revivals and preaching in the history of his nation. What he has just discovered has thrilled him, and he is attempting to share the whole thing with Rosie, his wife..."

"Rosie, this is so cool! Finally, I think I have found the missing link that I have been spending so long trying to find!"

"Link? What link, dear?"

"The link to why famous preachers of old like John Wesley, Jonathan Edwards, Charles Finney, and others were allowed by the people of their day to preach such strong and fiery messages. I had to do some serious digging to find it, but it's all here, one thing confirming another!"

"What, what did you find? I'll admit, hon, I sometimes wonder when you get to preaching your heart out if that's really God or if it is you and that passion of yours for the Kingdom of God!"

"Well, I love how the Holy Spirit is such a wonderful teacher and counselor and so very practical in what He shows us. For instance, I had a strange urgency to try to find copies of very old English dictionaries. You know, like the ones they would have used during these nineteenth-century revivals. That was combined with the Spirit of God prompting me to read over and over again 1 Corinthians 14:3 (NKJV): 'But he who prophesies speaks edification and exhortation and comfort to men.'"

"Rosie, that is the wonderful three-part ministries of the Holy Spirit in prophetic gifts. We know what edification is, right?"

"Right, yes!"

"That's to build up! It's also a no-brainer as to what comfort is, that is, to comfort someone who is hurting. Of the six ministries that Jesus lists that He has in Luke 4:18–19, two of them have to do with healing the brokenhearted. That means one-third of Jesus's ministry while on earth, if given equal proportions, focused on people who were hurting. So, one-third of the Holy Spirit's ministry, according to Paul, had to do with the same thing: healing the emotional wounds of people. However, that third word, 'exhortation,' is where my focus in seeking the truth here was drawn, and wow, did I discover something big here!"

"What, honey? What did you discover? What did you discover about exhortation?"

"Well, first of all, Rosie, over half of the modern Bible translations that I could find interpret the word 'exhortation' to mean 'to encourage,' including the translation that most churches today are accepting as the best translation for most people to understand. But do you know what I discovered in those old English dictionaries?"

"What, Blangdon? What? You are driving me a little crazy here, honey. What did you find? Remember, I must take the kids to their soccer game tonight! Don't forget you promised them that you would finish up your study time today to get there in time to watch them play!"

"The word 'exhort' or 'exhortation' did not originally mean to 'encourage.' As a matter of fact, to say that to exhort means to encourage and have it harmonize with any extremity of the word, it would have to mean, 'I encourage you to stop that!' Because it means to charge, challenge, or even rebuke. I know, Rosie, I know that the Holy Spirit led me to look in these old dictionaries. You see, these old preachers would not have had access to the Hebrew or Greek meanings of Bible words the way we do today. They would have, however, been able to get access to a dictionary as almost every place of learning and most homes had one for their children's schoolwork. But it gets even better!"

"Mom, we are late; we gotta go!" one of the kids yells out.

"Be there in a minute, kids!"

"Look here on my notepad, in the Vine's Dictionary of New and Old Testament words... The words '*exhort, exhortation*' under A. Verbs Page 390:

'*Parakaleo*: Primarily to call a person to the side, to call on, to entreat, see. *Beseech* (b): to admonish, exhort, or urge one to pursue some course of conduct (always prospective, looking to the future, in contrast to the meaning to comfort, which is retrospective, having to do with trial experienced).' Then Vine lists a ton of scriptural references and recommends the student cross-references in his dictionary to the word '*beseech*'! Then, when you do that, you find that the word 'beseech' that we equate with pleading or begging in our understanding refers back to 'exhort'!"

"Don't you see, honey, how the old English dictionaries, with their references to charge, challenge, or rebuke, derive their strong interpretation of the word from the original Greek?"

"Yes, yes, I see it now. But, honey, really, I gotta go!"

Just at that moment, one of the kids yelled out, "Mom, Mrs. Williams just called and said that the game had been postponed one-half hour because of thundershowers in the area, so we don't have to leave right now! Can we run back in and get some snacks and drinks to bring with us?"

"Yes, go ahead! Grab that small picnic cooler to put everything in!"

"Okay, Mom!"

"Well, Blangdon, I guess I have a few more minutes now?"

"Great! This will only take a few more minutes, and it explains everything! It explains why both people in the scripture, as well as revivalists of old, could preach such hard sermons and still be within the threefold balance of the Holy Spirit's ministry found in 1 Corinthians 14:3! God, you see, has a threefold balance of ministry, not a twofold balance the way many modernists want us to believe. Those modern translations of the Bible that interpret the word 'exhort' to mean to encourage have gone to a great extreme to take only one far-reaching possible interpretation of the word, and if it means to encourage, it would have to mean 'I encourage you to stop that' whatever it is that is being addressed by the word!

"Now take a quick look with me at the verb *parineo*, primarily, to speak of near (*para*, *near*, and *aineo*, to tell of, speak of, then to recommend)[94]; hence, to advise, exhort, warn is used in Acts 27:9, 'admonished,' and verse 22: 'I exhort.' See *admonish*.

"Okay, Rosie, wait until you hear this! Under the word 'admonish,' it is even clearer! As a noun *nouthesia*, lit., putting in mind (nous, mind, *tithemi*, to put)[95] is used in 1 Corinthians 10:11, of the purpose of the Scriptures; in Ephesians 6:4, of that which is ministered by the Lord; and in Titus 3:10, of that which is to be administered for the correction of one who creates trouble in the church. *Nouthesia* is 'the training by word,' whether of encouragement or, if necessary, by reproof or remonstrance, which the dictionary translates as 'a forcefully reproachful protest'[96]!

"Don't you see, honey, all of the criticism that I have faced through the years of preaching too strong was all because of the effect of the lukewarm churches in America having a wrong interpretation of this precious word for decades! The Lord has shown me in prayer that this attack has been so complex from Satan that he took a slow and subtle process that spanned decades to gradually literally change the meaning of this word in the English language. That is why the Holy Spirit led me to seek out dictionaries from the 1800s to see what that word used to mean to preachers of that decade!"

"Wow, Blangdon... Wow! So, it wasn't your zealous passion or heightened enthusiasm that caused you to preach so strongly! God was actually using you under an anointing of exhortation to try to warn a gradually backsliding denomination, who call themselves a fellowship, to turn away from their worldliness and turn back to seeking God with their whole hearts!"

"Yes, dear. The Congregation of God started powerfully as one of many denominations that got their start from the Azusa Street Revivals in California at the turn of the century! However, over time, their focus turned towards appealing to people with a softened, less spiritual message, and now it's hard to find a church within their ranks where the Spirit of God is allowed to move freely anymore! Not only is strong exhortative preaching for today, but it's also desperately needed now, in this season of the church!"

"Oh, dear Jesus! Blangdon, do you realize what this could mean if the church world in America or even worldwide discovered this cover-up by the forces of darkness? I mean, the devil obviously had to use willing people who wanted a softer message and would rather believe in a less confrontational God. Blangdon, this, by itself, if it just got to the masses so that church folk could understand it and pastors felt the liberty to teach and preach it, could spark even a worldwide revival! Praise God, honey. Praise God!"

"Yes, Rosie. Look, I know you have to run the kids to the soccer game. Now, my dear Rosie, as you go, please be praying that God will help you stand by me in this. I have already written an article about it, and when I finish my final edits, I will be printing off multiple copies to hand out at the National Ministerial Conference in Denver this year. This goes much deeper than I had time to even talk to you about today. There is also very clear-cut evidence that some of the modern Bible translations or transliterations were done by theologians who leaned towards a more liberal Gospel in their personal statements through articles, op-eds, books, and periodicals. Some of these men, with help from professional women, obviously intentionally, wherever they could, soften the meaning of interpretations of biblical phrases. Again, one clear example of this is using wording translating, 'to exhort,' 'to encourage,' instead of stronger, more confrontational language, intensifying the effect of teaching and preaching any chosen subject.

"However, Rosie, we must prepare ourselves for opposition because, as Christ said, 'Let him who is able to receive it receive it' (Matthew 19:12; paraphrased). But there will be many who will not want to admit they are wrong in their theology, their belief system, and, for some, even their favorite Bible teachers and preachers on television who have promoted this erroneous doctrine. Historically, revivalists have been strongly persecuted, sometimes by their own extended family members. God does promise to give us grace for such suffering, but perhaps you can see now that the days of being indifferent about the importance of a dedicated personal prayer and Bible study time have to be over. We must see ourselves as if we are preparing for war because we are—a spiritual war!"

With that, Windrose once again raised his right hand to turn off the omnisciscreen and temporarily suspend their trip into the nineteen nineties. He knew it was time to further explain to the souls something that was of utmost importance concerning their future revelations of everything that they were being taught. Especially as it related to the spiritual battles that would be waged against Jesus's bride, the church. They had just heard Blangdon explain to his bride, Rosie, that she must brace herself for the spiritual battles that they, as a couple, were about to experience. Now it was time that the souls were reminded that all of their preparation in all of these lessons was to supernaturally equip them for the future, and the future of dismantling Satan's deceptive strategies to prevent the preparing of the bride and to hinder the days coming when he will be judged and cast into the bottomless pit prepared for him and his angels!

"Souls, do you recall that in the very beginning, you learned that God the Father was an all-seeing, all-knowing, and ever-present God? He knows the beginning from the end. He can look backwards into the past or as far forward as He wants into the future with perfect comprehension of what things are going to happen in the future! It is so imperative that you understand that God, in His foreknowledge, knew that each one of you would one day make a choice of your free will to accept Jesus Christ as your personal Savior. Then, you would choose to make Him Lord of your lives. To make the mistake of thinking that you were somehow pre-programmed to get saved does not line up with eternal love. Such thinking leads to an evil of spiritual pride, which is the very attitude that brought Satan down to his fall. God, out of His love for us, gives every man and woman a free will! Within that space of free will, millions will one day hear the gospel of Jesus Christ and be converted to Christianity. From those millions will come one concerted 'type of' that will become His bride. She will be chosen and taken out at the Rapture to enter His heavenly abode before His one day coming in power to rule and reign on the earth. God the Father has already revealed to me that in the not-too-distant future, the souls will take one final journey far into the future and will witness the night that the world will stand still! The bride will not be any one denomination or country or people group. It will be the bride who has prepared herself for Him, made of men and women from all over the world."

"Windrose," Jonah-42 asked, "will all the souls that have been trained for these assignments complete their assigned duties?

"Sadly, no, Jonah, which in its simple complexity further proves that God the Father is, has, and always will honor the free will of His creation right up until the last of the last days on the earth! Even among you, who He knows will willingly accept the gift of salvation, and similar to the equal love shown to the very one who will betray Him just prior to His crucifixion, He will show all of you in your lives equal love. Even though in His foreknowledge He knows some of you will be of those who will fail in their duty to do as they have been taught both here in the arena of souls and in your eventual growth and training as biblical believers once on the earth."

The sounds of the souls expressing their sorrow over considering the facts that Windrose had just given them were a somber mix of groans, extended "ohs," and included some phrases such as: "Oh, I pray it isn't me, Lord," "Nos," and "Lord help me to succeed…"

"Be encouraged!" Windrose responded, "Faith is believing in God and His help that will be ever present to those who choose to walk with Him on a daily basis! You all have not been brought here to fear but to prepare you to believe and succeed! Now it's time for another trip on the omniciscreen to the most powerful Christian conversion that has ever occurred. Recently, you endured watching Stephen, the faithful martyr, get stoned to death by the very men he was called by God to confront with the truth. Some of you here will one day be called to be martyred for Christ, but with that calling, be certain that God's supernatural grace will be present at that time to help you endure it! Now, the very man who supervised that stoning will have his world turned upside down for the gospel's sake. For this next lesson, we are going to take a trip to Tarsus for an unusual meeting between two well-known Bible characters. However, in this scene, the one has been recently converted to Christianity by Jesus Himself. Luke, hearing from the other disciples of the conversion of Saul of Tarsus, is traveling to that city to write down a fresh report of what happened to this former persecutor of the early church! Let's look to the omniciscreen and focus on that meeting now."

"Saul, Saul, is that you? Welcome, welcome, my new brother in Christ, to the 'way'! I am Luke, a physician and a follower of Christ myself."

"Yes, it is me, Saul, or Paul, by my Roman name, whichever you prefer to call me. I had to flee from Damascus and that region as there are already many zealots who seek to take my life! Oh, the shame of what I have done… However, Jesus's love consumes me every time I think about it; it is almost as if it never happened!"

With a quill pen in hand and a fresh scroll on a large table in the room, Luke begins to write some beginning thoughts, the flickering light from a former ceremonious seven-light Jewish menorah that Luke found and lit when he arrived there. The room had formally been used by the local priests to keep the Jewish temple worship instruments clean and working properly. Luke felt it was all too fitting to light the room to indirectly celebrate the conversion of such a Hebrew zealot. A little sunlight shone through the corner windows, and with this lampstand handy, it created the perfect amount of light needed to write down the account of this extraordinary conversion.

As Luke began to write, stopping only to ask Saul questions to get everything exactly right, the wonderous peace of the Holy Spirit of God filled the room. Both men knew that something that would change the world was being written down in that room. Both Luke and Saul were realizing that the whole way that the Jewish leaders had been believing and teaching the people had greatly drifted off track through the years. Religious practice focusing on man's rules and the doctrines of men had overshadowed the compassion that God the Father had for both Jews and Gentiles for years. Jesus had come and told the multitudes such things as "I and the Father are one"[97] and "If you have seen me, you have seen the Father."[98] He had demonstrated a love for God's people that had been long lost by the strict laws and rules of the disconnected scribes and Pharisees. Both Luke and Saul wanted to make sure that they got every jot and every tittle correct in their description of what had just happened on that road to Damascus.

As Luke was still writing down the account as Saul was describing it, Saul interrupted Luke and said, "Luke, can I ask a favor of you? Once you get this written down, could you read it through to me out loud so that I can hear it?"

"Absolutely, Saul! I would consider it an honor to do so!"

Windrose pauses the omniciscreen to take a minute to address the souls in the transition of time of Luke and Paul's dialogue.

"Souls, I am going to move the scene ahead on the omniciscreen to the place where Luke has finished writing down Saul's account of his conversion;

therefore, as we join back in now, Luke has taken one more dip of his pen in the ink and popped it down at the end of his sentence."

"Okay, Saul, or should we start calling you Paul now because you have become a brand-new person in Christ? I have it all written down. Do you still want me to read it to you?"

"Yes, Luke, please do. You can refer to me as Saul or Paul, but somehow, I feel you are right. I feel that my Roman name, Paul, may become my new name as a Christian."

"Okay, let me put a little more oil in this lampstand, and then once it is full, I will begin reading it to you."

"*Akkkem,*" Luke clears his voice and then begins.

Then Saul, still breathing threats and murder against the disciples of the Lord, went to the high priest and asked letters from him to the synagogues of Damascus, so that if he found any who were of the Way, whether men or women, he might bring them bound to Jerusalem. As he journeyed, he came near Damascus, and suddenly a light shone around him from heaven. Then he fell to the ground, and heard a voice saying to him, "Saul, Saul, why are you persecuting Me?"

And he said, "Who are You, Lord?"

Then the Lord said, "I am Jesus, whom you are persecuting. It is hard for you to kick against the goads."

So he, trembling and astonished, said, "Lord, what do You want me to do?"

Then the Lord said to him, "Arise and go into the city, and you will be told what you must do."

And the men who journeyed with him stood speechless, hearing a voice but seeing no one. Then Saul arose from the ground, and when his eyes were opened, he saw no one. But they led him by the hand and brought him into Damascus. And he was three days without sight, and neither ate nor drank.

Now there was a certain disciple at Damascus named Ananias; and to him the Lord said in a vision, "Ananias."

And he said, "Here I am, Lord."

So, the Lord said to him, "Arise and go to the street called Straight, and inquire at the house of Judas for one called Saul of Tarsus, for behold, he is praying. And in a vision, he has seen a man named Ananias coming in and putting his hand on him, so that he might receive his sight."

Then Ananias answered, "Lord, I have heard from many about this man, how much harm he has done to Your saints in Jerusalem. And here he has authority from the chief priests to bind all who call on Your name."

But the Lord said to him, "Go, for he is a chosen vessel of Mine to bear My name before Gentiles, kings, and the children of Israel. For I will show him how many things he must suffer for My name's sake."

And Ananias went his way and entered the house; and laying his hands on him he said, "Brother Saul, the Lord Jesus, who appeared to you on the road as you came, has sent me that you may receive your sight and be filled with the Holy Spirit." Immediately there fell from his eyes something like scales, and he received his sight at once; and he arose and was baptized.

So when he had received food, he was strengthened. Then Saul spent some days with the disciples at Damascus.

Immediately he preached the Christ in the synagogues, that He is the Son of God.

Then all who heard were amazed, and said, "Is this not he who destroyed those who called on this name in Jerusalem, and has come here for that purpose, so that he might bring them bound to the chief priests?"

But Saul increased all the more in strength, and confounded the Jews who dwelt in Damascus, proving that this Jesus is the Christ.

Now after many days were past, the Jews plotted to kill him. But their plot became known to Saul. And they watched the gates day and night, to kill him. Then the disciples took him by night and let him down through the wall in a large basket.

And when Saul had come to Jerusalem, he tried to join the disciples;

but they were all afraid of him and did not believe that he was a disciple. But Barnabas took him and brought him to the apostles. And he declared to them how he had seen the Lord on the road, and that He had spoken to him, and how he had preached boldly at Damascus in the name of Jesus. So, he was with them at Jerusalem, coming in and going out. And he spoke boldly in the name of the Lord Jesus and disputed against the Hellenists, but they attempted to kill him. When the brethren found out, they brought him down to Caesarea and sent him out to Tarsus.

Then the churches throughout all Judea, Galilee, and Samaria had peace and were edified. And walking in the fear of the Lord and in the comfort of the Holy Spirit, they were multiplied.[99]

"Excellent, Luke! Yes, that's perfect, that is exactly how it all happened; thank you so much for reading it to me!"

"I have a feeling, Paul, that what I just wrote will one day be read by people all over the world to help them find both the forgiveness of Jesus and the hope that God can use them in ministry no matter what sins they have committed in their former lives!"

"Amen, so may it ever be, brother, or should I call you 'Dr. Luke'?"

"'Brother' first, Paul, 'brother' first, always....."

"May God go with you as Saul to reach your Jewish brethren, and as Paul, to reach the Gentile world and your Roman family and friends with this life-changing gospel of Jesus Christ."

"Amen, Brother Luke, amen, and may God go with you as well..."

With that, Windrose closes the omniciscreen and turns to address the souls again. "The Apostle Paul will go on to be the most single-used person in history to touch more lives than any person ever could without the Holy Spirit. He devoted his life to Jesus wholeheartedly and went on to suffer many, many things in his life, to which he will one day respond in his letter to the Philippians, 'Yet indeed I also count all things loss for the excellence of the knowledge of Christ Jesus my Lord, for whom I have suffered the loss of all things, and count them as rubbish, that I might gain Christ.'[100] You, as instructed souls, will have varied levels of suffering for Christ in your life. Some here will even be like Stephen and be martyred. Some will have to endure many smaller losses and heartaches as those that you love reject the changes in your life. For some in leadership positions, you will have to endure the rejection of some community members of the cities that you pastor. What you must realize is that, as Paul will also pen to the Roman church, 'All things work together for good to those who love God, to those who are the called according to His purposes,'[101] if you focus on the *eternal* good being done by your Sovereign God and Father in heaven, then you will be able to endure all things...

"Now, souls, we are going to visibly travel back into the future to Blangdon's life and ministry. As he moves ahead within his denomination, he will find himself having regrets. Regrets that he ever told his Congregation of God's brethren that he felt called to bring a message of revival to them. He had since realized that they took that as an insult rather than a blessing of help from the Lord to springboard into being revived spiritually. Even though they would all acknowledge privately that they knew that their fellowship of ministers was backsliding in a direction that every other major denomination had gone.

"Some of the professors in their theological seminaries actually taught and believed that these things were unavoidable processes and a natural and an acceptable occurrence within even every spiritual movement. It didn't matter that Blangdon had spent years studying revivals of history. It didn't matter that he could clearly show that a moving towards spiritual lukewarmity was considered by all of the apostles in their writings something to be avoided but also taught clearly by Jesus Himself in John's letters to the seven churches in Revelation. Also, it didn't matter that Blangdon maintained himself as a man of humility and integrity, spending much of his adult life in underpaid youth ministry, always having to maintain additional employment, including his wife, who had to work to provide necessary support. It didn't matter that Blangdon prayed daily for the Congregation of God churches and traveled at his own expense to their ministers' conferences, often spending considerable time at the altars praying for himself and his brethren. Even with all of this, he realized that they did not acknowledge that he had been sent by God as a revivalist in their midst. Then, through all this, Rosie and the kids were taking the rejections the hardest. Blangdon could tell that Satan was building up an attack of doubt in Rosie's mind. He not only loved her deeply and began to seriously fear losing her, but he also knew full well that the destruction of marriage caused a huge setback in any man's ministry. He began to talk with her privately about them getting counseling specifically designed for ministers and their wives. As she reluctantly agreed, what came out of their first sessions shocked Blangdon. On the way home that night, Blangdon knew in his heart that it was time for a conversation that he had been putting off for a long time. Rosie had just poured out with crying and tears her inner growing resentment towards God's calling on their lives, the struggles that the whole family had to endure because of that, and how when she became a Christian coming out of upscale economic family, she never 'signed up' for 'this'!"

"Rosie, for years, I have shared with you almost all, if not all, the wonderful revelations that God has given me in prayer. Am I right?"

"Yes, Blangdon, sometimes over and over again."

"Although our upbringings were so very different, we both came out of very worldly practices when we prayed to receive Christ. Is that also correct? I mean, you went to a large Christian university, and I ended up taking a correspondence Bible study program to become a licensed minister. However, I came from a small town in the Northeast, and you came from a large city. My ancestry basically goes back through generations of hard-working blue-collar workers, and yours follows generations of college-graduated professional people. My point is that culturally, we are sort of like people from two different planets. Do you agree?"

"Yes, Blangdon, and I do love you. I want you to know that, but..."

"But what, Rosie?"

"I'm just not sure I believe the same as you do. I mean, you seem to love knew that I didn't know, so I began to seek Him diligently to find out why."

"I know, Blangdon, God has shown you a lot, and that is the reason why you do what you do, but it's more than a motivation with you; it's like some kind of a fire burning inside you! I'm sorry, but I just don't have that, Blangdon. To be honest, most of the time, I relate more to Judy and my friends from work than I do you!" With that, Rosie began to cry and said, "I'm sorry, Blangdon, I'm so sorry!"

Blangdon began crying too and reached across and hugged Rosie and began to say, "It's okay, honey, we can work things out, and I believe it will start when you realize that this next thing that will only take a few moments, I feel is the most important thing that God has ever revealed to me has the answer not only for us but for countless thousands and, maybe, millions of people worldwide.

"You remember the story of Saul of Tarsus, who became the Apostle Paul, right, Rosie?"

"Yes, yes, of course; who wouldn't? He ended up writing over half of the New Testament!"

"What did he have, Rosie, before he was converted? I mean, he really felt he had been doing the right thing. He very much believed in God, and within the framework of that belief, he was very zealous for him. What driving force was pushing Paul in the wrong direction? I mean, Jesus, when He appeared to him, and I'm paraphrasing, 'Saul, why are you kicking against a sharp pointed object?' Or you could also interpret that to mean, 'Why are you doing something that is obviously bringing great pain to you?'

"In other words, Jesus was rebuking Saul's behavior and trying to get him to see how ridiculous it was. The whole time, Saul felt he was some kind of a hero for God, capturing, imprisoning, and sometimes sending to their death these new followers of this new, from what he saw, 'anti-Jew' religion.

"Saul had to recognize just what kind of a person he truly was in order for him to die to himself and surrender himself fully to Jesus. Rosie, do you think that it would be fair to say that Saul had to die to himself, that is his own way of thinking, that day, to actually begin to live for Christ?"

to pray and read God's Word. You do it every day joyfully, and you are always coming to me and sharing with me some fresh thing that God has revealed you from His Word."

At this point, Blangdon pulled over into a vacant store parking lot.

"Blangdon, what are you doing?" Rosie asked.

"I know we have to get home to the kids, and this will only take a minute but I did not want to try to drive and talk about something this serious." Blangdon put the car in park and turned the engine off. It had started to rain small raindrops that were covering the windshield and side windows, so it was as if they were closed into their own little world for a short time. "Rosie of all the things that you remember that God has taught me as it relates to revival coming not only to our church but to America, which one I felt was the most important?"

"Oh, there have been so many. I remember you have shared that Jeremiah 33:3 was one of your main foundations for life."

As Rosie began to recite it, Blangdon joined in, and they quoted it together: "'Call to Me, and I will answer you, and show you great and mighty things, which you do not know.'"[102]

"Yes, Rosie, yes, and after I was radically saved out of a very worldly life, being frustrated growing up with such a seemingly boring Christian life by those around me, I first wanted to tell the world about what I had found! However, when I realized that the established church and specifically the Congregation of God congregants did not want to hear what I had to say, I then began to do what Jeremiah said there to do. I began to pray, 'God, what is going on in the world? Why do so many people seem to not want to hear my testimony and all of the wonderful and exciting things that You are doing in my life?' I mean, Rosie, I knew Him; for the first time in my life, I knew Him. His wonderful Holy Spirit was by my side every hour of every day, and Jesus literally was my best friend. I could tell that they did not have a clue as to what that was. Either that or, if they once knew Him that way, they had allowed the ways of the world to creep in, and they had grieved Him away. I

"Oh, yes," Rosie responded, "that's very clear."

"Do you know what, again, the greatest truth that God has shown me concerning the current church in America and the answer to the reason why so many people, perhaps even you, Rosie, do not get excited about serving Jesus? About reading their Bible and loving to pray?

"It's that, like Saul, we have to die to ourselves first to ever become truly born again. For far too many in America, within our microwave, want it quick, society, they have been coerced by a convincing sermon not to become truly born again. Not to be actually convicted of their own kicking against the sharp objects of the sin that they have allowed to be in their lives, not to even feel much of any conviction about the choices they have made but coerced to pray a 'repeat after me' prayer that makes it easy to be, and again, 'saved' where no true inner conversion ever takes place. God becomes a 'sugar daddy' type of God who wants to spoil them with a wonderful life full of good stuff. Then, like in the Parable of the Sower, the seed falls upon stony ground and does not properly grow. The soil of the heart has not been properly prepared by truthful, well-balanced preaching of God's Word. So, either the enemy, like 'the birds of the air,' comes in and plucks the seed, or the cares of the world come in and choke the Word, and it becomes unfruitful.

"In my life, Rosie, I knew in my heart that I was a rotten sinner in desperate need of a Savior. So, I desperately cried out to God for all He had for me, including a desire to be filled to the max with His Holy Spirit. I wasn't just 'saved,' like signing this conversion card, and you are in. I was truly a broken man who willingly died to himself in a deep understanding of my sinful nature and was 'born again'! Rosie, one of the most powerful scriptures that God has shown me to preach is found in Paul's writing to the Romans. I believe it is the springboard that any spiritually lukewarm believer can grasp and allow its truth to rock your world to God's best for your life. Romans 7:9 states, 'I was alive once without the law, but when the commandment came, sin revived and I died.'[103] The whole chapter is filled with awesome examples that build up to that life-changing truth. I kind of compare it to being shot in the heart with a bullet. 'Bamb' the Word of God by studying the Ten

Commandments, one by one, shoot bullets of truth into our understanding until down, down, down we go. First one causes us to put our hands over our hearts. 'Oh, I have been shot.' The second one goes through our lungs, and we gasp and drop to our knees. We spin around only to get shot again, and we realize we have yet broken another one of God's laws. Then, we flop to the ground, speaking figuratively. Dead. So strength to stand. Nothing to stand on. Then we fall on God's mercy, pleading Him to forgive us for breaking several of His commandments and worthy of nothing but His designed eternal punishment of hell. With what little bit of consciousness we have left, we plead for His mercy. Just then, He reaches down, takes our hands, and pulls us up as we thank Him for His gift of salvation, as we realize that He has just delivered us from eternity in hell's lake of fire. We move from being dead in our sins to being resurrected by the gift of eternal life by Jesus paying the price of dying on the cross and paying our sin debt over two thousand years ago. Now, a child of God. No longer a slave to sin. No longer serving the devil. Now, a brand-new creature in Christ with a new name written in the Lamb's Book of Life! That's why, Rosie, I love Him so much. That's why I want to pray to stay in communion with Him. Because He is God, I trust Him to run my life. Because He is God, and that's why I want to do His will. Then also because He is God and now my Heavenly Father, I love Him, I adore Him, I cherish Him. Don't you see the cheap copy so many people are handed lacks all of that?

"I'm worried, Rosie, that once you were handed a cheap copy of the real thing of being truly born again! I'm worried that you have never had the death experience to your old nature and never really recognized how evil religious practice is. You never were truly born anew, born afresh, born again, transformed into a new person. A heavenly person with a heavenly address. You mentioned feeling closer to your friends than to me. James, the half brother of Jesus, warned in James 4:4b: 'Do you not know that friendship with the world is enmity with God? Whoever therefore wants to be a friend of the world makes himself an enemy of God.'[104]

"Now, I know that you do not want that, honey, but that one can kind of creep up on us. I mean, well and innocently, we little by little begin to make friends at work or at a school that we may be in. Then, one day, before we know it, we find out that, in reality, our closest friends are worldly people! Sometimes, it is because we did once sincerely know the Lord but have let the cares of this world creep in, and we become unfruitful. Other times, it is just because we have let offenses in the church or our extended family creep in, and our lack of forgiveness of those offenses creates a blockade of Jesus's grace reaching us. Whatever is the case with us, Rosie, can we just take a minute here in the car and pray for God to redeem us from whatever hole we have dug ourselves into?"

"Yes, Blangdon, yes, please do; I want to do something really radical. I truly feel this in my heart. Your parents' cabin up in Green Ridge mountains on Crane Lake is usually vacant this time of year. If you think you could manage with the kids for a few days, I would like to take my journal, which I have not used in way too long, and go up there. It's still warm enough this fall that I should not have to keep a fire. I want to just go there and do something that I have never done. Separate myself completely from the distractions of this world and just spend a few days with Jesus!"

Tears began to run down Blangdon's face as he quietly began to thank God for this most wonderful idea he was sure that God had given Rosie. It was a very safe location, and they had spent many weeks together with the family there. He secretly began to plan a complete food fast for her while she was gone, asking God to give him the grace to do so, knowing that he would be cooking full meals each day for the children. He was confident that the years of ministry that God had given him for so many others were about to powerfully affect the one earthly person that he loved the most.

Windrose approaches the omniciscreen again, and while turning off the future projection, he asks the souls an interesting question that, at first, seems preposterously detached from what they had been seeing in their recent travels between two millenniums of time.

"What common belief system do you see between Rosie, Blangdon's wife, and Saul of Tarsus in post-resurrection history?"

Windrose fully understood that answer to the question would be way beyond the souls' ability to completely understand, but he was setting them up for a learning experience that would best be yet served over two thousand years from that day. Yet he knew that the Father had created this very scenario to try to help future potential believers sidestep one of Satan's greatest pitfalls. The pitfall of religious practice versus a true relationship with Him through Christ.

Wendall-27 speaks up and says, "Windrose, how could there possibly be any common thing between a twentieth-century pastor's wife and a first-century Hebrew zealot? Please, Windrose, I mean no offense, but this question seems like a setup to something where there is no answer! But why would you do that? Surely, there is an answer!"

"Excellent response, Wendall! The important thing to always remember is that the difference between religious practice and having a living, vibrant relationship with God is that religion attempts to do things for God to earn His favor. In a true born-again relationship where you actually are spiritually converted into a child of God, you do things with Him because you have His favor already by being His son or daughter! There can be many contributing reasons why some people end up in religious practice. The main one is ignorance of the truth, having never learned about the free gift of salvation through what Jesus did on the cross for the sins of the whole world. Being ignorant of that, many try to find God through religious effort, but the most self-seductive is the fact that far too many people slide into religious practice in rebellion against the truth. The crucified life, once found, where Christ, the Chief Cornerstone, sets for us the example, is not an easy life. Sidestepping dying to self once an individual has accepted the gift so that one becomes totally dependent on the power of the Holy Spirit both to seek and to do God's will is a step many people take. At that point, they begin to do things 'for God' instead of 'with God' in a fruitless effort in the early stages of their growth of understanding once they have received the gift of eternal life."

Emma-16 speaks up and asks, "Windrose, is that what Rosie did at some time in her early experience with her growth in Christ, and maybe Blangdon did not? Is that why Blangdon seems to love praying and reading God's Word and Rosie does not?"

"Emma, I don't think you discovered that possibility on your own, but I believe the Father revealed that to you for everyone's benefit today. The truth is that as you will one day observe religious practice in others, only God truly knows the heart of every individual and what caused them to make the decisions that they made. But, yes, that is very much a possibility in Rosie's life, as it is very much a possibility in countless people's lives. The truth is that people who truly are led by God's Holy Spirit, because they are truly born again and have willingly laid their lives down for the gospel's sake, are a great blessing to the kingdom and the Father's will being done on earth as it is in heaven.

"On the other hand, people who are still alive to themselves, people who have resisted dying to their own will to follow their own wants, likes, and dreams, are often very oppositional to those who have died to themselves to follow the will of Christ. Everything from inner family conflict to churches being divided in their thinking and decision-making to major problems in government structures is all part of religious practice based on man's brain and understanding versus Holy Spirit-led decisions that have eternal souls at the heart of every decision."

Windrose takes his finger and once again draws the whiteboard in the air. He begins to write an important part of this lesson as his finger lights up green. He then says, "Souls, I am using the color green for this because green is often associated with prosperity, such as in the springtime when everything is sprouting up new. Or in times of harvest when the stalk of corn is tall or in the middle of the delight of summer when the trees are full of bright green leaves. The most prosperous thing that can happen in any family, church, community, or country is when there is unity among the people who live within that particular framework. Therefore, I am going to write in big, bold, capital green letters the following truth:

'UNITY DOES NOT COME FROM EVERYONE AGREEING WITH ONE ANOTHER; UNITY COMES FROM EVERYONE AGREEING WITH GOD!'"

With that statement, the souls began to clap and cheer and shout "amens" to what Windrose had just shared with them. It was such a powerful truth, and the thought of any family, church, community, or even nation being unified under God's divine wisdom brought sheer joy to their hearts.

Then Rosie-11 shouts out, "Windrose, it would be so wonderful if you could tell us that Rosie is going to find a brand-new refreshing relationship with Jesus Christ as she spends those three days in the mountain cabin!"

"Is this a personal hope, Rosie? Ha-ha," Windrose interjected with heavenly joy and laughter! You do realize that this is not necessarily you, correct?"

"Yes, Windrose," Rosie replied, "but it never hurts to hope, right?"

"No, Rosie, hope is always, always good, especially when you hope and pray that God's will will be able to be done!"

With that statement, Windrose made souls all through the arena just turn and look at each other and say, "What did he say? I don't understand," and such comments that they all knew would be soon explained in their next lesson.

CHAPTER 13

A RAINBOW OF INSTRUCTION, THE CHOIR ABOVE THE THRONE, AND A ROMAN GUARD GRADES SEVEN CHURCHES

Windrose, realizing that the souls are probably now on the most important topic, other than salvation itself, wants to do something to help them recognize the importance of this lesson. This time, he uses both index fingers to draw something above the whiteboard. He reaches up with both hands and both index fingers to a point high above the center, pulling down in an arch-like fashion from both sides. As his fingers move, an incredibly beautiful rainbow suddenly appears.

"The rainbow," he says, "was God's first symbol of hope. He gave it to Noah following the worldwide flood, a flood that brought about the destruction of the extreme sinfulness that had developed on the earth. Through the rainbow, God promised to never again destroy the earth with a flood. The reason I chose it today is that even though man, through the years, will attempt to deflect its true meaning, nevertheless, through heaven's vision, the rainbow will always still represent the eternal promise of a loving God. It will always be a reminder that He called a simple man named Noah to build an arc for the saving of the human race. God, the loving Heavenly Father, always has the plan of salvation for all who will believe and receive it!

"In this case, I chose it because the seven colors, fused together, also remind us of the importance of unity *'in God.'* In God is the only place you will ever find true unity! His Holy Spirit, when allowed to fill man's spirit, is the unifying force that inspires and leads men and women, confirming the important specifics of the will of God in every God-called situation.

"Red, orange, yellow, green, blue, indigo, and violet are all different colors, yet together they form something very beautiful!" Windrose then reaches up and turns on the omniciscreen and says to the souls, "Behold from a distance the very throne of God!"

Suddenly, spectacular combinations of countless multiple shades of white, accented with brilliant golden trim, appear everywhere. By God's design, the souls' ability to see the Father and the Son seated on the throne is slightly skewed because He understands that they are not yet ready to see them in their entirety. However, what the souls can see and hear is a magnificent giant rainbow arching over the throne of God and a sound of praise and worship that seems to come from the area of that rainbow, yet they specifically cannot as yet clearly see what is creating the music.

All at once, the omniciscreen begins to allow them to get a closer view, not of the throne itself but of the rainbow and how the music is being created.

"Souls, you are looking into the future. As I allow you to see closer, although you will not be able to see their faces, you will see seven tiers of balconies enveloped in shining robes of the different colors of the rainbows. This is the eternal choir of the martyrs of the faith who have been honored to sing above the throne of God in this heavenly choir. It is one of the highest places of honor for any who will one day give their lives for the sake of the gospel. As you look closely, you will see a man off in the distance in a golden robe. That, dear souls, is Stephen, the first martyr of Christ's church, who has the unique privilege of directing this choir!"

A roar of praise and thanksgiving arises from the arena of souls, which seems greater than at any other time since their very first lesson. Windrose just waits patiently, allowing their expressions of awe to continue for a lengthy time period before he steps back to his rainbow-crowned whiteboard and begins to teach them more about the importance of unity.

Windrose then begins to write on the rainbow-covered whiteboard. He starts by writing the number one, saying, "Souls, we just discussed this, but it is number one on the list of important things to remember about unity! Once again, as you just saw the whiteboard without the rainbow above it," he uses the color green to write,

"UNITY DOES NOT COME FROM EVERYONE AGREEING WITH ONE ANOTHER; UNITY COMES FROM EVERYONE AGREEING WITH GOD."

Then, Windrose asks the souls a question, "How could it be possible for everyone to agree with God? In your earliest lesson, you were allowed to see out in front of the throne of God the illuminated words that the angels fly past every time they are dispatched from heaven: *'Thy will be done on earth as it is in heaven!'* How is it possible for someone to know the will of God or, for that matter, for two people to know the will of God, such as in the case of Blangdon and Rosie, who are married and in the ministry?"

It almost seems as if it was in perfect unison that hundreds or possibly thousands of souls shout out, *"Through prayer!"*

Windrose once again bursts out in holy laughter, offering up praises to God for the fact that he knows that this is the foundation for all that he had been teaching them from the very beginning, lessons that have repeatedly taught them this truth. Yes! The Father had revealed it to them, but more than that, by their enthusiasm, "they got it"! All the journeys into the future through the omniciscreen, all of the examples, all of the future scriptures that were quoted, and even the fact that demons believed and trembled over the power of communicating to God through prayer have taught them this foundational truth! This delights Windrose, as he knows that the equipping of the souls, albeit tucked away in a process only fully understood by God, would indeed one day be productive.

Then Windrose writes an intriguing question under that very important quote:

"HOW MANY SHADES OF GREEN ARE THERE?"

The souls look puzzled as if they do not seem to have access to the answer to that question, in spite of the Father's special infusion of information about such things as an understanding concerning future cultures, etc. One of the souls blurts out, as they all sort of look at each other, "We don't know, Windrose. How many?"

Windrose smiles with that warm heavenly smile and says, "It doesn't matter. My point is that when it comes to unifying thoughts around any topic, the natural human mind's thoughts are as varied as the almost endless shades of green. Only through praying and earnestly seeking the heart and the mind of God in every situation can everyone come to a common conclusion. Imagine seeing a bright light on the top of a very tall tree. Picture seventy-seven people all surrounding that tree discussing with each other a decision that the group has to make. The conclusion of what should be done concerning that decision can be as varied as the number of people present in that discussion. However, if the unifying answer can only be found by everyone there looking up to that bright light, and that bright light is God, then they will all agree, if they always look to God."

Windrose then writes in a different shade of green point number two:

2) "PEOPLE WHO PRAY A LOT AGREE A LOT!"

He goes on to say, "One day, there will be a common phrase among married couples in the church: 'People who pray together stay together,' and that will prove to be a true saying because as any two people draw close to God, they also in the process symmetrically draw closer to each other. Souls, the same thing is true for groups of people, large and small. For example, some churches decide to have ongoing regular prayer meetings, and I don't mean once a month unless a holiday comes or the weather is bad. I'm talking about churches that discover the power of fervent prayer meetings. They may start as once a month but soon grow into once a week. Then, from the resulting joy and the miracles experienced by entering into the presence of God, on a whim, someone decides to start meeting for nightly prayer! Then, getting community attention, more and more people begin to attend, bringing both their own needs but primarily focusing on the fact that the wonder of God's Holy Spirit's visitation is that He will come as often as He is invited! Then, the unifying effect of the number of people praying together again becomes a symmetrical process. Imagine everyone looking up: in a family, in a church, in a community, in a state, or even in a nation! The truth is that point number two is that people who pray a lot agree a lot!"

Then, Windrose puts up point number three, using his finger and, strangely to the souls, in yet another shade of green! As he recognizes their concern, he takes a minute to explain.

"I bet you all are wondering how many points there will be. If I am going to go through all of the colors of the rainbow and all of the different shades of the different colors, just how long is this lesson going to take? Well, I will take a minute to tell you that all of the colors are important. However, we are not going to have a different point for each color or each shade of each of the colors of the rainbow. We are using the multicolor example for effect. God will one day speak to Abraham concerning how many people will be in his lineage and use the number of the 'stars in the sky' and the number of the 'grains of sand' on the seashore. Here, we want you to understand the vast number of people groups, cultures, educations, creative thought processes, damaged emotions, individual pride factors, intellectual capabilities, and so on of so many people can only lead to confusion and, sadly, chaos as decisions about almost anything are being made. Therefore, the Father wants me to show you that just as there are a limitless number of colors in the world, by using the rainbow as the basis for this lesson, He also wants you to recognize the beauty of each individual person whom He will one day create. He will blend all of their gifts and talents. The beautiful unifying effect of prayer numbers, groups, tens, hundreds, thousands, and even millions of people can be drawn together in family love, church harmony, community consensus, state leadership, and national congruency! People who pray a lot agree a lot!"

The souls do something at that point that they had not done from the beginning of the very first lesson. They all stand and applaud this wonderful and glorious truth combined with the complex beauty of God united by His truth and prayer. Shouts of "yes" and "amen" resound, along with other various expressions of affirmation. It was not possible for Windrose to smile any wider and any brighter than he had smiled before than on that day, at that moment, over the very demonstration of the unifying effect of learning about the power of prayer bringing unity itself!

After allowing a very pleasant time period of the souls' exuberance over this last firmly established truth, Windrose says, "Therefore, let us visibly travel back now into the future and look in on Blangdon and Rosie and see how the latest decision for Rosie to spend some time in prayer at the family cabin has gone. We see Rosie in the kitchen washing up a few dishes that the kids had left soaking in the sink from their after-school snacks. Blangdon comes, walking through the door excitedly. In his hands are sixteen beautiful bright red roses he had picked up at the flower shop to be a welcome-home gift for his wife. Grinning from ear to ear, he gives Rosie a big hug and a very tender, loving kiss. He can hardly contain himself because of something that he has just witnessed."

"I can't wait to tell you, I just can't wait to tell you what happened at church today, but first, Rosie, what can you tell me about your prayer sabbatical at the cabin, that is, unless it's something that you just want to keep between you and the Lord?"

"Oh, no, Blangdon, it was really very wonderful. Piece by piece, I would like to share it with you over the next few days, but first, what happened today at church?"

"Well, last week, Pastor Bloom felt that he had something for me to do for him, a little out of the ordinary. He later told me that primarily because of your and my ages being similar to the Hayes family, he thought that I might be a good one to do some marriage counseling with them. Pastor Bloom had also encouraged me to include you if I felt it would be helpful. They have had a lot of stress in their marriage since Jaydon got laid off from the gasoline engine line at the auto factory. I guess they had been promised jobs with the new electric car production; however, that is not growing in popularity the way they had hoped. Nancy got a job at a local daycare center, but she barely makes minimum wage, and with their four kids, it has put a great strain on them as a couple."

"Wow, honey, that's wonderful, but I really don't see how I could help. We are really talking about two totally different worlds here, with me being a teacher, and, honey, need I remind you that we are still trying to work out some of our own problems in our marriage?"

"Yes, Rosie, yes, I know, but here is where this gets totally cool! You see, I felt in my heart that God wanted me to say yes to the pastor and at least start to talk to them. So, we met today at the church, and I did the only thing I knew to do: I asked them how much time they spent every day praying together! They both looked at each other and, with a bit of a sheepish look on their faces, admitted that they rarely prayed together. So, I looked at both of them and said, 'Then I know a great place to start in our counseling time together! Follow me!' With that, with puzzled expressions, they both shrugged their shoulders and said okay.

"As we were walking towards the church sanctuary, I explained to them that we were going to begin today by praying together and for each other. As we walked the aisle, I reminded them that on a very special day, their wedding day, they individually walked the aisle and met at the altar before God and exchanged vows, which were led by the pastor and witnessed by all of those who were present that day. I then asked them if they felt comfortable kneeling side by side at the altar and holding hands as they prayed, and they each said no.

"Rosie, I then took a moment to pray for them and then suggested that they pray out loud. I reminded them that Jesus died for all of our sins on the cross, then rose again three days later, demonstrating that the power of the Holy Spirit could give us victory in those areas. I then suggested that they both individually and quietly before God ask Him to forgive them for any and all sins, both known and unknown. I then gave them some quality time to sincerely pray that prayer. I then asked them if they realized that the Jewish people once a year had a special sacrifice they offered that was designed to cover any unknown sins that were in their lives. They said they had not heard of that sacrifice but agreed it was a wonderful prayer to pray. I then proceeded, asking Jaydon to pray for Nancy first.

Then, I asked Nancy to pray for Jaydon. It was beautiful. I could distinguish their voices cracking in tender emotions as they asked for God to help each of them in their marriage and to be a more loving and patient spouse, especially during this difficult financial time in their lives. Rosie, what I witnessed was one of the most beautiful spiritual things I had ever seen. After they had finished praying, they both stood up and hugged each other, both having streams of tears flowing down their faces. As we later left the altar and proceeded to walk towards their car, I noticed that they both stood by it for a lengthy period of time, talking. Then, once again, they hugged each other and shared a beautifully lengthy, tender kiss. I could not tell for sure because I was a distance away, but it looked like tears were flowing there too. Get this, Rosie: Jaydon called me a little later, thanked me for taking time with them, and referred to me as a miracle worker. I reminded him that I was no miracle worker but that the Holy Spirit had just worked through the miraculous power of prayer!"

Rosie then begins crying herself as she cups her head in her hands.

"Rosie, what's wrong?" Blangdon asks.

"Nothing, honey, nothing is wrong; as a matter of fact, everything is wonderful. God has been so good to me and to us. This was one of the very things that He revealed to me during my prayer sabbatical. I went there, Blangdon, with a full knowledge of all the things that you had shown me, which God had revealed to you through the years. I have to be honest, honey. I just ignored most of that stuff as it related to my own personal life. I know that in my college years, I heard a lot of mockery of people who were fully committed to God. Also, deep spiritual experiences in the Holy Spirit are psycho-schematically explained away as emotional experiences ramped up in people's minds. While God, over and over again, led you by His Holy Spirit in ways that were to me amazing, I just let my own flesh and will govern my life so that I could have my own way. Over those three days, sweetie, it's very sad for me to say that God showed me that through the years, I have been a spiritual hindrance to you and to what you felt God was calling you to do. I was guilty of not praying through about those things myself. It even affected my love for you because, in my mind, you were just as I had been taught by men and women who had PhDs that you had some form of mental illness, especially your strong preaching, which, I now clearly see, was demonstrated time and time again throughout the Bible, turned me off because I have been a strong-willed individual who wanted my own way.

"Blangdon," Rosie states as she blurts out crying, "I know that I have been a rebel in God's eyes, and the scripture states that rebellion is as the sin of witchcraft!"

With that, Rosie drops right there in their kitchen to her knees and cries and cries and cries, pouring out her heart before God.

"I always wanted to believe the right way. My heart was saying one thing, yet I was doing another. It was almost like a tennis match between me and the truth, where I was playing against myself, hitting the ball over the net, and then trying to run to the other side and hit it back. Blangdon, the beautiful thing is that my eyes have been opened, and now I can see why you pray the way you do, why you love spending time in God's Word, and why you so passionately share God's truth with others. It's all true, it's all real, all of it, all of it is real," Rosie proclaims emphatically! "I love you, Blangdon, I love you, I love you, I love you, and I want to labor by your side in this ministry of trying to get others to receive the revival message. You have just been trying to get people to see that there is more of God than they have ever experienced. You have been trying to get many to see that they have never been truly born again and that some experience of being touched by the Holy Spirit years ago is not enough. Jesus went to the cross so that we can become filled and stay full of the Holy Spirit all of the days of our lives!"

"Yes, Rosie, yes," Blangdon responds as his joy over what he had just heard Rosie say begins to cause joyful tears to run down his face. "We must begin a whole new ministry together, sharing our joint testimony. I have heard of this new way of ministry called 'podcasting,' and in addition, people have been doing 'audio blogs' on the internet for a few years now. It would be very simple for us to put up pre-recorded broadcasts, and it would be an excellent way for us to get our message out! We have that video camera your parents bought us for Christmas to film the kids a few years ago. What do you think, honey?"

"Fantastic idea, Blangdon, but I will need to go shopping to get some new outfits for that!"

"Yes, of course, Rosie, of course," Blangdon said while laughing and praising God for the wonderful transformation that had happened in Rosie's life and the joy of knowing that their relationship was about to go into wonderful places in God!

The souls began once again thanking and praising God with simple songs of worship, as they had all just witnessed through the omniciscreen a couple transformed over several years by the Father's introduction of truth into Rosie's life.

At that point, Windrose approaches the omniciscreen and says, "Souls, we are now once again going on a journey to the isle of Patmos. We will zoom in on John the Beloved, whom we visited some time ago, and Markus, his Roman guard."

Antonio-65 speaks up and says, "Yes, I remember Markus because he ended up receiving Christ as his Savior that day, right?"

"Yes, he did, Antonio, and you will be happy to know that because of that decision that day through the years and the power of one person accepting Christ and then teaching their family generation after generation about the wonderful plan of salvation, 11,123 people will receive Christ following the 1,988 years of his life!"

Hallelujahs, amens, and countless worshipful expletives fill the arena as the thousands of souls from different time periods and spiritual dimensions are made aware of that astonishing numerical fact. The thought that just one faithful witness, placed at just the right time and the right place, could affect so many lives for eternity is incredibly astounding!

Windrose shouts out while laughing, "Grandpas and grandmas, great-grandpas and great-grandmas who are now but souls, don't ever stop telling your little ones the stories of the Bible and, most importantly, the wonderful stories of Jesus!"

Markus-3 shouts out loudly, "*Amen!*" which causes quite a commotion among the souls.

"Huh?"

"What?"

"Could he be?"

"Even he will never know!" Windrose responds while laughing in that heavenly jovial expression of his happy heart!

With that, Windrose points once again to the omniciscreen and says, "We are returning to the isle of Patmos, yet it is a full two years later, and Markus had been sovereignly by God-given charge over all of John's scrolls. According to Roman jail rules, prisoners were not allowed to keep any of their personal items in their cells at night. Markus, in his newly found faith and curiosity, had been reading and studying John's scrolls at night. As we zoom in, we find John quietly worshipping the Lord down at a favorite spot of his at the oceanfront. On a clear day off in the distance, he can see sailing ships passing by. In addition, there is a lot of marine life displaying the glory of God's creation at that particular spot. From time to time, he can watch a mother seal and her two pups frolicking in the surf between the jagged rocks. Dolphins often appear, and he has even seen sea turtles swimming just off the coast. John takes delight in all this as his interaction with the other prisoners is limited. He loves the sense of freedom of God's creation and hopes that one day, like the ocean dwellers, he, too, will once again be free to leave the island and enjoy life's natural surroundings unhindered by prison restrictions."

As Markus approaches John, he shouts out from some distance away, "Greetings, John! Isn't God's creation glorious?"

"Yes, yes, Markus, and greetings to you as well! I was just enjoying a bit of liberty as a part of my gift for good behavior. I love coming here to hope, to think, and to pray!"

"John, there is something that I have been wanting to share with you."

"Yes, what is it, Markus?"

"Before I became a soldier, I was born in a financially prosperous home. My parents were able to afford to send me to a Roman school. This was something that was not afforded by all children. As they recognized my giftings, the school began to suggest that I enroll in a higher level of learning to become a teacher. In that environment, however, there were also a lot of sports competitions and, eventually, chariot races and gladiator competitions. Because I did very well in the latter, I was assigned to military duty, but I never forgot the things I learned in school."

"Yes? Very fascinating, Markus, please go on..."

"Well, you know that at night, I am required to take your scrolls from you and then return them to you the next day? Because I was taught the Greek language, I have been reading the scrolls in my room. I find the letters to the seven churches most amazing. I hope I am not violating some holy principle of God or offending your privacy by reading them, John!"

"Oh, no, Markus, no," John says while laughing with delight. It is my prayer that the whole world may read them someday, so read them all that you want, and certainly, no offense taken. I am really honored that you would want to read what I have written."

"Well, there is something I find very interesting regarding the order of the churches in Asia that Jesus uses in addressing His various concerns. I suppose it's the strict educational standards I was raised with, or maybe something else. Jesus lists them in the following order: Unto Ephesus, unto Smyrna, unto Pergamos, unto Thyatira, unto Sardis, unto Philadelphia, and unto Laodicea. However, I have a different order, based on my many years in the Roman education program. Could it be that Jesus is giving His churches certain grades for different reasons?

"Could it be possible, John, that Jesus has, as He mentions, some 'hidden manna' of truth for those churches that would want to be graded by the Master Jesus in order to motivate them to be all that they can be for Him? If they just study closely, they may discover this nugget of truth that could compel them to seek Him more diligently."

"Markus, believe me, I traveled with Him everywhere He went, and if all the things that He did were written down, there would not be enough books in the whole world to contain them. Nothing, Markus, absolutely nothing that

He might choose to do under the Father's inspiration would surprise me! Yes, yes, yes, most noble and intelligent Markus, please tell me more!"

"Well, John, for instance, the first church listed that Jesus gave you in this powerful revelation is the church at Ephesus. However, in the possible grading order of excellence, I see the first church would be the church at Smyrna. I took the liberty, John, to memorize all of these letters because I could never be sure when my superior officers might discover what I was reading and confiscate them from my keeping."

"Ah, Markus, I can see already that God's wisdom as a young believer is upon you. I am so impressed by your diligence, and as you mentioned, you are a gifted learner."

"Thank you, John, so as I remember the letter to the church of Smyrna, it goes like this:

> *And to the angel of the church in Smyrna write, 'These things says the First and the Last, who was dead, and came to life: "I know your works, tribulation, and poverty (but you are rich); and I know the blasphemy of those who say they are Jews and are not, but are a synagogue of Satan. Do not fear any of those things which you are about to suffer. Indeed, the devil is about to throw some of you into prison, that you may be tested, and you will have tribulation ten days. Be faithful until death, and I will give you the crown of life.*
>
> *"He who has an ear, let him hear what the Spirit says to the churches. He who overcomes shall not be hurt by the second death."'*[105]

"John, in this letter, Jesus literally has not one criticism for Smyrna! He starts by saying that He can see all of the good works that they are doing, all of the struggles that they are going through as a church, and how they are struggling financially. This obviously implies that, according to the world's standards, they are in poverty; however, He says they are rich! Jesus goes on to say that He sees the blasphemy of those who say that they are Jews but are not and tells them that those same people truly are of the synagogue of Satan. In His conclusion, He admonishes them not to be afraid of the fact that the devil is going to cast some of them into prison, that their faith may be tried, and that they would have tribulation for ten days; He tells them to be faithful unto death and that He would give them a crown of life! John, from the perspective of an educated man who was raised on a strict grading system, our Lord Jesus gives Smyrna an 'A' grade! Then, as with every church, He concludes with something similar: 'He that has an ear, let him hear what the Spirit says to the churches.' In other words, the way I take that is for anyone who truly wants to know the truth. If they listen to what He is saying, they will find it! John, I know I did!"

"What a wonderful observation, Markus. Please continue…"

"Then the second church in the revelational order given by Jesus is Smyrna, which I have just quoted. However, in a grading order from an educational perspective, the second church that I see in this placement is the church in Philadelphia:

> *And to the angel of the church in Philadelphia write, 'These things says He who is holy, He who is true, "He who has the key of David, He who opens, and no one shuts, and shuts and no one opens": "I know your works. See, I have set before you an open door, and no one can shut it; for you have a little strength, have kept My word, and have not denied My name. Indeed, I will make those of the synagogue of Satan, who say they are Jews and are not, but lie— indeed I will make them come and worship before your feet, and to know that I have loved you. Because you have kept My command to persevere, I also will keep you from the hour of trial which shall come upon the whole world, to test those who dwell on the earth. Behold, I am coming quickly! Hold fast what you have, that no one may take your crown. He who overcomes, I will make him a pillar in the temple of My God, and he shall go out no more. I will write on him the name of My God and the name of the city of My God, the New Jerusalem, which comes down out of heaven from My God. And I will write on him My new name.*
>
> *"He who has an ear, let him hear what the Spirit says to the churches."'*[106]

"John, as I read the evaluation by Jesus of the church in Philadelphia, I see another church that is doing very well in the Lord's eyes. He first declares His lordship, firmly setting in place His ability to not only judge and evaluate their condition but to also execute whatever corrective measures He seems fit to put in place. Jesus then goes on to assure them that He sees the good works that they do and that He has set before them an open door, I assume of opportunity, in Philadelphia to have a church, and declares that no one will be able to shut that door. John, that's when, as a soldier and a former gladiator, I feel He gives just a hint of an admonition that they should work on getting stronger. He says that they have a little strength. John, I have never heard anyone ever speak about having a little strength as any kind of compliment or encouragement in all of my training and education. It is always used to encourage someone to work on becoming stronger. I believe that moves them just a small notch below Smyrna in any grading evaluation as a motivation to do better for the next test. Like any really good teacher, however, Jesus quickly focuses again on the good that they are doing. He points to the fact that even though they have had a little strength, obviously, as for us all, by finding His strength, they have kept His Word and not denied His name. He then concludes this awesome address to the church in Philadelphia by announcing several precious promises of coming rewards for their faithfulness. He tells them to hold fast so that no one takes their crown and promises that he who overcomes He will make a pillar in the temple of God! Wow, John, yes, we must, in my understanding, give Philadelphia an 'A-' grade, slightly below Smyrna, yet still a great evaluation from Jesus Himself."

"Markus, it is amazing to me that you can use the things you learned in your Roman education and apply them to this Christ-sent revelation! Please continue; I'm eager to see who you place at number three in your grading!"

"Yes, John; well, in my opinion, that would have to be the church in Ephesus! Jesus is quick to commend the Ephesian church for some very powerful things that they were doing right! It is hard for me to understand how, but they had some people who were claiming to be apostles but, however, were not true apostles. Perhaps they were just trying to build up a name for themselves. Only God the Holy Ghost knows for sure, but Jesus reports that they had proven themselves to be liars and that the Ephesian elders had exposed them for that. He also commends them for bearing long in patience and that, for His name's sake, they have labored and have not fainted. However, John, Jesus, like any good teacher, also slaps the back of their hand with His righteous measuring ruler by telling them that they have left 'Him' their first love in intimate closeness to His heart and leading. In a way, Jesus is warning them that they are becoming like His most vehement enemies, the self-righteous of the scribes and the Pharisees. They are becoming religious in practice when they once were primarily religious in relationship! Just as every generation in biblical history has moved over time in maturation, not all wine grows sweet with age, especially if the air of this world is allowed to leak in around the bottleneck's cork that seals it!"

"Markus, only God the Holy Spirit could be revealing these things to you as you have read the scrolls I wrote while caught up in the Spirit!"

"Yes, John, my life took a huge spiritual jump when you first led me to find faith in Jesus as my Lord and Savior, then another huge and, in some ways, bigger jump forward as far as perceiving spiritual truth when you led me to the baptism that John the Baptist told about, that when Jesus came, He would baptize people in the baptism in the Holy Ghost and fire! Since being baptized in the Holy Spirit and fire, the deeper things of God are much clearer to me!"

"Yes, Markus, that was a few months later, but I could tell that you were ready and wanting to receive all that God had available to you!"

"Well, John, Jesus concludes His warning of the Ephesians by calling them to repent and do the first works, which was to restore their personal relationship with Him, 'or else'! Now, in the world of Roman soldiers and formerly gladiators where I come from, when someone says that you had better do something 'or else,' it's quite clear that you do not want to ignore the warning to find out what the 'or else' entails! In this case, Jesus warns them that He will remove their candlestick! I'm sure through the years, for their own convenience, many will interpret this metaphor in a way that will soothe their wayward consciences. However, I would not want Jesus to ever remove my candlestick from heaven, no matter what it represents! John, as you continue to pray for me, will you please pray that I will never ever let my relationship and love for Jesus grow cold and that I permit God to add to my life whatever it takes to keep me on my knees before Him?"

"Yes, Markus, I surely will. And, Markus, I would ask that you pray the same prayer for me!"

"John, you? Well, you are an apostle, and you would never need such a prayer; why you are one of the—"

"Markus, stop! I am only a man like any other, yes, having the highly rare and special privilege of being one of the Master's chosen twelve, yet needing the power of His Holy Spirit through prayer and must remember to keep my own relationship and 'first love' alive and fresh daily like anyone else! So, what grade, Markus, would you give the Ephesian church?"

"Well, Jesus identifies one more positive factor before concluding His evaluation. He mentions that they hate the deeds of the Nicolaitans. Just what was that, John? I am not familiar with this sect."

"Markus, the Nicolaitans taught that your body could be sinful as long as your spirit was clean before God. It was a twisting of truth to form a lie, and what it did was provide a justification in people's thinking about practicing sex outside of marriage and other immoral sexual acts, one of which was so evil in God's eyes that it caused His fiery judgment and wrath to be poured out on two cities during the time of Abraham. Markus, Markus! Oh, that people would search the scriptures to find out what truly blesses the Father and also the things that are so evil that they bring His righteous judgment to fall. As Jesus so frequently taught, men might know the truth, and then the truth would set them free!"

"Amen, amen, John. Well, the last good thing that the Ephesians were doing was obviously because they studied the sacred writings of the prophets of old! They hated not only the teachings of the Nicolaitans but also the immoral deeds that this false doctrine taught. They could not be in the 'A' category because of the wrongs they were doing, but they did have many right things. I would give them a 'B' grade in the grading order of the churches in Asia that Jesus spoke to you about, John!"

In the middle of John and Markus having this discussion, Windrose steps up and pauses the omniciscreen in order to address the souls. He can tell by their facial expressions that they are troubled by what they are hearing and that it just wasn't making sense to them.

"Souls, you must realize something that you will hear John address shortly in his discussion with Markus. Paul will one day write as he also will address one of these churches in his letter to the Ephesians, actually years before John wrote the Revelation, that in speaking of Jesus, 'And He Himself gave some to be apostles, some prophets, some evangelists, and some pastors and teachers, for the equipping of the saints for the work of the ministry, for the edifying of the body of Christ.'"[107]

With that, the souls seem to relax back in their seats, and you could hear a solemn "oh" go through the arena, with many "amens" and affirmations of thanksgivings and words of praise to God, who always does all things well.

Windrose approaches the omniciscreen again and says, "Now, let's go right back into this conversation," and takes them back into John and Markus's discussion.

"Markus, you have to understand something about God's people throughout history. They have always had to have a prophetic voice to keep calling them back to the place that they need to be in God. Even though God's plan is to send His most precious possession, His own Son, as the greatest act of love that He has ever shown towards His creation, that you would think would have everyone continually thanking Him, worshipping Him, and seeking Him and His will for their lives for all of their lives, man's sinful nature still sadly allows himself to backslide into a spiritual slumber. The Apostle Paul will one day write to the Ephesian church, one of the churches that Jesus just addressed in these seven churches we are discussing."

The souls listen as Markus continues his evaluation in order by grade, scoring the seven Asian churches.

"Then, John, Jesus concludes His evaluation of the Ephesian church with a rare and unique promise: 'He who has an ear, let him hear what the Spirit says to the churches. To him who overcomes I will give to eat from the tree of life, which is in the midst of the Paradise of God,'[108] promising to restore what was lost in the Garden of Eden, which, of course, is eternal life!

"Then, based on everything that I can read here, the church of Pergamos comes in at fourth place in a grading order. Jesus did acknowledge the fact that they had a large potential of difficulty there because they lived where Satan's seat was. He tells them that He sees the fact that the persecution against them was so great that a man named Antipas was martyred there. In spite of the fact that it's obvious that some were willing to die for Him, sadly, others were permitting the doctrine of Balaam to be taught there. I can remember in studying foreign religions classes that Baal worship was essentially the worship of earthly gain or getting wealth through corrupt means. Wasn't there an Old Testament prophet named Balaam who was chastised by God?"

"Yes, Markus, Jesus not only taught the purest form of godliness but modeled it with His lifestyle of daily trusting God in every area of His life. Doctrine that promotes things that contradict what Jesus taught and lived, however good it may sound to the flesh of the hearers in any church, is a great abomination to Him. You are correct in your memories of your Roman studies."

"Thank you, John. Jesus specifies that the church at Pergamos also taught that it was acceptable to eat meat that had been sacrificed to idols and to commit fornication. Again, He repeats the 'repent or else' phrase, but this time, He says He will come and fight with the sword of His mouth! John, this should put the church in a place of holy fear of judgment because just as Jesus pronounced judgment of the temple, everyone throughout this whole region knows that it was destroyed by our army seventy years after Jesus prophesied it! What Jesus says with the sword of His mouth happens exactly as He says that it will!

"It seems to me, John, that Pergamos had too much of the world and its philosophies in it to be able to truly know God's sweet presence in their every service. I had a captain in my soldier training who would chastise the men by telling them that they had too much of the easy life of Rome to be a good soldier and too much of the pains of battle to ever be a normal Roman again. I believe that these so-called believers at Pergamos had too much of the world to enjoy God and too much of God to be able to do the things of the world any longer with a clear conscience! Jesus goes on to say that they also had another doctrine of the Nicolaitans, which, if I remember this correctly from class, taught that the spirit could be clean even if the flesh was dirty. I guess that is how they justified their having sexual activity outside of the covenant of marriage?"

"Yes," John replied, "there is a sifting process that takes place with every believer, and it started back to Adam and Eve. In this wonderful period of time, believers are extended a great level of grace never before given to mankind through the death, burial, and resurrection of the Lord Jesus Christ. God offering His only Son provides all of mankind the opportunity to not only be saved from their sins through faith but every believer is given the opportunity to be baptized or totally immersed in the Holy Spirit to help them have the power to overcome the temptations of the world and the lusts thereof. Sadly, even with all of this, there will always be some who try to form corrupt teachings that originate in the plans of demons as humans seek them and deceitfully soothe their consciences. However, these false teachings can ultimately send them to eternal destruction that was originally prepared for the devil and his angels!"

"Well, John, with this, I give Pergamos a grade of a 'C-.' I pray that no man or woman will ever, ever place this church in a position as an average church because it is in a middle placement, but somehow that is what I fear will happen!"

"Markus, once again, you appear to be wise beyond your years. I know that God has a powerful ministry for you one day throughout Rome!"

"John, that takes us to the church at Sardis. It appears that as churches slide back away from the Lord, they slide fast. Although Sardis apparently was once a recognized name that did have some life, Jesus now declares that it is a dead church! He says that He knows their works but that their works are not perfect before God. John, it sounds like a church that does things for God but does not seek Him in prayer to know what He wants, so they are not doing things 'with' God! Such a church cannot bear good fruit because whatever has built up its membership has been man-made and earthly-focused and not God-inspired and eternally focused! Jesus tells them to remember what they learned in the past. It's obvious, John, that at one time, they did know how to do things right! Like so many, they allowed the world to creep in! He tells them to hold fast and to repent. If they do not watch, He warns that He will come on them like a thief. Here again, we see the 'or else' type warning. He concludes by complimenting a few of their congregants and gives them a wonderful promise for their redemption, and as with every church, He concludes, 'He who has an ear, let him hear...' In other words, if you really care, you will listen to what I am telling you! The church at Sardis is mostly a dead church, with just a few in it who were truly seeking their God! For the little life left, I give them a 'D.'

"Thyratira, it's better for you that you place here and not last in the seven churches, although not by much! John, I know the prophets of old spoke very strongly, and Jesus, when it comes to exposing evil and warning of different levels of evil, does not pull any punches either. He quickly establishes His authority, declaring, 'These things says the Son of God, who has eyes like a flame of fire, and His feet like fine brass.'[109] He says, 'Thyatira, I see all that you are doing. I see your works (that are good when they are led by the Holy Spirit); I know your works, love, service, faith, and your patience; and as for your works, the last are more than the first.'[110] John, there is something here that I feel the Spirit of God is speaking to my heart, and it has to be by illumination and not by perception because most of my Christian growth has been here on this island with you. I mean, it's not like I have been a part of any church. But do people sometimes try to cover up their sinful practices with religious works? I mean, here, Jesus is clearly commending them for several things. Somehow, their last works were better than their first. Could it be that their first works were something they did to cover up something that they shouldn't have been doing? We know that good works are works that are inspired directly by God. I'm guessing that over time, they learned to be eternally fruitful by spending time in prayer, seeking direction for every step that they took. Therefore, their latter works were more pleasing to God."

"I think that is a very good point, Markus, and very much a possibility. Consider this seductress, for instance, who Jesus says is the strongest threat. Maybe she was an attractive class teacher or a music leader. It's very possible young men wanted to be part of her class or music lessons to get close to her. It's also possible that she used this opportunity to seduce these young men. Evil, Markus, can take on many forms and wears many faces. To be sure, in this case, Jesus said that she 'called herself a prophetess' and that she was teaching 'His' servants to have physical intimacy outside of marriage, most likely with her! There is one thing for sure, and that is it's easy to see His intense anger concerning this activity."

"I know in the military training, John, it was driven home to our understanding that these areas of weakness in soldiers could and would lead them to be vulnerable and easy prey for a seductress working for the opposing army. I'm sure Jesus knows the destructive power of sin, and that is why He speaks so strongly against its practices, especially against someone who is teaching that something like fornication is okay for a believer. Thyatira gets an ugly 'D-' but is also given the chance to repent, as Jesus concludes by saying to them, 'He who has an ear, let him hear what the Spirit says to the churches!'

"Then, John, Laodicea was last on the list of seven. It seems as if they should represent a list of what not to do as a church because Jesus had absolutely nothing good to say about this church! John, I believe that people should put their whole heart into whatever it is that they do. Especially if they are being observed by their leader. I know that we, as gladiators, would have this man thing, and I believe it is true with almost all men. Each one tries to outperform the other. I am in no way implying that such a competitive spirit should exist among Christians, but I only draw attention to the fact that we should do our best, especially when we know our overseer is watching! The manager and trainer of our gladiator training was known as the Lanista. We were trained to perform our best, fight our hardest, and endure the mental stress and the fatigue of the Colosseum, and we did so, especially when we knew he was watching. If anything, once I was promoted to become a Roman centurion soldier, we were taught to fight as if all of Rome or the emperor himself was watching at all times. Sadly, John, it almost seems as if the Laodicean church is living their lives like no one is watching, in spite of the fact that we see here that the King of kings is watching everything they do! He starts by establishing just who it is that *is* watching!

"John, I just have to quote to you the whole thing, even though I know you were inspired to write it; every word is so very important! I then want to point to key righteous judgments by our Lord! 'And to the angel of the church of the Laodiceans write, "These things say the Amen, the Faithful and True Witness, the Beginning of the creation of God."'[111] John, Jesus here is powerfully declaring who He is! He is saying, 'Yes, I am watching you, Laodicea, and all the churches for that matter. *I am the true witness to the beginning of the creation of God!' Wow!* Now, if I were a member of that church, *that* would get my attention! It seems that Jesus spoke the strongest about His authority to this church than any of the others!

> *"I know your works, that you are neither cold nor hot. I could wish you were cold or hot. So then, because you are lukewarm, and neither cold nor hot, I will vomit you out of My mouth. Because you say, 'I am rich, have become wealthy, and have need of nothing'— and do not know that you are wretched, miserable, poor, blind, and naked."[112]*

"Even though, John, Jesus is saying in a very plain way, 'Laodicea, you make Me sick,' yet out of His amazing eternal love, He offers them the solution to get it right!

> *"I counsel you to buy from Me gold refined in the fire, that you may be rich; and white garments, that you may be clothed, that the shame of your nakedness may not be revealed; and anoint your eyes with eye salve, that you may see. As many as I love, I rebuke*

and chasten. Therefore, be zealous and repent. Behold, I stand at the door and knock. If anyone hears My voice and opens the door, I will come into him and dine with him, and he with Me. To him who overcomes I will grant to sit with Me on My throne, as I also overcame and sat down with My Father on His throne.

"He who has an ear, let him hear what the Spirit says to the churches."[113]

"Then, once again, and for all of eternity, He says to all who will desire His will, '*He who has an ear, let him hear what the Spirit says to the churches*'!"

"Yes, Markus, yes, that is the most incredible thing about walking with Jesus every day for over three and a half years. It was His unmerited favor that He showed everyone all of the time! *He is Love!*"

With that, Windrose approaches the omniciscreen, laughing and dancing and spinning around and around, praising God, which the souls realize is more expressive than anything that they have ever seen him do before.

"*Praise God! All praise be to God! God is good; God is so good,*" Windrose shouts. "Curl your toes over the edge of your sandals, tighten your robe ropes, and get ready for the most exciting journey in the omniciscreen you have ever been on! God the Father is about to unveil it all to you. You will be changed for all of eternity, for the good of all mankind, for the good of every person that you will ever know, and for the ministries that God has for you all, and to completely undermine all the schemes of the evil one turning all things, even his wicked things, around for the eternal good! *Praise You, Father! All my love and thanksgiving extends towards You today and forever more!*"

CHAPTER 14

THE GATHERING

Windrose was still trying to maintain the pose that he assumed after his obvious celebration of something that the souls were still trying to figure out. The puzzled looks on their faces reinforced to him that he needed to give them some sort of explanation, but without taking away from the joy that he wanted them to feel in the moment that they would see what he knew was all about to come together!

"Souls, today we are taking a trip way into the distant future on a very special Christmas Day. It will be the day that people will celebrate Christ's birth as a baby on the earth for centuries of time. This particular Christmas Day, however, will have its own level of importance. In a way, it will combine many of the events relating to the salvation of mankind on the earth. That is why the year that we are traveling to cannot be known at this moment, even by me. Only the Father knows this year and day. Still, He is allowing us to visibly travel there because the seed sown in your heart today will have such a stirring impact that it will compel you, although not always knowing why in the moment, to prepare yourselves and others for this wonderful future gathering!"

As the omniciscreen opens, it reveals eckons of time into the future, causing the souls to gasp with delight. One of the souls says, "What is that over there? I hear a lot of shouting praises unto God, and people are coming and going out of that room with huge expressions of joy!"

Windrose responds, "Oh, that is the omniciscreen that is in heaven, where people go and visibly look back in time of all the things that the Father did for them that they never knew! Sometimes, it was when they were the most discouraged or the most worried and thought perhaps their prayers had gone unanswered! In heaven, God the Father will have endless ways of revealing the multiple times that just like any good parent, He did things for His children that they knew nothing about!"

Once again, the souls shouted with cheers of praise and thanksgiving at the unfathomable riches of God! They realize that they are looking into the city of New Jerusalem in the kingdom of heaven. It was just as beautiful as the areas that they had seen before, yet somehow even more beautiful than they remembered. What struck them as clearly different was the fact that there were people standing around in every direction, appearing to be waiting for something or someone. From time to time, someone standing there would ask, "Can you see anyone coming yet?" Or "Has the Father given any hints yet as to what is going to happen today?" Some respond, saying, "No," or "Not that I have heard about!" Everyone there seems to be talking with someone or asking each other about this upcoming event that they, as the citizens of heaven, have been invited to.

All at once, music begins to play softly at first. It is worship music, and for good reason, as the Father and the Holy Spirit then appear together in the central court. Some of the people who are waiting in great anticipation have already been living there in heaven for eckons of time. All have been informed that Jesus will be joining them later for His part of the *gathering*. He has not yet arrived because He has some preparation that needs to be done. Everyone there is, of course, also familiar with the Holy Spirit. For the sake of this coming together that day, the Father has allowed the Holy Spirit to be visible to everyone in attendance. Because the Father, the Son, and the Holy Spirit are all God, and each One is also God, their visible size is variable depending on which manifestation they are portraying. For today's *gathering*, the Father, and also the Son, when He arrives, will be the same size as all of the human souls gathered there. The Holy Spirit would appear slightly larger as He moves in and around and through the crowds of people. His presence would only accentuate the heavenly atmosphere and in no way be overbearing or over-expressive. As a flame to a candlewick or a gentle sparkle of a star, He would just be as He always is: wonderfully, beautifully, and heavenly expressive of God's majesty!

Windrose pauses the omniciscreen for a moment while addressing the souls concerning this once-in-all event of eternity.

"Souls, it is going to take great restraint to contain yourselves during every part of what you are going to witness here on this journey. I fully understand that you are going to be at a maximum expressional disposition because every part of this experience will thrill every part of your emotional makeup. If every part of the universe were filled with stars that you knew by name and you had a favorite star out of all of those stars, you would see that star today. If every sunset that you could ever experience could have a name, and you had a favorite sunset, you would see that sunset today. If every waterfall God created on earth had a name and you had a favorite waterfall, you would see that waterfall today. Therefore, it is only natural that your internal person, the very fiber and the center of your being as souls, the utmost laughter, the utmost joy, the utmost love, and the uttermost exemplifying of all of those things are in some cases all going to want to come spilling out of you all at once!"

With that series of statements, the souls all just look at each other in total amazement, yet bright, sparkling heavenly-type smiles cover everyone's faces because they know that whatever Windrose just described is going to be awesome! They know that, somehow, they are going to have to contain themselves so that they will not be a distraction to others. They also know that the most important thing that needs to take place that day is that God is the One who needs to be glorified!

"Souls, just to prepare you, you are about to see the Father speak to what the scripture will one day call 'The great cloud of witnesses.' It refers to all the people who are already in heaven. As God allows, they will view eternally important events that are taking place down on earth. The Father is going to address them all concerning who they are and what they are about to see. May He be glorified as He introduces the 'who's who' of heaven! Again, try to maintain calm composure because, as said before, this is going to be very exciting!

"Let's go back now to the omniciscreen and pan in on what is taking place on this special day called '*the gathering*.'"

"*Hello, everyone!* Greetings to you on this very, very special day in heaven's history! We are all going to see, and some of us, for the first time, key *eternalgens*, which is a heavenly word that describes the citizens of heaven once they permanently arrive here. I believe our first couple is waiting behind those shining white curtains to my right. This precious couple was My first created beings. Adam and Eve, would you step out and receive everyone's warm applause today?

"My first Adam! Adam, *ha-ha*," greeted with the Father's holy laughter, "is joined today by His lovely bride, Eve. Gentlemen, please hold your gasps of expression in the recognition of her beauty. Yes, I made Adam's bride look very gorgeous, as Adam is a very handsome man. Everyone here is familiar with their story, or you would not be here! Yet with My great mercy and grace, with their repentant hearts, I have forgiven both of their transgressions so that mankind can follow a future pathway to forgiveness. Remember, everyone, it was by their failure that My great prophetic declaration came forth, that with Eve's seed's heel, I would bruise the serpent's head! I had to create mankind with a free will, of course, or they could not have chosen with that free will to love Me and serve Me. I could have made automatons that could be simply programmed to do exactly as I desired, mechanical beings with no thinking process, no feelings, or desires. But how, then, would that be love? I had to create a godlike creature who could love but with that also have the capacity to not love or even to hate, a capacity to heal but also a capacity to hurt, a capacity to give but also with a capacity to steal, a capacity to work hard but also a capacity to be lazy, a capacity to serve others but also a capacity to be self-serving, a capacity to live for others' benefit but also a capacity to live only for their benefit, a capacity to understand sacrifice and to have it motivate them to make great sacrifices, but also a capacity to recognize sacrifice yet reject the desire to make sacrifices themselves for others. This platform of all of Earth's existence is a proving ground for true love and true faith. It separates the wheat from the chaff, the good from the bad, and those who embrace light rather than follow evil.

Because of my eternal love, I will offer to all mankind the gift of eternal life through the perfect sacrifice of perfect love demonstrated by My only-begotten Son, Jesus Christ. Those truly open in heart to receive that gift, either through immediate or prolonged revelation, will, by that gift, inherit eternal life, as have those who are here with us together today. Those who reject it will, very sadly, spend eternity with the one who I also created, the one who rejected it because he thought that he could overthrow Me and My kingdom. I created a place of eternal judgment for the devil and his angels in another place called hell! Those who reject My gift of salvation and the great sacrifice that My Son, Jesus Christ, made not only on the cross but throughout His whole life will also spend eternity in the place called hell."

Windrose, at that point, chooses to pause the omniciscreen to allow the souls to spend some time contemplating the complexity of the truth that they just heard the Father declare. "Souls, through heaven's vision, everything, and I mean everything you will ever do, see, feel, touch, or have, has to do with eternity. As long as you keep eternity as your main focus, keeping the main thing as the main thing, it will keep you lined up with God the Father's holiness and His plan for His creation. Once you become humans and start to live out your lives, should you choose to focus on temporal, earthly, and worldly things, your life will become filled with the potential for discouragement and disappointment. One day, a man named King Solomon will pen the words, 'The fear of the LORD is the beginning of wisdom.'[114] Having God and His eternal plan and time clock at the center of your everyday lives is what the fear of God is! Accepting that He always knows what is and will be best for your lives right up until what He decides is the end of life for you is the attitude that will bring you the greatest peace. It will also give you the greatest ability to thank Him for everything that comes your way in life. You will not remember this specific trip into heaven or these wise words of the Father; however, they will come back to you through His Word as you read it every day. One day, you will be allowed to ask the Holy Spirit to fill you, and, should you decide to say yes, even more of the revelation of God and His spiritual realm and truth will be accessible to you. Now we will return to the future and back to the very special day in heaven called '*the gathering*'!"

As the omniciscreen comes back on, Adam and Eve are making their way past the crowds who are cheering them, shaking their hands, and giving hugs as time allows. The Father once again approaches His speaking platform. His voice is not loud but is nevertheless powerful. Everyone can clearly hear every word that He says as He begins to speak once again.

"Next on today's list of special guests for *the gathering* will be another famous person and his family. Noah, would you please bring your wife and three sons, Shem, Ham, and Japheth, and come out and greet the people today?"

As Noah and his family come through the shining white curtain, heaven is filled with applause and worship and praise to God for His beautiful plans to save mankind.

"People of heaven, this is the man I chose for one of the hardest tasks that anyone ever undertook on earth in all of human history. As much as I show My creation My love and teach them the importance of spiritual things, generation after generation tends to allow the temporal things of this life to draw them into the sinful ways of those who do not know Me. The riches of this world can never compare to the eternal riches of heaven. The ability to live forever and ever millions of years without end in a golden city that has no more sickness, no more pain, no more tears, and no more sorrow lacks earthly words to describe its value. Yet for far too many, even after they have tasted heavenly gifts and experienced *My* reality, they trade in momentary pleasure for eternal bliss. Sin grows like an unchecked cancer, spreading all around just as it did in the days of Noah.

"My creation followed Adam and Eve, even though I set down a pattern for the sacrifice for sin and showed both My forgiveness and love. Although I then showed My ability as their Heavenly Father to deal with them as children, both to bless obedience and to discipline sin and wickedness, they continued to grow more wicked on the earth. I knew that I had no other option but to pour out My wrath and destroy the earth with a flood and start over again with a new godly line through Noah's family.

"Noah, say hello to the heaven's family today, and please explain why your beard is so long that it almost touches the ground!"

With that, all the citizens of heaven begin to laugh and nod their heads yes, indicating that they would like to know why.

"Ah, my sons used to pick on me, and if I did not cut my beard more often, I would have to start wrapping it around my waist. I would tell them that I was saving it up in case we ever had to use it to weave a rope to tie up an unruly goat!"

With that, Noah starts laughing, and so does all of heaven, joining in at Noah's wonderful sense of humor!

Shem speaks up and adds, "Father, don't you wish that all we had to worry about was a single unruly goat?"

"Yes, yes, when momma elephant got upset, it rocked the whole boat!"

With that, all of heaven starts laughing again, including the angels, the Father, and the Holy Spirit! Heaven is such a place of joy that when one of the well-known Bible characters tells a funny story, it sparks laughter that is already present within everyone's heart.

Noah then adds, "However, thanks be to God that we made it through every day in spite of any and every problem that the animals and we, the passengers, had along the way."

The Father then speaks up and asks Noah a question. "Noah, I am sure everyone here would love to ask you what the most difficult thing you encountered was from the time you started building the ark until the very last day when the waters subsided and you found yourself on dry ground."

Noah's head drops, and he says, "Well, I do not even have to think about that answer, for it haunts me to this day. The one thing that I am sure of is that God designs a life for us in which we need Him. He does that because He understands the necessity for us to stay close to Him. Without Him, I could have never endured the experience I am about to mention. The most difficult thing for me was that the day it began to rain, and the door was shut, all of the people that I had been preaching God's righteousness to all of those years had refused to come inside when they had the chance. My heart was so saddened, even though my whole family and all of those animals were saved! Thankfully, God's peace though came so warmly and comforted my heart. I knew that He, too, shared my sorrow and my heartache over all of these lost people whom He had created, just as He had the animals."

"And that, Noah," the Father replied, "was why I chose you, son, a simple vineyard dresser, because I knew your heart and that you would pray for My strength, obey My leadings, and also feel the same sadness I feel whenever a single person is lost for all of eternity! What is so sad is that even though I make a way to escape, just as I did with the flood, many choose not to follow it!"

With that, all of heaven explodes into praise to God and celebration of His goodness and love for all of mankind.

"Noah, thank you and your wife and dear family for being faithful for all of those years to My heavenly calling and for saving the population of planet Earth. I'm sure as you walk among the people over the next few thousand years, many will love to sit down with you and have you tell them the stories surrounding the building of such a massive vessel and your experiences with all of the animals.

"Now, next for today's *gathering*, a person that I'm sure you are all familiar with, Abraham, and his dear wife, Sarah, will you please come out and greet all of heaven this Christmas morning?"

With that, Abraham and his lovely wife come from behind the shining white curtain, and thunderous applause echoes through the streets of the golden city. Sarah and Abraham emerge holding hands and wave to everyone, smiling from ear to ear.

"Abraham," the Father says, "come and greet the people who spent their lifetime reading about your marvelous journey with your dear wife and the difficult calling I called you both to. Your life is similar to every life I fashion; it was designed to need Me to make it through. Your precious Sarah, although she had her doubts, prayed and prayed for you, Abraham, and endured more than almost any wife who ever lived through the many trials and years that you both had to wait to see my promises fulfilled. Come now, both of you. Know that you can speak freely, as the eternalgens long to hear from your hearts."

Abraham starts to encourage Sarah to go first; however, she insists that he does.

"Dear eternalgens, forever citizens of this beautiful golden city, where there will be no more sickness, no more sorrow, and no more tears, it is my delight to have the opportunity to speak with you today. I must say right from the beginning that God truly chose a nobody from the land of the Chaldeans when He appeared to me in Mesopotamia in His shining white glory. As Noah already stated, I wholeheartedly agree that the Father creates for us a life in which we need Him. God truly wants to take the finest diamond, the purest gold, and the finest silver and place it inside a vessel of plain clay when He chooses to use someone. He is that diamond, that gold, and that silver that He places inside us through His Holy Spirit. Each piece has a bright and glorious light that shines forth from it, all to make an ordinary man glow with His brightness over time as He works Himself in and through and out of us into the lives of those around us. To Him be all the glory for His wondrous works!

"I also was guilty of a lot of doubting God through those many years of waiting for His promise to be fulfilled. Sarah, who I so dearly love, with her tender heart, had to endure so many hardships, including believing with me for the fulfillment of the Father's promises. Through it all, she remained faithful to me and even allowed her own heart to be broken, trying to give me a son through her handmaiden, Hagar. How I prayed for another way, and I'm sure that I was much too easily swayed to take Hagar to conceive Ishmael, and yet even in that, God promised to build a great nation of twelve leaders from him. God is such a merciful God as Adam, Eve, and Noah have all demonstrated through their lives in that as they endeavored to live for Him even in their mistakes, which were often in response to evil Lucifer's temptations, the Father turned them around and made something good in the end!"

"Thank you, Abraham. While man looks on the outward appearance, I look on the heart. I chose you from before the foundation of the world because

I knew your heart through My foreknowledge. I knew that through every difficulty, even though you often doubted Me and at some times were even frustrated with Me and My plan, you would bring it to Me in prayer. Then I could guide you, and the mission I had designed for you to be the earthly father of the Jewish people would be fulfilled. Sarah, now it's your turn. What would you say today to all the eternalgens in heaven this morning, especially to all of the women who are called to stand faithfully behind their husband's calling and ministry while on the earth?"

"Good morning and blessed Christmas morning indeed to all my fellow eternalgens in this wonderful golden city! Ladies who are here this morning and who have stood faithfully beside your husbands through thick and thin, I think today that we all know what our shared secret was. It was prayer! Praying for our husbands as it is impossible to stay mad for very long at someone that you are truly praying for," Sarah says as she laughs!

With that, all of the ladies of heaven and some of the men as well joined in hilarious laughter and giggling, as they knew exactly what Sarah was referring to.

"God's ways are certainly higher than our ways, and His thoughts are not our thoughts. As my dear Abraham said, God has designed us to need Him in this life and calling. We all remember those days when the soup pot of our anger was boiling over inside, but we took it to God in prayer. During that prayer time, He touched us with His grace and whispered a word of understanding to our hearts with His still, small voice that kept us loving our husbands and standing with them."

With Sarah's statements, a great amount of applause echoes all through heaven. The ladies all stand to their feet in a standing ovation to honor the person whom they considered the mother of the Jewish people.

So, with that, the Heavenly Father says, "As I know, you and Abraham have been chatting back behind the shining white curtain before you came out. Isaac, would you please come out and join your mother and father and speak for a moment to all of the eternalgens of heaven this morning?"

As Isaac walks out, God does something amazing. Isaac walks out as a teenage boy, and Abraham and Sarah light up with great joy and chuckle. As he goes and stands between his mother and father, they each put an arm around him. In the next few moments, Isaac begins to transform before everyone's eyes into his adult self. The Father does that to help everyone see Isaac for what he was and then for what he became as he grew older.

"Isaac," the Father says, "come now and speak for a few minutes to heaven this morning, and then when you are ready, invite your beautiful Rebecca out to stand by your side."

"Thank You so much, Father God. I, too, stand in line with God's chosen imperfect ones because even though I was born of this wonderful godly couple, what a joy it is when we enter heaven and get to see our loved ones again. Mom, I missed you so much! I, as much as any man, had to pray and seek the mind of my Heavenly Father in everything. Even as my dad, Abraham, took me that day on that journey to Mount Moriah for that well-known sacrifice, I had many doubts along the way. I finally asked my father, 'Look, the fire and the wood, but where is the lamb for a burnt offering?' When he replied that God Himself would provide the ram, I was comforted for a moment, but when he bound my hands and my feet and laid me on the altar, I knew that, in that moment, I was the chosen sacrifice. As I closed my eyes, trusting God completely, I was flooded with His heavenly peace, and I knew that whatever plan God had was going to be all right. But please know, fellow eternalgens, I was but another man that God chose to use for His glory. Now I understand that the Father was simply displaying what one day He Himself would do by offering His only-begotten Son on that same mount for the sins of the whole world. This was the most perfect act of love the universe would ever witness!

"Rebecca, my beloved, please come out and join me by my side and greet all of heaven this morning!"

With that, all of heaven gasps as God allows Rebecca to come out in her youthful beauty, adorned with some of the jewelry that Isaacs's servant gave her when he went with her to meet her family. Just as God did with Isaac, God supernaturally matured Rebecca into the woman of God that she became as she stood by Isaacs's side in their life together.

Rebecca starts by bowing her head for a moment to gather her thoughts. Then she lifts her head and smiles and starts by saying, "Fellow eternalgens, I, too, must be quick to give God the Father all of the glory for what He was able to accomplish in our lives. I realize I was not so much of a success story as my wonderful mother-in-law, Sarah, here today; however, although not many of my life stories were recorded in God's Word, I, too, had to be a woman of prayer. I had to be dependent on God every day and fully and regularly realized what a great act of mercy it was for God to choose me, a simple servant girl who agreed to water a few camels in answer to a fleece my husband's servant had asked of the Lord. My innocence and my beauty were all gifts totally due to God's grace because, as a young woman, I had all of the struggles of any other woman in my culture. Once the Apostle Paul arrived in heaven, his writings were available to us here, a real preternatural honor that the Father allowed as we all prayed for the development of the early church. We were all informed of God's design and its creation. I love what Paul wrote in his letter to the Roman church and am so thankful to God and His Holy Spirit for allowing us who lived our lives under the old covenant days to be able to read the hearts of some of the new covenant personalities. I have memorized it by heart because it is so meaningful to me and my imperfections.

'For what I will to do, that I do not practice; but what I hate, that I do. If, then, I do what I will not to do, I agree with the law that it is good. But now, it is no longer I who do it, but sin that dwells in me. For I know that in me (that is, in my flesh) nothing good dwells; for to will is present with me, but how to perform what is good I do not find. For the good that I will to do, I do not do; but the evil I will not to do, that I practice. Now if I do what I will not to do, it is no longer I who do it, but sin that dwells in me.

'I find then a law, that evil is present with me, the one who wills to do good. For I delight in the law of God according to the inward man. But I see another law in my members, warring against the law of my mind, and bringing me into captivity to the law of sin which is in my members. O wretched man that I am! Who will deliver me from this body of death? I thank God—through Jesus Christ our Lord!'[115]

"Isaac and I just love reading the words of Paul together, as we do the rest of the apostles' writings. Jesus, Jesus, Jesus, died for the sins of us all, even those of us back to the beginning of time."

With that, Adam, Eve, Noah, his wife, Shem, Ham, Japeth, Abraham, and Sarah all shouted out with arms raised in praise, as did multitudes of other eternalgens in that moment who had lived during those days before Christ.

A very loud "*thank you!*" then echoes throughout all of heaven, which once again makes everyone laugh and praise God. As it was previously explained that Jesus was somewhere else preparing something for later in the ceremony, He wanted everyone to know that even though He was not right there, He could still hear everyone's testimonies, so it was He who voiced those loud words.

Rebecca continued, "I know that many of you are familiar with my story of showing favoritism to Jacob and deceiving Isaac as he was old and going blind. Deception is never right in God's eyes, and I have fully repented in my heart for my sins. God, in His infinite wisdom and grace, was able to turn even that around and use it for the eternal good. It humbled me, and it humbled Jacob over our whole lifetimes. God our Father is so good at using imperfect, broken vessels to do His perfect will. Although we should never plan ahead of time to sin, sometimes, with our best intentions, we fall short and make very bad choices. John, another one of Jesus's disciples, stated that 'if we confess our sins, He is faithful and just to forgive us our sins and to cleanse us from all unrighteousness.'[116]

"I stand here today with my husband, Isaac, a forgiven woman of God's handiwork, chosen by His grace to be the mother of two twins, one who would be named 'Israel' and would later father twelve sons who would become the fathers of the twelve tribes of Israel for God's glory."

As Rebecca starts laughing, in her desire to make others laugh, she says, "The way I look at it, God only needed a womb to birth a couple of babies. He just happened to pick mine! Ha-ha-ha! To God be all the glory for His excellent greatness!"

As all of heaven's eternalgens were at this point roaring with laughter and praise, the Father stepped forward laughing Himself. "Thank you, Rebecca, but believe Me, you were much more than just a womb! You worked hard raising those two boys and blessed your husband by aiding him through your years together. My love for every one of My creations goes beyond anyone's comprehension. You were not only chosen by Me; please think about this: you were designed and created by Me. Tell me, Rebecca, how much did you love those two boys the very day they were born?"

"More than life itself, Father. There are no words to describe how much I loved those baby boys!"

"You loved them because you and Isaac made them in an act of great love for each other. Then, they were a part of you for nine months. You see, when you create something, you have an affinity towards what you have created. However, when you make someone, you love them with all of you. So when they came into this world, you loved them more than words can describe. That, Rebecca, is the same way that I love you. You are not just a 'thing,' not just a 'womb' to give birth to two boys, but someone more precious than words can describe. I, too, so love all of My children and so love them that I gave My most precious gift in giving them My only-begotten Son, Jesus the Christ!"

Windrose pauses the omniciscreen for a moment, drawing all of the souls' attention to remind them of the enormous importance of this trip into the future and what a very special day it is indeed.

"Souls, as I have already told you, this opportunity to listen in on this day is a gift that you one day will remember. But you will only remember it if you indeed do make the right choices in life because if you do, *you will be there on this day*! You must accept Jesus into your hearts as your Lord and Savior when you are given the opportunity. Then, follow that decision by getting water baptized, which is not a requirement for salvation. However, by honoring John the Baptist's example, you send a powerful testimony to all those who know you. Then, of utmost importance is that you ask Jesus to baptize you in His Holy Spirit; John taught that Jesus would be the baptizer in the Holy Spirit. The Holy Spirit will give you the power to live pure and godly lives and to be able to pray with an unction that is far beyond any prayers that you could pray without Him! However, the truth is that the fact that you are here in this soul training does not and cannot buy you any special favoritism. You are merely souls with a free will yet to become humans that God has chosen for special training, but as you make the right decisions in life, one day in the future, on that Christmas Day, you will actually be here among the eternalgens enjoying *the gathering*. Now, let's go back to the omniciscreen and see who the Father is going to introduce next!"

With that, the omniciscreen zooms in again on the ginormous number of people in heaven on Christmas Day somewhere way off into the future at a date only the Father knows. The Father once again begins to speak, addressing the citizens of heaven, saying, "Next I would like to call Jacob to come out and greet the eternalgens of heaven," at which Jacob comes out, waving to the people and clapping his hands over his head and giving praise to God!

As the Father addresses Jacob, He says, "Jacob, waiting out behind that white curtain are your twelve sons with Leah and Rachel, but what comes to your mind in your journey of walking through your life in serving Me? What stands out as the most important thing you experienced or realized as you look back over your lifetime?"

"For me, yes, I can relate to what the others have testified, yet standing out the most is that no matter what you experience in life or how you try to influence other people's decisions, God is still God. There is almost an innate part of us that tries to change God! We foolishly start out in life like a small baby wanting to get their own way by pitching a tantrum, somehow imagining that we are making God afraid or somehow that by making Him angry by doing this or that, He will change our circumstances. However, just the opposite is true. He, in His infinite wisdom, ends up changing us! God indeed does design for us a life that we need Him in! Once we let go of the ropes that we are trying to turn Him around with and simply submit to His will, we finally have calmness and inner peace from our struggle. Throughout my life, I believe the story most people remember and relate to is my wrestling match with God at the river Jabbok. However, Jabbok was just a culmination of what my life had been all along. I was always trying to wrestle my way out of things with God. It was only at Jabbok that God finally showed me how easily He could win!

"But guess what, folks?" Jacob says as he starts running back and forth in front of all of the people, jumping and leaping and praising God. "In heaven, there is no more sickness or pain and no more tears, so even though I had to walk with a limp throughout my whole life on earth, here in heaven, I am whole. Here in heaven, His will is always done, just as it said in Jesus's prayer as He taught His disciples to pray, 'Thy will be done on earth, as it is in heaven'! The wrestling match is over, folks! God is completely in charge of everything said and done here."

"Yes, yes, Jacob. Indeed, My will is done here through everyone here acknowledging Me as God. Now, please invite your wives and dear family out for everyone to meet. Then, Joseph, as you come out, you will be given your own chance to speak in a bit, but I am going to introduce you and your brothers first in their youth with you wearing your coat of many colors. I want the people to see just how beautiful it was! Leah, mother of Ruben, Simeon, Levi, Judah, Issachar, and Zebulun; Bilhah, mother of Dan and Naphtali; Zilpah, mother of Gad and Asher; Rachael, mother of Joseph and Benjamin; please come out now and greet the people. In a few moments, watch My ability grow them up before your eyes, just as I did with Isaac."

As they walk out through the shiny white curtain as boys, all of heaven once again begins cheering as Joseph, wearing his coat of many colors, waves and does a three-sixty spin with a big smile, which makes everyone laugh. Then, the Father raised His hands, and they all began to mature into grown men right before everyone's eyes. However, surprisingly, Joseph's coat grows in size right along with him.

The Father comments, "Joseph, the coat your earthly father, Jacob, made you was a temporary coat. Your brothers ripped it and covered it with lamb's blood to deceive your father, Jacob. However, the blood of the Perfect Lamb, My Son, which has purchased eternal life for all who are here today, brings forgiveness for your brothers and a grace that will make that coat last forever in heaven. Wherever you walk in heaven, Joseph, I would like you to wear this coat so that people will recognize you and can stop you and ask you to tell them the story of your father's love for you." This statement brought even greater "ohs" and "awes" from the eternalgens than when they saw it with Isaac because they are watching all twelve brothers go *ᵣᵣᵣᵣᵤᵤmmph*, growing from young boys to young men, and their parents mature from their younger years into more mature parents.

The Father smiles and asks, "Is anything too hard for God?" And in response, all of heaven again breaks out in laughter.

"Leah," the Father calls rather abruptly.

"Yes, Father God?" she replies.

"I have a special gift for you today. I recognized how your adult life brought you a lot of rejection and pain. It hurt you when Jacob wanted Rachael above you. You were fully aware of your dad's manipulation on Jacob's wedding night and had to hide your tears as you knew that Jacob thought that he was coming into Rachael's bed chamber. You were a faithful daughter, so you agreed to Laban's deceptive plot. When the morning came, and Jacob realized that he had been deceived, you cried a thousand internal tears, telling yourself that over time, you would win Jacobs's love.

"Each time you had another baby boy, you gave them names that revealed hope. First, it was Reuben; you said, 'Because the LORD has looked upon my affliction; for now my husband will love me.'[117] Then it was Simeon, at which time you said, "Because the LORD has heard that I am hated, he has given me this son also.'[118] Then thirdly came Levi, and you said, 'Now this time my husband will be attached to me because I have born him three sons.'[119] You named your fourth son, Judah, saying, 'This time I will praise the Lord,'[120] hoping that would do it. With the birth of number five, Issachar, you felt I had rewarded you for giving your servant to Jacob. Right up to the end of your childbearing years, you still hoped for Jacob's love because you called your last son, Zebulun, saying, 'Now my husband will honor me, because I have borne him six sons.'[121] Yet in all of that, Leah, you still faced Rachel finally conceiving Jacob's favorite son, once again wounding your heart." *However*, God says with a loving but firm voice, "I have a special shining shawl made with a heavenly silk that has six colors, honoring your six sons in it for you to wear anywhere and everywhere you go throughout heaven for all of eternity. Red for all the blood that you shed through each childbirth, maroon for the suffering of your years of heartache. Blue for the sadness of your heart that you rebounded from each time to be a good mother, turning it into the bright blue sky. Yellow for the bright sunshine that you brought to My heart each time I saw that your inner beauty was far more beautiful than anyone's outward beauty could ever be. Green representing the prosperity of your sons, orange representing the sunrise and sunset of each and every day you did show love to Jacob in trying to get him to love you, and pink representing the mouth of that wonderful smile that smiled over and over again for the benefit of your boys and others who needed it, even though you were deeply hurting inside!"

Leah, struggling to hold back her great expression of thankfulness, is interrupted by a touch on the shoulder and a statement from the Father. "It's okay, Leah. There are indeed no tears of sorrow in heaven, but there are lots of tears of joy!"

"Okay, thank You, thank You, thank You," she says as tears begin to flow down over the beautiful, shining, multicolored shawl that the Father had just given her. She then begins to sing, "Hallelujah, hallelujah, hallelujah, hallelujah," as all of heaven joins in singing, "Hallelujah, hallelujah, hallelujah, hallelujah, hallelujah!" For several hours, heaven continues to resound with the sound of singing, worship, and praise.

At the end of that time of singing, the Father steps out and says, "There are many phrases that you will never hear in heaven: One is, 'For the sake of time!' Another is, 'Because time is limited.' Or, 'Let's move through this quickly!'" To this, everyone starts laughing and shouts countless amens in response. "Let's now invite Rachael to come up and greet the eternalgens."

As Rachel moves towards God, the Holy Spirit can be seen moving right alongside her. As she recognizes this, she smiles, and the Father says, "Rachel, you know, don't you! You know why I allowed you to see Him."

Then the Holy Spirit says, while also smiling, "Yes, because Rachel was always sort of shy about speaking to any group of people, she would always pray for courage, and You would always send Me to go with her, and today she can see My form."

As the Holy Spirit was speaking, Rachel was smiling and nodding yes, indicating that what He was saying was just exactly what she was thinking.

"Eternalgens, please know that I, too, agree with what has been declared by the others here today. Yes, God very much created a life for me that was designed to need Him. Even as Jacob fell in love with me, almost at first sight, I fell in love with him too. I was contented for all of those fourteen years before we were finally able to be married, only through the strength that God, by the Holy Spirit, can give. I longed to be with him as much as he longed to be with me! It is so wonderful how the Holy Spirit can seem like He is holding you up, I guess because He is," Rachel says while laughing and praising God, which caused all of heaven to join in the laughter and praise with her because everyone there had experienced the Holy Spirit's help themselves at different times of difficulty in their lives.

"To me, the most wonderful thing that happened once I got here to heaven was that I had the hope of seeing Benjamin again someday. My sorrowing was intense during the painful delivery and the hours surrounding my death after the delivery. All of it hit me at once. I knew that not only was I probably dying, but I could see what was happening with my body. I knew I would be saying goodbye to Jacob, Joseph, and the rest of the family, but my entry into paradise was so beautiful that I knew I would be joined soon by others that I had to leave behind. Once Jesus died on the cross for all of our sins, then delightfully, we became able to enter into this beautiful golden city forever and ever! The most wonderful part about meeting our Heavenly Father, Jesus, His only-begotten Son, and the Holy Spirit face-to-face is that we also get to see again those we love and who we had to let go of on earth when we passed. Especially special for me was seeing Benjamin, whom I died giving birth to! I saw how terribly heartbroken Jacob and my dear teenage son, Joseph, were as they knew I was in life-threatening labor. I was praying and praying for them as I was going in and out of consciousness during my suffering. Seeing them and Benjamin now every day is so wonderful! God the Father gave me the delight of watching Benjamin grow up. Not every minute of every day, of course, but during different highlights of his life, God would give me a peek into the natural realm! I'm still not sure if He does that for every mother who passes in childbirth. I only know that He did it for me and little Benjamin."

The Father then speaks up loudly but kindly, "Joseph, come on up front of your mother now. You are next! All of the eternalgens are looking forward to spending time with you so that they can discuss all of your life stories and the various adventures that you found yourself on in person."

"Coming, Father God!" Joseph replies, now humbly wearing the coat of many colors that his Heavenly Father had recreated for him.

"Joseph, say a few words to the people regarding what you have heard your forefathers and their wives say about their lives as they lived out the plans that I had for them!"

With that, Joseph bows his head for a moment as if to think about what he might say first.

Windrose takes that opportunity to pause the omniciscreen again to address the souls as they are processing huge amounts of revelation from everything they are hearing and seeing. The solemn look on their faces causes Windrose to realize that he needs to address something.

He starts by talking about a general concern that he knows will exist throughout all of mankind's history regarding what life would be like in heaven.

"There are times when on the earth folks will become concerned about whether or not they will be able to spend eternity worshipping God. The truth is that because God is such an eternal God, continually blessing people and caring for them on the earth, the conversations about God's faithfulness will continue. Thanking and worshipping God all of the time will just be something that happens naturally as everyone continually talks about the Father's faithfulness! As you are witnessing here on Christmas Day, eckons of time into the future Bible personality after Bible personality will be introduced and given a chance to share just a brief portion of their lives.

Consider the fact that all of the myriads of souls that will be saved for all of the years of earth's existence will all be greeting and talking with each other, not to mention the fact that discussions with the countless numbers of angels all of heavenly conversation in itself will be enough to kindle continuous thanksgiving, praise, and worship. The enemy of all souls will always want to keep people in doubt about the joy of heaven. There will be a reflection of earthly trust of faith, and so will there be a heavenly trust of faith. All of it forever will be by God's eternal design. Just think about that, and any concerns about worshipping for all of eternity will be laid to rest. Also, just as there will be earthy bodies with earthly needs that will be temporary, there will be heavenly bodies with heavenly eternal needs, which is impossible even by divine revelation to comprehend yet. For instance, if the Father began to equip you with knowledge concerning your ability to fly as humans, you would be stunned by even the perception of being able to fly. Jesus will not take the time to explain to the disciples when He will be here on earth how His resurrected body will be able to pass through walls with closed doors or fly up into heaven with the angels the day He ascends into heaven! You see, some matters will have to do with a heavenly faith concerning things that will have to do when you are in heaven in glorified bodies."

At that point, the arena is once again filled with nonverbal expressions of awe and splendor as all present react to information so impressive that it is outside the realm of human verbal expression.

Windrose goes on to say, "The purest form of worship between man and God has no human words. It is a melody that flows from the heart, expressing the majesty and great splendor of God! Souls, with that said, I think you are now ready to hear from one of the godliest men who has ever lived besides Jesus Christ. I am talking about Joseph, the eleventh son of Jacob. With that, Windrose lifts his index finger, and once again, the omniciscreen powers up to let them see eckons of time into the future to that very special Christmas Day!" The souls listen carefully as Joseph starts to address the eternalgens.

"Eternal citizens of heaven, what a delight it is to gather with such a distinguished group of individuals from God's planned strategic historical journey of time on the earth! One can only say after the fact that it is a pure joy when God sets aside years of someone's life for His divine purposes. I do admit that through the years of having to do without all of the things that seemingly normal people have, there were days of struggle! There were days when my faith was tested. There were times when I felt angry with God for giving me the life that He gave me. When that happens to you, however, the day will come when you realize that our wonderful, loving, gracious Heavenly Father has only been using you in that way to help thousands or perhaps millions of other people!"

Then Abraham, Sarah, Isaac, Rebecka, and families start shouting amen with Jacob and his wives and other sons, shouts that are quickly joined by all of the eternalgens! It is plain to all who had read Joseph's stories and to the eternalgens who had been allowed by God to travel through time as another unique heavenly blessing to actually be among the unseen people and witness these events take place firsthand that even as God is an eternal God and His love is beyond measure, so are the blessings that are in heaven for all of eternity for those who live there.

"Thank You, Heavenly Father, for the privilege of being chosen from before the foundations of the world in Your divine and eternal planning for mankind. Even though, Father, there were times that I doubted You, and there were times that I found myself feeling very lonely and afraid as I prayed, You were always there by Your Holy Spirit to give me the strength to make it through one more day. Sometimes, one more day was all that was needed to have one more piece of the puzzle unfold to give me hope for a better tomorrow."

"Joseph, although I knew that the sacrifice that I was calling you to make in your life was great, I also knew that I had planted deep down inside you the necessary components that would motivate you to pray and receive from Me My strength and bring you forth for the purpose of saving many lives! Down through the years, there would be another One that I would call to an even greater sacrifice, for the saving of even more lives, for the saving of those more lives, not only to keep them alive here on earth but to grant them the gift of eternal life so that it would be for the saving of many more lives eternally!"

With that, Windrose raises his hands and slowly fades out the omniciscreen view of many eckons into the future and a very special Christmas Day, a Christmas Day that the souls were also about to find out was also to allow them to meet a very special person, the most special person of all time. They do not yet realize he has been closer to them than they ever realized!

CHAPTER 15

THE LAUNCH

Windrose starts to address the souls once again as he understands that there is a lot that they are supposed to gain from seeing this gathering, and at the same time, there is a lot that they cannot fully comprehend yet. Perhaps many things that they were going to see this day they will never be able to appreciate until they have lived out much of their lives on the earth in the future. Then, with that, God, in His righteous understanding, will realize what things they are seeing they should be allowed to remember one day and what things they should not. It would never be fair to the rest of humanity, nor just in the struggle between good and evil, to equip some individuals with a great amount of spiritual revelation and others to not. Only in what He knows is a fair balance and for the good of fighting evil will He one day reveal small pieces stored away in the souls' minds at just the right time to help them make the right decisions at just the right time to accomplish His will on the earth. This will also help them to recognize good over evil and truth over deception.

"Souls, again, it is impossible for you to comprehend the significance of hearing these people's stories and recognizing the greatness of the beauty of heaven this early in your pre-physical conception. You can see what you are being allowed to see and understand what you are being allowed to understand. There is a part of something that can and hopefully will be one of the main things that you practice when you are born and raised on the earth. It's called faith. In the future, when the scripture is written down, it will be a book of sixty-six different books compiled by many different authors. It will be divided one day by what they will call the Old and the New Testaments, which technically means the Old and the New Covenants between God the Father and mankind. In the Old Testament, the word 'trust' is used often, but the word 'faith' is introduced in the New Testament. The point of interest here is that they are similar words that mean almost the same thing. To have faith in God is to have complete trust in Him. Souls, I say all of that to draw you to the fact that in everything you are doing and seeing, what is most important is that you trust in God or have faith that whatever He does or is doing is for your 'eternal' good! Not only for your good but for the eternal good of all those He loves and that you love around you.

"Therefore, souls, as you are meeting all of these wonderful Bible characters and hearing pieces of their life stories, simply try to trust that God knows that it is for your good and for the good of those you will know and love in your life's future. If God allows you to, remember this during times of questioning circumstances, which every believer has. If you put the word 'eternal' each time you are asking if something is good, it will help you sort things out. Although what you are going through may be difficult temporarily, it will be that it will have eternal gain."

Liling-97 speaks out and says, "Windrose, is there a reason why God does not just implant within our minds the entire writings of the Bible so that we might have a better understanding of what we are seeing and hearing from all of these characters?"

"Liling, I see that God's intuitive wisdom is already working in you, and you do not have your human body yet! Think of it this way. The Bible will be known as the 'Word of God,' and it will be a precious gift given to all of mankind. It will one day be the most published book in the whole world for many decades. What God the Father expects is that as an act of mankind's free will, if they have any interest in knowing about God or knowing Him personally, they will obtain a copy and read it for themselves. Liling, if all the souls had the Bible implanted or what will one day be called downloaded into their minds, that would not be fair to the rest of humanity that had to find it and read it on their own, would it?"

"No," Liling says. "And yes, that does sound like common sense."

With that, all of the souls acknowledged that they agreed with Liling, and Windrose proceeded to point back to the omniciscreen.

"Souls, we are now going to listen to Joseph share an intimate conversation that will never be written down as many private talks between father and son or father and daughter are done. Pay close attention because, hopefully, it will one day soak into your inner consciousness if it is God's will to do so to help you understand His love for all mankind. Jesus will one day teach through John's Revelation that to him who overcomes, He will give to eat of the hidden manna, and God, in His giving of precious gifts to those who love Him in precious ways, does reveal some things to some people that are not revealed to others. Hopefully, souls, for each of you that you might love the Lord your God with all your heart, mind, soul, and strength, you might discover the hidden manna that will fall on your lives from heaven."

With that, the omniciscreen lights up again, exploding with the splendor of the heavenly city and the multitudes of eternalgens in the middle of applauding God's plan through Jacobs's sons and setting in place the foundations for the twelve tribes of Israel. Joseph begins once again to speak.

"There are precious things that are shared in all of our lives between ourselves and our parents that seem to never get written down anywhere. My father, Jacob, had lived an extremely adventurous life. He had interacted with many people as well as God's angels on a couple of occasions. Being perhaps the less masculine of the two brothers born to Isaac yet the more intuitive to human nature, his strengths seem to surround thinking about another person rather than bullying them when it came to accomplishing things important to him. His life subsequently seemed to be in and out of constant turmoil, some of which were storms of his own making.

"My father so desired that all of his sons would be able to have harmony in the family. However, if there was an area he perhaps lacked wisdom in, it was that he had such a tremendous capacity to love that it spilled over into a 'pot of stew' of life that left a bad taste in many others who tasted it. So, I think it was with my precious father. In his being a parent, he was trying to come up with an idea that he hoped would promote unity among the brothers, but instead, it created strife. His coat of many colors was a gift to me, but it produced an object of many jealousies. At my young age, I had yet to learn ways to temper others' negative feelings, and in my enthusiasm of receiving such a beautiful gift, my enthusiasm was an oil that made the flame of jealousy burn hotter. In a way, I brought my brother's wrath upon myself; however, God, in His infinite wisdom, used all things working together for good to bring me to the very pit that would eventually lead me to Potiphar's house and then providentially to the Pharaoh of Egypt. The very place where God the Father could give me favor and raise me up as second in command over Egypt and protect tens of thousands from famine, including His own Hebrew people."

Someone may have thought that it thundered that day in heaven as the great rush of thanksgiving and praise roared out from all of the eternalgens with a fully eternal revelation of the Father's awesome workings on the earth. With that, a great whooshing sound passed by the crowds, which made them all cheer. Windrose realized that though this was a regular occurrence for the eternalgens, the souls had yet to witness this taking place, so he took a minute to pause the omniciscreen and speak to them again.

"Souls, one of the awesome eternal things you will learn about the Father is that He created laughter, He created joy, He created love, He created fun, He created family, He created adventure. As a matter of fact, every positive life experience in the thousands of years of pre-creation was part of His endearing design for those He would love so much. Therefore, as a part of everyone's eternal reward, they will be able to take time to travel back to spend those wonderful moments of life that everyone longs to relive. I'm not referring to those things that are only momentary pleasures of one's physical experience but those things that everyone longs for living again for just a short season.

"That whoosh that you just heard was the 'live and love again' time capsule taking another individual, group, or family back in time to relive their most awesome moments. For some, it will be the moment that they first got saved and their eyes were opened to the Kingdom of God for the first time. For others, it will be the place they were at when they first learned of and were baptized in God's Holy Spirit. For others, it will be that hole-in-one on a golf course or that trophy fish they caught on a trip with their son. For some, it will be the moments in the ladies' room while they help their daughter get ready for their wedding or when they see their daughter accept their diploma and graduate from medical school. Because life itself is an eternal path, in reality, the options to visibly travel back in time are truly without number. However, I do not want you souls to think of it as leaving heaven for even a moment because nothing on earth will ever compare to anything in heaven once you are here. Just the same, there are moments in time that seem almost heavenly, but they are so good. The Father simply gives a supernatural 'replay' of those events for all to enjoy here. There are many, many surprises in eternity that you will only discover once you are here. Just know that the phrase 'God is good' can be rewritten millions of times throughout eternity by all of those who come here and experience His goodness. The people one day on earth will have a very limited perspective of heaven…"

All the while Joseph was speaking about him, Jacob, later named Israel by God, was standing with the other well-known personalities off to the side, nodding his head yes in agreement with everything that Joseph was saying.

"My abba Jacob, when presenting me with the coat of many colors, explained to me that he had been making the coat secretly for many months. The coat he pointed out actually had many different color tones as a representation of all of the different members of their family. He told me he knew in his heart that God was going to use me for some special and very unique calling. He was concerned there would be jealousies and strife between all of his sons, but he had planned over time to use it to teach everyone the importance of loving all people of different skin color and race. He wanted to tell over and over the story of the strife between himself and Essau, to try to teach his children to love each other despite whatever negative emotions were stirring inside of their hearts at any given season of their lives. He knew that in his tremendous capacity to love, it was obvious to all how much he had loved Rachel, and everyone knew the years that he had worked so that he could have her as wife. He also shared with me how greatly saddened he was that the whole plan that he had with the coat of many colors almost immediately created a storm of negative feelings with the other brothers and how he was in the process of trying to come up with a new plan to undo the damage that had already been done. He shared with me, with tears running down his cheeks, that he struggled with guilt that once more, although he had earnestly prayed about the idea, another one of his plans in life had seemingly failed. I know how much everyone has heard about how much my father, Jacob, loved me, but I also loved him very deeply, even though our personalities were quite different. Many times, someone's motives can be from the purest of loves, yet have the circumstances of deep sorrow." With that, Jacob and Joseph ran towards each other, jumped into each other's embrace, and wept tears of joy and love on each other's shoulders. Then they walked together to a huge huddle-like group hug with all of the members of the rest of the family!

At that point, something white began falling from the air in heaven. The souls looking on from the omniciscreen and those standing there in the golden city all started laughing and said at almost the same time, "What is it?" With that, the Father reached out both of His hands and caught some and said simply, "*Yes!*" Then He started laughing jovially. He then said as He tasted some, "Sweet like honey, sweet like My love for all My children."

Initially, no one recognized what was happening, but when introducing Moses, the Father chose to have manna fall out of the air, which sparkled in the light of God's glory like golden snowflakes.

As this began to happen, Windrose raised his hand and paused the omniciscreen and began once again to teach the souls about something that would happen in the future to the children of Israel in their wilderness experience after they were delivered out of Egyptian bondage.

"Souls, God the Father will provide everything that the children of Israel will need one day when approximately two million Jewish people in one night will be called to pack up all of their very necessary belongings and leave Egypt and head into the desert with Moses as their leader.

"Manna was the daily provision of a heaven-sent bread that God sent the children of Israel in the forty years of wandering in the wilderness. The scripture would one day teach that it was sweet to the taste of honey. The word 'manna,' literally translated, means 'what is it?' That is why it brought such laughter when the Father simply said, 'Yes!' It will be, beyond the shadow of a doubt, one of the most spectacular of all Bible miracles because it will happen every day for over forty years. It came from seemingly nowhere, yet God's creative miracle power sent it. The children of Israel would be instructed to only gather enough for one day except for the day before the Sabbath's rest. On that day each week, they were to gather enough for two days. If they tried to gather more than they needed for one day, it would spoil and stink before the next day came. The Father knew that on this Christmas celebration, which was the actual day of Christ's birth anniversary, not the traditionally celebrated one, this falling down of manna would be representative of something that He was going to do later in this ceremony. The Father's plans and timings are always perfect."

Then Moses walked through the shining curtain followed by his two wives. "Moses, throughout the past couple of thousand earth years, those standing in pulpits have declared you a miserable failure in the desert for striking that rock instead of speaking to it. In so doing, this portrays Me as a short-fused, angry, unreasonable God. However, there have been a small percentage of pulpiteers throughout history who recognized that it was all part of My plan for you to be sent into Moab's mountains so that nobody could find your burial place. Come here and stand beside Me; let's share with them a little secret about what mountain you got promoted to!"

With that, Moses smiled from ear to ear, walking with a large once wooden staff that was now pure white ivory and glowing brightly with the glory of God, which illuminated all of heaven. The Father, lovingly laughing, put His arm around Moses, and, filled with heavenly joy, Moses joined Him in laughing about something that they both knew had happened several thousand earth years earlier. The crowds of eternalgens burst forth with thanksgiving and praise unto God, applauding the man Moses as one woman commented, "He does not look anything like Charleston Heston!" This made thousands laugh hilariously. However, many had no idea to whom she was referring.

"Tell them, Moses, what mountain most Bible teachers forget that you were promoted to from your wilderness wanderings for over forty years and your rebellious yes, but not unforgivable striking of that rock with your staff. They somehow seem to forget that there was a time when I was so frustrated with the children of Israel Myself that I was going to destroy them all and start over with a new people group. However, your precious intercession in prayer pleaded for Me to give them another chance. To keep you from becoming an icon. To keep you from becoming a man who would be, one day, worshiped yourself. I chose to use this act of your disobedience to both teach you the importance of obedience and launch forth the necessity of a new leader from among this next generation who would be going into the Promised Land. So, tell all of heaven this day, what mountain did you eventually get the honor of being promoted to?"

Moses takes a moment to gather his thoughts, knowing immediately what the answer is but contemplating just how he should describe it.

"Father God, it was the wonderful day that You called Elijah and me to go down to a mountain that would eventually be called the Mount of Transfiguration. Jesus had brought Peter and John up to a summit near where they were ministering as you pre-planned to have them witness firsthand Jesus being transfigured into glorious glowing white garb."

"Joshua, come on out here and stand beside Moses. Aaron, also come out now, please, and stand here with your brother. Yes, Moses, I chose to honor you by bringing you with Elijah to the mountain where John and Peter witnessed My Son, Jesus, transfigured with a glowing white garment before their eyes. All of your further rewards will be here in heaven for all of eternity for your faithfulness to your heavenly calling and known as the greatest of all the Old Testament prophets."

More and more angels began arriving and positioning themselves in tiers surrounding the city. Their ability to hover in one position in what seemed like standing on air amazed all of the eternalgens. All of their armor shined with brilliant silver and gold, and the light from the glory of God that filled heaven, reflecting off of that armor, was brilliant but not blinding. Gentle, loving smiles were on all of their faces.

"The manna that I sent down from heaven was My provision, and yes, I tested them for over a week before the manna came because I knew that they had brought their own provision and it would take that long for them to come to the end of their plan. Oh, how I wished that My children would have learned at a faster pace that heaven's provision is so very dependable. That faith is what I am growing in them all of the time. That good things come to those who wait on the Lord to see just how I am going to work all things together for the good. For the eternal good of those who wait on Me!

"Eternity, eternity, eternity, is what it is always all about. The Kingdom of God, forever and ever and ever without end in the spectacular bliss that you see now here all around you. No more sickness, no more crying, no more tears but tears of joy! However, I do remember that My children were made of dust, and I remember their frame. The passing from the temporary pleasures of this life into the eternal pleasures of the life to come is a process, often a very long process, that involves difficulty. It involves suffering. It involves self-denial, self-sacrifice, and sometimes downright tragedy to put someone in a place in the earthly existence where they simply have no choice but to let go of the things that they can no longer hold on to. It is in those places where they discover the heavenly realm. It's in those places that they discover the complete reliance and dependability of the Holy Spirit. But it is in those places where I am the most often doubted. It is in those places where I must listen to murmuring and complaining against Me. Sadly, it is in those places where far too many walk away from their faith in Me. Holy Spirit, would You now speak to the eternalgens about the sifting process as You have many roles, but most profound is Your role as a teacher to those who will desire to be baptized by You and stay close to You all of the days of their lives."

With that, the glorious translucent person of the Holy Spirit moves in close to the Heavenly Father and begins to speak to crowds in heaven. His voice is gentle and yet firm. Almost a whisper and yet loud enough for all of those who are listening to hear Him clearly.

"Ah, yes, Heavenly Father, here is where the chaff is separated from the wheat. Here is where the wolves are separated from the sheep and the good fruit from the bad because all love to be proven as real love must be tested. In romantic relationships on the earth, a husband and wife grow closer as they go through trials together, and the one remains faithful to help the other. Times of lack come, and the one is willing to do without so that the other can have. Times of sickness come, and the one is willing to work sometimes two or even three jobs so that the other one can get their needed rest to take time to heal. In many of these same ways, a person's love for God is proven through trials during their earthly stay in their life's process.

"The children of Israel were in Egyptian captivity for those 400 years and had gotten accustomed to their slavery even as difficult as it was. The Egyptian idolatry had wormed its way into the Hebrew's spiritual lives as well as the advanced methods of developing delicious food. Even though they did not have physical liberties to travel as they would or come and go as they pleased, their diet was rich with tasty meats. Often, people are willing to trade off a close walk with God in exchange for things that appeal to their senses. God the Father knew that for His people to experience Him in the fullness, He had to lead them into the desert. The only thing beautiful in the desert by His design is God Himself!

"A very high percentage of the time, as people slide away from a close walk with the Father, they gravitate into one form or another of religious practice. Doing things for God the Father instead of with Him. The first can be completely accomplished with prayerlessness. The second requires a life full of prayerfulness. Jesus taught, as recorded in Mark's Gospel:

> *He answered and said to them, "Well did Isaiah prophesy of you hypocrites, as it is written: 'This people honor Me with their lips, but their heart is far from Me. And in vain they worship Me, teaching as doctrines the commandments of men.'*

For laying aside the commandment of God, you hold the tradition of men, the washing of pitchers and cups, and many other such things you do."

He said to them, "All too well you reject the commandment of God, that you may keep your tradition. For Moses said, 'Honor your father and your mother'; and, 'He who curses father or mother, let him be put to death.' But you say, 'If a man says to his father or mother, "Whatever profit you might have received from me is Corban"—' (that is, a gift to God), then you no longer let him do anything for his father or his mother, making the word of God of no effect through your tradition which you have handed down. And many such things you do."[122]

The Holy Spirit recognized that what He was teaching was probably one of the most important truths that could ever be taught to believers. Recognizing that His audience was to the eternalgens already in heaven, He pauses to make this amplified declaration.

"These things I am reminding everyone here to prepare you for what you are about to witness is number three in succession of the greatest heaven-sent events that have ever transpired. So please pay close attention to what I am about to remind you!

"People never like to hear that it is possible to hinder the Creator of the universe through different forms of unbelief. I just quoted you one of many recorded in the scripture, according to Mark. Now, I would like to show you how it also carried throughout the Old Testament. Recorded in the Psalms."

The eternalgens were amazed as the Spirit of God, in His visible but translucent state, reached up one of His hands, and a glowing golden scroll appeared, which He unrolled with His other hand and started reading to them.

"This," He said, "is one of the most powerful passages of scripture ever written, which reveals the broad scope of the Father's love and His patience in working in spite of His displeasure, with His children whom He had called forth out of Egypt. It will help everyone better understand the hugely important proclamation that will come later today and how He knew people had to learn to fear Him, or they simply would not fight off multiple temptations to sinful practices that could indict their souls for eternity.

"The psalmist Asaph writes in this Psalm, as I inspired him to see the truth:

Give ear, O my people, to my law;
Incline your ears to the words of my mouth.
I will open my mouth in a parable;
I will utter dark sayings of old,
Which we have heard and known,
And our fathers have told us.
We will not hide them from their children,
Telling the generation to come to the praises of the Lord,
And His strength and His wonderful works that He has done.

For He established a testimony in Jacob
And appointed a law in Israel,
Which He commanded our fathers,
That they should make them known to their children;
That the generation to come might know them,
The children who would be born,
That they may arise and declare them to their children,
That they may set their hope in God,
And not forget the works of God,
But keep His commandments;
And may not be like their fathers,
A stubborn and rebellious generation,
A generation that did not set its heart aright,
And whose spirit was not faithful to God.

The children of Ephraim, being armed and carrying bows,
Turned back on the day of battle.
They did not keep the covenant of God;
They refused to walk in His law
And forgot His works
And His wonders that He had shown them.

Marvelous things He did in the sight of their fathers,
In the land of Egypt, in the field of Zoan.

He divided the sea and caused them to pass through;
And He made the waters stand up like a heap.
In the daytime also He led them with the cloud,
And all the night with a light of fire.
He split the rocks in the wilderness
And gave them drink in abundance like the depths.
He also brought streams out of the rock
And caused waters to run down like rivers.

But they sinned even more against Him
By rebelling against the Most High in the wilderness.
And they tested God in their heart
By asking for the food of their fancy.
Yes, they spoke against God:
They said, "Can God prepare a table in the wilderness?
Behold, He struck the rock
So that the waters gushed out,
And the streams overflowed.
Can He give bread also?
Can He provide meat for His people?"

Therefore, the Lord *heard this and was furious;*
So, a fire was kindled against Jacob,
And anger also came up against Israel,
Because they did not believe in God,
And did not trust in His salvation.
Yet He had commanded the clouds above
And opened the doors of heaven,
Had rained down manna on them to eat,
And given them of the bread of heaven.
Men ate angels' food;
He sent them food to the full.

He caused an east wind to blow in the heavens,
And by His power He brought in the south wind.
He also rained meat on them like the dust,
Feathered fowl like the sand of the seas;
And He let them fall in the midst of their camp,
All around their dwellings.

So they ate and were well filled,
For He gave them their own desire.
They were not deprived of their craving;
But while their food was still in their mouths,
The wrath of God came against them,
And slew the stoutest of them,
And struck down the choice men of Israel.

In spite of this they still sinned
And did not believe in His wondrous works.
Therefore, their days He consumed in futility,
And their years in fear.

When He slew them, then they sought Him;
And they returned and sought earnestly for God.
Then they remembered that God was their rock,
And the Most High God their Redeemer.
Nevertheless they flattered Him with their mouth,
And they lied to Him with their tongue;
For their heart was not steadfast with Him,
Nor were they faithful in His covenant.
But He, being full of compassion, forgave their iniquity,
And did not destroy them.
Yes, many a time He turned His anger away,
And did not stir up all His wrath;
For He remembered that they were but flesh,
A breath that passes away and does not come again.

How often they provoked Him in the wilderness
And grieved Him in the desert!
Yes, again and again, they tempted God
And limited the Holy One of Israel.

[The Holy Spirit said in a booming voice to emphasize what was being said.]

They did not remember His power:
The day when He redeemed them from the enemy,
When He worked His signs in Egypt,
And His wonders in the field of Zoan;

Turned their rivers into blood,
And their streams, that they could not drink.
He sent swarms of flies among them, which devoured them,
And frogs, which destroyed them.
He also gave their crops to the caterpillar,
And their labor to the locust.
He destroyed their vines with hail,
And their sycamore trees with frost.
He also gave up their cattle to the hail,
And their flocks to fiery lightning.
He cast on them the fierceness of His anger,
Wrath, indignation, and trouble,
By sending angels of destruction among them.
He made a path for His anger;
He did not spare their soul from death,
But gave their life over to the plague,
And destroyed all the firstborn in Egypt,
The first of their strength in the tents of Ham.
But He made His own people go forth like sheep,
And guided them in the wilderness like a flock;
And He led them on safely so that they did not fear;
But the sea overwhelmed their enemies.
And He brought them to His holy border,
This mountain which His right hand had acquired.
He also drove out the nations before them,
Allotted them an inheritance by survey,
And made the tribes of Israel dwell in their tents.

Yet they tested and provoked the Most High God,
And did not keep His testimonies,
But turned back and acted unfaithfully like their fathers;
They were turned aside like a deceitful bow.
For they provoked Him to anger with their high places,
And moved Him to jealousy with their carved images.
When God heard this, He was furious,
And greatly abhorred Israel,
So that He forsook the tabernacle of Shiloh,
The tent He had placed among men,

And delivered His strength into captivity,
And His glory into the enemy's hand.
He also gave His people over to the sword,
And was furious with His inheritance.
The fire consumed their young men,
And their maidens were not given in marriage.
Their priests fell by the sword,
And their widows made no lamentation.

Then the Lord awoke as from sleep,
Like a mighty man who shouts because of wine.
And He beat back His enemies;
He put them to a perpetual reproach.

Moreover He rejected the tent of Joseph,
And did not choose the tribe of Ephraim,
But chose the tribe of Judah,
Mount Zion which He loved.
And He built His sanctuary like the heights,
Like the earth which He has established forever.
He also chose David His servant,
And took him from the sheepfolds;
From following the ewes that had young He brought him,
To shepherd Jacob His people,
And Israel His inheritance.
So he shepherded them according to the integrity of his heart,
And guided them by the skillfulness of his hands."[123]

With that, the Holy Spirit rolled closed the golden scroll and raised it, releasing it from His grip. It disappeared in the same miraculous manner that it had appeared to begin with.

"Thank You, Holy Spirit," the Father says as He turns to address the huge gathering of the eternalgens that day. "I am delighted to inform you that Jesus will be joining us shortly for this great day of celebration. This is going to be a special day for Him, and I know that you all will be so delighted when you see Him again today. All of you who have arrived through the years into heaven have personally enjoyed His company on multiple occasions as He loves to just take whole E-days at a time with His children. His omnipresence, which is difficult to understand even in your now heavenly bodies, allows Him to be in multiple places at one time in His fullness. It will always be one of His favorite things to do and to discuss stories of His working through some of life's toughest challenges for that person while they were still on Earth."

With that, an enormous expression of powerful cheers of praises unto God and exuberant declarations of excitement and unrestrainable worshipful verbal praises to Jesus created such a loud noise that all of heaven felt the golden streets below them vibrating in a gentle hum that seemed musical in nature. Some of the eternalgens who had been musicians from large orchestras began quietly discussing between themselves, and it reminded them of when everyone was warming up before a large concert with the tone in perfect harmony of expression.

At that point, angels began to appear, flying in from various completed assignments and positioning themselves in tiers that the eternalgens did not even know existed before. It seemed obvious to everyone that they were arriving in different groups in preparation for something big.

With that, Windrose pauses the omniciscreen and approaches the souls, clapping his hands and giving exuberant praise unto God. The souls are immediately inspired by his enthusiasm and, in the moment, also begin to jointly praise God for His goodness and His wonderous works, which the scripture would one day declare were past finding out by any non-inspired human process. Only the Holy Spirit can reveal the Father's plans and that last trip far into the future eckons of time away where they got to actually see the Holy Spirit instruct the eternalgens concerning something very big that was about to happen that day.

"Souls," Windrose says to pull back their attention to something very important he has to share with them now, "what you have seen through these times together is that the Father, in His secret plans for the eventual equipping of His children, as I told you from the very beginning, will not be able to be remembered by you in total once you become humans and have your temporal bodies on the earth. One day, by making the right choices on earth with the same opportunities as any other earthly person, you will be able to receive the gift of eternal life through the Lord Jesus Christ and His substitutionary sacrifice on the cross. Then you may actually be in this Christmas Day celebration, depending on what period of time the Father has for you to live in. In order for all of this preparation to be a just deed on the Father's part, He cannot allow any of you to have any special favors that no one else will ever have. Only seeds of thought and pieces of instruction that you have received in these classes. If, however, you are faithful to do with what you have been trusted with and be obedient to the Holy Spirit's leading in your lives, then the Father has shown me that you will one day, once in heaven, be able to remember all of these classes and have eternal fellowship with the other souls that you got to know while here. He can offer this as a gift to you.

"At the end of this Christmas Day celebration, which again is the actual Christmas Day, the actual anniversary of the day that Jesus was born on the earth, which has been kept a secret throughout time to keep people from worshipping the day above others rather than worshipping Jesus, the reason for the day. Every story you witnessed, and all of the individuals that you met through each story at different points in history will continue with their lives in the time period that they lived. Some of you were in those stories, as we hinted, and yet that could not be revealed as anonymity was so vitally important so as not to affect your ability to rightly process the lessons that you needed to learn from each story.

"As we come to the end of you watching this celebration from a point in history from before the foundations of the world, I would like to quote to you a scripture that Paul will one day write to the Ephesian church: 'Just as He chose us in Him before the foundation of the world, that we should be holy and without blame before Him in love.'[124] The holy Word of God declares that He chose all of the believers from before the foundation of the world! However, just as I taught you in the past in the multi-time dimensional levels of classes and the thousands of souls present, only God knew. That way, some of you very possibly could be in our midst from a point in the future eckons of time even beyond this Christmas Day, so it is possible that for those souls, more classes are yet to come. However, for many, and it's safe to say for most, these classes will conclude today following your viewing of this next procession and celebration honoring Jesus in the most special way. So, once again, souls, tighten up your sandal straps and your robe wraps for the most thrilling thing that you have ever seen!"

With that, Windrose raised his hand and pointed his finger, which began to glow with a beautiful golden luminescence this time as the souls were given full view of the heavenly celebration, continuing with the Father speaking to all of heaven.

"I am no less in authority whether I am standing here in the midst of heaven or sitting on My throne. *I am that I am!*" says God. "And I delight in spending time with My children.

"Moses," the Father says again, "please take the lead along with Aaron and Joshua for what is going to be a 'Procession of the Prophets.' Aaron and Joshua, although you were never officially named as prophets, you operated similarly to the office of a prophet on many occasions; therefore, the three of you will lead this procession. Will now all of the prophets from both the Old and New Covenants time periods and those who were used in ministries similar to a prophet come out and begin to line up one behind the other in rows of two, please?"

So then, all dressed in brilliant white robes came through the shining curtain one by one. Adam, Enoch, Noah, Abraham, Isaac, Jacob, Miriam, Deborah, Samuel, Nathan, Elijah, Elisha, Jonah, Isaiah, Jeremiah, Ezekiel, Daniel, Hosea, Joel, Amos, Obadiah, Jonah, Micah, Nahum, Habakkuk, Zephaniah, Haggai, Zechariah, Malachi, followed by the twelve close disciples of Jesus, Peter, James, John, Andrew, Philip, Nathanael, Matthew, Thomas, James, Thaddeus, Simon the Zealot, and Matthias, then followed by the New Testament prophets, John the Baptist, Agabus, Judas Barsabbas, Silvanus from among the prophets, Barnabas, and Paul the Apostle.

Then, the Father said, "I want you to form two lines. Now, move to the outer edge of this main golden street and face each other," which they did.

These prophets and disciples were hardly strangers by now, having spent for some of them hundreds of earth years in heaven together. They often chose to gather and exchange stories of their various challenges and miracles. The one often in the highest demand was Jonah, as everyone wanted to know what it was like to be inside that great fish for three days! So, as they moved about and got into position, there were some expected handshakes and small talk conversations between them. The Father quietly waited, smiling, as one of His greatest joys was to see the comradery of His chosen men and women of God have warm fellowship with one another in heaven. One of the greatest joys of having the honor of entering heaven will be for everyone the ability to move about and talk with all of the famous Bible personalities and discuss with them their adventures in carrying out God's will for their lives. The Father knew, however, that this was no ordinary day. As a matter of fact, it was one of the most important days that heaven will ever have. It still was not time yet to announce just what that event was, but it was shortly coming. Everyone could sense it; some were speculating what it was, and others were hoping for what they thought it was because it was indeed that one giant celebratory event was about to take place. Possibly the biggest one heaven had ever seen.

About that time, Michael and Gabriel flew in from different directions and landed near the head of the procession of the prophets. They had both just finished their most recent assignments, which the Father knew would give them the liberty to be there. Many of the eternalgens were in awe as they had never seen them in their beauty standing next to each other.

Windrose knew he needed to do something. He then paused the omniciscreen again for just a few minutes as there was so much chatter between the souls that he had to calm their excitement. He also knew that he needed to go and be somewhere else shortly, so he felt it best to take a minute to talk.

"Souls, one of the greatest acts of revealed love that will ever take place in the universe's history is about to unfold here. You will sense a profound peace coming over you from the Father to help you contain your enthusiasm. When you see me leave the platform, there will be one more view into the future on the omniciscreen that will be a sign to you that the Father is going to place you in a short period of time in a type of supernatural sleep, awaiting your birth as children in your place in history. There will be no sense of the passing of time while you are in this place. A type of supernatural soul pod in which your beings as souls will be forever protected by the armies of God until your time comes. Have no fear and just consider this fact: If God took all of this time to take you through all of these lessons to prepare you for your future lives and to help the future lives of others, doesn't it serve to reason that He will with that make sure that you are protected while you in a type of deep sleep until your day comes? It will be like in one minute, you are asleep, and the next minute, you will be in the loving arms of your parents on earth. There will be zero recognition of the passing of time. God, by His miraculous power, can and will do this!

With this, Windrose raises his hand and once again points his finger, which a second time begins to glow with a beautiful golden luminescence, and once again, their view is launched into the future by eckons of time to that perfect day that will be kept a secret. The anniversary of that true first Christmas when Jesus Christ was born after being conceived in Mary supernaturally by the Holy Spirit nine months earlier. The souls noticed that Windrose somehow had slipped away from their view, and because he had just told them that it was going to happen, they were not alarmed. Just as he said, they could sense God's wonderful peace flooding over them, giving them that assurance that everything was going to be all right.

The first thing that the souls see is that the Father once again begins to speak to the eternalgens concerning the lining up of the prophets on both sides of the main golden street that runs through heaven. Michael and Gabriel had positioned themselves one on one side and one on the other of the rows of prophets. Then the main street of gold began to slowly move and the end where the archangels were standing and the prophets, starting with Moses and Aaron on one side and Joshua on the other, gently began to develop a cross golden street down about one-quarter distance away from the top forming the shape of a golden cross. To everyone's amazement, the prophets and disciples did not have to change positions, but once the golden cross-shaped street formed, they made a perfect connection from one to another, completely lining the perimeter of the whole cross! Then they recognized that the top of the cross was now perfectly aligned with the white shining curtain that everyone else that day that had been introduced had walked through! There was only one opening in the complete line of people around the cross, and that was right at the shining curtain. Only at that moment, it began to glow with the golden glory of God!

The Father took a few steps from where He was standing and beckoned with a roll of His arm for the Holy Spirit to come and be at His left side, leaving a space open on His right. He then shouted, "*Yeshua, Jesus the Christ, the Lamb of God, the Word, the Messiah, Lord of all, Emmanuel, the Alpha and the Omega, the King of kings, the Light of the world, the Good Shepherd, the Bread of Life, the Way, the Truth, and the Life, the Prince of Peace, the Wonderful Counselor, Mighty God, and most of all My precious only-begotten Son—come forth!*

"*These eternalgens and the souls viewing from a far distant past is the manna I sent down from heaven. He is the Bread of Life, and He is the Friend who will stick closer than a brother!*"

With that, Jesus walked forth through the now golden shining curtain onto the golden cross-shaped street lined with all of the prophets and disciples. The Father then asked Him, "Jesus, I once granted You one special blessing for all of Your willingness to leave the glory of heaven and become a man. To endure the great suffering of over thirty-three years, the half of which has never yet been told: the emotional rejection, the persecution, the attacks from the evil one, and so much more. I once asked years ago, 'What special extra blessing would You ask for as a special gift of honor once You completed Your obedience?' Would You like to tell everyone within the sound of Your voice today what Your wish was that I have granted You over the years since Your time spent in obedience to My heavenly calling on the earth?"

Jesus responded, "Father, I had asked You all of that eckons of time ago, if it were possible, please let the day of My birth and the day of My resurrection be also a special day for children all over the world for every culture that welcomes the foundations of My truth. Thank You, Father, for although You did not create that specifically, the enemy of all souls, in his best attempt to deceive people away from My truths in not knowing what he was doing, actually did something that ended up being loving days for children all over the world. It ended up being another example of another one of his evil plans blowing up in his face. Thank You, Father, that in a world full of much suffering, You once again showed that You can and do work all things together for the good of those who are called according to Your purpose. Songs around My birth and songs around My resurrection were also sung all over the world during certain seasons, which created excellent faith-witnessing platforms for all who believed." With that, Jesus looked in the direction of where He knew the omniciscreen was viewing and waved and said, "Hello, souls!"

As soon as the souls see the Son of God through the omniciscreen, which He had left running, they all gasp and excitedly start praising Him with great joy: "*Jesus is Windrose!*" some say. While others say, "*Windrose is Jesus!*" Great tears of joy flood their faces, and holy laughter fills the arena as excited conversations fill the air! Shouts from every direction in the arena began to shout back, "Hello, Jesus! Or Windrose," which caused some discussion. "Should we call Him Jesus or Windrose now?" "Jesus, Jesus, Jesus, of course!" everyone seemed to emphatically declare.

Jesus just started laughing with jovial heavenly laughter over their enthusiasm. "Because all of the life lessons that you learned with Me had to do with the Father's will and direction, I chose to use the name of a face and working parts of a compass as My class instructor's name. Now that you know who I am, yes, please call Me by My biblical names!"

Anne-77 says to a group surrounding her, "Can you believe that we have been in the process of being taught by Jesus the whole time, and we did not know?"

Then Terry-23 says, "You know, I think that He was trying to throw us hints along the way but knew that if He told us that, we would feel intimidated or something."

Anne-77 responds, "Well, one thing I know for sure is that if He knew it was best not to tell us it was because He and the Father are One, and this whole learning process was planned out by them, and it would just be foolish to think that it should have been done differently!"

Terry-23 quickly directs everyone's attention back to the omniciscreen that Windrose/Jesus had left running. "Let's not miss anything that comes next because if God has not put us in our sleep state yet, then He wants us to see what's going to happen next!"

As Jesus proceeded to walk out on the golden road in the shape of a cross, all of the prophets were applauding and praising God even though many of them throughout time had already spent time with Him in heaven. They knew everything the Father was doing that day to bring everyone together, for this type of celebration had to be leading up to something big.

Some felt they knew what it was. Others acknowledged that even though they had been God-called prophets, this had not yet been revealed to them.

At just about that moment, the Father began to place an additional eternal blessing upon His Son. "Jesus, My one and only-begotten Son, indeed in You I am well pleased. Your heart has been perfect in all Your ways. In order for You to fulfill Your mission as the second Adam and to be able to take back from Satan the keys of death, hell, and the grave, You had to be filled with sinless blood. In order to do that, You had to live a sinless life. Not just a sinless life but a sinless life as, yes, the Son of God, but as the Son of God born of a woman and be both God very God and man very man. Your only special tools that You could accomplish this with was through the knowledge of the Holy Scripture, which You had to learn first as a child, then as a young man, and then as an adult. Then, as a man, You had to choose to be baptized in My Holy Spirit."

As the Father was telling Jesus this, the Holy Spirit, standing beside the Father in His translucent state, was nodding His head up and down, signifying yes and smiling, which caused everyone to applaud and break out in holy laughter, expressing thankfulness to God the Father.

"If You did not fulfill the sinless life as a man or by some supernatural means other men did not have access to, then it would not be a just substitution! Adams's access to My presence was to walk with Me in the cool of the garden every day. He could have consulted Me before he partook of the forbidden fruit offered by Eve, but he did not. Adam chose the counsel of the woman more credible than My counsel. Adam sinned and ignored My clear commandment to not partake of the forbidden fruit. He indirectly obeyed the serpent's counsel through Eve rather than My own. Therefore, the second Adam had to obey Me perfectly, and for You, it was all the way through a life of suffering and being rejected by Your own people. The denying Yourself the pleasures of ever having a wife or children or the grandchildren that followed and all the way through the horrible suffering surrounding the crucifixion. Your perfect, sinless blood was an acceptable atonement for the sins of mankind. The most precious substance that the world ever would see. More precious than diamonds, rubies, or the finest gemstones. More precious than gold or silver or the purest ore. More valuable than any other tangible thing on planet Earth was Your sinless blood that You paid the highest of all prices for! Holy Spirit, will You remind us of the many places where Jesus's blood was shed in the twenty-four-hour earth day surrounding the crucifixion?"

"It would be My honor, Heavenly Father. The first place He shed His blood was when He went to the Garden of Gethsemane to pray the night before He had to go to the cross. It is written in Luke's gospel,

> 'And He was withdrawn from them about a stone's throw, and He knelt down and prayed, saying, "Father, if it is Your will, take this cup away from Me; nevertheless, not My will, but Yours, be done." Then an angel appeared to Him from heaven, strengthening Him. And being in agony, He prayed more earnestly. Then His sweat became like great drops of blood falling down to the ground.'[125]

"Then secondly, when He was brought before Caiaphas, the high priest, He was punched in His face while they mocked and spat on Him. This brought bleeding in His nose and mouth. Thirdly, they made a crown of thorns and rammed it down on His head, causing blood to drip down from those thorns poking through His skin and dripping to the ground."

As the Holy Spirit continued to share the list, both the souls listening through the omniciscreen and the eternalgens listening in were all verbalizing their emotional feelings of sorrow, overhearing all that Jesus had to suffer.

The Holy Spirit continued to list the rest of the eight different places where Jesus's perfect blood had touched the filthy dirt of planet Earth. "Then, they ripped off His bloody garment, threw it to the ground, and cast lots of gambling over it. His precious blood touched the ground through His bloody robe that He wore. Then, the fifth thing they did was they laid thirty-nine whip lashes on His back because, by Roman law, any more than that would kill a man or drive him to insanity. Then, number six, they laid His already badly torn back on a very rough hand-hewn cross. And number seven was to proceed to drive a single nail through both feet overlapping and two other nails, one in each wrist, with blood dripping down from each puncture wound. Satan laughed with glee along with his demonic imps, but he would have been crying if he realized that it was the worst mistake that he had ever made. Then, number eight was that a Roman soldier rammed his spear up into Jesus's side through His rib cage into His heart to try to make sure that His heart had stopped beating. The scripture records that blood and water rushed out of the Messiah's side down on the ground. What Jesus endured to pay the price for the sins of mankind was some of the worst torture any human being could ever suffer!"

As all of the souls were very quiet and the eternalgens already knew the story, they also expressed a somber attitude, and the Father stepped up and stated, "This, My children, was the greatest act of love ever demonstrated in the history of the universe and untold numbers of people will spend eternity in this beautiful place all because of what My Son, Jesus, was willing to do to pay the price for their sins! This is not a time for sorrow but for celebration! This is not a time for sadness, for the suffering of the Son of God is behind Him now, and today is My day to give Him what I have been promising Him for eckons of time.

Jesus, today is the day when You get to travel to Earth and bring back Your bride!"

It is believed that heaven had never seen praise and celebration like what they were experiencing following that statement. Jesus started laughing and dancing and praising God by singing unto His Father, and the Father, Son, and Holy Spirit were singing songs of celebration that day. In those moments, those who heard it said that never before had any music been made or produced that equaled the beauty and harmonious tones of that music.

As that continued for what no one knows for sure how long, shofars were sounding off in the distance. Angelic choirs were again singing songs that they had not sung since that first Christmas Eve before the shepherds who were watching their flocks by night. "Glory to God in the highest, and on the earth peace and goodwill towards men." It had been hundreds of years and eckons of time, but only the Father knew for sure how long. Jesus was about to go and bring forth His bride, His true church, which meant that countless in numbers, only the Father foreknew, would all be coming into heaven at once that next day.

The Father once again begins to speak directly to Jesus, "My Son, I know You have chosen wisely but share with the eternalgens and the souls who are listening in today, from a very far away time, how You chose Your bride, the true church, from so many different belief systems currently on the earth. In this moment, what the church world refers to as the Rapture, how did You choose Your bride, which will be made up of thousands of thousands of believers?"

"I chose her looking way beyond the long list of false brides who tried to enter into the gate another way. Their leaders, pastors, and prophets tried to create a way that was broad to be my bride; such is the way of the promiscuous woman who was with many and faithful to not one. Such attempt to build My kingdom for numbers' sake. Rather than being virtuously mine only, she left her womb open to many. Rather than producing children for My kingdom, she became intimate for pleasure only, mothering none, nurturing none, and the fruit of her womb was corrupted by her own selfishness. But my bride has been longing for this day for eckons of time. She is the one who has been preparing herself with a beauty so rare that a thousand words cannot describe her." With that, Jesus quoted from the Song of Solomon with a slight adaptation, "'You have ravished my heart, my sister, my bride-to-be!'[126] Not visibly religious but radically obedient to My every calling. My every nudge, My revealed desires, keeping herself spotless by My sacrifice.

"Her beauty, first of all, primarily is the beauty of her heart. No natural beauty could ever compare to what she has. Her most beautiful attribute is her unquenchable love for Me. Her unwavering commitment. Her continuous longing for My coming to get her. Her sacrificial obedience has required her great personal cost throughout her whole life. She is My spiritual bride who is made up of the men and women of My church over the past eckons of time. She has watched, she has prayed, she has waited, and now, Father, it is My time to go and get her and bring her back to Me. She has sought for and kept her lamp full of the oil of My Holy Spirit. We will eventually celebrate the Marriage Supper of the Lamb. She shall be with Me continually in preparation, in training, in equipping until the time comes when I shall return to earth with My bride made up of tens of thousands of My saints to rule and reign with a rod of iron with My righteousness for a thousand years. Until the kingdoms of men become the kingdoms of our God! Until it can truly be said, 'Your will finally will be done on earth as it is in heaven.'"

When Jesus said those words, the beautiful and glorious banner that hung across from the throne of God, where angels flew past as they left heaven for every mission, started flashing in brilliant golden light. The choir of martyrs over the throne of God began to sing songs that had never been sung before until that moment. A series of seven majestic songs glorifying Jesus that had been written and compiled Himself by the Father for that special day.

The prophets and the disciples all raised their hands in the direction of Jesus to honor Him, and, as senseless as it might seem to some, prayer was so much of their everyday life for so many years that they all prayed for the Father's blessing over His journey to earth.

With that, Jesus launched into the bright blue heavenly sky with Gabriel and Michael and a few chosen angels that were with Him when He made His heavenly ascension from earth. They launched out of sight into the earth's dimension, preparing to sound the trumpet at His appearing.

The souls were permitted to see Him launch, and with thousands of goodbyes for now from the arena, some yelled, "I will see You soon in my heart, Jesus!" and such affectionate comments as they had so gotten to know their Windrose, who was secretly all the time their eventual Savior, their Jesus. Someone whom they dearly loved and missed already. To whom Jesus responded, "I will see you the next time in your childhood dreams." One by one, they all slowly drifted into their heavenly sleep in the safety of their God-made soul pods, which were invisible until that moment.

One of the hundreds of angels assigned to guard the heavenly-designed citadel they were in said to another, "Do you think that they will fulfill their assignments?"

The other angel responded, "If they only learn early to completely submit to the Father's will and trust Him through everything, then yes; yes, they absolutely will!"

Although Christmas celebrations on earth for another year had already long passed, this was one Christmas Day no one on earth will ever forget. They will eventually find out the actual day Jesus was born because it will have been the same day He returned when an uncountable number of people vanished from the earth. Cemeteries all over the world find unexplainable open graves with no bodies left inside. The world's best scientists will scramble to try to explain what happened. But in the twinkling of an eye, those who had spent their days after they were truly born again longing for Jesus's return will be in another spiritual dimension today. The place that had been watching them all along through the supernatural multidimensional God-designed viewtrons. Through the eternal continual vision of heaven's love! Hallelujah! Forever now, without end!

GLOSSARY

DEFINITIONS OF FICTIONAL WORDS UNIQUE TO THIS BOOK, AND CERTAIN COMMON WORDS WITH NEW MEANINGS

THE SOULS are the dozens of characters in *Through Heaven's Vision* explained in more detail for the readers understanding.

Eph 1:3-5 NKJV states *Blessed be the God and Father of our Lord Jesus Christ, who has blessed us with every spiritual blessing in the heavenly places in Christ, just as He chose us in Him before the foundation of the world, that we should be holy and without blame before Him in love, having predestined us to adoption as sons by Jesus Christ to Himself, according to the good pleasure of His will,*

The above scripture clearly says that God knew us from before the foundation of the world! These are the huge numbers of individuals in the book with first names and an identifying number which act sort of like a last name. In the fictional story line, souls are being taught by the main character Windrose things that by Gods supernatural ability will be locked away until they become humans and what God the Father understands is the perfect times revealed to their understanding. Sort of like what some people call an illumination or a revelation.

In the story line God being perfectly holy and righteous having to combat the lies and deceptions of Lucifer is justified in teaching the Word ahead of time because Jesus is the Word, and the Word has always existed. Borrowing truth from the future is perfectly ethical because that truth always existed. Satan's evil nature to lie, cheat, steal, deceive, mislead, create false religions, send false teachers, and so on in *Through Heavens Vision*, must be combatted with truth.

The author after years of prayer felt that God gave him this concept but as the introduction will state in no way does he believe that any of these classes ever actually happened. It merely provides a platform for a group of teachable souls to develop what may be Heaven's vision. Possibly you will find your first name in the list of many "Souls" in *Through Heavens Vision?*

3 DIFFERENT TITLES GIVEN TO THE SOULS BY WINDROSE AT DIFFERENT TIMES:

<u>Soldiers</u> in a spiritual battle for truth and promoting the seeking of Gods will in all that they do.

<u>Defenders</u> of the truth of God's word. Of the reality of Jesus Christ, and His death and resurrection purchasing the gift of salvation for all who will believe. Defenders of the proper interpretation of the balance of Gods Holy Word of both Old and New Testaments.

<u>Stewards</u> of God's Word and the responsibility of carrying out the perfect will of God by seeking that through prayer and treasuring the truths of Biblical Christianity. Also stewards of embracing the revivals that He has sent in history and is still sending.

<u>TRINITOTALUM</u> is a book created word describing the Trinity.

The Ongor, the Tydrum and the Grimple trees are made up trees in the Garden of Eden for the book and do not actually exist anywhere

<u>OMNICISCREEN</u> is created from the word omnipresence of God. In the story it allows Windrose is able to take the Souls on visual trips of time travel. They are watching events in the past or future on the omniciscreen. Pronounced "om-nis-i-screen."

<u>OMNISEECAST</u> is the unique name of the new TV intentional satire similar to Gods future projection system in Archer the youth pastor's home.

<u>EMOTILLIANCE</u> is the central thinking process of the Souls. As they are yet without bodies, and they do not have a brain they rely on something that God has created that has information storage capabilities. As the soul is made up of the mind, will, and emotions one day when they receive their God given human bodies their emotilliance will be able to upload to the mind part of their brain to allow retention for whatever the Father in His foreknowledge knows that they will be faced with in their future existence. As the soul is made up of the mind, will and the emotions. Emotilliance is a created word for the book representing those three things.

CROSSPAC factors of the emotilliance activation has to do with the souls mind being activated in the soul realm not yet human so that when they time travel they understand the culture of the time period that they are viewing into. Acronym for "Cross Reception of Superior Societal Placement Accepting Change."

CYLINDRICON is the 3D viewer place in the book that allows the souls to view 3d images of such things as the building of Noah's Ark.

DEMONITRAC A device that interprets the demonically garbled language for the Souls to be able to understand as they are viewing discussions taking place by demons in their dark lair.

TRICOMPLEXIUM is a three-way view or effect of a teaching by Jesus! It suggests that Jesus's teaching has such wisdom that it is has the potential of three interconnecting truths.

ETERNALGENS were once Earths citizens that represents the name for citizens of Heaven in the future of our story line who are now in Heaven.

ECONS of time are eternal time periods created so as to keep in the Father's heavenly secrecy how long eternal time periods are.

EDAYS are a heavenly time period measurement that's equivalent to one day on Earth!

SOULPODS are the cocoon like crystal glass like pod created by God that would house them until born on the earth in our story line.

VIEWTRONS are a type of cameras that are in Heaven that lets those under God's command to view occurrences that are taking place on earth such as Jesus going out to bring home His bride.

ENDNOTES

1   Genesis 9:25–27 (NKJV)

2   Genesis 3:22 (paraphrased)

3   John 3:2–21 (NKJV; paraphrased)

4   John 1:29 (NKJV)

5   Proverbs 30:20 (NKJV)

6   Matthew 21:9–17 (NKJV; paraphrased)

7   James 5:10 (NKJV)

8   Isaiah 1:11–17 (NKJV)

9   Psalm 51:15–20 (NKJV)

10 2 Peter 2:1–3

11 John 3:17–19 (NKJV)

12 2 Peter 3:1–9 (NKJV)

13 Revelation 2:24 (NKJV). Hereinafter, emphasis added.

14 1 Corinthians 2:9 (NKJV)

15 John 14:1–3 (NKJV)

16 Revelation 21:23 (ESV)

17 Colossians 1:9–18 (NKJV)

18 Revelation 21:1–5 (NKJV)

19 Matthew 6:9–13 (NKJV)

20 Romans 8:18–23 (NKJV)

21 Matthew 7:13–14 (NKJV)

22 Acts 1:1–11 (NKJV)

23 Haggai 1:8 (NKJV)

24 John 1:11 (NKJV)

25 Acts 1:2–3 (NKJV)

26 1 Corinthians 15:3–8 (NKJV)

27 John 14:18 (KJV)

28 John 14:16 (NKJV)

29 John 19:30 (NKJV)

30 Acts 14:12–15 (NKJV)

31 Acts 19:2a (KJV)

32 Psalm 69:25 (NKJV)

33 Psalm 109:8b (NKJV)

34 Acts 1:24–25 (NKJV)

35 Ecclesiastes 3:11b (KJV)

36 Jeremiah 31:31–34 (NKJV)

37 John 1:29b (NKJV)

38 Jeremiah 31:33 (NKJV)

39 Acts 2:1–13 (NKJV)

40 Acts 2:14–47 (NKJV)

41 Hebrews 11:6 (NKJV)

42 James 4:2b (KJV)

43 Luke 23:34a (ESV

44 Malachi 3:6a (KJV)

45 Mark 16:17 (KJV)

46 Hebrews 13:8 (KJV)

47 1 Corinthians 14:22a (NKJV)

48 John 3:3 (paraphrased)

49 John 3:4b (paraphrased)

50 John 3:6–7 (paraphrased)

51 Acts 11:26

52 John 3:16 (NKJV)

53 John 3:18 (NKJV)

54 Jeremiah 17:9 (NKJV)

55 Jeremiah 17:9 (paraphrased)

56 Isaiah 64:6a (NKJV)

57 Matthew 6:33 (paraphrased)

58 Acts 7:51 (NKJV)

59 Revelation 2:1–29 (NKJV)

60 John 4:24 (KJV)

61 John 8:44a (KJV)

62 John 14:9 (paraphrased). Hereinafter, brackets added for clarity.

63 Genesis 1:26a (NKJV)

64 Genesis 2:21–23 (NKJV)

65 Acts 20:26–38 (NKJV)

66 Jeremiah 17:9 (NKJV)

67 Jeremiah 22:29 (NKJV)

68 Matthew 5:18 (NKJV)

69   Revelation 2:24

70   Mark 12:30 (NKJV)

71   1 Corinthians 11:19 (NKJV)

72   Ecclesiastes 3:7 (paraphrased)

73   Matthew 12:33–37 (NKJV)

74   Isaiah 53:2 (NKJV)

75   Matthew 13:24–30 (NKJV)

76   Matthew 13:36–43 (NKJV)

77   2 Corinthians 10:4–5 (NKJV)

78   2 Corinthians 1:8–11 (NKJV)

79   Hosea 4:6 (paraphrased)

80   Luke 22:24–27 (NKJV)

81   Luke 22:28 (NKJV)

82   Matthew 6:10b (KJV)

83   James 2:19 (NKJV)

84   Acts 6:1–8 (NKJV)

85   Acts 7:1b–53 (NKJV)

86   Psalm 116:15 (NKJV)

87   Acts 7:54–60 (NKJV)

88   Luke 23:34 (KJV)

89   Acts 7:60 (KJV)

90   2 Thessalonians 1:6 (NKJV)

91   Acts 7:49 (NKJV)

92   Acts 7:51–52a

93   Acts 7:52b

94   Vine's Complete Expository Dictionary

95   Ibid.

96   Ibid.

97   John 10:30

98   John 14:9

99   Acts 9:1–31 (NKJV)

100   Philippians 3:8 (NKJV)

101   Romans 8:28 (NKJV)

102   Jeremiah 33:3 (NKJV)

103   Romans 7:9 (NKJV)

104   James 4:4b (NKJV)

105   Revelation 2:8–11 (NKJV)

106   Revelation 3:7–13 (NKJV)

107   Ephesians 4:11–12 (NKJV)

108   Revelation 2:7 (NKJV)

109   Revelation 2:18b (NKJV)

110   Revelation 2:19 (NKJV)

111   Revelation 3:14 (NKJV)

112   Revelation 3:15–17 (NKJV)

113   Revelation 3:18–23 (NKJV)

114   Proverbs 9:10a (NKJV)

115   Romans 7:15b–25 (NKJV)

116   1 John 1:9 (NKJV)

117   Genesis 29:32b (ESV)

118   Genesis 29:33 (ESV)

119   Genesis 29:34 (ESV)

120   Genesis 29:35 (ESV)

121   Genesis 30:20 (ESV)

122   Mark 7:6–13 (NKJV)

123   Psalm 78:1–72 (NKJV)

124   Ephesians 1:4 (NKJV)

125   Luke 22:41–44 (NKJV)

126   Song of Solomon 4:9a (paraphrased)

Milton Keynes UK
Ingram Content Group UK Ltd.
UKHW051057151024
R3709500001B/R37095PG449372UKX00003B/5

9 798893 332995